Praise for *Long Change*

"An ambitious book. . . . It's a testament to Gillmor's writing that these stories . . . are as real and exciting in his novel as they would be if I were hearing them from a driller on a slow day. . . . The action in the novel is relentless . . . you can allow yourself to be pulled from page to page, confident that you won't be kept waiting for a payoff." *The Globe and Mail*

"*Long Change* displays Gillmor's talents for beautiful prose, strong storytelling and character development." *Winnipeg Free Press*

"An intimate epic, a tightly focused personal narrative set against one of the most powerful economic forces of the twentieth century. . . . *Long Change* is a window into a world which few readers will have really considered, a deeply embedded critique not only of the oil industry—certainly a ripe subject for such examination—but of the North American myth of success, a warning of the shaky ground where money overshadows and subverts passion, the quicksand where dreams slowly suffocate, long before the bullets start to fly." *National Post*

"The interior life of an oil man—what a daring book. Ritt Devlin is a decent, stalwart, sympathetic public enemy with an intuitive understanding of the earth's depths but legitimate questions about his own. A novel to take you places you fear to go." Padma Viswanathan, Scotiabank Giller Prize finalist for *The Ever After of Ashwin Rao*

LONG CHANGE

A NOVEL

DON GILLMOR

VINTAGE CANADA

VINTAGE CANADA EDITION, 2016

Copyright © 2015 Don Gillmor

Published by Vintage Canada, a division of Penguin Random House Canada Limited, in 2016. Originally published in hardcover in 2015 by Random House Canada, a division of Penguin Random House Canada Limited, a Penguin Random House company. Distributed in Canada by Penguin Random House Canada Limited, Toronto.

Vintage Canada with colophon is a registered trademark.

www.penguinrandomhouse.ca

LIBRARY AND ARCHIVES CANADA CATALOGUING IN PUBLICATION

Gillmor, Don, author
        Long change / Don Gillmor.

ISBN 978-0-345-81415-9
eBook ISBN 978-0-345-81416-6

        I. Title.

PS8563.I59L65 2016   C813'.54   C2015-902013-1

Book design by Andrew Roberts
Cover image: © Frank Scherschel / Getty Images
Printed and bound in the United States of America

10 9 8 7 6 5 4 3 2 1

Penguin
Random
House

For Grazyna

From so simple a beginning endless forms most beautiful and most wonderful have been, and are being, evolved.

Charles Darwin, *On the Origin of Species*

But the day of the Lord will come like a thief. The heavens will disappear with a roar; the elements will be destroyed by fire, and the earth and everything done in it will be laid bare.

2 Peter 3:10

CALGARY, ALBERTA

DECEMBER 2004

To the west the lurid twilight lingered above the Rocky Mountains. Below him, the city was laid out in an optimistic grid. Ritt examined his wife, the curve of her neck, which emerged swan-like still. It had held such fascination, her marvellous geometry. Where does that go? The marvelling, the animal quickening that love brings. Perhaps he was simply at an age where he no longer saw the world contained in a woman's hips, a relief and a tragedy, if that were true. Alexa's drink had disappeared and she held up her glass and waved it subtly, the cubes touching in Pavlovian chime. Ritt got up and took her glass and walked to the teak bar and poured out the last two ounces of Snow Queen vodka over her ice.

The first bullet hit him high, in the shoulder. The next four were more difficult to place, as they came in quick succession. Ritt fell forward, slumping heavily onto the bar, then sliding to the floor.

Alexa walked toward him and picked up the drink that was sitting, miraculously intact, on the bar. She was surprised to see her hand shaking. She was still holding the gun and when she looked at it, she thought, *the murder weapon*, and then she placed it uncertainly where her drink had been. She was wearing black pants, heels, a black top, and the silver necklace he'd given her for their fourth anniversary. She stared at the blood slowly pooling beside her husband. They had argued, of course, drunken battles that had become ritual, become foreplay. She had emptied the clip though missed with two of the shots. He was the one who had taught her to use a handgun. At the shooting range, her arm had sagged under the weight. The targets, curiously, were paper outlines of men, concentric circles diminishing within them, and at the centre that unreliable heart.

He was her second husband and she was his third wife. It was her fifth or sixth (or seventh) drink. They had been so joyous when they met, Alexa at the sour end of a failing union. That first night at the Crystal Ballroom they'd danced and laughed and drunk and both of them went home thinking: this is how it's supposed to be. They'd been together for thirteen years, a number that left Alexa at what she felt was an unfortunate age.

She took a sip of her drink and watched the last pink glow die in the west. Lights spread across the foothills, clusters joined by thin lines that resembled constellations. The wind picked up, a bellicose chinook curving over the mountains. She was out of bullets and out of ideas and Ritt lay there bleeding.

"Alexa."

The word was slurred and thick. She didn't respond. It hadn't occurred to her that he wasn't dead. She looked at him and immediately wondered if she'd imagined her name. A trick of the wind, or his body settling, final sighs escaping.

"You have to call," Ritt said.

"Call," she repeated, wondering if she was having a conversation with a dead man.

"Call the ambulance."

She took a sip of her drink. "Why would I do that?"

"It's our only chance."

"Our only chance or your only chance?" She didn't dare look at his face. She might be a drunken woman talking to a dead man.

"Alex, you don't want to spend your life in prison."

"Why aren't you dead, honey?" It sounded like a plea.

A fiery pain arced across Ritt's back like the forked lightning he'd seen as a boy growing up on the plains of West Texas. What he now saw were the fibres of her white carpet, enlarged grotesquely. He wasn't sure if he could move and felt it would be better not to. He had been raised in a country where you could sit in your home in Houston or Newark and know that in some clapboard bungalow with a slant six engine rusting on the lawn a boy was torturing insects or pouring lighter fluid on a cat, and that boy would grow and drift and at some point, on a highway, or in a brightly lit convenience store, or walking along Elm or Oak or Main with a handgun in the Gap bag, he would present you with the random death that was your birthright. But here he was in the Peaceable Kingdom, alone with a woman he had once loved, his blood pooling into view.

He tried to picture Alexa, her slurring elegance, her anger and confusion. A gun? Who could have seen that coming?

Over the course of their marriage she had slowly become unmoored and Ritt had simply watched her drift away. Her routine, alcohol-fuelled explosions were proof that she existed after all those arid afternoons alone, Ritt dealing with the endless challenges of his company. It had been a few years since he'd had the energy to engage with her temper; he'd watched their battles as if he was a remote third party. He could have done more, the refrain of every marriage. But he was distracted with his own problems. *Maybe divorce isn't the way to go,* she'd said a week ago, *we just need to talk this out, hon.*

Now he was dying, and he imagined himself hovering above the foothills, though ascension was unlikely. He would likely head downward, past the places he had spent his life exploring, through all that accumulated time—the Gelasian, the Zanclean, the elusive Devonian. Familiar adversaries that had offered up their disappointments. To the east, the promiscuous Bakken.

Oil was civilization's subtext, but it was showing its age, dirty and unwanted, an ancient embarrassment farting in the parlour. Gas was the logical refuge before sun or wind or hydrogen failed to save the world. To the south, shale beds held gas and trilobites and the dead societies of articulate brachiopods, the petrified testimony beneath us, the certainty of geologic time. The Cretaceous was glorious—those lumbering tyrannosaurs in a lush world that was already breaking up; Pangaea still separating into continents to give everyone their own room. Then the Paleogene, to freeze it all like a child's lunch that got taken out and warmed up millennia later.

In 1938—a geologic blink—his father finds Jesus outside an Abilene speakeasy. *Except a man be born again, he cannot see the kingdom of God.*

Ritt saw a woman beheaded in Africa—1990?—kneeling in the dust, on display for the foreign oilman, her sins abstracted in the morning glare. The images arrived randomly: a polar bear crumpling, in slow motion it seemed, a second after the bullet entered its unsuspecting head; biscuits cooling in the kitchen; standing in a Wyoming motel room scrubbing bloodstains out in the sink; that short miraculous walk to the barn with Oda, his first, his love, his virginity on its last legs.

Ritt stared at the carpet. What had he left this world? Add up the good and subtract the bad and see if anything remained. What was best in his life had already been buried. He understood he would simply be another layer of sediment ten thousand years from now, buried with his oil and his loves and the separate resentments that bound them all. He wondered if Alexa had more bullets.

THE
PALEOCENE

ONE

WEST TEXAS

1951

he wind carried grit that scoured Ritt's face in the sickly rig light. He was working a slow-drilling graveyard shift and stood smoking by the wellhead with Bobby Purdue, the eighteen-year-old motorman.

"I figure two more connections till daylight," Bobby said. He had a pitted face and eyes like a lizard. He was already married unhappily to Jody Watts, a former majorette who had mapped their future down to the minute.

Ritt took a drag of his cigarette and looked at the stars in the boundless sky. The August heat had cooled. The driller was asleep in the doghouse and had told the boys to wake him in time for the next connection and to quit smoking near the goddamn wellhead.

"Sunrise around seven thirty," Bobby said.

Ritt checked his watch: 4:21. His father would be asleep still. In another hour he'd be up reading his bible. His mother had named him Rittinger because she thought it was a grand name, remembered from a book she'd read as a girl, before her marriage to Del Devlin and their Pentecostal adventure, which had banned all books except the Lord's. She would be up at six, the two of them moving warily in the dark, avoiding one another. His father read the bible out loud at the dinner table and that was pretty much it for conversation.

Ritt was only fifteen but because he was over six feet tall he could pass for eighteen, and the driller had hired him on as a roughneck for the summer. He was supposed to be heading back to school in two days and as he stared up at that sky, with its ancient sense of possibility, he knew that he wouldn't be going back to school, or back to the house that wind and sand had ground down to the grey boards.

For the past week Ritt had been carrying all his savings on him. He had a bag with a change of clothes in his rig locker. In his head were unwanted images of the Fourth of July just past. As the country had celebrated with gunpowder and flags his father had taken off his belt and folded it in half as he walked toward him. When Ritt put up his arms in defence, his father dropped the belt and bore down with his fists. His mother stayed in the kitchen, forcefully singing a hymn to drown out the sounds: *Jesus, lover of my soul, Jesus I'll never . . .*

His father's face loomed, twisted with rage over Ritt's transgression: buying a new pair of cowboy boots with his first paycheque. He'd kept the boots hidden under his bed and had never worn them, except in his bedroom, standing on the bare floor, afraid to walk because of the sound those heels would make. He just stood in that mirrorless space and imagined himself walking. He put them back under the bed, where his mother must have found them while she was cleaning. She would have stood there, assessing her loyalties. When Ritt realized that this time his father wasn't going to stop hitting him, he delivered a hard right to his nose. He heard a sound like a branch breaking. His father crumpled, sitting down hard on the floor then rolling slowly to one side, blood leaking out of his broken nose. Del was almost seventy and lying there on the floor he was suddenly an old man. Ritt was flooded with anger, guilt, fear, surprise, relief. His mother came out of the kitchen and looked at Del and the blood that was dripping on her floor, then looked at Ritt and said, "Oh god, oh god," and knelt and wept.

Since then, through the long summer while Ritt had worked at his first real job, there had been an uneasy truce between him and his father and a new, complicated, silence.

Ritt said, "I think this may be my last shift. I'm taking off."

"You don't want to give this some thought?" Bobby said. "Maybe sleep on it. Two three days. Or until puberty maybe. You got some place you need to be?"

"I do."

"Jesus, Ritt. You only got this job because I told the driller you was eighteen. You ain't going to find another."

"I'll find one."

"You ain't going back to school?"

"No." Ritt threw down his cigarette and stepped on it. He'd miss school, oddly. It was a refuge. He was grateful for the information the teachers gave. He was quick with numbers and had skipped a grade. The classroom was where the world made sense. But he couldn't imagine two more years in that house.

"And this new life of yours?"

"Texas isn't the only place with oil."

"You light out like this you might never be able to come back."

"That's the good part."

"What's the bad part?"

"I'll come to it soon enough."

Bobby flicked his cigarette into the desert and watched the wind take it in a quick orange arc. "Tell you what, studhorse, I'll drive you to Abilene. We'll get drunk. You'll meet a girl, get your ashes hauled. You'll be so goddamned grateful you'll marry her then find the Lord and regret every sinning thing you ever done. It's the natural order of things. You need to join the human race, Ritt."

The sunrise was still struggling when shift changed at eight a.m. and the day crew banged their lockers open and unhappily put on their rig clothes. Ritt and Bobby drove down Route 20 in Bobby's truck, Eddy Arnold's "It's a Sin" playing on the radio. The eventless land passed unnoticed, the colour of the deer Ritt and his father shot each fall. This land only had one meaning and it was hidden a mile underground.

It took more than three hours to get to Abilene. They had breakfast at a diner then sat in the booth and ate pie and drank coffee and smoked cigarettes, too tired to talk.

The only two couples Ritt had witnessed were his parents, who exchanged about six words a week, and Bobby and Jody. He'd gone to their wedding. Bobby drunk and grinning with his arm around Jody as they left the church. That was eight months ago, and they were already on their way to killing each other.

After breakfast, they drove around Abilene for an hour. Bobby let Ritt drive because he was tired of it. Ritt didn't have a driver's licence but had had a lot of practice. He pulled over in the shade and they slept in the cab of the truck. When they woke it was after six. Ritt fumbled with the keys and started the truck.

He drove back to the same restaurant and they went in and ordered chicken and biscuits. The waitress remembered them from the morning, and asked if they were with the Air Force since just about everyone in town was. "No, ma'am," Bobby said.

"Then you the only two who ain't. You'll probably want to remember that if you boys intend to go out on the town."

By 7:30 they were standing in front of a bar. Bobby told Ritt to just walk in like it was something he did every day after work. Ritt was tall and solid and had a face that looked a lot older than fifteen. His mother had once told him he was an old soul. This was after his father had laid a whipping on him and Ritt had sat and stared at the wall in his bedroom while she'd sat on the bed and stared at him.

They found a table and Bobby ordered a couple of Lone Stars.

"Where is it you're in such a hurry to go?" Bobby asked.

Ritt had to admit he didn't know.

There was no real destination in his head. But he knew he didn't fit in to all of this somehow. Bobby did. He'd work the rigs, fight with his wife, get drunk on Saturday night, maybe find religion himself if things got bad enough.

Bobby kept at him. "You're a bit green to just light out."

"Maybe."

The bar filled up. There were some girls but mostly it was guys from the Dyess Air Force Base, either veterans or locals who were working there or had signed up, feeling their odds of not getting in another war were pretty good. Ritt sipped his beer, the third of his life, and tentatively looked at the women in the bar. Hard and wild-looking, another species. He felt a table of men staring at him and when he briefly met their stare they didn't look away. While he hadn't spent any time in bars, he could feel a barometric change, the tenor of surrounding conversations rising in pitch, the evening building toward something.

Bobby slow danced with a girl and Ritt stayed put, taking small sips of his beer, trying to enjoy himself and not really sure how. When the song ended, Bobby came back to their table and sat down heavily.

"That girl could tempt Jesus," he said.

"Bobby, we should head out."

"Afraid you're going to have fun?"

"That's not what I'm afraid of."

Bobby looked over at the table of men staring at them then finished his beer.

One of the men walked over to them. He was short-haired, his face etched with the discipline of the military.

"You like to dance?" he asked Bobby.

"Some."

The man stood over them, staring them down. "Maybe time for you boys to get on home. You can dance with your sister."

Ritt glanced around the bar; they wouldn't be getting any help here. After a few long tense minutes, he and Bobby got up and headed for the door, trying not to walk too quickly. Ritt felt nauseous.

They got to Bobby's truck before the Dyess boys caught up with them. There were four of them. The parking lot may as well have been on the moon; the whole town was empty.

"What asshole place you boys crawl out of?" The one who talked was the biggest. There was a tattoo of a knife on his wrist. Ritt backed against the truck. He draped one hand into the bed as casually as possible. There was grit on the corrugated metal surface and he felt along its length, his hand moving down until he came to the cold steel sitting in the wooden tray Bobby had built. The four faces shone in the pale street light like masks.

Three of them fell on Bobby and he went down and they laid into him. The fourth walked toward Ritt with a wide smile. Ritt brought the tire iron around in a clean hard arc that caught him on the side of the head and Smiley went over and his head bounced on the gravel with an otherworldly sound. Ritt went after the three who were on Bobby and got in a clean shot on the big one, who sank to his knees holding his head, screaming as blood started down his neck and onto the ground. The other two backed off, leaving Bobby curled on his side. Ritt tried to get him up, but he wasn't up to it. Smiley was still lying on the ground, his head opened up, blood spreading in a terrible circle.

One of the Dyess boys screamed. "Jesus, oh Jesus."

Ritt got the door of the truck open and dragged Bobby up and stuffed him in as best he could, Bobby crawling a bit, like a snake that had been run over. He closed the door and ran around to the driver's side. The two still on their feet were tending to Smiley, as the big one lay on his side, moaning.

One of them screamed at Ritt, "You fucking killed him. Oh god, Jimmy."

Ritt found the keys in Bobby's pocket and had trouble getting them out. Bobby was half on the seat, half on the floor. Ritt got the key into the ignition and started the engine. One of the men ran toward the truck. He kicked the door and then grabbed for the handle and suddenly his face was there, mottled and insane. Ritt shifted into first and lurched ahead and the face disappeared behind him. A rock clattered in the truck bed. He took the main street then turned quickly onto a side road. He kept the lights off and moved past untroubled houses. His head was roaring. Smiley—Jimmy—was likely dead.

Would they think he'd head south to Mexico? That's where you disappeared. That's what he'd heard anyway. Ritt turned north. He kept on the side roads and drove hard, using the pole star to get a rough position.

What would those boys do? First off, they'd call the law. So the troopers would be out. Then the boys would head back to Dyess and get the cavalry and they'd get in their trucks and fan out with their hunting rifles. Either way, his life was finished.

Ritt glanced at Bobby, slumped against the door. He was breathing hard and there were pale bubbles of blood on his lips. One eye was closed and blood was turning dark on his face. He might need a hospital but if Ritt went to the Abilene hospital he was done. He'd stop in Oklahoma. That might be far enough away.

He stayed on section roads, moving in a jagged line toward Wichita Falls, speeding past the sleeping poor. His mother had raised him on Thessalonians—*the dead in Christ will rise first*.

Ritt stared up, out the window. The black dome of endless stars was free of rising dead. Clouds bunched in the west. Jesus wouldn't take him now. Perhaps he never planned to. Religion filled his house like a plague, his father using the bible as a sword, cutting down everything until he saw a world small enough to live in.

He'd need gas sometime soon and he couldn't chance a station even if there was one open, which there wouldn't be. He wasn't sure about these blown-dead farms; they'd have dogs that would set on him if he tried to sneak some fuel.

In Seymour he stopped at the top of a small rise and turned off the engine and listened. The air was cool and still. Dark houses sat on the street like missing teeth. Bobby was asleep, issuing harsh rattling breaths. Ritt opened the door softly and got out and pushed on the frame and when the truck was rolling he got back in and let it drift down the small hill and coast to a stop beside a DeSoto that sat beside a well-tended house. He took a length of hose from the truck bed and undid the gas caps and moved the hose up and down until he got a flow and siphoned some into Bobby's tank. He kept his eye on the house, waiting for a dog or a shotgun to come out that door. He forced himself to stand fast; he didn't know where the next tank would come from. Two minutes went by like a century. There was no sound whatsoever except the gas moving through the hose. He felt his fate was hanging in the balance of this moment. If whoever was in that house called the law, his life would be prison, plain and simple. One of those men you saw chained together on a road crew. He stared into the black sky that curved above him and thought, without irony, that he was in God's hands. When he figured he had most of it he closed both caps and then started the truck and drove, checking his rear-view to see if lights were coming on in the house.

He crossed into Oklahoma not far from Burkburnett and figured the first thing he needed to do was get rid of the Texas plates. In Lawton he found a car outside a hotel and he took the tools from Bobby's truck bed and got the plates off and then drove out of town and pulled over and took off Bobby's and hid them in the flatbed and put the new ones on.

He got through Oklahoma, crossing into Kansas at Alva. When the sun was up it started to get hot. He saw a country store and parked down the road so no one in the store could see what he was driving. He reached into Bobby's glove compartment and took out the buck knife he had there and made a careful cut on his left hand. He went into the store and asked where the bandages were—damn toolbox, he said, holding his hand. He bought the bandages, two sodas, a map and a loaf of bread and said it looked like fall was coming. The store owner was half asleep and Ritt could smell liquor on him. He drove away breathing hard. It was the first person he'd talked to and he'd had to work to slow himself down, not talk too fast. He found the most godforsaken part of Kansas and pulled off the road into a stand of stunted trees. Bobby was awake and Ritt gave him a soda but it hurt his cut lip and he put it down.

"You should eat something," Ritt said. He handed him the bread but Bobby waved it away. He gave him the bandages and Bobby examined his face in the rear-view mirror.

"Where are we?" Bobby said.

"Kansas, I figure."

Bobby sat up stiffly and looked at his bloodstained shirt.

"Those boys had a mind."

"They did."

"They after us?"

"They are, but they sure as hell aren't in Kansas."

Bobby stared through the dirty windshield.

"Anything broken?" Ritt asked.

"My insides ain't feeling too good."

"You need a doctor?"

"Could we go to one if I did?"

"I could leave you there. You didn't do anything."

"What did you do?"

"I came around with that tire iron."

Bobby thought about this, his face ghostly with pain. "That boy hurt pretty bad, is he?"

"I figure maybe. Can you drive?"

"I think so."

Ritt got out and Bobby slid awkwardly over to the driver's seat. He poured some soda into a handkerchief and used it to clean off the blood. Ritt put a bandage across a cut on his forehead. Bobby took another sip of the soda and tried a biscuit. They looked at the map.

"I figure we go north," Ritt said. "Maybe Montana. They might be drilling up there. I've got to sleep, but if you can take it for a few hours, I expect it's best to get as much country between us as possible."

"Ol' Ritt. Got it all figured out, do you?"

"You can go back if you want to," Ritt said. "I've got that money I've been carrying. It's enough for a bus." And a lot more.

Bobby examined Ritt, and Ritt could see him weighing everything—what he owed Ritt for saving him back there, his unhappy union with Jody. On the other hand, because of Ritt, he was back to square one in the middle of nowhere.

"I'll drive for a bit, see how this settles out."

In the end they drove for twenty-seven hours, through the nights, on small highways and back roads. The air cooled. A man in Billings said they were drilling in Alberta, place was swimming in oil. They crossed the Canadian border on a section road near Cut Bank and drove past farmland. A billboard outside Medicine Hat welcomed them to town with a faded drawing of a man reaching out to shake their hand. It took four more days of driving around to find work on a rig drilling shallow gas wells just north of Medicine Hat. The first paycheque made them feel like millionaires. They checked into the Corona Hotel and bought new clothes and ate a steak dinner and got too drunk to walk.

The next day Ritt stood on the drilling floor that was slippery with mud, his head heavy and listing like it was filled with mercury. He wrestled with the breakout tongs and twisted the pipe apart as his feet slid on the floor. He tied the line around the pipe and they jacked it up and dangled it over the floor and Ritt stuck it into the pipe that was sitting there and Bobby let go with the spinning chain, dirty water spinning into Ritt's face.

The afternoon shift moved into grey twilight. By nine p.m. the temperature had gone down and the wind picked up. The first drops came like needles, driven at an angle. Within ten minutes the rain was a monsoon. Ritt could hardly see the rig lights. And he could feel the bit grinding. They'd have to pull it out and change it, most likely.

Ritt wondered if graveyards would even come out to relieve them in this. Driving would be hard. If they had to do a double shift in this mess it would be a long night, and he had already eaten the lunch he brought. There wouldn't be anything until breakfast.

Alf Lang, the driller, came out on the floor, his troll face dark and angry like it always was. Lang was in his forties with a thin blond pompadour, a career rig pig who had a hostile relationship with everyone on earth. "We're going to have to pull her. Get to it, girls."

Bobby said, "Jesus, I mean why don't we just shut her down, come back tomorrow when this blows through. Can't see fuck all."

"This don't suit you two, you can head back to Texas."

Alf went to the mud shack to wake up the derrickman, Pete, who had likely been drinking, expecting a slow shift. Ritt watched Pete come out of the shack like a hibernating animal emerging in spring. He climbed slowly up the derrick. It would be worse up in the stick. The thought of another eleven hours out here was crippling.

They started pulling the pipe. Ritt kept his head down and didn't think about the time and got into the familiar rhythm. Watch the pipe rise out of the hole, mud sliding down it, throw in the slips, ram the tongs into place, unscrew the pipe, lay it down, fourteen hundred feet of pipe coming out thirty feet at a time. He tried to remember the lyrics from a Merle Travis song, "Nine Pound Hammer," but couldn't keep them straight. He wished he had a girlfriend because the thought of her would be a comfort. He'd only been out of Texas for a month and it seemed like a lifetime. He wondered if that man was dead. They would have got him to a hospital. Maybe he was fine now, back at the base, re-telling the story to put him in a different light. Maybe he was simple from the blow, and sitting on his parents' porch where he'd stay for the next fifty years. The rain came down so hard he couldn't turn his face to it. He was wet through and cold. Nothing was visible beyond the rig; they laboured in a dark cocoon, drilling mud splattered on the steel floor.

When the bit finally came up, the teeth were worn right down. Ritt twisted it off with a chain wrench and they hauled a new rock bit out and spun it in. It was midnight and Ritt had made peace with the fact that the guys on the graveyard shift wouldn't show in this weather.

Across from him Bobby stared hopefully into the blackness, looking for headlights. Midnight came and went. The rain was violent, bouncing off the steel. The noise was deafening.

"Sonsabitches ain't coming," Bobby screamed to Ritt above the engines.

"I just hope days are here at eight," Ritt said.

Bobby looked like he'd been punched. If the day shift failed to show up, then they'd have to work through to their own afternoon shift, thirty-two straight hours with no food or coffee or dry clothes. "I'll quit," Bobby said. "I swear it."

"And go where," Alf yelled. He hated the rig owners, two men who were exactly as evil-tempered as Alf, but he wouldn't leave the rig unattended because it would mark him in the oil patch.

"We shoulda never left Texas," Bobby said, sliding around the floor, struggling with the tongs. "We shoulda never gone to Abilene."

"But we did," Ritt said.

Ritt could see that Bobby was saying something more but the words were obscured by the engines and the rain. Bobby started screaming but Ritt couldn't make it out. Bobby let the tongs dangle and stepped toward him and took a swing. He caught Ritt's hard hat, sending it spinning along the floor. They were at each other but were so waterlogged they couldn't do much. Up close Bobby's face was red and old-looking. "You ruined my life," he screamed in Ritt's ear, and then they fell, with Bobby still trying to punch him. Alf came over and started kicking the two of them with his rig boots and yelling at them to get back on the goddamn tongs. One of his kicks didn't connect and then Alf was suddenly upended beside them, pulling at Bobby and punching his head. Their hard hats were gone. Ritt tried to stand but the rain and drilling mud on the steel floor made it impossible. He slid to his knees and was pulled down. He swung blindly. The exhaustion of battle finally set in and they all gave up, lying on their backs in a row, breathing like Clydesdales. Above them the rain moved in the derrick lights and hammered on their faces, wrenched by the wind into kaleidoscopic patterns that disappeared in the void.

TWO

MEDICINE HAT

JULY 1952

L ying on his bed in the Corona Hotel, sweating in the oppressive July heat, Ritt stared at the stained ceiling and examined his options. He had saved some money. That was the bright side. He was sixteen, and in his cowboy boots—the closest he'd found to the Justins that his father had thrown onto the fire—he stood six foot four. He was filling out. He could fool a great deal of the world as to his age, though sometimes he felt like he was operating a giant machine that belonged to someone else. During the day, he could hold his aloneness at bay, but in those moments when sleep wouldn't arrive, a quiet panic crept into him. His dismal room seemed to expand in four directions until there were miles of prairie on all sides and he lay on that small bed in the centre.

The sweat snaked down his chest even though he wasn't moving a muscle.

He was coming to understand that oil was a living thing, it breathed and moved and gathered like a lynch mob, and to find it took a combination of science and voodoo. A geologist had come out to the rig to take core samples and while he was examining those cylinders of marbled rock, Ritt had asked what he saw there. Everything, the man said. You learn how to listen, rocks will tell you every damn thing. It occurred to Ritt that the oil game had two sides: on the surface there was unreliable machinery, drunken roughnecks and decent wages. But the real story was below.

Bobby would work the rigs forever. But Ritt decided he wanted to be one of the people who went down there and found that oil.

Geology is the story the earth tells itself, the geologist had said.

People tell stories.

The difference is, the earth can't lie. Every story is true.

Slow drilling graveyards were the best. It was cool in the night. Ritt could walk out into the farmer's field and get away from the noise and from Bobby, although they'd made peace of a sort. They hadn't mentioned their fight, just gone back to things as usual.

During the day it hit a hundred degrees and the steel of the rig was too hot to touch. They had spudded in two days earlier, moving the rig from Brooks to north of Redcliff. Bobby hadn't chained the water tank down to the flatbed properly and it had rolled off into a farmer's alfalfa crop and they'd had to drive through the field to winch it back up. The farmer saw them out there and roared away in his truck and came back with a rifle and put three holes in the water tank. Ritt had spent an hour patching it.

He wandered out into the cheat grass and examined the night sky, locating Orion's Belt. He felt caught in its celestial undertow, as if the sky could uproot him and carry him off.

He had felt that way when he was seven and his father took him down to the river to be reborn. The preacher had stood knee deep in the water facing Ritt and his father, who had led him farther into the river. The current tugged at them and Ritt was worried it would pull them both away. It was June and the sun was high. The preacher and his father pushed him over backwards, the water suddenly swirling above him. He opened his eyes and saw the sun sparkling on the surface. A handful of people stood on the banks, ready to receive his new soul. None of them were familiar, flinty sentinels sent by the church.

At that moment he had only the slightest acquaintance with sin, if you didn't count what had happened in that parking lot. He had yet to covet or steal or lust. He'd been afraid of his father and wondered if this was a sin. Hitting him likely was. He had fired a rifle and learned the alphabet and buried a pet dog. When his mother baked biscuits he sat in the kitchen and when they came out of the oven he waited impatiently for them to cool enough so he could fill his mouth with soft heat. Within a day they'd be hard as dirt. At the dinner table one night he'd told his mother they *were* hard as dirt, and his father had picked him up from his chair and whipped him with his belt. His mother sat on at the table, her voice raised in a hymn: *You are the river running through my soul. You are the river that makes this body whole.*

The land northwest of town reminded Ritt of Texas, patches of desert with small cacti growing and rattlesnakes sunning themselves on the flat rocks. The winter had been harsh, and now the summer was as hot as Texas, which didn't seem fair.

The wind was dry and some of the farms to the west still hadn't come out of the Dust Bowl completely and everyone talked about rain.

Ritt had heard a lot about Leduc; they were drilling all through that oil field and hitting nine times out of ten. He imagined the country there to be less empty than where he was. There might even be girls, though what kind of girl migrated to a rig town?

Bobby walked toward him and offered him a cigarette and they lit up and exhaled upward.

"I wonder if we should be heading to Leduc," Ritt said.

"Every roughneck on earth is already there."

"Maybe."

"Truth is, Ritt, I'm thinking about going home. I'm not interested in passing another winter here."

"Texas."

"Maybe Dallas. Anyway, I didn't do nothing wrong. Maybe that guy's all right and it's forgotten. It's his own damn fault anyway."

"I don't think that's a chance I want to take."

"I'm thinking of marrying Darlene."

"Congratulations. Again. If you take her with you, you'll want to steer clear of Jody."

"I wanted to steer clear of Jody a week after we got hitched. Look, it's long change and me and Darl are going to that dance. You should come, maybe find yourself a girl. It ain't healthy, your life alone."

Long change was the closest they got to a day off. They got one Saturday night every three weeks shifting from graveyards to afternoons. It was Ritt's only chance to meet a girl. But he hadn't met one; he didn't know how. His experience was limited to falling in love with every waitress who brought him a hot meal and called him honey. Once, when he was thirteen, he'd gone to a church social and a girl who was his age walked him through a field to a stand of trees and then pulled down her pants and said he had to show her his because she'd showed him hers. He felt she was getting the best of the deal—her mysterious line, a quick slash of the pencil, seemed anticlimactic, though something about it lit him from within. He did as she asked and the two of them stood there for a moment without speaking as she examined him like a scientist. Then she pulled up her pants and marched back across the field as he stared after her.

Girls his age were still in school and would be for a few more years. Bobby said he should just pay for it but the only prostitute he knew of was a forty-year-old woman who chain-smoked at the Legion and he wasn't going to part with his wages for that experience.

At seven a.m. the sun was still welcome. Ritt drove them back to town in Bobby's truck while Bobby slept. Up ahead Ritt saw Pete the derrickman's pick-up, parked on the shoulder. Pete lived in the Corona Hotel, too, with a woman who worked in the diner. They'd gotten thrown out a few nights earlier after a drunken battle that woke half the hotel. Pete was prone to trouble with his women. He'd told Ritt that his most recent ex-wife had bought a Floyd Tillman record and played it all day long drinking rye and Coke and weeping. Pete finally broke the record, slinging it across the room into the wall. She bought ten copies the next day and hid them and he eventually broke all of them. And then the marriage was broke.

Pete was bent over beside his truck. He had something in his hand and was flailing away. Ritt parked and got out of the truck and there was Pete, hammering a rattlesnake with a tire iron. The snake's tail was pinned under the tire of his pick-up. What were odds of that, Ritt thought. Pete stood up and stretched backward like he'd been shovelling snow and his back was sore. He was sweating heavily and Ritt could tell he'd already had a few beers.

"Fucking rattlesnakes," Pete said.

It was a squiggly dark line, its flesh exposed where the tire iron had opened it up.

"Teaching it a lesson, are you, Pete?"

"You might fucking say."

They were surrounded by useless scrub and semi-desert. Small cacti grew by the shoulder. There wasn't a sound. Pete had to be near sixty. He was wearing a Western shirt with the sleeves cut off and tattooed onto his withering bicep were the names of his three ex-wives, each with a shaky line drawn through it: ~~Amy, Flora, Cindy~~. On his forearm a new tattoo read "Marie You Bitch." Pete, the ladies' man.

Then the half-dead snake coiled up and struck Pete in the leg. His face filled with fear and surprise and a sense of resignation, like some part of him knew he had it coming. He lifted his pant leg and saw the mark on his cowboy boot. He swore and slammed the tire iron down on the snake, sparks flying where the steel hit small rocks on the shoulder.

Ritt's head filled with the unwanted image of himself swinging a tire iron. The odd sound it made. "Jesus, Pete, the damn thing is dead."

Pete straightened and held his back again. His face was mottled and sweaty and primal. "You saw that. Fucking rattlesnake."

Ritt nodded and walked back to the truck. Bobby had somehow slept through it all. Ritt drove to the café on the highway and woke Bobby up and they went in and had breakfast and Ritt fell in love with the waitress. When they were leaving, Bobby turned to the other diners, mostly truck drivers, and said loudly, "We already done our eight hours."

Ritt slept until five in his poorly ventilated room at the Corona. The transom was open but there wasn't much cross breeze and he couldn't leave the door open because he didn't trust the other men who stayed at the hotel. They'd take his money or his boots. He showered under cold water and was hot before he finished dressing. Outside, the hottest part of the day hit him in a wave. He walked to the Chinese restaurant and ordered a turkey sandwich and a Coca-Cola. At seven Bobby came by with Darlene and the three of them drove to the dance. Darlene was wearing so much perfume it formed a cloud. She had a small face and fading blond hair and was shaped like a bowling pin—the physical replica of Jody.

"We're going to find you a girl," she said to Ritt.

"What kind you going to find me?"

"A good one," Darlene said.

"He don't want a good one," Bobby said. "Plenty of time for that later. Right now he needs a bad one."

"There will never be a shortage of bad women in this world," Darlene said.

"Amen," said Bobby.

The band was playing something by Bob Wills. A few couples were dancing already, farmers and their wives, heavyset people who could really dance. Ritt had only been to one dance before, at school. Most of the kids he knew had learned to waltz from sisters or mothers and had some idea, but dancing was a sin in Ritt's household. He couldn't even imagine his mother waltzing. In the school gym he had lingered at the edge, feeling the music, the happy fiddle and the melancholy steel guitar. He had watched couples spin like dervishes and looked at the line of girls gathered at the opposite wall. To walk over there would have taken nerve. And even if he'd had the courage, what would he say? He couldn't ask them to dance. The girls were laughing as if they were in a play, checking to see if they were being watched. Pretty girls who'd spent two hours getting ready. Their brushed hair and fresh dresses, the promise of softness. He'd watched as they paired off with other boys and then he'd left and walked home, seven miles, angry that something that was supposed to bring joy had brought something else entirely.

Bobby brought back two beers, and a gin and Coca-Cola for Darlene.

"You're not getting me drunk, Bobby, if that's what you're thinking," she said.

"That's part of what I'm thinking." Bobby pointed to a large woman in her forties in a gingham dress on the dance floor. "There's your future wife, Ritt, right there. I'll bet she can cook some."

Ritt didn't bother to laugh.

When Darlene started to tell them about how all the other people at work didn't do their jobs and she basically did everything, Ritt got up and said he was just going to look around. He wandered behind the tables and watched people spinning gracefully in patterns, large circles and small circles. He went to the bar and got another beer and stood there swaying to the music. A girl came up to him then and asked him his name and Ritt was so surprised he had trouble remembering it.

She was probably twenty, very tall, not necessarily pretty but with a kind face. She introduced herself as Oda. "You're not from here," she said. "That accent."

"Texas," Ritt said. "I came up to work in the oil fields."

"I can see the rig lights sometimes from my bedroom at night. They look like Christmas trees. Is it wonderful to be out there in the dark?"

"I don't think anyone has ever called rig work wonderful," Ritt said.

"Is that what you want to do?"

"No, I sure don't. But it pays, and when I get enough money, maybe I'll figure out what's next."

The band started playing "Chained to a Memory" and Oda asked Ritt if he wanted to dance.

"I'm not much of a dancer."

"Neither were any of them before they learned," Oda said, indicating the people on the dance floor. "It's not hard."

"I don't know that I want to learn in public."

But she took his hand and led him to the dance floor and he was filled with fear and gratitude. They found a corner away from the tables and she stood with her right hand raised, as if she was swearing on a bible and Ritt understood he was to take it in his left. They began to shuffle around in a small circle.

"Just follow me and the music," Oda said, her voice quiet

next to his ear. He held his other hand lightly on her lower back and felt overwhelmed, but by the end of the song, he was moving his feet in some kind of time with the music.

She led him back to a table. "There," she said. "That wasn't so bad, was it? No one ever died from dancing."

"A few in the Pentecostal Church came close."

Oda laughed. "You're Pentecostal."

"Not anymore. But I was raised in it."

"Ritt's a different name. Like Oda, I suppose."

"It's short for something."

"Short for what."

"I'm not going to tell you."

"Writ Large," Oda said, laughing.

"What."

"Nothing. It's from a book I read."

He danced with Oda a half dozen times that night and told her a little more about Texas. She lived on a farm just west of town, but she said she didn't intend to stay there. She'd let her brothers work the farm and share its miseries. She was going to Calgary to become a librarian. She confessed she read constantly, studying his face to make sure that this didn't turn her into an oddball in his eyes. Her world was in books as much as the farm. She was five foot eleven, a slim woman with hidden grace, and as the evening went on, Ritt divined the prettiness in her face that he hadn't seen when she first approached him. She had lovely skin and a laugh that was infectious. Her nose was long and thin and this suddenly became appealing. When her two hulking brothers came to collect her at the end of the night, she kissed him quickly on the cheek and said, "Goodnight, Ritt Large."

After Bobby dropped him off at the hotel Ritt lay on his bed for an hour, not sleeping, thinking about Oda, replaying her voice in his head, the feel of his hand on her back while they danced. He tried to remember everything she'd said, trying to reconstruct her in words.

The Sunday afternoon shift was bleached by the sun. It was 102 degrees and the landscape looked like an overdeveloped photograph. Pete didn't show up for the shift and Alf swore and kicked the metal door of the doghouse twice and cursed the owners for hiring a half-dead rummy living in the saddest country song ever written. He turned to Ritt and said, "You're going to have to go up the stick. Fucking Pete must've died of natural causes."

It wasn't that unusual to lose a worker to long change. They got thirty-two hours off every three weeks and in that brief vacation they got as drunk as possible, cramming all their living into that one Saturday night. In the crippling hangover of Sunday, some of them realized there might be more to life than rig work.

Ritt climbed up the steel derrick ladder to make a connection. When he got to the platform he tied a rope around his waist and then used a clove hitch to attach it to the railing. From that height he could see a few farms on the plain and he wondered if one of them was Oda's. She was the only thing he thought about. He wanted to be sitting in the shade somewhere, listening to her talk. He leaned forward over the drilling floor and added a stand of pipe and they made a connection

below him. Ritt climbed back down and went to the shack
that held the sacks of drilling mud and went in cautiously. One
of the idiots from graveyards had caught a rattlesnake and put
it in the mud shack a few weeks ago and Ritt thought he was
easily stupid enough to do it again. He listened for the rattle
and stepped lightly. He found a sack and dragged it out and cut
it open with his folding knife. Bobby sauntered up.

"So what do you think? You gonna get hitched to Olive
Oyl?" Bobby said, as Ritt began sifting the drilling mud into
the sump pit. Ritt knew Bobby was mad because Alf had sent
Ritt up the stick and not him. It was a recognition that Ritt
was more suited to being derrickman, despite the fact that
Bobby was three years older. "I just might," Ritt said.

"You have a lot to learn about women."

"That may be true but you sure as hell aren't the one to
teach me."

"Don't fall out of that stick, studhorse," Bobby said, "You do,
you'll die a virgin." He walked off, searching for his cigarettes.

In September, Bobby got married to Darlene at City Hall and
Ritt stood as an uncomfortable witness. Darlene's parents
didn't look too happy either. It was hard to believe this marriage would end any better than the first one. The next day,
Bobby and Darlene drove south to Texas in the same truck
he'd driven up in. Standing outside the hotel Ritt wished
them both luck and they shook hands and Ritt knew he'd
never see Bobby again.

"Find out what you can about Abilene," Ritt said.

"I'll write you when I know something. Maybe he's alive and kicking and you can come back."

"Maybe. But if he's done with, it won't ever be safe. They burn people for murder in Texas."

Ritt watched them pull away and realized that was the last of Texas, though he couldn't say he was sad to see Bobby go.

On the Saturday afternoon of his next long change, he drove out to see Oda. Her father and brothers had all gone to the livestock show in Calgary. They sat in the kitchen, drinking lemonade. It was warm for late September and the sun came in and shone on the spotless linoleum. It was just her and her father and brothers. Her mother had died when Oda was six.

Her father was a big man, like her brothers, and when Ritt had come by to pick her up for a date the three of them had been sitting in the parlour and he felt like he was rescuing a princess from some awful giants in a fairy tale.

"Hard to believe you're related to them," Ritt said. "You don't look like them. You like to talk, they haven't said three words to me."

"They're better with animals than people."

"I can see why you want to get out of here."

"They're not bad men. But this isn't the life I want for myself." She made a gesture that was meant to include the whole area. "Come on, I'll show you the farm." She took his hand and led him outside.

They walked to the barn, not talking, still holding hands. Years later, he would look back on this moment, the short walk to the barn in the pleasant autumn sun, and realize it was where his future really started.

She led him to the loft. She took a blanket down from a hook and laid it on the hay. It was warm up there. The sun came through the cracks in the boards and straw dust was suspended in the light. She kissed him and they lowered themselves onto the blanket, still kissing. She took off her top and her bra and undid her pants. Ritt just stared.

"You could take yours off, too," she said.

He did, and when she reached to touch him, he felt like he was entering another world. He wanted all of her at once. They kissed again and she pulled him on top of her and looked into his eyes as he entered her. For a moment, he was afraid to move. She shifted her hips, and he started slowly. "There," she said, "like that."

Afterwards they lay on the blanket and for a while all Ritt could do was stare up at the grey arch of the barn roof. But then he propped himself up on one elbow so he could examine her long body. She was slim and small-breasted with long legs. Her skin was surprisingly white for a farm girl in September.

They fell asleep then, curled together in the warmth of the loft. When they woke up they made love again then got dressed quickly, suddenly worried that her giant brothers could return at any moment.

Ritt drove home in a state he couldn't describe. His life had been so quarantined in Texas that he didn't have the words for what had just happened with Oda. Maybe no one did.

THREE

MEDICINE HAT

1953

In November, with the first bitterness of winter, the caustic winds blowing the topsoil before the snow came and settled things, Alf Lang drove his white Cadillac into a semi-trailer head on. He was angry and drunk and wanted to get somewhere in a hurry. His body was found thirty yards from his car, laid out on his back, one of his boots missing.

After the sparsely attended funeral, one of the rig owners, Shane Pruitt, stood outside the church and told Ritt that this was his chance to take over as driller. He looked at Ritt and said, hopefully, "What are you, twenty-one?"

"Yes sir," Ritt lied.

"Young for a driller but I think you're up to it. I'll get you set up, work a few shifts with you. Alf told me you've been up in the stick. You'll get on to it."

Pruitt needed Ritt because every driller with any experience had decamped for Leduc and finding experienced hands in the gas fields was becoming a full-time job. The wind cut into their faces. Grey clouds were low in the sky.

"You have a girl?" Pruitt asked.

"Yes sir."

"Well, if you're drilling, you're making good money. Damn good money. Get married if you've a mind. Alf got killed driving a Cadillac, remember that."

Ritt had gained some understanding of the machinery, but it was old and often broke down and there were always problems. He came to appreciate that you had to be creative to keep a rig running.

People were another matter altogether. He was sent a succession of rig hands who turned out to be useless. An English alcoholic who fell into the sump pit and had to be rescued and then sat baking like pottery by the heater in the doghouse. Two students who had dropped out of university and who quit on the first day and walked nine miles back to town. A man named Sikes fell out of the derrick after failing to properly tie himself off. He landed on the steel drilling floor, broken in a dozen places and Ritt had to drive him into the hospital as he drooled blood, one arm at a terrible angle. Against his best judgment, he hired Pete, who had just been fired from a Big Indian rig. The devil you knew.

He and Oda had a secret Christmas together in his hotel room on Boxing Day because her family wouldn't invite Ritt to theirs. She brought him leftover turkey, and some mince tarts she'd made. They gave each other books for Christmas—*The Grapes of Wrath* for him; he bought her *Jane Eyre* because the woman at the bookstore had recommended it. They made love all afternoon and then Ritt drove her home.

She planned to leave in June, had already found a job working in a library in Calgary and was going to share an apartment with a friend then start school in September.

Ritt realized he'd better plan his escape too. He liked the responsibility of being a driller and he liked the money, but the idea of being here after Oda left depressed him.

He loved being her only admirer. Where others saw a tall gangly bookworm, he saw grace and beauty. He loved to hear her tell him about a book she'd just read, in her beautiful voice. She would describe the plot and deliver lines of dialogue and Ritt couldn't imagine that reading the book on his own would ever be as interesting as this. Others would eventually figure out what Oda had and there would be men in Calgary who would fall for her as he had and he despaired at this thought.

Ritt had no context for the courtship of Oda Zephron Otros, a name descended from Andalusian farmers, an exotic name that belied its peasant roots. Ritt's parents had refused to provide any details about how they met because they had met in sin. He'd been told one time by his paternal uncle, Horace, that his father had gotten drunk at the roadhouse where his mother worked. Maybe they had loved recklessly, then somehow ended up in the Pentecostal Church, praying for forgiveness. There were no books in his house except the bible, which wasn't big on romance.

His only real reference point was *Duel in the Sun*, the only movie he'd seen in Texas. He'd gone with his mother to the Bijou Theater when his father was away on one of his ill-fated cattle-buying trips. Ritt often thought about how Jennifer Jones and Gregory Peck had loved each other but shot each other in the desert and died in one another's arms. At the time, Ritt had thought this might be the best possible outcome for many marriages. It would certainly have been the best one for his parents.

Oda, for all her natural authority and curiosity, had only books to guide her. Nothing resembling romance had ever entered her house. She told him her brothers would take wives at some point, pairing off strategically with women on nearby farms. They would approach the task of finding a mate with the same dispassion they used when buying livestock. They would find women who could cook and run a household and fix a water pump and whose notions of romance extended no further than their own. Her father hadn't acknowledged any woman after her mother died.

So Ritt and Oda's romance was constructed from pieces of Jane Austen and Jennifer Jones and the conviction that they were utterly different than anyone they knew and therefore perfect for one another.

Spring arrived several times, giving a sense of relief before another blizzard came and punished them for relaxing. When it finally stayed it was too short to celebrate and a long dry summer was already on them. In June, Oda got ready to leave for Calgary. Everything she needed was in a suitcase. Ritt picked her up and drove her to the bus stop and she gave him one last kiss and he watched the Greyhound pull away and resisted the temptation to get in his car and race after it. The plan was Ritt would finish the summer and come out in September and find a place and then they'd be together.

In late July Pruitt sent them to drill some holes in the British military compound, an area west of town where contingents of three hundred British soldiers at a time did training exercises in the semi-desert. Sons of the working class, short pugnacious men with shaved heads cursing the heat.

On a slow-drilling shift, Ritt walked out into the scrubland to get away from the noise of the rig and heard an incongruous whistling noise with a descending cadence. A mortar shell landed somewhere to the north and there was a muted explosion. Fifteen minutes later another one landed somewhere to the south. Ritt walked back to the rig. A third landed, closer now.

"They're finding their range," Pete said. "Limey bastards."

When the fourth one landed two hundred metres away, the roughneck got in his truck and drove off.

"He's hightailing it," Pete said. "Shit-bag clown. They want a fight they come to the right fucking place." Pete went off to get his .22 out of his truck.

Ritt got on the field phone in the driller's shack but he couldn't get through. He walked quickly to the toolpush's trailer and knocked on the padded door twice. He opened it and went in, enveloped by the smell of linoleum and bacon and sleep. In the small kitchen there were dishes in the sink and an empty bottle of Jim Beam on the counter. A girl came out of the bedroom. She was wearing a cowboy shirt that belonged to the push. Her thin bare legs were the colour of skim milk. She brushed hair away from her face. She might be eighteen. The toolpush was in his fifties.

"Arnie's kind of out cold," she said.

Ritt looked at the empty bottle. "Yeah, I figured."

"So is there some kind of war or something?"

"Apparently."

They assessed one another in the dim light of the trailer.

"I better go see about those bombs," Ritt said. The push wasn't going to be any help.

"Go get 'em, Tiger."

Ritt drove his pick-up fast down the gravel road. He figured the men shooting off the mortars were out in the field somewhere and he'd never find them. So he went to the barracks, a collection of wooden buildings not far from the front gate. He heard another bomb land.

He told the man seated at the desk that there was a rig out there with five men working on it and those bombs were getting pretty damn close.

"You're the man in charge?" the officer asked, assessing Ritt, his alarming youth.

"I will be, you hit that rig." Ritt imagined the toolpush blown to bits as he slept. His teenage girlfriend gone.

"Yes. Right."

He got on the field phone and gave clipped instructions. There were two other men in the room. They all had moustaches and short military haircuts and brown uniforms. There was a map on the wall. It reminded him of Oda's bedroom. She had a map of the world on her wall with small pins in it, all the places she wanted to see.

Ritt drove back to the rig. The push was still asleep in his trailer, his girlfriend sitting on the padded bench that ran along the wall hugging her knees into her chest.

"Did the good guys win?" she asked.

"The world is safe again."

"I wouldn't go that far."

In mid-September, Ritt told Pruitt he was heading back to Texas. His mother was ailing, he said, and needed him. He thought this lie might make his departure easier but he underestimated Pruitt's celebrated meanness. He called Ritt a lily-assed pussy and reminded him that he'd shown him the ropes, put his goddamn faith in him and he didn't appreciate that this was how he was being repaid. The world was full of ingrates.

Ritt stood and took it, and when Pruitt ran out of steam, said he'd give him the full two weeks and help set up someone new if it came to that but he expected his final paycheque to be ready for him when it was time to go.

Pruitt grunted and returned to his paperwork and Ritt left.

The two weeks passed slowly. He went to pick up his cheque and was surprised that it was there. He had money and he had a girl. He could taste fall coming, a coolness that carried on the wind.

In Calgary, Ritt found an apartment that wasn't far from the one that Oda was sharing with two girls, within walking distance of the Bow River. He took correspondence courses to make up for his missing high school, and hired a seedy lawyer to get him documentation. Oda had already started her library studies. It was three months before Ritt got up the nerve to tell her that he was only seventeen, not twenty-one like he'd told her. He confessed he'd lied because she was three years older and he had been worried she'd lose interest.

"It will be the only lie I ever tell you," he said. He didn't count the fact that he'd told her his mother was dead. For all he knew she might be. But he didn't want this lie about his age to haunt them.

Oda examined Ritt, weighing this information.

"I'm turning eighteen in March," he said.

"You have to do penance. Maybe you're too *young* to understand the concept."

He insisted he was clear on the idea of penance. Her version was making him read Leo Tolstoy's *Anna Karenina* to her. She spent most nights at Ritt's and every night before they went to bed, he had to read ten pages out loud. Ritt agreed to this before he found out the paperback edition was 811 pages of small print.

He began that night. "All happy families resemble one another, each unhappy family is unhappy in its own way," he read, then looked at Oda's face on the pillow beside him. "I don't know that that's true."

"It was true for Tolstoy."

"That doesn't mean it's true for me."

"How many happy families do you know?"

Ritt shrugged and continued. "Everything was upset in the Oblonsky house."

He read five pages then stopped to ask why, if Tolstoy was a count, would he even bother writing books.

Oda looked at him like he was a slow student, then said, "He had no choice. He had to write. It was what was inside him. And you can't interrupt and ask questions and disagree with the author all the time. You have to read me ten pages without interruption."

But there were nights when neither of them wanted to read and nights when they slept in their separate apartments. Sometimes Oda would read (Ritt's favourite arrangement) and her voice brought something to the book that he knew his own voice didn't. By the time they reached page 300, Oda was reading most nights, and Ritt suspected it was because she was impatient with his wooden delivery.

It was five months before she read the last sentence: "My reason will still not understand why I pray but I shall pray, and my life, my whole life, independently of anything that may happen to me, is every moment of it no longer meaningless as it was before, but has an unquestionable meaning of goodness with which I have the power to invest it."

With these lines, Ritt's debt was paid. They were married in the spring at City Hall, joined in matrimony by the distracted monotone of a skinny Justice of the Peace in a brown suit, their vows witnessed by a stranger.

With his high school equivalency done, Ritt had applied to study geology at the Calgary branch of the University of Alberta. He was accepted, and on a grim Monday morning in

September, in an over-lit lecture hall amid the scrubbed, tired faces, Ritt found his calling. At the front of the room the professor, Niles Stamp, tall and languid, a pale Brit in a white shirt and black knit tie who stared at the class over horn-rimmed glasses, paced and spoke over his shoulder as if the students were all trailing behind him. He had a gap-toothed smile that lingered a beat too long and he used it as punctuation. The continents, he told them, fluttering the thin fingers of one hand, have been on a long, slow walk for billions of years and they have no intention of stopping.

Ritt found Stamp was both passionate and distracted, as though he'd be doing this even if no one else was in the room.

"We were the centre of the universe until Copernicus and Galileo came along," Stamp said. "Newton explained that we were totally unnecessary. Darwin challenged God to a duel and won, more or less. Nothing is static. The land and seas will continue to rearrange themselves. One day we will join the dinosaurs. Let me assure all of you, we won't have the run they did. Our day will be shorter. Our end just as violent, likely more so. But there won't be anyone to study us fifty million years from now. The rocks alone will survive. And in them is a record of every random stupidity that we have celebrated as progress."

Ritt glanced around the large lecture hall. People doodled and twitched and a few students were sleeping. He didn't know how they could. This was a mystery being revealed. Ritt was captivated as Stamp described the planet as it existed four billion years ago, indifferent to the life that oozed and fought and evolved on its surface. This was merely the façade, its public face. Its real personality was down below. Every war and every scar is there, the liquified remains of a species that was never able to grasp its vulnerability. More's the pity, Stamp said, in that comforting accent.

"But we're no better than the dinosaurs. We rule like blind kings. We're addicted to mystery—and into that void we have thrust a hundred gods. But if you peel back the layers of this earth, every hard truth is revealed.

"And that is why geology is so dangerous. Because it *is* the truth. Mind you, it began as heresy. Until the seventeenth century there was only one truth, and that was religious truth. Nicolas Steno was the one who opened our eyes. It was Steno who invented time. Until Steno, there was no such thing as geological time. In the Christian world, God made the earth and everything on it. In 1656, Christian scholars more or less agreed that the world was 5,660 years old. The actual day of Creation was pinpointed as October 23, 4004 BC. This was the exact *day* that God made the world, or at least rolled up his sleeves and got a start on things. How did they arrive at an actual *day,* you might wonder. Indeed. What they did was add up every *begat* in the bible, a book that contains the hazy recollections of unreliable Bronze Age drifters. They followed Adam's line down through Seth, his third, and least famous, son."

Ritt vaguely recalled the bloodline from church. Adam was 130 when he fathered Seth, a detail that had stayed with him. At the time, he had wondered what their father/son world looked like. No tossing the football with Dad for Seth. Then Enos, Jared, Enoch and Methuselah, who ate up 969 years on his own. Then Noah, a 600-year-old drunk, passed out naked for his son to look upon. Ham, Canaan. He'd missed a few.

"Genesis foretold that the world would last for six ages," Stamp said, pacing the room, "and Christian scholars decided that an age was a thousand years. Why? Why not? When you're the only game in town you get to make the rules. Which would mean that the world would end in . . .?" Stamp let the question hang, surveying his somnolent crowd.

"1996. Not much time. And who knows, at the rate we're going, perhaps the scholars were right. But then Nicolas Steno, a Dane—he was born Niels Stensen—and a curious man, asks a simple question: How did fossils of seashells end up on mountaintops?

"This is the question that launched geological science."

It was warm in the lecture hall. An incubating heat. More heads nodded downwards.

"The most obvious explanation was, of course, the Flood. Noah sails around the world for forty days and forty nights with that mythic, well-mannered menagerie. Tempers beginning to fray, one imagines. The lions and the gazelles perhaps not as chummy as they had once been. The waters subside and some of the shells end up on the tops of mountains. But that didn't explain how the shells got *inside* the rocks. Religious scholars put forward the idea that they *grew* there. Steno lived in Florence at this point, a religious town. You couldn't walk ten feet without hitting a saint. No one wanted to go against the clerics. But Steno did.

"In the Christian world, the bible had been the only narrative. Steno gave us a new story. The story of geology started as an act of imagination. Steno shook the world. He realized that the earth was created by forces other than God, that layers had formed, one on top of another. That this process had taken millions of years. The rocks were here before God."

Ritt put up his hand.

"Yes, Mr. . . ."

"Devlin. What happened to Steno?"

"An interesting story, our Steno. In the end, mystery claims most of us, I suppose. He created a science that refuted God, then converted to Catholicism and became a priest. He went on to become a bishop and took a vow of poverty. He lived on bread and beer . . ." a few chuckles from the men in the class. "He fasted three days a week. He wore rags, became emaciated. It killed him, finally. He was forty-eight years old."

Ritt wrote all this down in the notebook Oda had bought for him.

"In the fourth century BC," Stamp said, "mercifully free of the constraints of an as-yet-unimagined Christian god, Aristotle posited that the earth changed at such a slow pace that these changes weren't evident in one person's lifetime. His protege, Theophrastus, pushed this idea further, establishing that fossils were the petrified remains of organic matter. The torch was passed to Pliny the Elder, who gave us the *Naturalis Historia*. Alas, he perished when Vesuvius erupted, a witness to all that igneous rock. This was in 79 AD, just when Christian scripture sales were starting to pick up. Not coincidentally, science didn't flourish in the wake of those sales. It wasn't until the eighteenth century that the word 'geology' was coined. You can't have a science without a name, can you? We finally had something to put on university curricula, something that would thrill a room filled with distracted hormonal forgetful youth."

Stamp paused and offered that smile of his.

"Some of you are here against your will," he said, looking around the classroom. "Perhaps you needed a science course to complete your degree and geology seemed the most innocuous. Most of you will leave this course with little more than a few memorized facts. Years from now you'll remember sedimentary, igneous, metamorphic. You may even remember what they are."

Stamp stared upward, as if addressing the heavens.

"Perhaps," he said, "one day you will hike up to the Grassi Lakes in the mountains and see for yourselves one of the world's best preserved coral reefs, several thousand feet above sea level and you will remember the martyred hero of geology, our friend Mr. Steno. Though, frankly, I doubt it.

"But a few of you will begin to understand what geology is. It is both history and philosophy, it is the *bedrock* of science, pun intended. Our only reliable record. Every civilization is buried eventually. Every love is fleeting. Every book forgotten, every king buried. Brought down by hubris or vanity, but a victim, always, to geologic time. Govern yourselves accordingly."

Stamp's lectures were the high point of the school year, the world explained in a way that Ritt understood. He discovered a version of himself that surprised him, both curious and competitive, wanting to grasp everything. In the evenings, he studied at the dining room table they'd bought in a thrift shop, Oda at the other end, studying too, or sitting on their battered couch, reading, her legs tucked to the side.

The next summer, Ritt found another job on the rigs. He worked in the camps up north because he could put in twelve-hour shifts for two weeks straight then get a week off, flown home to Calgary by the company. With the money he made in almost four summer months, he was able to make the mortgage payments on the bungalow they wanted to buy and pay his tuition.

In the last week of August, before they both had to head back to school, they drove up to the mountains in the service-able Ford Victoria Ritt had found them. They pitched a canvas tent on the banks of the Bow River and fished for trout in the cold, glacier-fed water.

"Do you ever miss Texas?" Oda asked, as they cast their lines.

"Parts, I suppose. Sometimes I'll hear an old country song on the radio and I'll feel this pull."

Oda often asked about his childhood, his family, and Ritt struggled with the answers. *So what made you leave, and so young? I thought I killed a man.* That was not an answer he wanted to give. He played up his father's Pentecostal anger, killed his mother (a lingering cancer), keeping as close to the truth as possible. But every time Texas came up, he felt he was betraying her.

"We should go there sometime."

"We will." Though not while his parents were alive. He did want to show her where he grew up, but he wanted it to be like the diorama of an Indian encampment at the museum—a harm-less reproduction. Showing her the house he grew up in, the church where his aunt had fallen onto the wooden floor to speak in tongues. Steering clear of his parents, Abilene and the police.

As evening drew near, Ritt made a fire and put the pan on and dropped in two trout.

"I'm going to start an oil company," he said.

"What are you going to call it?"

"Oda Oil."

She laughed. "And the world will know my name."

Ritt adopted a preacher's tone. "Now this is eternal life, that they know you. I bring you glory on earth. Glorify me in your presence, my child."

It was still light when they crawled into the tent. After Oda fell asleep, Ritt got up and went outside and pissed with abandon, staring up at stars barely visible in the pale night sky. He was comforted by the mountains. All that violence brought to the surface for inspection. The dramatic folds, the patterns of collapsed stone and eroded shale.

In the morning, it was cool and they built a fire on last night's embers and Ritt boiled water for oatmeal. After breakfast, they hiked in Healy Pass and came across a female grizzly bear turning up the grass to expose flower bulbs, then sitting like a giant teddy bear and eating them. They watched for a while then climbed to the summit and made love on a warm rock that overlooked the valley, God staring down at them. You don't want to get too inventive with that audience. Despite his purging of the church, pieces of it still lingered.

Afterward, he watched her for a time, stretched against the rock, basking in the warm sun, then he got up to stand naked at the edge of the rock and survey the valley below. He thought that if he wasn't religious at this moment then he never would be.

In September, Ritt was back at university, taking another class from Niles Stamp. Stamp's avowed and public atheism had caused some unrest at the end of the spring term. By October there was a growing opposition to his teaching style. Ritt's class contained several devout Christians who sent the professor a letter demanding that Stamp stick to science and leave religion out of his geology lectures.

Stamp read the letter, which was signed by several students as well as three professors and a dozen church officials and three elders in the Mormon Church, to the class.

"I understand that I have offended some of you, that my . . ." Stamp read from the letter, "'often offensive, inaccurate, personal views on the subject of religion' have caused some discomfort, and in some cases, outrage. I would argue, gentlemen and ladies, that discomfort and outrage are part of a first-rate university education." Stamp punctuated this with his gapped smile. "Let me offer my assurances that none of you will be getting a first-rate education. Not here, not now. But at the very least, you should have some sense of what a first-rate education looks like. It involves debate, it means challenging accepted views, and it should include battles against dogma and ideology. It places the burden of original thought on your broad Western shoulders. I am *glad* that I have made you uncomfortable. It is part of my job. In turn, you should be making *me* feel some discomfort. You should challenge my views, stand up in this classroom and thunder and stamp your feet and raise your voice. I suppose," he said, holding up the letter, "that this rather timid document is a step in that direction."

He took a moment to examine the shiny faces turned up to him, some of them Christian. Ritt tried to indicate his support for Stamp with his complete attention. Stamp wasn't done yet. "If you absolutely *must* believe in a bearded, irrational deity who was only gainfully employed for six days out of several millennia—not counting the odd vengeful plague—and whose lack of any kind of social life has perhaps not made Him an ideal candidate for His chosen line of work, and who watched His only son die and didn't really do the right thing as far as Mary went, if you can embrace a god that sent boils and frogs as sleight of hand to impress the heathen then went off golfing while the holocaust raged, if your faith *still* nags, then I ask you to see yourselves, here in this class, as 'God's accountants.' Tracking His work, documenting all the fury He has wrought upon the world, His final fury, of course, being man."

Stamp gathered his papers and left the class. Ritt noticed grumbling from the Christian students and a conspiratorial huddle of the three Mormons. Four people remained asleep.

Before the Christmas break a group of students drew up a petition to have Stamp fired. When they asked Ritt to sign, he refused, saying they'd be lucky to find another professor like him. Certainly his other professors weren't like Stamp, but steady lifeless men standing in front of black-and-white images of rocks projected onto a screen. They droned and pointed and Ritt joined the sleeping dead, his chin on his chest.

Ritt went directly to Stamp's office to let him know there was a petition going around asking for his dismissal, citing blasphemy as the central reason.

His professor smiled that smile at him. "I should be flattered, I suppose, to join the ranks of those heretics who have come before me." His office smelled of pipe smoke. "Blasphemy. It has such a quaint, medieval ring to it."

Ritt wondered then why a man as smart and passionate about geology as Stamp wasn't out in the field, working with the layers of rock he so eloquently described. A man for whom rocks were living things, who saw the breathless inevitable narrative they formed. He hesitated before asking, "Did you work in the field, Professor Stamp?"

Stamp smiled once more, staring at Ritt for an uncomfortable moment. "You mean, that would certainly be preferable to lecturing sleep-deprived undergraduates and angry Christians." He finally said, "I was in the field, briefly. A year or so. Ages ago, watching the Cretaceous unfold." He gave a tiny snorted laugh. "There are many nights when I wish that I could have stayed there." He looked like he was going to offer Ritt an explanation. Instead, he said, "We sometimes pay a dreadful price for what seem like small failures at the time. I am trusting that you won't make this mistake. Steel yourself, Mr. Devlin."

FOUR

MACKENZIE RIVER, NORTHWEST TERRITORIES

AUGUST 1959

he river was almost a mile wide, the western bank a distant, undramatic line. The current flowed in a long soft arc. Overhead an eagle ascended on a thermal. Ritt was in the stern, paddling indifferently, letting the river carry them, Oda in the bow. They had flown to Fort Good Hope on the Mackenzie River and planned to paddle to the Arctic Ocean. Ritt had graduated in the spring and this trip was partly to celebrate that fact. They put in upstream so they could see the Ramparts, a seven-mile stretch that cut through limestone leaving steep cliffs. They were extraordinary, though Ritt had the feeling someone was watching from above, and was glad when they emerged onto a flat wide vista.

Oda had immersed herself in northern exploration literature in preparation for the trip. This was her habit, to exhaust a specific genre or niche or author. It had been the Russians when he met her. He had seen Southern Gothic come and go (Faulkner, Tennessee Williams, Flannery O'Connor). Dickens had lingered for months like an unwanted guest; she'd told Ritt he reminded her of a Dickens orphan. Then it was on to Emily Dickinson's quietly determined output. Herman Melville had been a bust: "I don't need a fifty-page whaling tutorial, I'm not actually going to go out and *do* it." Though she did actually want to paddle to the Arctic Ocean; the trip had been her idea.

"Alexander Mackenzie was on this river in 1789," Oda said, resting her paddle for a moment. "He thought it would take him to the Pacific Ocean. Lots of energy, not a great sense of direction. He called it the River of Disappointment."

"You get the feeling that most explorers basically didn't end up where they thought they were heading. Didn't Columbus think he'd discovered India?"

"Martin Frobisher thought this was China."

"Like life—you never know where you're going to end up."

"Where did you think you'd be right now? When you were a teenager in Texas? You must have dreamed a life."

Rotting in a federal prison, Ritt didn't say. "All there was was oil and God. I just thought I'd be gone. I didn't work it out much further than that."

"Well you can't get more gone than this," Oda said, staring serenely around her.

They camped on the bank, hard-packed sand flanked by low pines. Large flat rocks sat in the water as if they'd been dropped. The summer sun didn't want to set. At nine p.m. the sky was colourless and epic. It was the last week of August and cold enough at night to see their breath.

While Oda read more about Alexander Mackenzie, Ritt gathered driftwood and made a fire. He'd seen a few fish jumping and spent an unsuccessful hour trying to catch one. They ate canned stew.

"Can you imagine what it's like up here in January?" Oda said.

"I'd have you to keep me warm," he said and pulled her toward him. They made love inside their zipped-together sleeping bags in the protracted twilight. Afterwards, Ritt lay thinking of his mother. He rarely thought of her, but when he did, he felt a rush of guilt, a sense he'd abandoned her. Though he would have left in any event, and surely she knew that. Another year, two at the most. Perhaps she had left Ritt's father by now, returned to her old life, whatever that held, with its own fears.

Ritt checked to see that Oda was sleeping, then got up and left the tent, walking to the edge of the water where he sat by the dying fire. What kind of ingenuity did it take to live off this land, this daunting barrenness. Though his father's small acreage in Texas had been equally barren. They had kept chickens on their farm, a handful of them in a small coop in the yard. When he was nine his father had made him kill one of them, holding the squirming thing on the stump, hatchet poised. The blow decapitated the chicken and it fell off the stump and made a quick circle around the dusty yard, an act that was both miraculous and frightening. "That's what most people's lives are," his father had said.

In the morning they were stiff with cold. Distant hazy clouds obscured the sun, the featureless sky. They ate oatmeal and drank terrible coffee and packed up the canvas tent and loaded the canoe.

They paddled silently for hours on the wide and placid river. A ribbon of trees followed the water northward, the water's moderating influence allowing them to grow. Beyond the trees was tundra that stretched for hundreds of miles. The sun gained power, a hint of real summer in its heat.

Five days went by, blurring into one another without the stark line of night. It was almost midnight by the time the sun set. They read in the tent in the evenings. Oda had brought an account of the Franklin expedition. Ritt was reading Hemingway's terse wartime prose. The mosquitos were worse than he had expected, a torment. It seemed unfair to venture to this lofty latitude and still have to deal with tropical pests.

There was something about this empty land that made him restless. How was it possible that they were the only ones for miles? One night he left the tent and stood outside and looked at the pines, ghostly sentinels. Something moved, a shock. There were two of them, pale wolves, soundless, padding on the sand. He glanced quickly around to see if there were others, but they appeared to be the only ones. They stopped and glanced at Ritt, indifferent. Certainly they weren't surprised. Perhaps they'd followed along behind the pines as he and Oda drifted down the river. Wolf attacks were extremely rare, he knew, and most of the alleged attacks were old wives' tales spread by ranchers who wanted to shoot them with impunity. He felt some affinity with these creatures as well as a trickle of fear. He had a hatchet and a long knife in the tent. Would they be looking for caribou? They moved off along the sand bar. Ritt lowered his long underwear slightly and started to piss. He took a step then walked, spraying in arcs around the tent. A little splashed on the canvas.

"Ritt, what are you doing?"

"Marking our territory."

"We don't have any territory, Ritt. That's why they call it wilderness."

"All right. So I'm keeping the demons away."

He slept fitfully with the knife and hatchet at his side. In the morning there was no sign of the wolves.

The next afternoon, Oda took a break, making a comfortable spot for herself and lying with her back against the bow seat, reading her book. Ritt paddled sporadically. They had made fairly good time and were in no rush. He watched the landscape drift past, soothed by the high wide sky and monotone palette.

When the river changed its cadence, Ritt failed to register the subtle shift. His hand was cold where it met with the water, the skin red and chapped, and he was thinking only about how uncomfortable he was. As they came around a wide bend, he saw small white specks on the river, rapids that hadn't been marked on his map.

"Oda, there's some fast water coming up. I don't think it's much to worry about but you should get back in the seat and get your paddle in the water."

Oda nodded, and carefully put her book in the steel, water-tight container and screwed on the lid. She glanced behind her to gauge her room to move, stood up partially and twisted around, then lurched to the side that Ritt was paddling on, his weight snug against the gunwale. She dropped to one knee awkwardly in an attempt to get her weight lower but her hand missed the gunwale and she went over the side and took the canoe with her.

They were both in the fast water and they flailed, trying to get hold of the canoe. Ritt yelled for her to get upstream from it so she didn't get between the canoe and a rock. The weight could crush her. Oda lost her grip on the canoe when it threatened to push her under and Ritt instinctively let go and went to her.

They swam together, not talking, saving what energy they had. The water was cold enough for hypothermia. The river was wide and they moved with the current, angling, hoping it would push them to the bank. When they got to the shore they struggled onto the sand, heaving, exhausted. Oda's lips were blue. Ritt had never been this tired in his life, an exhaustion that made every movement monumental. He crawled to Oda and held her.

"We need to get warm," he said. She was unresponsive, eyes fixed on something else, her own struggle. Ritt rubbed her arms and back and whispered her name into her ear.

He remembered the belt that he had wrapped around his waist. It held two small waterproof compartments. Inside one was a map folded into small squares. In the other, matches.

"Fire," he said simply, and stood up with difficulty in his waterlogged clothes. Oda lay down on the sand. She looked like a drowning victim. He moved as quickly as possible to get warm, and searched for driftwood and dry sticks. His arms seemed alien, without strength or feeling. He piled some driftwood in the sand near the trees then went to Oda and tried to pull her to her feet. She had difficulty standing but staggered with him to the driftwood. Ritt talked to her as he struck one of the matches and held it shakily to the kindling. He blew carefully on it, his breath coaxing, but the flame died. The air was cool. Without the sun it didn't have the power to heat them. Oda lay curled and shivering. Ritt used four matches, all with the same heartbreaking result, watching the first optimistic glow falter. He examined the next match, wondering if his life depended on it. They needed to dry their clothes or they would die. He took off his shirt and strung it on pieces of driftwood to dry and form a wind break. His skin was mottled. His arms seemed to have shrunk.

This time the flame caught, and Ritt added more kindling, carefully arranging it, calculating the breeze, estimating what the fire could handle, what it wanted from him. He moved Oda closer to the flames and struggled to take off her shirt and pants. He took off the rest of his own clothes and when he was confident the fire had caught he lay beside her and held her to him and wondered if this was how they would be found.

The heat grew menacing, but he welcomed it. Oda stirred, mumbling, clutching him. He wasn't sure how long they lay like that. He got up every now and then to add more wood to the fire. He knew they needed to try to recover the canoe or at least some of the gear that had spilled out.

Their clothes were drying quickly. Oda rolled over to expose her front to the heat. Ritt stood and jumped up and down and waved his arms. His head ached. The sky went from pearl grey to a deep grey-black. They didn't get much rainfall up here. He hoped they wouldn't be getting any now.

"Ritt," Oda said. The first word she had spoken. "Do we have anything from the canoe?"

"No, but maybe some of it went ashore where the river curves."

"We can't walk it. There's no food."

Ritt wondered if they would experience what those early explorers experienced, wasting away as they trudged obediently, bickering and praying for deliverance. They had one thing the early explorers didn't, which was hope: some other party might come down the river and help them. Though they hadn't seen anyone so far.

When they were dry, they got dressed and started to walk. Ritt guessed it was near six p.m. The river sprawled ahead and he wondered where the wolves were.

After two hours they found a waterlogged canvas bag that had washed onto the sand bank. In it were wet clothes, and a steel container that had a bag of oats and Oda's book about the Franklin expedition in it. They reasoned that they didn't have time to stop and make another fire to cook the oats so they poured some of the oatmeal into the lid of the container, added some water from the river and ate the mess cold as they walked.

The light of day had become an otherworldly twilight, the sun near the horizon but refusing to set. Ritt had guessed the overturned canoe would wash up on the bank; he hoped it would be this bank. He wasn't sure he could swim the river.

"The thing is," Oda said, "with these wilderness stories, you get the feeling that the most dangerous thing out there is *us*. People turn against one another, they fight, they kill each other, they *eat* each other. They go crazy. They find God, or give up on God. I wonder if they suddenly see how small they are, how indifferent the world is. Some kind of truth lands on them in the wilderness."

"It might land on us."

"We'll find the canoe, Ritt. Or some people will find us."

"There might be some kind of outpost, some trapper, someone around." Ritt stared down the river, surveying the unwelcome emptiness. "Which was the one where they started eating each other?"

"Franklin. You thinking of eating me, Ritt."

"Always."

He thought of the surviving members, back in England, sipping tea, the last remnants of an undigested colleague moving through them, and shivered.

They continued on in silence for a few hours, determined to make as much distance as they could before stopping to rest. Ritt could feel the dampness of the clothes on his back. Close to dawn, he saw something up ahead on the sand. A paddle. He picked it up.

"Half the battle," he said, and used it as a walking stick. Farther on they came to a bend in the river where driftwood had piled. They found small dry branches for kindling and carefully arranged it all. Oda gently tore three pages from the Franklin book and she crumpled them and laid them at the base. They huddled together and formed a wind break and Ritt bent to light the paper. It caught and after some artful management, the driftwood started. They pulled out the wet clothes and arranged them near the fire and lay down. Neither of them could sleep, despite their exhaustion.

"Franklin led one of his expeditions on this river," Oda said. "He may have stopped on this very spot."

It finally occurred to Ritt that Oda felt responsible for this. "This is not your fault, Oda."

"Well, you're wrong, Ritt. It certainly is." She began to cry and Ritt held her.

"We're going to get out of this," he said. "We're not Franklin."

After she'd calmed down, he got up and walked along the shore where he found two large pieces of dry wood he hauled back to the fire. He put one of the logs on and they watched as it slowly caught. A few clouds moved against the pale sky.

The men on that last expedition must have known they were going to die, Ritt thought. At some point you lose hope. Nineteenth-century Englishmen still thought they owned the world. But at some point you're simply another animal trying to survive.

Ritt dragged the second piece of driftwood into the flames and at last they slept. They woke hungry, several hours later, their faces swollen from mosquito bites. They decided they weren't cold enough to use their precious matches to start the fire so they ate the last of the oats mixed with river water. The sky was blue and mocking. They packed what they had into the canvas bag and walked.

They found the canoe two days later, the current nudging it into the sand of a bend in the river. It was undamaged. Roughly half their gear was gone. They only had the one paddle. Most of the food was gone. But the tent was in a bag lashed to the thwart. A water-tight tin container contained two boxes of matches.

Ritt gathered wood for a fire and they took everything out of the canoe and laid it out to dry. They pulled the canoe up and set up the tent so it could dry, too, and Oda fell asleep and Ritt lay awake and wondered what would have happened if they hadn't found the canoe.

They took turns with the paddle and after two days the delta came into view. The largest in the country, almost forty miles wide where it met the sea. There were thousands of small lakes contained in it, which shifted or disappeared or grew depending on the changing river sediments. The delta was a living thing, in flux, moving uncertainly, but always in motion.

Ritt wondered if there was oil down there. So much oil had been found in the world's deltas: Mississippi, Orinoco, the Persian Gulf. He could be paddling over underground rivers of oil. Would they have died without the canoe? Perhaps. But they had survived, and that fact filled him with the sense of possibility that survivors felt—a sudden freedom to engage the world. He really would form an oil company. He would come back here.

To the west the Richardson Mountains gleamed. The trees had been getting smaller as they moved north, the spruce stunted. But in the delta there were white spruce that were fifty feet tall, thriving on the rich nutrients that came to rest near the sea. Everything came to the delta. It was full of muskrat and fish and life. The channels were calm, a gentle maze that led to the Arctic Ocean. They paddled silently past the trees.

In Tuktoyaktuk, they checked into a hotel and stayed in the bath together for an hour. Over dinner they managed to laugh about the trip and basked in their closeness, now strengthened by the bond that survivors shared. Two days later they caught a plane south to Edmonton, then changed to a larger plane to Calgary. The city seemed more humane, dirtier, a refuge.

FIVE

CALGARY

1962

Mackenzie Oil operated out of their kitchen; Ritt was the only employee. He spent weeks going over geologic maps, looking for some piece of Alberta farmland that had been overlooked, hadn't been seismically plumbed, yet hid something of value. Geology was art as much as science. He dreamed of drilling in the Mackenzie Delta, but it was far too expensive and too complicated.

The maps were laid out on the Formica table, and Ritt traced his finger along peraluminous intrusive complexes that yielded biotite quartz monzonite fading to granite. Tight, mean-spirited formations that wouldn't hold his oil. He had hiked up to the Grassi Lakes to see the coral reefs exposed on the mountain, reminded of Niles Stamp and his blasphemous lectures.

Most petroleum geologists fought with the rock: they assaulted it; it was the enemy. You needed to understand the rock, see that its permanence was an illusion. *As solid as rock.* But it wasn't. It shifted and moved. It got tired and gave up and let itself be subsumed by ambitious strata thrusting up from below, seeking the light. We quarry it and puncture it and blow it up because we can. But to get it to truly release its secrets, you need to ask it the right questions.

Ritt leased a small piece of unsung farmland that undulated over gentle synclines through the abandoned Daedalus field. Wells had been drilled in the Daedalus years earlier, in the 1940s with an old steam rig. The region produced briefly and weakly then was abandoned and reverted to farmland. Ritt had examined well logs from the area around it. It looked like everyone who had drilled there had gone too deep, passing through a seam of high permeability that might hold oil. He only had enough money to lease a small parcel, but no one else was there and if he hit oil, he could get hold of the land around it.

To finance the hole, he had to use all of his savings, borrow from the bank using their house as collateral, and invite a mid-sized company in for half the profits.

Ritt also came to an unusual agreement with the drilling company whereby he would work as driller on the rig. It gave him an income and kept him on top of the operation. He was financially overextended, fretting in the fast disappearing autumn. He was convinced that his and Oda's future depended on this hole. If he found something, it would be enough to turn his company into a real company.

The rig had wrapped up a hole for someone else near Swan Hills and Ritt went there to help move it to his lease. They tore the rig down, loaded the pipe onto the flatbed, laid the derrick down carefully, winched the water tank up in halting, grinding movements. When they had it all loaded up and cinched down, Ritt got into his truck with Shanty Macleod, the derrickman.

"Jesus, this cold," Macleod said, blowing on his hands.

"Yeah, and now we have to put her all back together."

Ritt turned up the fan until the cab was overheated. Macleod was a solid worker. He'd hired a roughneck who was a local farm kid, sturdy and willing to learn. But the motorman, Matt Sabo, was a sour presence, the kind of man who brought discontent to every relationship he had. A familiar type in the oil fields.

Ritt drove slowly down a section road, behind the trucks carrying the rig, a daisy chain of flatbeds moving slowly. They drove for almost two hours then circled in a low snow-dusted swale that bordered a farm. At the fence a dozen cattle observed dumbly as they unpacked all that iron and set it back up. It took most of the night. Small pellets of snow fell. The deeply resented cold of November, before you got used to it.

They drilled and Ritt listened to the engines, detecting small changes in pitch as they laboured through stubborn sand. He examined the tailings, played with the muddy rock, held it up to his nose to sniff, rolled it in his hand. His longest conversations were with the earth itself, walking the rolling farmland and muttering to the world beneath him, trying to divine where it hid its fuel. Once, during a connection, he put his ear to the open pipe standing on the rig floor, then yelled down threats that gave the roughnecks pause. What if there wasn't anything down there? What if he was wrong? In a week he would know and he wasn't sure he could bear any bad news.

In the doghouse, Ritt examined the charts that were spread out on the steel desk. They were an hour into the graveyard shift. Matt Sabo came in and lit a cigarette.

"Put it out, Matt," Ritt said, without looking up.

Sabo was in his fifties, a career rig worker, inexpertly tattooed, occasionally drunk.

"I don't think we need to worry too much about gas," Sabo said, taking a long drag. "I think we're heading for dust. This thing hits dust you're done, that be about right?"

Ritt straightened up and looked at Sabo. "You're, what, fifty-three, still working motors for a half-assed outfit out in bum-fuck Egypt. Put it out, Matt, or pack your bags."

Sabo stared at him for twenty seconds. Ritt could tell he was thinking that he didn't need to take any shit from this twenty-seven-year-old Texas dickhead: Should he put it out or take a swing? Ritt watched his face; you could almost see the thoughts lumber through his head. Sabo took another long drag then flicked his cigarette against the steel wall of the doghouse where it bounced onto the floor. He kicked open the door and left it open and stomped down the stairs like a teenager.

A light snow started to fall. An hour later it was a blizzard. Ritt could feel the bit slowing down, its teeth worn out. They'd have to pull the pipe and put a new bit on.

Sabo came back into the doghouse and rubbed his hands, his face misshapen from the cold. He took off his hard hat and his hair was flattened to his head like it had been ironed.

"Need to pull her," Ritt said. "Round trip."

"Not in this," Sabo said.

"No choice. Bit's gone."

"Ride it until the day shift arrives."

"Take five minutes. Get some coffee. (

"I ain't." Sabo stared at Ritt. "Fuck thi

"You go down that road, don't come ba

Sabo wavered, stuck in the moment.

turning points, which way did you go? R

appointment, the thought of three hours of backbreaking
work, frozen through, working in the dark in the middle of
nowhere. Work that was as forlorn as you could ask. Sabo
didn't know whether to quit or pull pipe. But you up and quit
and then what? Ritt knew he should say something to sway
him but he couldn't find it in him. He was at his own turning
point. If this well was dry he didn't have anything left. If it was
dry it meant he had miscalculated, had misread the geology.
He had persuaded himself that he had a gift, persuaded Oda.

"Fuck you, Ritt," Sabo said at last. "Fuck you and your
duster."

Ten minutes later Ritt saw the tail lights of Sabo's truck
going up the lease road, disappearing quickly in the snow.

Shanty Macleod came in. "Sounds like she's done."

Ritt nodded. "Have to pull her. We're going to be a man
short."

"Pitter patter, let's get at her."

In the morning, the sun rose weakly in the parched sky. Ritt got
in his car and drove toward the rundown motel where he was
staying. He saw light reflecting off something on a hill to the
south. He stopped his truck and stared up at it. There was movement; someone was up there. He wondered if it was a scout.

drove around the section roads in a long circle and came up on the hill. A truck was parked there. Ritt stopped, turned off the motor and approached slowly. He looked in the truck. There were charts on the seat and a plaid thermos. The keys were in the ignition and he took them out and put them in his pocket and walked carefully up to the low scrub that grew near the crest. Through the branches he could see a man sitting on a blanket. He was looking through a pair of binoculars and he let them hang from the strap around his neck and wrote something in a notebook. Ritt realized he was counting the stands of pipe, timing their progress, watching to see if they flared off any gas. Someone had hired him to see if they were going to hit oil out here; if they did then that company would snap up the surrounding land at the next sale. Ritt didn't have the cash to buy any more land; he needed the money from this well if there was any.

"You getting what you need?" Ritt asked.

The man turned around and stood up and backed away a step. "Jesus." He was short, dressed in a barn jacket. His face was flat and open with blinking blue eyes, vaguely Scandinavian. Maybe twenty-five years old. Someone's nephew, getting his start in oil.

"I'm . . ."

"A birdwatcher. That be it?"

"This is a free country, mister."

"And this is my land."

"I don't want any trouble. I'll just be getting in my truck." He walked past Ritt with his head down, as if Ritt might not notice him. Ritt watched him get in his truck, the look of relief then the look of surprise when he checked for the keys and they weren't there. He patted his pockets, looked on the seat, on the floor.

Ritt walked up to the door and the man locked it. Ritt took the keys out of his pocket and held them up.

"I'm not getting out," he said, his voice muffled by the closed window.

Ritt took out the folding knife he carried in his jacket and knelt down and stabbed the front tire.

"Jesus Christ," the man yelled from the cab. "You got no right."

"That's my hole down there. And you're a spy. You're not in a great position to talk about rights. Who you with."

"I'm independent."

"You sure are. You're about as independent as it gets. Twenty miles from the nearest town. No truck. Who is it that's so curious about what I'm doing out here the middle of nowhere."

The man looked at him defiantly.

Ritt looked in the truck bed. He picked up an old sheet wrapped around a four-foot jack that lay there, tore a strip from it then twisted it and unscrewed the gas cap and stuffed the sheet down into the tank. In the breast pocket of his jacket he took out a book of matches that said "Dew Drop Inn" on them.

"You can't do that." His voice high and barely audible.

Ritt tore off a match and lit it. "The good news is you're going to warm right up."

The man jumped out of the truck and backed away, both hands raised and Ritt tossed the lit match to the ground.

"They never said *this* could happen," the man said. "They never." He looked like he was near tears.

"And who is 'they,' exactly."

"You hurt me, you're in trouble, mister. *Big* trouble. I'm with Alhambra."

A big outfit looking to get bigger. If this man reported back that they were on to something, Alhambra would buy up the land around his lease. They certainly had the money.

"You know," said Ritt, "north of Medicine Hat, they found a scout watching a Big Indian rig. The boys locked him in the mud shack with a rattlesnake for two days. Dark enough in there you can't see your hand in front of your face."

The man looked around, hoping somehow help was going to arrive.

"I got rights," he said.

"You do. What you're short on is options. C'mon, I'll give you a ride into town."

The man stood there for a second, as Ritt turned and walked back to his truck. Then he followed. They drove for half an hour listening to a phone-in show where a woman described the washing machine she was selling, how it had done right for her family but now they were all out on their own, including her useless husband, doing god knows what.

At the Dew Drop Inn, Ritt pulled into the parking lot and knocked on number nine. A big man came to the door, unshaven, unhappy, the motorman from the afternoon shift, Dave Tindal.

"Sorry to interrupt your beauty sleep, Dave. I've got a present for you."

"What the hell I want with this."

"This is a scout and I want you to babysit him for the next five hours while I sleep then I'm going to collect him. Make sure he doesn't use your phone. He won't tell me his name so I'm going to call him Loretta." He turned to Loretta. "You try and get in touch with Alhambra and you'll be in the mud shack for two days in the dark freezing your ass off."

"You . . ."

"And that's enough talk about rights, Loretta. You want to steal another man's play then you forfeit your rights."

"You even look at that phone I'll twist your head off and spit down your neck," Tindal said to him. Then he turned to Ritt. "I'm getting paid for this, time-and-a-half. I ain't babysitting this idiot for free."

They kept Loretta until they finished drilling the hole. There was oil where Ritt thought it would be and this news lit him up inside. The seam had good permeability and strong porosity and it probably moved in a band for twenty miles to the northeast. It might give them fifty barrels a day, half of which was his. And this territory would give up more oil, he was sure of it.

He phoned Oda from his room. "It looks like we hit."

"And now we're rich," she said dryly.

"Beyond your wildest dreams."

She laughed. "When are you back?"

"Be there tomorrow."

"What are we going to do with all that money?"

"I'm going to take you to the bookstore, you can pick out any book you want. And if there's any left over, we'll go out and have a nice dinner."

Their hostage had spent the four days of captivity watching soap operas, eating the sandwiches they supplied. They bought him a toothbrush and clean underwear. Ritt finally drove him out to his truck.

"You learn anything watching *Search for Tomorrow*, Loretta?"

"That Eunice is a piece of work."

Ritt gave him the keys and left him to fix his flat tire. "You're still in for a world of trouble," Loretta called after him as Ritt walked back to his own truck. "You can't kidnap people. It's a crime."

"And spying is a sin. I'd say we're about even."

Alhambra might already be buying up land. Ritt thought he'd be able to borrow more based on the test results and he'd try and lock up some more of it.

On the road back to Calgary, wispy snow blew across the highway, obscuring the edges. When Oda opened the door, he was overjoyed to see her face, but he noticed that she looked tired. They embraced and had a long dinner and made love and afterward lay in bed, talking. Ritt revelled in that moment, her skin touching his, that length, the comfort of his own bed, the hypnotic timbre of her voice, perhaps the thing he missed most when he was away.

"I'm pregnant, Ritt."

It took a moment to register. He almost said, "Congratulations."

But then he wrapped her in his arms, said into her neck, "That's wonderful."

"We'll have a baby."

They gushed through possibilities until they fell asleep: boy, girl, scholar, athlete, world leader.

Ten hours later, Ritt woke up to a new world. The practicalities of a child suddenly loomed. He didn't know anything about raising one other than to steer it away from religion. They wouldn't be getting any help from family. Ritt's company was still precarious. But he wasn't going to rain on Oda's parade. Over breakfast they decided to name the child Mackenzie, after the river, after his company, a name that would suit a boy, and could be stretched to fit a girl.

He dreamed his oil company the way he dreamed his child—growing, gaining strength. His company still only had one employee but it had cash flow. At least for now.

Within two weeks of Ritt's discovery, Alhambra had leased most of the land that bordered his play. He'd managed to get just one more small parcel. Then he'd gotten a call from Shanty Macleod, who was doing some more work up there, and Macleod told him that Alhambra had set up three rigs right on the border of Ritt's lease and started drilling; they were going to drain the formation. This was the way Alhambra operated. A vulture company that used spies and financial clout. They sometimes bought up the company that they'd pushed to the brink of bankruptcy, if it had any assets.

With a child coming, Ritt suddenly was thinking of the future in a more urgent way. He wanted to get somewhere others couldn't so easily follow. He'd written to the Geological Survey people in Ottawa earlier in the year, after he'd heard the government was mapping the North. Three weeks after learning he was going to be a father, he took a cab to the airport and flew to Ottawa and checked into a cheap hotel. In the morning he took a cab to the drab building that housed the Geological Survey department and asked to see those maps. He was led into a room with long tables and metal filing cabinets with horizontal drawers that held charts. He was shown to the stereoscope and allowed to look at aerial photographs. Some of them were almost featureless, as if they hadn't been developed properly. Ritt spent six hours examining geological charts and correlating them with the aerial photographs.

He saw what he guessed were unmetamorphosed sedimentary rocks in the Lower Cambrian, which wouldn't be of any help. To the east of them lay a faulted piece of the Arctic Platform. The Sverdrup Basin might yield something. He submersed himself, rising and falling, snaking around the deformed earth, moving downward.

He came back first thing the next day and stayed until the department closed. He was hopeful there was something on Ellesmere Island. Or Melville maybe. He would need to file for drilling permits. He wanted to get in before the stampede, when the big companies would buy up blocks even though they wouldn't do anything with them. Nail down land so that others couldn't. Oil was a chess game, the world ruled into squares, hundreds of companies quietly dividing millions of square miles.

In the evening he walked along the canal in the December air. Skaters moved along the ice, the sound of their blades carrying in the winter air.

He stayed in Ottawa for six days, examining charts, filing claims. He phoned Oda each night, checking in. On the plane home he thought about their unborn child, hoping it would inherit the best qualities from each of them. From Oda, a deep curiosity, a willingness to meet the world head on, a sense of adventure. And what were his own best qualities? Independence. Nothing else came to mind.

Calgary finally came into view, the City on the Plain, its tower thrusting up like a fist, threatening God.

The next day he got a call from Peter Manchauser, president of Alhambra Oil.

"You kidnapped one of my people," Manchauser said.

"Happy to extend him our hospitality."

"That was my nephew, my wife's sister's kid. I don't have to tell you kidnapping is against the law. People go to jail all the time for it."

"Trespassing's a crime too, I hear. Not to mention stealing information."

"You don't want to get too rigid in your definition of theft, Devlin. It's bad for business."

"It's working out pretty good for you, I hear."

"We'll see." There was silence on the line. Manchauser finally said, "Look Devlin, I've got something I want to talk to you about. Meet me at the bar at the Palliser tomorrow at five."

The next day Ritt arrived at five and Manchauser was already there. Ritt recognized him from photographs in the newspaper. He was a particularly unattractive man, tall and ill-formed, his chinless face scarred by acne, dominated by a large menacing nose. He motioned for Ritt to sit, one over-sized hand hovering over the chair.

"You kidnapped my nephew," he said, again.

"You're draining my formation. I'd say you got the better of the deal."

"That's how you stay alive in this business, by getting the better of the deal. How did you know to drill there? The received wisdom was it was drilled out twenty years ago."

"Most of what's received in the oil patch isn't wisdom, Mr. Manchauser. Sometimes it's just pure horseshit."

Manchauser leaned in. "I want you to come work for me. I'll put you on the payroll as a geologist. Cut you in on the plays you develop. You'll make a hell of a lot more money than you're making with your midget company."

"Would you have taken this deal fifteen years ago when you were starting out?"

"No one offered me this deal."

"I'm doing all right on my own."

"I'm going to drain that play. I'll set up as many rigs on the border of your lease as it takes. You don't have enough capital to survive. Maybe you can keep buying small parcels, you can keep bringing in some mid-sized ham-and-egger to back your play. But I can wait. I'll pick you off, and when I do, my next offer isn't going to be as lucrative. This is a take-it-or-leave-it thing, Devlin."

"I'll leave it," Ritt said, getting up.

"You're going to regret that decision."

"Give my best to Loretta."

Oda had been sweating heavily in the night and was tired and her stomach hurt and she assumed this was all part of being pregnant. She was so ill on Christmas Day Ritt took her to the hospital, the emergency ward quiet, draped in red paper streamers and cut-out Santa heads. A few people huddled, nursing sprains and cuts and broken fingers.

"It might not be anything serious," she said.

"It better not be."

Both of them knew it was serious. They sat with their accumulating fear until a nurse led Oda away. Ritt waited where he was for a while, then got up and paced, then inquired at the desk, then paced some more. He was afraid to form any concrete thoughts. Oda finally emerged from the pale green door, her face drawn.

"They did some tests," she said. "We'll know in a week. Let's go home."

Nine days later they were sitting in a doctor's office. The doctor was in his fifties, unsmiling, staring at his hand spread out on the desk in a patch of January sun streaming in the window. There was cancer in her liver, he told them, looking up.

"But there's hope," Ritt insisted.

The doctor shook his head slowly. "Two months, maybe three. I'm sorry."

"The baby," Oda said.

"I'm afraid the fetus won't be sufficiently developed . . ." He trailed off, then looked out the window.

They left the hospital, walking into the cold air, the sun a remote blur behind the cloud. The appointment hadn't lasted fifteen minutes, that tiny span taking everything. Ritt didn't have any words and neither did Oda. They walked, numbed by the news and the cold.

In bed that night finally they cried, each consumed by shuddering sobs that lasted for an hour before they were both exhausted and fell asleep.

It took two days for Oda to become practical. They had only a few weeks, she stated flatly. Her pain would increase and then the drugs would take something of her she'd never get back. Ritt stopped going to work. They walked during the days, noting the last geese flying south, spying a coyote in the park one evening, grateful for the cold wind on their faces. They watched the river coagulate, the chunks of ice grinding against one another, fighting before finally knitting together. They went to bed early and Ritt read to her. And just as she'd said, as those weeks passed, Oda quietly disappeared, eating less. Ritt lost his appetite as well.

It was the end he had envisaged on their northern canoe trip, watching one another waste away. But afterwards, Ritt would still be alive. He considered going with her, and Oda, reading his intentions, made him promise not to.

They hadn't been able to talk about their child, but Oda finally said she had become convinced it was a girl. In one stricken moment, they both imagined this girl who would never be: tall, like her mother and father, forthright in her dealings with the world, a tomboy who tossed a ball with Ritt in the backyard. She always had a bandage on her knee, she loved her dog. She would grow up to inherit the oil company that bore her name.

It was only seven weeks. Oda died in the hospital, gaunt, her belly distended, her eyes wide, her skin a stubborn yellow. Ritt held her lifeless form, breathing in the last of her, weeping and thinking of that day in the barn years earlier when he'd first touched her miraculous skin. He slept a few fitful hours and the nursing staff let him be. When he woke up, it was still night.

He kissed Oda on the lips and pressed his forehead to hers, then left his wife and child. Outside, he turned away from a harsh west wind. He stood in the parking lot for a long time, staring up into the blackness.

The funeral was four days later in a small wooden neighbourhood church with a handful of people. Oda's father and brothers were there, their rural bulk uncontained by the pew. Useless giants with their grief.

He recalled sitting in the church in Texas, its lulling heat, fighting sleep. He wondered if that man he'd hit with the tire iron had died, and Oda had been the price he'd needed to pay. An eye for an eye. But God had taken two lives in compensation, the vengeful Old Testament God that his father had so admired. Ritt stared blankly at the minister, his generic pieties drifting through the small cold space. Ritt's tears were of anger as much as sorrow.

He buried her in a graveyard in the northwest part of the city, even though he couldn't bear the idea of Oda in the ground.

The rest of the winter was spent in blackness. Mackenzie Oil languished. Ritt slept poorly, ate little, walked long distances in the city. If he walked, he didn't think.

In March he drove toward the mountains with his camping gear and hiked deep into the bush. He made a bed out of spruce boughs and set up the small tent on top of them. The ground was too frozen for tent pegs, so he used rope to suspend it from four trees. He chopped firewood from a deadfall with a hatchet and gathered dry pine twigs and cleared a hole in the snow to make a fire pit. The fire he made was excessive but he took comfort in it. The night sky was clear, and northern lights danced briefly. He fried some canned corned beef and ate a little and threw the rest on the fire.

In the morning, he rebuilt the fire and made coffee and toast then put some food into a pack, along with a large knife and his compass and some matches and set out. The deep snow made walking difficult in the woods, and Ritt was relieved to come out finally onto the Elbow River, frozen and with a light snow cover. He walked along that for several hours.

The day was overcast and he trudged without looking up, allowing himself to relive those weeks he'd had with Oda between finding out she was pregnant and finding out she was dying. A week of it spent away in Ottawa. They had been together for ten years, and thought they'd be childless. It had hovered in the background, a quiet lack. With the announcement that she was pregnant, every moment, however mundane, became magical. He had walked her to work in the mornings, and in the evenings they made dinner, then mapped their lives. Ritt's new company was filled with possibility, their lives on the verge of flight. Ritt still had Oda's voice in his head, and as he trudged through the snow, he replayed it like a tape, over and over.

It was almost dark when the first snowflake hit his face. Ten minutes later, it was a snowstorm, taking the last light of day.

Ritt turned back on the Elbow. He guessed he was four miles from camp. He kept his head down against the wind, as it picked up, moving the snow on the ground as well. He kept his eye out for signs of his footsteps leading off the river back toward camp. He saw a lynx move into the woods and felt solidarity rather than fear. Two animals facing nature's wrath.

He found a spot that looked familiar, but by now his footsteps were obliterated by the snow and wind. He weathered the moment of panic that descends on those who are lost in the woods. He knew people died because they gave up too soon. They were found half a mile from the road or camp or their car.

He stopped to cut a walking stick to help in the snow. His hands were cold as he worked the knife to cut it to size. He decided he would give it another hour before taking his chances where he was. He'd look for shelter at the base of a large spruce. His limbs were heavy, and he moved mechanically.

He remembered hunting with his father in Texas, a cold fall day, wishing he was at home in the kitchen eating warm biscuits. They sat silent in a duck blind, his father sipping coffee, offering Ritt some, the first he'd tasted, hot and bitter. They had a bird dog that was old and almost useless. An hour went by in silence, Ritt occasionally examining his father's profile in the dappled light of the blind. His eyes were rheumy with the hour and with age, grey bristles on his sagging jaw, his canvas coat stained. Ritt shivered in the dawn as his father recited Isaiah, *The earth is defiled by its people . . . therefore a curse consumes the earth; its people must bear their guilt.*

They shot six ducks. Ritt brought one down, the shotgun kicking his shoulder like a horse. At the end of the day, they stopped at a farm, a house with peeling paint, a listing grey barn. The fields were dust. His father got out and took one of the birds out of the trunk and headed for the house. Ritt stayed in the car. A woman came to the door. She had dark hair tied back, a few wisps on her face. His father went inside. There were two girls playing a game in the yard. They were a bit younger than Ritt. They had thin cotton dresses with pale flowers and he thought they must be cold. He couldn't tell what the game was, but they skipped in tandem then stooped to pick something out of the dirt. They saw him in the car and did a funny impromptu dance for him, their feet moving quickly, their dresses fluttering, their faces expressionless, their thin mouths set. His father came out thirty minutes later, his mood improved. Ritt didn't know what he had been doing in there but figured it was more bad than good.

The trees offered a little protection, but he could see only a few feet in front of him. His weariness sat on him like a thick blanket. Though he was without fear.

Yea, though I walk through the valley of the shadow . . . We don't need the devil, we have You. *In your anger do not sin.* Ephesians. Does that ring a fucking bell? All You know is anger. That is what You are, the accumulated anger of two thousand years of mankind eviscerating itself. *Man's anger does not bring about the righteous life that God desires.* Book of James. But You don't desire the righteous life, do You? You're in love with violence, it's good for business. You don't want to guide us through the valley of the shadow of death, You want to be in a parking lot with a tire iron making someone pay. You can't kill me.

Ritt staggered through the drifts, his legs impossibly heavy. *You can't kill me.*

SIX

TEXAS

1964

From the plane Ritt looked down at Abilene, which was greener than he remembered. In the airport, he rented a monstrous immaculate Cadillac and drove to the offices of the *Abilene Reporter–News*. Twelve years ago he'd asked Bobby to look into what had happened to Smiley after the parking lot. He'd known even then that Bobby wouldn't and maybe he was relieved he hadn't.

If he'd killed that boy in the parking lot, if he'd been arrested and jailed, he might be out of prison by now. Starting his life at twenty-eight using whatever skills he'd learned in prison besides survival. Machinist, janitor, flipping burgers somewhere. Though seeing as how he'd attacked a soldier, they might've never let him out. Or they might have given him the chair; Texas loved its electricity.

In the newspaper's offices, a man directed him to the archives where he met with a woman in a cardigan who was smoking a cigarette. She looked over her glasses at Ritt.

"I'm looking for the newspaper for August 27, 1951," he said. "And the next four days. Please."

She hesitated and for a second Ritt thought she was going to ask why. *I want to find out if I'm a murderer.*

She made him write it all down on a small form, filling in the dates. He wondered if he should put his real name down, then decided not to..When he finished, he handed it to her and she disappeared for a longish time.

She came back with the papers and put them on the counter. "You need to stay at that table," she said, motioning with her cigarette. "I hope you find what you need."

For a few minutes he simply stared at the paper. It wasn't on the front page. That was good. When he finally turned the page, it was with the caution and dread people had when handling a dead animal in their backyard.

The story was in the August 28 edition. "Local Boy Target of Vicious Attack." He scanned quickly.

> Jimmy Dean Fayette, age 21, is in critical condition following a brutal attack on Saturday night. Witnesses say that two assailants sped away into the night, most likely headed toward the border. Police are searching for a green Chevrolet truck. Mr. Fayette is in Hendrick Medical Center and has not regained consciousness. His mother, Mrs. Lilly Fayette of Abilene, said her son worked at the Dyess Base and attended First United Methodist.

There was a picture of Fayette in uniform, short-haired, staring at the camera with clear-eyed malevolence. He could see Jimmy Dean coming toward him in that parking lot, his half-smile, a man in love with violence. Ritt looked at the next day's paper but there wasn't anything. Nor was there a story in the others. He brought the papers back and requested a few more. He went through them but there wasn't a follow-up story. This must mean he hadn't died. Or there would be more. Wouldn't there?

Ritt went down to the entrance of the building where there was a bank of phones and looked through the phone book. There were six Fayettes. No Jimmy Dean, but there was an L. Fayette, which could be his mother. He wrote the address down and walked to his car.

Abilene was pastoral in the summer heat, not the dark place filled with menace he'd held in his head all these years. He drove to the address he'd found for L. Fayette. It was a modest bungalow with a small porch at the front, a rusting truck on the gravel pad beside it. Weeds flourished on the brown lawn. Ritt sat in the car for a while, wondering what he would say if this was, in fact, Lilly Fayette.

While he sat there, two people approached on the sidewalk. A woman in her sixties and a man who might be thirty-five. They walked up to the house and the woman produced a key from her purse and unlocked the door. The man turned and looked around. It had to be Jimmy Dean. He was dressed for middle-age—Eisenhower jacket, T-shirt, khakis. Ritt sat in the car, fiddled with the radio, listened to part of a Buck Owens song, played with the dial and finally shut it off and got out of the car.

He knocked on the door without knowing what he would say. The man opened the door, his mother's voice in the background asking who it is.

"I don't know who it is," the man said without taking his eyes off Ritt.

"I'm looking for Jimmy Dean Fayette," Ritt said. There were those flat eyes that had stared out of the military photo. His hair was longer. A tooth was gone. An eagle clutching a snake tattooed on his forearm.

"What business you got with him?"

"I want to make sure he's alive."

"Far as I know," Jimmy Dean said. "And I'd be the one to know. Who the hell are you?"

His mother suddenly loomed beside him, a short sour-faced woman who emanated the same natural hostility as her son. Behind them, a faded couch, the sound of a TV game show. The manufactured joy of the studio audience.

"Just a concerned party," Ritt said.

"So get your concerned ass off my property," Jimmy Dean said. "Before someone puts some lead in it." His eyes had the bright anger they'd had thirteen years ago. Ritt guessed his gun wouldn't be far.

"Y'all take care," Ritt said, letting his Texas accent out.

"I'll take what I goddamn well want."

Ritt got in the car and started it. Jimmy Dean and his mother stood on the porch and stared at him. The relief wasn't as great as he'd hoped. But something lifted off him and was carried away.

The road to Midland was a blur. Everything that existed on this land was hard won. The Lord loved hardship; it was good for business. It was no surprise that the money was down where the devil dwelled.

Even his righteous father had dreamed of oil, but their property didn't sit on anything of value. Del must be dead by now. Or drooling under a plaid blanket in a religious hospice. He would be over eighty if he was still alive. Ritt was determined this visit wouldn't be a confrontation, though he knew he might be under-estimating his father's rage, his anger growing as his body shrank.

Approaching Midland, he saw the small church they'd gone to. Ritt recalled the divine healer who had come to the church one hot August Sunday, a woman named Eddie Lee. The afflicted assembled in the first pew and Eddie Lee spoke from the pulpit, her voice rising and then descending to a whisper, a symphonic lecture on damnation and the devil getting into our bodies and how sometimes his presence was a boil and sometimes it was an evil thought and sometimes it was a sick-ness that no doctor could treat.

One by one the sick hobbled up to be healed by Eddie Lee. She talked to them and felt their thyroid or their cancer or their unspecific misery and said a few words while holding her hand on whatever part needed curing. After an intense moment, the whole congregation rapt, Eddie Lee suddenly yelled for the demons to be gone and for Christ to take this sinner's pain. She put a hand to their foreheads then thrust them backward into the arms of a burly churchgoer who caught them and led them away, their eyes fluttering. Perhaps their torment was eased. Maybe just being the centre of things for that moment was enough, to share their suffering with the congregation. The brutal summer light came in the windows and baked them in their Sunday clothes, faces shiny with sweat, dresses damp. God teaches through suffering, his mother had whispered in his ear.

He had sent his mother a handful of letters over the years, most of them containing a cheque. He had written that he'd had some trouble in Abilene and had had to light out, that he was sorry he couldn't tell her more and sorry for the misery he had surely caused and hoped she could forgive him. He'd never added a return address, afraid of being tracked down by some vigilant trooper. His worries had been for nothing. Jimmy Dean had survived, a Lone Star misfit who lived with his mother. It was a wonder someone else hadn't taken a tire iron to him.

Their old place had been painted, the fence was new. Ritt could tell his parents didn't live here anymore. He knocked on the door anyway and a woman answered. She was in her thirties, wearing jeans and a Dallas Cowboys T-shirt.

"I'm trying to locate Alma Devlin," he said. "I'm her son."

"Goodness. We bought this place three years ago. I can give you her address. It's in town. We have it in case any mail comes for her. It makes it easier. Though there hasn't been much. Come in, Mr. Devlin."

"Thank you, ma'am."

He stood waiting as she went into the kitchen and Ritt could hear drawers being opened. The rooms had all been painted, the old wallpaper torn down. There was modern furniture and some sports equipment littered around. They must have a son. His father filled all these rooms with his rage.

The woman returned with a slip of paper in her hand.

"I knew I had it somewhere. It's a retirement home, I think."

His father must be dead. "You like it out here?" Ritt asked.

"Well, it has its ups and downs." The woman's face had a strained prettiness. This place, or someplace like it, had probably been a dream of hers or her husband's or both of theirs. They thought they'd get some land, no bosses, crazy in love.

Raise their kids away from the city. He wondered what she thought now, after three years.

"Thank you for your help," Ritt said.

"Good luck, Mr. Devlin."

He drove to Midland and found the address on the paper. It appeared to be a motel that had been converted to a rest home. The parking lot had only two cars. The two-storey building needed paint. Ritt went to the reception and spoke to a middle-aged woman who was reading a paperback and eating potato chips from a bowl. Her hand moved around the bowl as if she was looking for a particular chip. Hair coiled tightly in pink plastic curlers.

"I'm looking for Alma Devlin. I'm her son."

She put the paperback down and examined Ritt. "Alma's in number seven. She expecting you?"

"This is a rest home?"

"It is. We don't get a lot of visitors."

"How is my mother doing?"

"Alma? Well there's good days and bad days. You know. Her memory . . ." The woman tilted her head from side to side. "Some days she's fine, sometimes she doesn't have a clue who I am."

"Does anyone come in, if there's a medical problem?"

"There's a nurse comes by once a week, checks on everyone. And I'm here and the girl who does the beds and laundry. It isn't the Ritz but they're cared for." The woman looked Ritt up and down. "She told me about you. Left home and became famous. That's what she said. You ain't ringing any bells. What are you famous for?"

"I'm famous for leaving."

Ritt knocked on number seven. His mother answered and scarcely moved when she saw him. Her face was heavily lined, her short grey hair stiff as straw. She looked like a startled bird.

"Rittinger?" she said at last. Her eyes like buttons, unreadable.

"Mother." He stepped forward to embrace her and she melted slowly in his arms and hung on.

"My, my." She held him at arm's length and examined him, measuring the distance between the boy who left her and the man who stood here now.

She let him in and Ritt looked around the room. The light didn't quite penetrate from outside. The furniture had come from the house. The religious icons were gone, the painting of Jesus with the halo beaming above his head. She had a small kitchen; otherwise it was essentially a motel room. They sat in the only two chairs.

He was unsure where to start. He asked about his father.

"Oh, Del's been gone, what is it, twenty years now."

It couldn't have been twenty. Maybe ten, probably less.

"Remember we put him in the ground? Not much of a turnout." She leaned in conspiratorially and whispered. "And I don't know that they were mourning." She rolled her eyes like a vaudeville comic, and laughed.

"Tell me about Dad. He wasn't like that when you met."

"No, he surely wasn't." Her eyes were cloudy and red. She looked older than her years. "He was nothing but fun." She became more lucid as she told him about how Del's drinking spiralled after they were married and how he was fired from his rig job and then from another and then punched a driller, which left him fewer options in the local oil patch. After a particularly vicious night of drinking he passed out, shirtless, at dawn in the bed of someone's pick-up and woke in late afternoon suffering from alcohol poisoning and a severe sunburn that put him in the hospital. It was during that stay, his fever raging, his body in torment, the toxins leaching out, that he found religion. And after that, it was simply life's painful journey, walking on their hands and knees toward penance, pausing every once in a while to look skyward.

"Where is it you live now?" she asked. "Abilene, isn't it."

In his first letter he'd said he'd had some trouble in Abilene. She must be thinking of that.

"Bit north of there."

"Pretty country I hear."

He got up to use the bathroom. It was tiny and he opened the medicine chest to look at what was in there. There was something for arthritis in a prescription bottle. Two other bottles held pills but he didn't recognize the names. Painkillers maybe, or sleeping pills. He didn't see anything that might address her dementia, if there was anything that helped. At some point, she would need more care.

When he came out the afternoon light had changed, the brightness fading, her room deeper into a gloomy grey.

"Do they look in on you?" Ritt asked.

"Bethesda comes by, brings my groceries. We play cards. She asks me questions about the old days. She's a gem that one."

They sat for several more minutes, in silence. She didn't have much in the way of human interaction. She never really did. She and his father had barely talked, moving around each other like two snakes in a cage. After a while Del ceased to be a person, just some force of nature that you had to endure, like an ugly winter that won't end. She was used to living alone.

"When you arrived I was no longer alone with that man's rage," she said suddenly. "I had something to protect."

Though she hadn't protected him. His mother and her torn allegiances. Loving Del then afraid of him. Unable to protect Ritt. After the whippings, when Del's belt was safely back in his jeans, he and his mother would sometimes sit in the kitchen. She couldn't acknowledge it was happening, never looked at his cuts or bruises. And after he left, Ritt hadn't been able to acknowledge her; he'd told Oda his mother was dead.

"Do you remember going to see *Duel in the Sun*?" she asked then. "At the Bijou. When was that? Was it last summer?" Nineteen forty-six. "If Del finds out he'll beat us both till his arms get tired. Gregory Peck, now there is a handsome man."

Of course Ritt remembered, the messy Technicolor, bleeding orange and red, life more vivid than anything he'd seen around Midland.

"Who was that actress . . .?"

"Jennifer Jones," he said.

"That's who it was. They're in the desert and they love each other and hate each other and finally *shoot* each other. Remember the preacher—the 'sin killer.'" She laughed again. "But you can't kill sin."

Ritt remembered his mother made him promise never to talk about the movie once they got home, but in that seven-mile walk it was all they talked about. Ritt was overwhelmed by the size of the screen, by the loudness of the film. He loved the welcoming dark of the theatre. He fell in love with Jennifer Jones and would have died for her. Ritt could see them walking home after the movie, the dust coming up on the plains to the north. So much of their lives contained in one afternoon.

Ritt asked how his father had died.

"Out in the yard, chopping wood. I was at the kitchen window—that window right there—and I saw him go down. I just stood there, hoping my prayers had been answered. I made some biscuits, told myself not to look out there." She had a perfect memory when it came to Del's death. She'd probably replayed that tape a few times. "When the biscuits were done, I let them cool for a bit then picked one up and took a bite. I went out to him. He was gone and I thanked Jesus." She laughed again. "That was the last real use I had for the Son of God."

They sat in silence again. Soft noises came from outside, people talking in the parking lot. Ritt recalled a dinner at his house when he was twelve, one of the very few times they'd had company. Aunt Ettie with her gift for tongues and Uncle Horace visiting from Wyoming, his mother's sister and her large docile husband and their miserable son, back at a time when vacations meant driving a long way to put your own misery behind you in order to stay with relatives so you could bask in theirs. It was summer and they sat at the table eating an overcooked, unaffordable roast in the sweltering heat, drinking lemonade, and wiping their perspiring foreheads. His father's natural animosity ensured that their meal was shrouded in heavy silence. Ritt had looked up at the four adults, chewing with determination, staring in four different directions, a silence that filled not just the room, but his entire universe, settling in his stomach and spreading through his capillary system until by the end of dinner he wondered if he still possessed the power of speech.

He could see his mother had become lost in this particular silence. She finally broke it by asking Ritt if he was Horace's boy.

"No," he said, quietly. "I'm Rittinger." He looked at the floor, the worn carpet, the dark brown streak of a cigarette burn. "What do you do all day?" he asked.

"Oh I watch the television. That's what people do. Sometimes things can't be fixed, Del. They try, they surely do. I see it every day on the TV, people mending some grievance for the studio audience, hugging and thanking the Lord. But some holes you can't fill." She looked out the window.

"Del," she said, turning to Ritt. "Did you find oil out there? On our land. Tell me you did." She laughed then stared down and began to softly sing, *Jesus, lover of my soul, Jesus I will never let you go.*

Ritt got up heavily and walked to her and leaned down and kissed the top of her head. In the car he broke down and when at last he quieted, he drove away from Midland, Texas. He would not be back.

SEVEN

CALGARY

1970

Ritt found solace in geology. It was immutable, a foundation. Mackenzie Oil continued to punch holes with some success. He was getting a reputation in the oil patch as a contrarian and a magician, finding oil in areas overlooked by others. In the spring he joined a survey team on Ellesmere Island in the Arctic, a joint venture among several companies. The endless days of May appealed to him, an attenuated twilight where he was half-dead all the time. He worked twelve-hour days and when the crew flew out for some R&R he stayed in camp. He didn't leave until a month after winter arrived and survival became the subtext to everything. The darkness was oppressive. A polar bear circled the camp for three days before the Eskimo hunter hired by the team shot it from fifty yards away. For a second it seemed unfazed, intact, then it slowly crumpled into a pile, sprawled like someone's giant pet. When they examined it up close, it wasn't as white as Ritt had thought.

———

To get big enough to drill in the North, he would need to expand his company. But to do that he needed someone on the business end. He stumbled upon Jackson Tate at a party, the first he had been to since Oda died.

Jackson Lamont Tate was thirty-two years old and hadn't considered oil, though he was a local boy who'd grown up in its lengthening shadow. His plan had always been to live out East. He'd gone to law school in Toronto and worked so hard he'd hardly looked up in three years. He stayed there and worked for one of the large threatening firms with a WASP pedigree with the aim of making a great deal of money. And at some point he would. But in the meantime he was working brutal hours on someone's dull mess making a modest salary. When he was back visiting family he went to the party where he met Ritt, who told him oil was going to be the centre of the universe. That both the city and the industry were poised.

Ritt sketched the geological composition of the Mackenzie Delta on a napkin and explained to Tate where the oil was.

"This is a treasure map," he'd said.

"Does that make us pirates?" Tate had replied.

"It will."

Tate had a dishevelled frat-boy look. He was a determined smoker, a lapsed athlete who had retained that loose gait. His field was tax law, and he saw it as a form of jazz. Where there was complexity, there was opportunity, he told Ritt. It was Tate who first grasped that the key to growth wasn't simply a matter of geology; the tax code could be plumbed as well.

Tate hired an attractive secretary, found new office space that made Mackenzie look like a real company, and set up an empty subsidiary that was the corporate equivalent of one of those animals that puffs itself up to discourage predators. It was Tate who conceived and initiated the IPO, and Ritt who found himself with a script and a slide projector in Tate's office, woodenly rehearsing his speech.

"Oil is civilization's subtext," he began, reading from the text that Tate had written. "It is energy, politics and security. It binds . . ."

"More . . . I don't know . . . *conviction*." Tate was sitting in a chair, smoking. Beside him sat their secretary, Emily, who Ritt was pretty sure Tate was sleeping with. Emily nodded.

"It is energy, politics, security," Ritt continued. "It binds Christians to Arabs."

"You have to hit those notes." Tate said.

"What notes?"

"*Christians* to *Arabs*."

"Maybe *you* should be the *one* delivering the *speech*."

"That's better. No, it has to be you. You've got the credibility. You're the geological Jesus. And you've got that voice—you sound like the football coach for Texas A&M. They'll respect the accent. It means oil to them. I'm just an eastern-educated shyster who's going to burn through their money like a forest fire in July."

A week later Ritt stood in front of a room filled with prospective investors. He examined the faces: sagging, forlorn, a few blotchy with alcohol. Men who juggled paper and drank at lunch, swaggering through a city still clinging to its Kiwanis-shaped ideals.

"Oil," Ritt said, "is what holds Western civilization up. It is energy, politics and security. It binds Christians to Arabs. It starts wars and creates wealth.

"But I'm only going to talk about the last item on that list. The world's oil is concentrated in a number of deltas." He pointed to the slide behind him, an aerial view of the Orinoco gulf. "Orinoco, Niger, Gulf of Mexico, the Persian Gulf. These deltas have similar geological conditions to the Mackenzie Delta. I was trained as a geologist and I won't bore you with the details, but I could."

A polite ripple of laughter.

"The Arctic is the future of oil."

He paused after this statement as Tate had instructed him, but it didn't have the effect he'd hoped.

"Consider this: conventional oil plays won't last forever. We're punching holes down here like there's no tomorrow. America's oil fields are mature and may in fact be in decline though you won't hear anyone admit to it. Who's that leave? Well, you've got a cartel in the Middle East that has never allowed independent auditing of their reserves. Maybe the Saudis really do have two hundred and sixty-seven billion barrels in the ground. Maybe it's half that. Maybe it's a tenth. I don't know. Neither does anyone else. Most of the world's oil is in the Middle East, which can blow up without warning. It blew up in 1967, it will blow up again. That's what it does best. The Russians have oil. They also have short tempers, nuclear weapons and a national drinking problem." (The polite laughter that Tate had predicted and had offered himself during rehearsals.) Ritt clicked to a graph showing projected world oil prices. "In the short term, the North is a solid investment; in the long term"— click to a boldly coloured graph depicting world oil supply and consumption, two lines that re-crossed as they ascended—"it's a brilliant investment.

"Mackenzie is a small, extremely well-focused company looking to grow. You don't know me, but I am the man who discovered the Daedalus field. I was the one who opened up that play after every oilman in this town passed on it. They thought it was dead. It wasn't. You need to know where to look. I know where to look. I did very well with Daedalus. I would have done much better if I had had the capital. As it turned out, I wasn't able to nail down the land I needed and others profited from my intuition and expertise. My feeling about the North is the same as my feeling about Daedalus; others have misread it. I have a detailed understanding of the geology of the North, we have an innovative management team, and with sufficient capital, we will become one of the largest players in this city."

The next slide showed a diversified company with various red, aggressive-looking arrows snaking out to subsidiaries, only one of which existed, the dormant shell company that Tate had invented. "We are building a network of companies designed to sustain exploration and development.

"If this were a hundred years ago, I'd be talking to you about what the railway will do for this country. How it's more than transportation; it's a symbol. It will unify the country. It will *create* a country. The twentieth century is the American century because of oil. It fuelled the world wars, it is literally driving the

American Dream. But at some point America will run into trouble, as difficult as that is to conceive at the moment. The time to invest in the future is when things are good, when we're prosperous. Because that won't last. It never does." He sounded to himself like his old professor, Niles Stamp.

"That is what I'm selling here today. A vision. One that will keep the country secure. And most importantly, it will make shareholders a great deal of money. We have conventional plays that insure earnings and we have a unique vision for the future. With your help, Mackenzie will be the first in the Arctic. We *are* the future."

It was hard to read the faces in the crowd, to attach a dollar value to their interest. They were neither moved nor repulsed, a mob waiting for leadership. A few smiled noncommittally, some took notes. The applause was polite.

The next morning he and Tate flew to Toronto and gave the same pitch to a room filled with listless investment bankers. Ritt felt more comfortable with the speech. He found the inflections that Tate wanted. After two days of pitching, they flew to New York. The city was dying. Garbage strewn in the late autumn light. At a red light a bearded, mad-eyed man in layered rags approached their taxi. The cabbie rolled down the window and showed the man the baseball bat on the seat and the man turned away.

"It's going to be hard to raise money in this town," Ritt said.

Tate watched the city go by, chaotic and purposeful. "But it's here," he said. "We just need to pry it out of their jaded hands."

Two days went by in a blur of repetition. Emphasizing his Texas drawl as Tate had suggested, talking about his roots in the Lone Star State, how he was *born* unto oil. Ritt made a pitch for the North and looked out at impassive, meat-fed faces, money men who had sat through dozens of these dog-and-pony shows, listening to pitches for miracle drugs and hamburger chains. Mackenzie Oil was too far away, too small and risky. Why not just keep betting on Texas and Oklahoma.

They went to a midtown steakhouse for a late dinner and settled into their whisky. Tate flirted with the waitress. He flirted with all waitresses.

"Is it true this city is wicked?" he asked the woman. She was about thirty, dressed like a stewardess in a tight dress and pill-box hat.

"Only the good parts," she said then left with their order.

Tate turned to him. "Here's the thing. Those guys, they're not independent thinkers. This is herd mentality. You get the lead guy to turn, the whole fucking herd follows him right off the cliff. What we need to do is to leak some information to the top dog, watch the others follow."

"Information about what, Jackson? You don't mean make up test results."

"Not 'make up.'"

"Are these guys going to give a shit about promising surveys three thousand miles away in a country they can't find on a map?"

"They might if they think this is a bargain and they're on the ground floor, if we leak the idea you saw something in the Neutral Hills but we're trying to keep it quiet so we can nail that land. Geologic Jesus strikes again."

"Except we didn't find anything in the Neutral Hills and that's my reputation you're throwing away."

"It gives you time to find something real."

"You don't seem too concerned with the real, Jackson."

"Look, you think Pete Manchauser would worry about a little misdirection?"

"Manchauser would drown his mother in a burlap sack if it gave him an edge on the competition. That's not a model we want to copy."

"We aren't going to get enough to get you up north with this. But we'll get something. Enough maybe to attract a partner with deeper pockets. We'll be a legitimate contender."

"Here's to legitimacy," Ritt said, raising his glass.

"And knowing when to be illegitimate."

Ritt didn't have a clear picture of Tate leaving him. He didn't have a clear picture of arriving at this bar, the last in a dizzying sequence, each one more of a dive than the one before. He didn't have a clear picture of anything, except that Tate had led them here. And now he was gone. He'd left with a woman, a laughing maybe glamorous woman who kept taking Tate's cigarette out of his mouth and taking a drag and re-inserting it in Tate's mouth like she was feeding a baby.

They had been moving south and east on their bar crawl, and in his deeply compromised brain, Ritt felt these were the two worst directions. North and west, that was the way to go. They'd found the woman en route and Tate invited her to continue on with them, laughing, grabbing, kissing as they drunkenly walked. She found everything Tate said hilarious. Ritt examined his unfamiliar drinking mates, faces made of plasticine, moulded into lumpy red shapes, their mouths all moving at once; *Joe Namath—right here, in this bar, Broadway Joe. I shit you not.* How long had he been here?

Ritt wondered if he'd slept a little, his head on the bar. Time certainly had disappeared. His watch read 5:52. That couldn't be right. It was eleven when they'd left the steakhouse. He'd lost his suit jacket somewhere. He looked around the bar, a painful process, his brain moving half a step behind his eyes, sloshing inside his skull like bilge water. He got up heavily and walked uncertainly to the door and lurched out.

A reluctant light moved along the street. Was this Third? Papers rolled like tumbleweeds. Garbage on the sidewalk, the night's flotsam. A thin, stooped street cleaner picked unsuccessfully at the remains of a hot dog then sat on a bench and lit a cigarette. Ritt's head was thick and crowded, his mouth dry. He staggered slightly. Pieces of the evening's conversation came back, Tate telling him they were on the cusp, the *fucking cusp.* Tate would wake up in one of these towers with a woman whose husband was expected back soon. The streetlights all went off and the light was suddenly flat and unappealing. Ritt walked twenty blocks, counting them out loud. He didn't have any money and even if he did he couldn't trust himself inside a lurching stained cab. He passed signs that he tried to read through eyes that refused to focus—*The Catholic Center for Indifference, God Bargains! Fifth Avenue Fashions.* Stained wax paper wrappers blew by him. A man in a grimy coat was asleep on the sidewalk, a black dog tied to his ankle with a frayed rope. The sound of sirens and horns, the city waking up to new crises. A woman lifted her considerable skirt and pissed daintily over a sewer grate. Two rats rocketed by, hugging the curb. Black men congregated on the corner and his limbic Texas brain told him this was rarely a good sign. A faint moon was disappearing over the Hudson River. At last, his hotel loomed and he was filled with relief. He wavered in the elevator, almost home. When he hit the bed, he felt his world pitch and heave. He wondered if his company was turning into something he wouldn't recognize. Too heavy to lift, a burden.

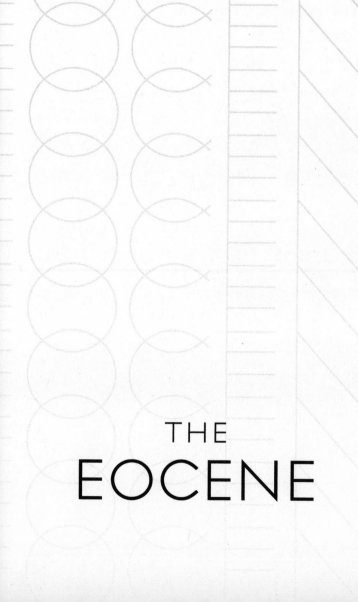

THE
EOCENE

EIGHT

ELLESMERE ISLAND, THE ARCTIC

1977

I t took three increasingly uncomfortable flights to get to Ellesmere Island. Ritt bounced awkwardly in the northern thermals as the plane descended through cloud cover, the barren landscape barely distinguishable from the sky. It was late September and there were less than two hours of muddy daylight this far north.

From the plane, the land was mountainous yet oddly undifferentiated, a white mass that stretched almost to the North Magnetic Pole. (The earth's magnetic field had reversed itself hundreds of times over the millennia, he recalled from his university days, going from south to north and back again, unable to make up its mind). The placid surface of Ellesmere was given to bouts of violence—twenty-five square miles of ice calving off to roam the sea. Below that surface, nine formations through the Upper Ordovician to the Lower Devonian, biostromal carbonate buildups that hid migrated hydrocarbons. Hid *my* hydrocarbons, he thought.

To see the romance of the North, you needed to be able to glimpse the underlying geology. The Arctic was distant and life threatening and prohibitively expensive; he had sunk $20 million of his own into this hole and still needed two slightly disgruntled partners to provide most of the financing.

The plane landed awkwardly on the crude runway and lurched slightly, the brakes pushing Ritt forward in spasms. He stepped out the door into air that twinkled, ice crystals suspended in the lights. The rig towered 150 feet into the darkness, illuminated by bulbs that ran up the derrick and gave off a light that was quickly absorbed. It was as isolated and hostile as a space station.

Manchauser had wanted a piece of this well and Ritt had rebuffed him, despite needing the money, because he figured the man was less dangerous as an enemy than as a partner. Now Manchauser was loudly denouncing this northern experiment as folly. And perhaps it was. Most explorations began as folly. Ritt was still certain that the North was the future. It retained a sense of the infinite, which is what oil depended on. Conventional fields in Alberta and Texas and Oklahoma were limping slightly. Three hundred thousand square miles that looked like a pincushion, oil dribbling to the surface like an old man eating soup.

Ritt walked into the camp, dropped his gear and went looking for the toolpush. He found Seth Shorten in the doghouse, examining a chart. He was almost sixty with a grey brush cut, an unflappable man who had seen most of the ways drilling could go wrong. Ritt asked if they were making any progress.

"Usual heartache. It's slow drilling but she'll get there."

"How is our schedule?"

"We're ballpark."

"And the samples. Where's that geologist?"

"Bit of an issue. I caught him smoking dope in his trailer. Says it helps him 'communicate' with the earth. I told him I catch him communicating again he'll be walking back to Calgary. Fucking geologists."

Ritt shrugged out of his coat and sat down, and they sipped stale coffee and looked at the charts that were tacked to the wall. A fold-out of Miss December was beside the drilling chart. She was wearing a Santa Claus hat, holding a wrapped present and winking.

"There's something you might want to take a look at," Shorten said. "In the morning. Bit south of here. Haven't seen it myself but apparently it's quite the deal. Let me know when you're up and I'll get the guide to take you."

Ritt slept erratically in his small room, legs extending past the short bunk, in and out of oppressive dreams. He woke feeling claustrophobic.

The guide was named Ikuk, and he was short and bow-legged, his face a ruin collapsed around a mouth half-filled with dark teeth. His skin was intricately lined, the lines sharply inter-secting, though his hair was black and lustrous. He spoke delib-erately and with economy, as if he had a finite supply of words.

They set out on separate machines, Ritt to one side and behind the guide, wearing a snowmobile suit, boots, a bala-clava and tinted goggles. The moon was almost full, a ghostly hole. The pale landscape gave off a weak light of its own, low hills of limestone and shale set against the horizon. They passed a sledge half-buried in the snow, a piece torn out of the bottom.

An Arctic hare suddenly sprinted. The Inuit had filled this emptiness with mythology, as all peoples did—mischievous crows and wise wolves and cleansing floods. They drove in the roar of their engines for two hours as the sun rose weakly and slid along the horizon as if it were lost.

The guide slowed to a stop and shut down his machine. Ritt pulled alongside and killed his too. Ikuk pointed toward the water. Ritt dismounted stiffly and started walking. In the struggling light he saw dozens of orange and yellow mounds sticking out of the snow. The tallest was about six feet high. When he got closer he saw that the texture resembled melted ice cream. Otherworldly growths slanting down toward the coast. They appeared to be the petrified remains of trees, ancient stumps. There was a patch where the snow had been cleared, revealing a black surface that looked like topsoil. When Ritt got closer, he realized it was coal.

He looked at the guide, who pointed toward the horizon. Ritt's eyesight failed to discern anything on the plain though he could hear an engine. Then a snowmobile came into view, pulling a small trailer on skis. The man turned off the engine and walked toward them. A white parka, a grey and brown beard, unfamiliar insignia. He shook hands with the guide then approached Ritt, introducing himself as Gunnar Stephansson. He said he was part of a multinational team of archeologists and paleontologists that was studying Ellesmere Island.

"Trees," Ritt said.

"They are fifty million years old. Eocene. Greek for Dawn of the Modern."

"How could they have survived months of darkness followed by a few months of constant light?"

"We don't know yet. We've also found fossilized remains—part of what appears to be a large crocodile, fragments of a skull."

"How large were these trees?"

"Maybe a hundred and sixty feet or more." Stephansson had very little accent, the English of an international scientist, veteran of a hundred conferences. "You're an oilman." It wasn't quite an insult.

Ritt smiled. "Different science. Same territory."

Stephansson shrugged. "Oil is so ordinary, no? You find it in jungles, in deserts. This forest has no modern analogue. It is a discovery. You people say you discover oil, but it is like discovering groceries at a grocery store."

Ritt didn't want to get into a pissing contest with a Scandinavian scientist. "That's coal?"

Stephansson nodded. "You can't drill here, of course. This is a protected area."

"I realize."

They both looked away. Ritt's guide stood there, the recipient of their gaze, the resource they both plundered. His teeth rotted from Fruit Loops and Pepsi, his way of life vanishing. Now we are the whales, Ritt thought, fat and sustaining, beached on this alien shore.

Ritt had sold the federal government on the idea that his rig would establish sovereignty in the North; the derrick was a flag. Ritt was an explorer, claiming the land for the queen like a sixteenth-century sailor. In return, Mackenzie Oil was getting an alarming tax break that Tate had aggressively leveraged.

"If you make a mistake up here . . ." Stephansson said, leaving it at that.

———

Ritt found Breton Allman, the geologist, in his trailer, mixing something in an industrial blender amid the incongruous, jungle smell of pot. Breton was bearded, wearing jeans and a faded T-shirt with an image of Laurel and Hardy on it. Pink Floyd was playing on his small cassette deck. He had ten candles going, giving a baroque light.

"If there's a sour gas leak the mask isn't going to seal over that beard," Ritt said.

"If there's sour gas, we're pretty much fucked anyway."

"You finding anything that's going to make us happy?

"Not yet."

Ritt had worked with Breton before, and tolerated his idiosyncrasies because he offered a unique perspective.

"How do those samples look?"

"A bit gassy, a flicker."

Ritt surveyed the space, which looked like a teenager's bedroom. "You like it up here?" he asked.

"Top of the world, Ma."

"You saw the petrified forest?"

"Ikuk took me out there a few weeks ago. Fucking mind-blowing, man." Breton picked up a tin from the worktable and sat back down. He unscrewed the lid and took out a joint and lit it from one of the candles and held the smoke in. "Eocene. That is wild." He let the smoke leak out and offered the joint to Ritt. "You should try this shit. Seriously. You will *become* the Eocene."

Ritt waved it away and Breton talked on about Jurassic-sourced hotspots and the Inglefield Uplift. "So there isn't a whole shit-load of stratigraphic info," he said. "During the Silurian, basin formation basically got its ass kicked by Caledonian plate margin deformation and plate-interior stresses. The way I see it, there is quiescence and there is revolution. I mean, that's geology, right."

"So where is that oil hiding?"

"Million-dollar question. This is where the puzzle is supposed to knit together. Pangaea. One world. Bob-fucking-Marley. Except you look at Greenland and Ellesmere and those coastlines don't match. Africa fits into South America—that all knits into one tidy land mass. But up here tectonics hits a wall, man. Baffin Island, Labrador, Greenland, they all fit like a jigsaw. The rock matches. But Ellesmere is an orphan. Like it was dropped from space."

Ritt's head was heavy with the weariness that Arctic travel always brought. Breton's trailer was overheated and smoke-filled and invited drowsiness.

"Those tree stumps," Breton said, "I counted eighty-three. Some kind of Sequoia. Man, it is all about cycles and we are heading back to giant lizards up here. Give it a few years, but this shit is already melting and if it's warm here you'll be frying eggs on your forehead in Miami and everything that can move will go north and where you and I are sitting will be the site of the Super Bowl two hundred years from now."

"Go Ellesmere," Ritt said dreamily.

Breton talked incoherently of synclines and volcaniclastic successions. Ritt tuned out. Breton got up and moved things around on the messy table. He came back to show Ritt a core sample that was two feet long, lying in a box, a gift.

"Listen to this, man, don't say anything. Just listen to what this beautiful fucker has to tell us." Breton stared at the core sample with the red-rimmed eyes of an accident victim.

Ritt looked at the perfect cylinder, a core sample from eight thousand feet down. It was dark, marbled with greys, and its surface shimmered in the candlelight.

"You hear that?" Breton said.

"What."

"You can't hear it? Like a murmur. Language, man. We are literally fucking the earth. Ooh baby do me all night long."

Ritt looked at Breton's expression, the concentration, straining through the effect of endless joints and profound isolation. There was a Carlos Castaneda paperback on Breton's bunk. Every day was the first day of the rest of Breton's life, a cycle that was not without its drawbacks.

"You draw those lines—the ancient lines, man, it all connects, right," Breton said. "Sulphide-bearing carbonate rocks on Baffin Island. The tectonic features of the Arctic Archipelago. Taglu breaks everyone's heart. Niglingtak gets everyone hard again. How many wells are going now—thirty?"

Breton was glassy-eyed. Ritt wondered how many joints he had smoked today.

"Big picture: three miles of Cambrian clastics and carbonates along a differentiated shelf-edge accumulate on a continental margin that is going to hell in a handcart. What I think is there is a long seam of paleo-oil-water contact and you could have ten billion barrels there. That shit has to go somewhere. You follow that geology, you sink your mind down into the revolution and when the smoke clears you're up to your tits in Cretaceous sandstone and then it is all pussy, brother."

Ritt watched the core shimmer between them. The candles flickered, casting fleeting shadows on Breton's lost face.

NINE

CALGARY

1979

B ehold the New Rome. Twenty-nine construction cranes were poised like carrion birds along the skyline. Every month, thousands moved here: welders, labourers from the East, professionals, criminals, women with tight jeans and damaged blonde hair who bought cowboy boots and drank shooters and hoped the city would shower them with love.

It was New Year's Eve and everyone in the office had gone home except Ritt. He'd stayed to mull over Tate's increasingly complex (and increasingly risky) expansion plans. Outside, a few cars moved through quiet streets. Everyone was saving their energy for later. Nineteen seventy-nine had been a glorious year, a drunken march into the future, staggering under the weight of new riches.

In three years, oil had gone from $14 to $35 a barrel, and that leap had made fortunes for a lot of people, including Ritt. Yet each time West Texas Intermediate crept up another fifty cents, he felt increasingly unsettled. One of the effects of expensive oil was it made people feel they were smarter than they were. Every half-baked junior with two producing wells was suddenly a genius. They convinced themselves it wasn't market forces (and some manipulation) that made them rich; it was wisdom and insight and corporate courage. And this kind of instant wealth made them feel like they weren't quite getting enough even as they were getting more than they ever had in their lives. It fuelled a sense of want, it redefined need, everyone living like Elvis. And the nagging remains of Ritt's Pentecostal upbringing felt a judgment coming.

From his view on the nineteenth floor, the city resembled a huge toy, a model of an urban landscape some billionaire had bought for his useless child, the scale reading one inch = one inch. Ritt took his tuxedo off the hanger and laid it on his desk, then stripped to his underwear. He stood in the window and stared down at the city, ironically recalling Matthew 25: *When the Son of Man comes in his glory, and all the angels with him, then he will sit on his glorious throne.*

He poured a small scotch and took a sip then returned to sway in the frame of the window. The towers were still lit, ten thousand empty offices glowing. Each one driven by a single belief: the world would always need oil.

Ritt put on his tux and finished his drink and took the elevator down to the underground parking lot. The party was at Manchauser's monstrous home. Ritt was surprised to have been invited given that his relationship with Manchauser was defined by an ongoing, almost simian hostility. At the party there would be government ministers, bankers, takeover targets, fat investors, a few people flown up from Dallas, journalists who were easily dazzled. There would be champagne and cigars and the men would talk government rumours and merger fables, horseshit that swaggered in the moment, dicks rolled out like garden hoses.

He drove slowly to Manchauser's place, trying to visualize Manchauser's wife, his third or possibly fourth. She had been carved into a humourless doll, as brittle and blank as ice. Her name might be Mandy. Manchauser had built a house west of town that had a theatre and a ballroom and an Olympic-sized indoor/outdoor pool and a legendary view of the mountains made possible by 120 tonnes of rock and soil added to a not-quite-impressive-enough ridge. Ritt tried to imagine himself having a good time and couldn't. A few snowflakes hit the windshield. The roads were still clear.

This was oil; five hundred people dressed in black evening clothes. In the dim light, they formed an amorphous dark pool; they *looked* like oil. And like oil, Ritt thought, they often flowed uphill (with a little help, under the pressure of gas) and here were hundreds trying to move uphill, hoping to make contact with those above their own station—a bigger company, a better connected wife, a board member. The party was a geological formation and—depending on permeability—people flowed toward the money. But like oil, some got trapped, in conversations with dullards, with people who were below them trying to move up themselves. They got stuck. Others got stuck there with them, forming a reservoir of itchy unhappy people who wanted nothing to do with one another. Rote conversations about Brent Crude and can-you-fucking-believe-the-Saudis. They blended and settled, every ambitious VP and grasping wife.

A colleague glided by. Anderson? Brillig? The name was gone. The man saw Ritt but kept gliding. Looking for the sun gods. Ritt would probably talk to him later in the evening, after the man realized he wasn't going to get any time with Manchauser or the other mandarins, after he'd spent long, humiliating minutes at the edge of conversations, unrecognized, not quite hearing, laughing when they laughed.

The ballroom had a wall of windows that faced west where the night sky lowered onto the jagged mountains. There was a deck outside that looked down onto the pool. Ritt asked one of the servers if she could find him a scotch. He scanned the crowd, looking for his wife. She was the reason he was here. Deirdre had wanted to come, thought it might be interesting. Why not go to the biggest party in town? Even if it's terrible, she said, it will be memorably terrible.

There was a country band playing, someone famous that Ritt should know and didn't. He was grateful for the noise, a cocoon. Some women on the dance floor gyrated carefully. The server returned with three ounces of peaty single malt in a heavy glass.

Ritt saw Tate working the crowd. Gliding through, shaking hands. It was an oddly voyeuristic experience to watch him operate; Tate's strength was in creating an instant intimacy. When he shook hands, he clasped his target's hand in both of his. He leaned in and often whispered something vaguely conspiratorial, as if he was sharing some new and meaningful secret. A gift for acquaintance. Tate had few actual friends and his girlfriends came and went. He was twenty feet away, his hand draped over someone's shoulder, leaning in to say something essential.

When he saw Ritt, he waved and came over. "That guy I was with, Fanshaw, he's in the premier's office," Tate said.

"I don't know that he's worth getting close to."

"We need someone in there."

"I hear he's roadkill. He's probably here looking for a job. You cozy up, you'll be getting a call from him in January is my guess."

"You talk to Manchauser?"

"No, and it would make my evening if I didn't have to."

"He's going after Ocelot. Going to swallow them up." Tate made a chomping movement with his jaws.

"He's got an ugly appetite."

"He'll come after us, Ritt. At some point those threats will become real."

"But you'll keep him at bay?" Ritt noticed that Tate was weaving slightly.

"The best defence is a good offence." Tate held up his empty glass and disappeared into the crowd.

Ritt saw his wife near the windows, talking to Jack Gordon's wife. Deirdre's dress was short, showing her truly wondrous legs. He walked up behind her and touched the small of her back and kissed her when she turned around.

"You remember Sheila Gordon," Deirdre said.

"Of course, how are you, Sheila."

"Already tired of this shindig," she said. She had honey blonde hair held up in a complex swirl. "I'd better go find Jack. You have to steer him around these things, otherwise he just drinks with the kitchen staff." She wandered into the din.

He and Deirdre shouldered through the crowd, shaking a few hands, kissing a few taut faces. They had been married two years and still retained that alchemy that made even the mundane miraculous. Ritt observed her dark hair and oval face, her purposeful walk. She was a welcome surprise after the lengthy, self-imposed romantic drought that had followed Oda's death.

She took his hand and led him to the dance floor. They slow danced, fitting together comfortably, gently circling in three/four time.

It seemed to Ritt as if people were trying to will themselves to have fun. Getting ready to inhabit an anecdote that would be told at the Petroleum Club next week, *then this crazy sonofabitch, he takes off his clothes and jumps in the goddamn pool holding a bottle of Dom-fucking-Pérignon.* They weren't in the present, they were trying to shape history.

"Do you know many of these people?" Deirdre whispered as they danced.

"That one," Ritt said, indicating with his head. "Tall blonde who thinks she looks like Jessica Lange because the surgeon told her she did."

Deirdre laughed.

"She's married to Dixon Trump, Badger Resources," Ritt said. "That's Dix over there, ignoring the person who's talking to him, hoping that Manchauser is going to walk over and anoint him with holy water."

"What about the guy in the Western-cut tuxedo. Talking to the woman with the evil smile."

"Middle management stiff at Imperial. One of those guys who gets up at five a.m. to jog four miles along the river. Doesn't drink, brings carrots in Saran Wrap for lunch. Works late, married strategically, went to every corporate retreat Arizona offered up, but he's stranded somewhere in the middle. The kind of guy who ends up blowing his head off in his basement rec room."

"God, Ritt, a bit morbid."

Ritt saw Manchauser approaching, waving one big hand in greeting, cutting the air with sausage fingers.

"Glad you could come, Ritt," he said, shaking Ritt's hand.

Manchauser grabbed Deirdre's hand and shook it. "Pete Manchauser. Welcome . . ."

"Deirdre," she said.

"Deirdre. I hope you're not wasting your affections on this man," he said, laughing and slapping Ritt on the back.

"I don't think they're wasted, Pete."

Manchauser openly assessed her considerable sexual worth with the leonine gaze of someone at the top of the food chain. That lazy authority.

"You still freezing your dick in those northern holes, Ritt?" Manchauser's smile was mechanical, as if he'd farmed the job of smiling to an outside agency. When Ritt had rebuffed him on the northern well, Manchauser had hoisted that smile and told him to watch his back.

"The last great frontier, Pete. But I think you're better off sticking your dick in these tired old holes down here."

"These tired old holes made me six hundred million last year."

"Glad to hear it."

Manchauser's face seemed stuck between expressions. He looked like LBJ's homelier brother.

"You two enjoy yourselves," Manchauser said at last and walked off, greeting people, basking in the accumulated fear.

Ritt turned to Deirdre. "Now you know why I didn't want to come tonight."

"You oil people are so charming with your dick metaphors."

"Quick, let's get out of here for a minute," Ritt said, tugging her down the spiral staircase to the pool area.

"It's almost midnight, Ritt, we should stay up here with everyone else. What is so important?"

"We are." Ritt took off his tuxedo jacket and hung it on one of the dozens of hooks along the wall. Then he sat down and took off his shoes and socks. He removed his pants and put his watch in the pocket.

"Ritt, you can't be serious." Deirdre laughed, the laugh that she'd had when they met. A conspiratorial laugh that invited you in. "You don't have a swimsuit."

"This pool is the size of a lake. We'll swim to the other end. Don't be a chickenshit."

Deirdre stood for a moment, assessing the downside, which was considerable; someone could steal her purse, for one thing. And she didn't want to leave her $1,400 watch unattended, nor did she want to test its advertised waterproof capabilities, which she thought might have been for her sport watch anyway. More critically, they would be the only naked people at a party that had several hundred fairly important people milling around upstairs.

"No one's going to steal your purse," Ritt said, guessing her thoughts. He took off his shirt and underwear and jumped into the shallow end and swam a few strokes. "Don't make me come get you."

Deirdre slipped out of her clothes and hung them up and walked to the edge. That natural glide, a sensual perfection that thrilled him. She sat down and slid into the pool.

"God I hope the party doesn't move down here," she said.

They swam to the far end where there was a barrier that came down to the water's surface. They swam under it and were outside. Steam came off the warm water into the cold air. Part of the pool was underneath the overhanging deck and so they weren't visible to the partiers. The water was deep but there was an underwater ledge that enabled them to stand, the water up to Deirdre's neck. They kissed for a while in the steam and Ritt lifted her up slightly.

"Ritt, this is such a bad idea." But she was laughing.

Then he was inside her and they turned to look west, the mountains dimly visible. It started to snow again, a few flakes that landed on the water in front of them. They slowly fucked as the band played above them, the lyrics muffled: whisky, unreliable women, Oh Lord.

After they finished they stayed locked together, Ritt holding her, effortlessly. "Can you see the Devil's Thumb," he asked, squinting toward the mountains.

"I can't see anything. That snow is really starting to come down. Maybe we should think about leaving. It might be a nightmare getting out of here."

Above them there was a loud communal countdown then a sustained cheer.

"Happy New Year," Ritt said and they kissed again.

There was splashing in the pool on the interior side of the barrier. Others had joined in. The noise grew. A few people ducked under to swim outside, their heads bobbing in the fog. There was a sudden loud splash as someone jumped off the balcony. A head emerged, a man in his twenties, fully dressed, whooping.

Ritt noticed a light to the south, a warm glow. He realized Manchauser's twelve-car garage was on fire, the flames visible through an open door. Ritt assessed the wind, which was brisk from the west, blowing the smoke away from the house. A gas tank ignited and the explosion wasn't as dramatic as he'd expected. He heard yelling from upstairs. The flames spread quickly.

"Jesus," Deirdre said. "We have to get out of here."

They swam back under the barrier. Ritt mentally calculated the cars that Manchauser would own; there would be a pick-up truck that had been driven once, two luxury SUVs that got quite a bit of use, two Porsches, probably matching, something being restored—a vintage Jaguar or Corvette. There would be least three exotic, unridden motorcycles. He'd have a sedate black Mercedes sedan, and something extravagant, a Bugatti or a 1923 Rolls or a Formula One car.

The inside pool was filled with people who didn't know what was happening outside. Above them the band had stopped playing. The people in the pool wore bathing suits taken from a locker that held dozens of them. When Deirdre got out all eyes followed her, the men in awe, the women in judgment. There were towels in a large built-in closet and they dried off. Ritt dressed quickly. Deirdre was a calculated beat slower. She put on her shoes first then took three strides to her dress and took it off the hook and this brief Helmut Newton snapshot of her in heels before she casually slipped her dress over her head would haunt many in the pool for a long time. She picked up her purse and followed Ritt up the stairs.

The ballroom was filled with the subtle joy that disaster brings. The guilty pleasure of destruction. Ritt looked for Tate and couldn't find him. He would be enjoying this. Ritt hoped he hadn't caused it. Hundreds of people jockeyed for position against the glass wall looking toward the garage, which was fully engulfed now and gave off a gorgeous light. Some of the people were out on the deck to get a better view. With every expensive explosion Ritt heard the awed noise people made at fireworks displays.

Ritt tried to find their coats, without luck. The staff were all in the ballroom, trying to see the fire.

By the time they got outside, it was snowing hard. Ritt took off his tuxedo jacket and draped it over Deirdre and took her hand and led her to their car. It was cold without their coats and Deirdre was shivering in the passenger seat as the interior warmed. They were almost hemmed in but Ritt was able to maneuver around and get free. More than a hundred cars were parked on the subtle grade of the foothills. Twenty vans that had been hired to ferry drunkards home stood in a row, the drivers illuminated slightly by the conflagration. Snow fell softly. No one else seemed to be leaving. He wound down through Manchauser's acreage and hit the 1A and drove east to the city.

"Someone must have set that fire, Ritt. Don't you think? I wonder who."

"The list of suspects is going to be the whole oil patch." Or Jackson Tate with seven drinks in him.

"Cars are his thing, aren't they. This is hitting him where it hurts."

"I suppose. A bit."

They drove on in silence. The headlights lit the snow so that it became the foreground, swirling flakes obscuring the road. Ritt wondered where police would be setting up spot checks, looking for drunken New Year's Eve drivers, of which he was technically one, though he felt clear-headed. There were sirens, and a fire truck barrelled by them, shaking their car slightly.

"That was fun, Ritt," Deirdre said softly. "In the pool." She leaned over and kissed him on the cheek and Ritt reached his hand out to hold hers.

"It's 1980," she said.

TEN

CALGARY

1981

eirdre Lennox came from an eastern family of quiet accomplishment and few emotions. She had thrown herself into law school, studying hard, rarely dating, keeping to a very small group of friends and emerging from those years as a hard-working, focused, not-very-well-rounded individual. A long relationship with another lawyer ended uneventfully. They were both ambitious and worked ludicrous hours and over the course of four years saw less and less of one another. During a rare dinner out, she examined her boyfriend's face, a man with whom she had lived for three of those four years and whom she sort of planned to marry and with whom she had had sex four times in the last twelve months, and she focused on his jaw as it chewed its way through an expertly aged, absurdly priced piece of steak, the sound of mastication oddly amplified, and she failed to recognize anything. It wasn't that she couldn't remember why they were together (though she couldn't): it was a failure to recognize him at all. He seemed a stranger, and she was on an awkward blind date with a blandly handsome man who at any moment might begin talking about the soft underbelly of real estate law.

She moved to Calgary as an act of self-discovery, leaving her quietly supportive family, her bewildered boyfriend, and her few friends. She cycled and skied and worked for a mid-level law firm and by the time she encountered Ritt Devlin she was thirty-seven years old and still single.

They met at a political fundraiser. Ritt was there simply as the visible proof of his modest contribution, to register the fact that he was supportive and that at some point, he might need support. Deirdre was a volunteer on the campaign team where her considerable organizational skills were prized. The fundraiser was a low-key event that spilled out of a voluminous boardroom on the top floor of one of the towers.

Ritt saw Deirdre standing by a window, staring west. The clouds were being pushed eastward, bunched into a chinook arch, the wind powerful enough to rattle the glass. Behind the arch—that perfectly drawn line of cloud—there was blue sky. Deirdre was wearing a sharply tailored suit jacket and skirt and heels. Her hair was drawn back with a severity that seemed punitive, a flamenco dancer's bun. Ritt approached and told her about the mechanics of chinook winds, how the adiabatic heating of downward-moving air produced the curiously warm wind that had once raised the temperature more than forty degrees Celsius in one hour. She listened dutifully, as campaign workers did to contributors, her face impassive. He was slightly overwhelmed by her presence, the way she cocked her hip slightly to shift her weight, the way she smoothed a few errant hairs that had escaped her bun. Then she laughed at a joke Ritt made, and her head went back and her eyes almost closed and she touched his forearm. He hadn't dated since Oda's death. He was smitten and everything that he came to admire about her was simply back-filled into a hole already deeply dug.

They were married eighteen months later in a small white rural church that sat alone in the foothills twenty miles west of town. Present were a handful of oil people and her handsome family, who withheld judgment on Ritt; his self-made status wasn't a recommendation and his absent family loomed large in their imaginations. They had expected an overblown, gaudy, easily criticized Western event and hid their disappointment that it was small and tasteful.

Three months before her fortieth birthday, Deirdre said she wanted to have a child. They tried to get pregnant, joyously at first, then arduously, then desperately. The first doctor they saw told them to get drunk and get a hotel room. The next doctor prescribed Clomid for Deirdre, but it didn't work. They were both tested, and the results singled neither of them out. Deirdre hovered over the decision to try artificial insemination. Ritt accompanied her on most of the appointments and went to his own, sitting in a small room, paging through *Juggs* magazine, which didn't contain any photos he could construct an effective fantasy around and ran directly counter to his preference for small-breasted women. He flipped through the pages. The models struck him as faintly oppressed, short heavy-breasted young women who had left abusive homes only to end up in a crummy studio in a strip mall being photographed by a creep. And that idea was no help, though he didn't want to go back to the receptionist and complain about their somewhat clichéd selection of soft porn. He hunted through the other three issues that were in the drawer and realized the stupidity of this search and was suddenly conscious of how much time had passed. Some other sad bastard was probably waiting for the room. So he abandoned the magazines and instead replayed a particularly lascivious scenario with Deirdre when they were first trying to get pregnant and she had an intense sexuality that looked, from Ritt's perspective, like she was possessed. He came grimly into the plastic container and brought it out to the weary nurse who had probably been handed a thousand of these.

The artificial insemination didn't work. Deirdre decided on in vitro. She researched it with the same kind of single-mindedness she had applied to law school, and put up with the lengthy wait for appointments, the blood work, shots, and sonograms. They took eighteen eggs from Deirdre and successfully fertilized ten. They put one in and she and Ritt waited for a few weeks, not talking about it, before giving up.

"When you come down to it," the doctor said to them, "it's a question of odds."

Deirdre was acutely aware of the odds, which dropped precipitously as a woman aged. At forty, the odds of getting pregnant using IVF were 30 percent; at forty-one they were 20.5 percent. The chance of live birth was 12.6 percent.

"This is Darwinism at its most elemental," the doctor said, leaning back slightly in his chair. They sat on the other side of the desk, huddled like refugees applying for asylum. "Sink or swim."

Deirdre put up with the invasive procedures and awkward meetings. One day Ritt looked at her IVF journal, a spiral-bound student notebook she took to every meeting. It was crammed with notes on judging embryo quality, on morphological scoring systems, intrafallopian transfer, the prolonged use of GnRH agonists, all of it written in her neat, schoolgirl script. There were semi-familiar acronyms (ART, ICSI, FSH) and an ink drawing of an embryo that had tiny hands. He wondered if this was a doodle made during one of the unhelpful appointments. She criticized various doctors. ("There is a smugness to her. She's *hoping* I fail.") Most of all, her entries revealed a profound sense of isolation. Despite the fact that they went to most of these appointments together and held hands as the doctor delivered careful assessments of risk and hope and outcomes, Deirdre was waging war with herself and nature at a biological level, and Ritt was a bystander.

He had his own private war to fight. Oda had died when she was pregnant with their child and even as Deirdre and he strived to conceive, some primal impulse perversely equated the whole endeavour with death.

He felt like their lives were suspended, everything dependent on the outcome; they couldn't plan for either result, a combination of superstition and self-preservation. The second, third and fourth fertilized egg all failed. The doctor then inserted two and they both took, twins whose heartbeats were perceived in the ultrasound, though one was stronger than the other. She lost one after two weeks, a mystery; it happens, the doctor said. It may be better for the other. They weren't sure how to mourn.

A week later the second twin was gone, vanished without explanation or ceremony. The resulting D&C was the low point of the ordeal, a draining, tearful event. But they went through all the remaining fertilized eggs, each invested with a more desperate hope, those two weeks waiting for the results filled with quickly dismissed fantasies of being an alarmingly good and innovative parent, of reading bedtime stories in the dimly lit, over-decorated nursery. The final egg was anticlimax; neither believed it would take, a dark thought they kept to themselves. When it didn't, they slumped into a year of lengthening silences. They rarely spoke of the grief that had consumed their lives, despite being encouraged by a therapist to do just that. In the aftermath, they rarely made love and began accepting the social invitations they had avoided for more than a year.

Ritt's mother died just as this trying, desperate cycle was coming to its end. He'd gotten a call from the rest home and made the arrangements over the phone. He and Deirdre flew down in early winter. The service was in the church he'd attended as a boy. Nine people sat in the pews around him. He didn't recognize any of them. Deirdre wept, though it wasn't for his mother. On the flight back the next day, they didn't speak, but the thought that they had somehow buried their unconceived child in the barrens of West Texas sat there between them.

Deirdre didn't have the will to repeat the process with her fast-declining odds. Ritt didn't have the will either. He was conscious of the misery Deirdre carried inside, that was settled in now, a companion that would never leave her, a situation he was powerless against.

So Ritt rooted himself in the earth, moving down farther each day into familiar rock, moving back through geological time, descending into the late Eocene, cold air moving across the earth, the end of the epic, tectonic war that created the Rocky Mountains. The world settling down, reclaiming its ice, forming layer upon layer until everything was still.

ELEVEN

CALGARY

1982

Ritt sat in his large unadorned office with Tate, staring at the wreckage. The Saudis had flooded the market with cheap oil, and the glut that had been silently hovering finally crashed, the ruins sprawled across the continent. The price of oil plummeted. More than two-thirds of the province's oil rigs were idle. There were foreclosures and oil-field equipment auctions and a worrying spike in calls to the suicide hotline. The classified section of the newspapers bulged to record thickness; homes were for sale with all the furniture in them and the two cars in the driveway, people selling the lives they'd bought on credit.

Mackenzie Oil had taken such a hit that Ritt worried they wouldn't be able to continue their Arctic drilling program. The feeling of invulnerability that had fuelled the boom was gone.

"We need to get creative if we want to continue your experiment up north," Tate said. "I've been talking to Sakamoto at Japanese National. They're interested in the North; we can maybe get three hundred million from them. Two-fifty."

The company was now so diffuse it was difficult to work out the dimensions of the hit they'd taken. Tate had exploited the tax system with great esprit and their expansion had been complicated. He used a long-idle subsidiary—Mackenzie Exploration—to make a leveraged buyout of Resolute Resources using borrowed money. Mackenzie Oil then bought the assets of the takeover company from its own subsidiary. It needed to buy the assets rather than shares, Tate had patiently explained, because it gave Mackenzie Oil a write-down and allowed them to avoid taxes. They had built up an impressive pile of tax credits for their Arctic exploration, and when they took over Resolute, they applied those credits to the new company and all that tax money went into Mackenzie's pockets.

Ritt had sold the government on the idea that drilling in the Arctic was tantamount to a territorial claim. Now he worried that Tate's aggressive plays would affect his relationship with the feds, which had become a marriage of sorts: filled with argument and mutual gain and simmering resentment and stretches when you couldn't bear to touch one another.

And they had the National Energy Program to contend with, which had the stated aim of preventing foreign oil firms from taking profits out of the country, and which looked, to the Americans, like a half-assed South American socialist stab at nationalization. It provided government subsidies for Canadian-owned companies, regulated prices and imposed heavy taxes, and a barrel of Alberta oil quickly dipped far below world prices. This had the effect of driving certain small operators into bankruptcy and most of the majors into the US and overseas to look for more lucrative opportunities. The whole town complained of conspiracy and communism and letting the eastern bastards freeze in the dark, but as Tate pointed out to Ritt, there was an upside.

"The big guys are heading south, the little guys are dying," Tate said. "We hide out in the hills and come down and finish off the wounded. Some of them don't have the capital to survive in this environment."

"Do we?"

Tate shrugged. "As long as the banks think we're solvent, we're solvent. Money is psychology, not math."

Ritt stared up at the painting in his office, a crude depiction of a buffalo with the words "I roam" written in bold red letters across its body.

"I've got a plan," Tate said.

Tate had a specific look when he launched these plans of his, which had been, by turns, lucrative, vaguely larcenous and costly. The proximity to stupid money had made him realize just how much of the world was there for the taking.

Tate was probably the person whom Ritt was closest to and he found it odd they rarely saw one another outside the office. Ritt had never been to his house. The two of them had built a nascent, precarious empire, joined by this burden. Yin and yang, Tate had said drunkenly one night, and they tried to figure out which was which. When Ritt had asked him about the fire at Manchauser's New Year's party, Tate had shrugged and replied that it was a victimless crime—Manchauser got the insurance, his guests got a memorable night, and his enemies saw that the man could be burned. That was the message, Tate said, in his disturbingly amoral tone. They left it at that. Ritt realized he and Tate weren't really friends, a thought that depressed him slightly.

"I hope your plan doesn't involve borrowing more money," Ritt said, "because we are leveraged to the tits and I don't want any more liability."

"We take a run at Synoco."

Ritt stared out the window. "So you want us to take over, what are they—the tenth largest American oil company? About twelve times bigger than us." You couldn't fault Tate for lack of ambition. He preached a brand of counter-cyclical economics: to rush in when everyone else was leaving. But sometimes there was a good reason everyone was leaving.

"Not take over Synoco exactly. But here's the thing. Synoco owns a big piece of Maple Leaf Oil. We get that piece. With our government's brain-dead communist energy policy, we can get more out of it than they can. Their Canadian assets are now a burden. MLO has good flow, incredible land holdings, nice production. They're an ideal fit."

"And how do we get Synoco to sell if they don't want to?"

"We attack Synoco itself."

"What's their market cap? Ten billion?"

"Give or take. We talk to them, explain that their Canadian assets no longer have the same value, which they should have figured out. They turn us down, and we buy fifteen, twenty percent of Synoco's shares at a premium, which threatens their autonomy. We offer to trade the shares back in exchange for their holdings in MLO."

"Jesus. A lot of risk."

"Now is the time for risk. When everyone is too nervous to make a move."

"We'd be betting the company."

"You don't bet, you can't win."

Three weeks later Ritt flew to Dallas to meet with Jimmy Peterson, the taciturn CEO of Synoco. He looked more Ivy League than oil, a strong, tanned face with vertical lines that emphasized its rectangularity. Peterson didn't say much, just sat up straight while Ritt talked, like a schoolboy who was daydreaming. Ritt laid out his case: you could call the National Energy Program a socialist wet dream or whatever you wanted, but it was policy and that was that. Mackenzie puts in a tender for Synoco stock and exchanges the stock for shares of Maple Leaf, then Synoco avoids capital gains, retires the shares, which enhances the value of remaining shares. Win-win and fucking win. This was Tate's sleight of hand.

After Ritt was done laying it out, Peterson was quiet for a minute. He finally said, "Why do I get the feeling this is a threat, Ritt?"

"It's an offer that will benefit both parties."

"Well, I'll tell you, I don't feel benefited. I truly don't."

Ritt started to reiterate the upside for Synoco. Peterson played with his cufflinks and interrupted. "You came all the way down here to tell me your socialist government has me pinned to the mat."

"You can dream about an Adam Smith utopia or you can deal with the reality on the ground, Jimmy. I'm saying we can work this to mutual advantage."

"And I say fuck Karl Marx and the horse he rode in on."

Peterson stood up. Behind him Dallas sparkled, the Texas sun bouncing off mirrored towers. "I'm going to hang onto

Maple Leaf. Your people will come to their senses at some point and vote in a real government."

Ritt nodded. They shook hands and he left.

Twelve days later Mackenzie made a public offer of $62 a share for sixteen percent of Synoco stock, which was trading at $49.82. Peterson went to the courts to try to block the sale, though it was more bluff than anything.

When Peterson called, Ritt was in his office, staring west to the mountains, which had taken on the purplish hue you saw in bad paintings. They looked majestic and alarmingly close and fake.

"You want a fight you came to the right place," Peterson said.

"We were hoping this would stay friendly."

"Well that ship has sailed."

Ritt had a copy of the letter that Peterson sent out to Synoco shareholders. *We believe it is important that the US government take action so that American citizens are not victimized by foreign companies depressing the value of their investment on the basis of alleged tax benefits that are HIGHLY questionable.*

"I think we can both benefit from this, Jimmy. Right now you're spending fifteen grand a day on lawyers who are too well paid to tell you that there isn't any law that can stop a legitimate stock buy in a free market."

"What the hell you boys know about free markets?"

"I have to live with the policy, same as everyone else."

"You want me to hold still while you fuck me."

"I want you to do what's best for your shareholders."

"You go straight to hell."

Ritt re-evaluated the view from his office, tracing the jagged line of snow in the mountains. A stream of cars inched west.

"I might just sell Maple Leaf to one of your rivals," Peterson said. "You think of that."

"This isn't exactly a seller's market."

"Fuck you, Devlin."

Two days later Ritt flew to Beaumont, Texas, to take a look at the Arctic drill ship he had ordered a year ago and could no longer afford. It was a hardscrabble town with pumpjacks operating on the fringes and red brick buildings lining orderly streets. The sun was brittle, the faces worn. He'd bought a decommissioned 150,000-ton Japanese supertanker that was being converted into a drill ship here at a shipyard. They were putting a drilling platform in the centre, reinforcing the forward section, then they'd take it up to the Beaufort Sea. Manchauser had said it was pure stupidity.

Looking at the supertanker, a grey monster in dry dock, it was hard not to agree. Sparks flew as the massive industrial cutting torch moved slowly through the hull. The sound of steel on steel, an erratic tolling, echoed through the air. Grimy men dotted the cavernous space. Sparks formed spitting semi-circles. The industrial light deepened the gloom.

A stocky man came up beside him, a foreman he'd met before but whose name he couldn't recall.

"Hell of a thing," the man said. "Be the size of Rhode Island when she's done. I hope she floats."

"She'll float."

He was surprised by how comforting he found the familiar accent. A relief after the flat lustreless sounds north of the border.

Ritt drove to his hotel and lay on the bed. He wished Deirdre were here. They could go to a corny diner where everything on the menu was from 1955 and men with grey stubble and soiled cowboy hats drank coffee from cups that were half an inch thick and smoked cigarettes and talked about how much of a god Tony Dorsett was. They'd listen to Patsy and Lefty and she'd ask him to tell her all about Texas and then they'd come back and make love on this bed.

He called her, waking her up.

"I'm in Beaumont. You should see that ship. Looks like science fiction."

"It's late, Ritt."

"I know. Just wanted to hear your voice."

"That's nice. It's just, I've got a breakfast meeting."

"Well . . ."

"Givener. He thinks seven thirty a.m. is the ideal time for a meeting." He heard her moving around in the bed, the rustle of covers.

"Okay then. Sleep tight."

Ritt tried to sleep himself, then sat up and poured a drink and watched a black and white re-run of a sixties series on TV. He had another and watched a game show with the sound off, thinking about Deirdre. On the screen a woman jumped up and down, waving her arms. Lights flashed. The host gave her a professional smile. He and his wife were just in a lull, he thought. He hoped.

As the plane curved toward Calgary in the dark, Ritt looked out the window and saw the lines of red tail lights heading east. Perhaps it was the out-migration, a long parade of rig hands whose unemployment benefits had run out; professionals who suddenly found themselves without clients; families loaded into over-packed woe-filled station wagons heading back east; hard-luck girls who hadn't managed to land a cowboy and had been unable to grasp that they were essentially a marketing construct and the last oaf they took back to their basement apartment after closing time was about as good as it was going to get. The city settling into itself, assessing the mess after the guests all left.

TWELVE

DALLAS, TEXAS

1983

It was early April when Ritt and Jackson Tate flew
to Dallas to formalize the deal with Synoco, which
Peterson had unhappily and reluctantly agreed to
in principle. Synoco was boxed in; the easiest way
out of the mess was to get a good price for Maple Leaf.

"Here's the thing," Tate said, lounging on the leather seat of
the rented Gulfstream jet. "We're on their turf, this jet is going
to be in their hangar, we're driving in *their* limo from the airport, meeting in *their* boardroom. It could all be bugged. I'm not
saying they'd do it, but they could. So don't say anything that
you wouldn't say to their faces."

"What are they going to say to our faces?"

"Sticks and stones. They're going to get nasty, but at the end
of the day, we're going to walk out of that boardroom with
their company."

"Peterson wants more than the shares. How high can we go
with this?"

"We can go to a hundred and twenty-five million. Enough so he
won't have to fall on his sword at the next shareholders' meeting."

Ritt wondered what they would do at their next shareholders' meeting. Throw out a few magic words—*synergy, diversified*—and hope for the best?

They were flying low enough to see the endless curve of America through the window. Ritt dozed off and woke up with a start as they banked into their approach, Dallas suddenly splayed below them.

They moved slowly through traffic in the Synoco limo. It was the afternoon rush hour. Dallas went by, shiny as the future. In the expansive Synoco lobby there was a ten-foot bronze of a horse on its hind legs. In the boardroom waiting for them were Peterson and various VPs and lawyers in expensive boxy suits. The hard faces of men who had played a little ball at Texas A&M or Oklahoma, men who wanted to take some flesh out of this deal. Testosterone seeped out and filled the corners of the room like sour gas, seeking the ground. The table seated about forty. They stood up as Ritt and Tate came in and everyone was introduced all around and Ritt remembered none of their names.

He and Peterson re-assessed one another: Ritt with twenty-two million Synoco shares in his pocket and an unwelcome sense of financial exposure, Peterson with his rage. It was twilight, and dark clouds scurried east. Peterson had demanded an evening session. He likely wanted to see who still had something left at three a.m.

"It's late in the day so we'll lay it on the table," Peterson said. "You want Maple Leaf, I'll tell you right now, it's going to cost."

"I've got twenty-two million shares I can give you."

"That's a real good start."

It didn't take long before tempers began to rise. Ritt laid out a mutually beneficial scenario with great tact, then one of Peterson's Dobermans hammered his fist on the table.

"Let's put the facts on the table," he said. "You boys are stretched so thin you're fucking transparent. West Texas goes down another dime and you're going to topple."

Tate responded. "You want facts. Here's a few more. We are going after Maple Leaf, an asset that is basically dead weight for you. But we have twenty-two million Synoco shares in our hip pocket; we could go after *Synoco*."

"You don't have the muscle," Peterson said.

"We could partner up," Tate said. "You don't think someone in this town might want to get in on that. How many enemies you have, Peterson?"

"You boys don't have the money," Peterson said. "Plain and simple. And if you've got an imaginary friend in this with you, now would be the moment to bring him in. You're wasting our goddamn time. Give me *one* good reason . . ."

"I've got twenty-two *million* good reasons . . ." Tate said, starting to get out of his chair.

One of the lawyers said, "Maybe we should just all take a break and think about life for a few minutes."

Ritt and Tate walked down the hall to the lobby, where Tate passed him a note that read "lobby bugged" and so they talked about *The Godfather* movies.

"Basically, they're about management styles," Tate said. "You've got Don Corleone, he's got this wise grandfather thing going on. But it only works because he was a violent thug when he was young. So he can afford to sound like Mr. Rogers now. He helps the little people, which buys loyalty. Sonny, his management style is to beat you half to death with a garbage can lid. Effective in the short term, but a disaster in the long run. Fredo's a fucking idiot; he can't even manage himself. Which leaves Michael. The educated son, the war hero, the guy who doesn't want to be part of the family business. But he's perfect. You know why? Because he's got a lot of his father in him. He can be ruthless when he needs to be. In the end, that's what management is: intelligent ruthlessness. Michael has his own *brother* killed . . ."

On a piece of paper, Tate wrote "150—MAX" and handed it to Ritt, whose stomach dropped: an increase of $25 million in six hours.

"That's when it becomes clear: to *preserve* the family, you have to be prepared to *kill* the family."

"This philosophy isn't filling me with joy," Ritt said.

"Michael, not Sonny," Tate said, pointing to the boardroom. Ritt wasn't sure if he was referring to Peterson or to themselves.

When they finally hammered out a deal, the sun was coming up weakly behind them, the city coming into grey focus, still static. They had their prize, although they had paid a lot, too much. Ritt would give Synoco the twenty-two million shares plus $214 million cash for control of Maple Leaf. The final tally was north of $1.5 billion, all of it borrowed. On the way to the airport Ritt silently weighed joy and fear.

It wasn't until their unbugged jet took off that he and Tate spoke.

"We did the right thing," Tate said.

"We did." He wasn't sure they had.

"Go big or go home. We didn't have a choice."

We had a choice, Ritt thought. Now they were big but they were vulnerable. The python that swallowed the pig. Too fat to move, too poor to shit. "What if Manchauser tries to pick us off?"

"We're too fucking complicated now," Tate said, lighting a cigar. "It would be like trying to take over the Vatican."

Ritt was jangled from no sleep and the cresting and falling of adrenaline over twelve hours of argument. He poured a large scotch and looked at the landscape as the Gulfstream moved over the last of Texas. The route the jet was taking mirrored the one he'd driven a thousand years ago in Bobby's pick-up. What had become of Bobby? Working motors for an outfit out of Midland maybe, watching the Cowboys every Sunday as he drank his Lone Star. Darlene drinking Thunderbird in the afternoon, watching the soaps, talking to the screen, offering advice—*Why don't you just leave him, honey*. The land was laid out in squares, each farmhouse sitting behind a copse of trees as a wind break.

Below that tranquil surface (from this height anyway) the Texas Paleozoic had run riot. Permian seabeds filled with bryozoa and goniatites and the petrified imprint of the first restless sharks (he still heard all this in his head in Niles Stamp's encouraging accent). Then life as we know it is wiped out. Ninety percent of it anyway. There go the trilobites. But that remaining ten percent is still game for the fight. Ready to evolve. Put it all behind them. To the east, the Appalachians forming, waiting for hillbillies to arrive and inbreed. Giant ferns, wingless insects. What else happened in the Paleozoic? Reptiles and annoying flies. Forests creep back. Oxygen levels through the roof. Everything circling around the idea of oil.

Wyoming still had patches of white, but spring was moving up from the south. This might be Ritt's moment but he didn't know.

It was almost six by the time he got back, feeling hungover and exhausted. Deirdre wasn't home yet. He took a shower and heated some soup. He poured a small whisky and watched the news and went to bed.

In the morning, she was there beside him. He hadn't heard her come in. He used to be a light sleeper, the smallest noise waking him, but last night, he'd been dead to the world and dreamless.

She turned to him, propped up on her elbow. "You get everything you needed down there?"

"Most of it."

"And you can afford it."

"No."

"You'll want to keep that nugget to yourself."

It was Saturday and for once they had no plans. Ritt suggested they drive to Lake Louise, walk up to the tea hut, get some air, stay in the chateau, order a stupidly priced wine.

It was early afternoon by the time they got on the road, the sun angled into the windshield, the mountains lost in the glare.

They spent the two hours on the drive up listening to classical music on one of Deirdre's cassettes. As if they had better save all their conversation for dinner.

They checked in and decided it was too late to hike up to the tea hut. Instead, they walked beside the lake, passing elderly, fit-looking Germans. The sun was almost behind the mountains, the advertised turquoise of the lake muted.

Near the end of the path, on the rock face that towered above them, a climber was spread out, seeking purchase with his hands and feet. He wasn't attached by ropes, a free climber relying on the next tiny ledge or crack to leverage his weight upward. Counting on the strength in his fingers and arms. An act of faith. He was halfway up.

"I could never do that," Deirdre said. "God, my stomach gets queasy just watching him. What happens if there is no next piece of rock to hold on to? Or what if it crumbles? To take that kind of risk. For what?"

"The thrill, I suppose." Ritt watched as the man freed a hand to search above him, like he'd lost something in a cupboard he could barely reach. "And when you stand at the top and look down it must feel like a miracle."

"If we stand here and watch, he's going to fall."

"And we'll be responsible for his death."

"I'm serious, Ritt. We have to go."

The wine list was lengthy and wordy (*angular and earthy with tobacco tones*) and Ritt settled on a price—$432—rather than a wine. The dining room was half empty. It was the shoulder season and there were fewer tourists. They ordered and looked out to the mountains.

Deirdre was brooding. "The whole industry would love to see you fail. People are going to want to get close to you but you don't have any friends out there."

"I don't know how many I had before this."

"Manchauser is going to see you as a genuine threat now."

A sommelier arrived with the wine, and opened it with a flourish. He handed Ritt the cork and Ritt placed it on the table. He took a sip of the wine and nodded. The sommelier poured the wine, and Ritt could tell he wanted to say something that would let them know he had a bottomless and nuanced understanding of *premier cru* Bordeaux, but sensed this wasn't the moment.

"Is this what you wanted, Ritt?" Deirdre asked after the sommelier was gone.

Ritt shrugged. He wasn't sure. It was what Tate wanted. Ritt wanted to drill in the North and he'd need a company that could swing that kind of money around.

"I'm worried it's just going to mean more dreadful evenings with the industry," Deirdre said, "chatting with those wives about how the service at the Royal Hawaiian has gone to shit." She took a sip of her wine. "My job bores me to death but it's the only thing that gives me any definition right now. Maybe I should do some volunteer work. I don't know, Ritt, you're away half the time and even when you're home, your head is somewhere else."

"Most of the heavy lifting will be Tate's."

"Which is another problem. Has it occurred to you that he's out of control? Maybe he's got some kind of corporate death wish. Like those gamblers who secretly want to lose. You risked the *company*, Ritt."

"He's a bit aggressive . . ."

"He's the second coming of Pete Manchauser."

"But Manchauser doesn't have anyone to rein him in."

"You don't seem to be pulling too hard on those reins." Deirdre stared at him and the look on her face (a particularly lawyerly look) made him wonder if she was assessing him like a P&L statement. In one column was "good earner," "reasonable physical shape," "still in love." And in the other? "Aloof," "obsessive," "an unhealthy relationship with geology (*geology!*)."

And what did he see when he looked at his wife? A beautiful, determined woman who moved through the world with that dizzying linear stride. The inability to conceive had thrown up a roadblock, and now she was evolving, adjusting to the new environment. Five geological epochs had ended in catastrophe. And with each one, species died, new ones emerged. Sometimes it was adaptability that determined who was left after the upheaval. Sometimes it was simply luck.

Ritt looked out to the mountains. Eighty million years can age you. The limestone was holding up surprisingly well (the Cary Grant of rocks, Stamp had said), the softer sandstone and shale not so much. The shale valleys fell victim to every glacial bully that crawled through town. So much of the earth's surface was uneventful and conservative, disguising its revolutionary youth below. But the Rockies waved its youth like a flag; aggressive thrust faults still on display, oceans floors torn up and lifted to the skies during the throw-the-TV-out-the-ninth-floor-window party that was the Laramide orogeny. A maturing range that refused to grow up.

The aquamarine lake was now black. A few canoes bobbed at the dock. They finished their dinner, throwing aimless observations into the silence.

Back in their room after dinner, Deirdre spent a longish time in the bathroom. She emerged in the hotel robe and walked to the bed. He remembered this moment of anticipation, played out in other hotel rooms, when that short walk and the shedding of the robe shortened his breath. Tonight they made love mechanically, neither of them really wanting to, but neither wanting to face the truth not making love in this setting would reveal. The weight of expectation pressed them into service, their hands going through familiar caresses, their mouths making the usual sounds. When they finished Ritt kissed her goodnight and was asleep within minutes. He woke in the dark, nudged into consciousness by an awful dream he couldn't quite recall (a climbing accident?). Deirdre was at the far side of the huge bed, her reading light on, her back to him. He heard a page turn, then another, then he closed his eyes.

THIRTEEN

CALGARY

They were getting ready for a dinner party at the Higginses', Drew and Amy, though neither of them was dying to go. They had been out the previous eleven nights, fulfilling commitments that had been made months earlier. Each felt socially worn out, with the metallic edge that too much alcohol brings. Deirdre stood looking at the full-length mirror beside the closet door, barefoot, holding a dark dress in front of her.

"Do you know if the Hunnicutts or the MacKays are going to be there?" she asked, speaking to the mirror, turning her head and lifting her chin slightly to tauten her neck.

"Cecil MacKay most likely. Hunnicutt, I don't know."

"I wonder if I can get away with wearing this dress. I wore it to that nightmare fundraiser on Thursday."

"You can get away with it."

"Are you just saying that?"

"Yes."

"Is this sit-down?"

"I think so. They've got one of those dining room tables that seats about fifty people."

"This is the environmental whatever thing."

"Yeah." The Higginses had created a Western salon that brought in people from all walks of life to talk about oil.

"You know the first words out of anyone's mouth will be *Nowruz*," Deirdre said. The spill that had dropped 100 million gallons of crude into the Persian Gulf.

"Can't wait."

Ritt drove up the hill toward their destination on a road that had small patches of black ice; the tires slipped then grabbed jerkily. It was November and the light was gone. The city felt brown and recessionary. They were almost at the Higginses' when Ritt noticed that the radio wasn't on and that they'd been driving in silence.

They parked and then rang the bell and stood glumly in front of the Higginses' door, feeling the way Jehovah's Witnesses must feel, preparing to have the same conversation they'd had six hundred times. When Drew opened the door, both Ritt and Deirdre managed salesman smiles and walked in.

Higgins was lozenge-shaped and red-faced, an earnest, exhausting man whose heartiness taxed everyone around him. He thrust out a hand like a bear's paw.

"Ritt, there are some people here who want to disembowel you." He let out a hearty laugh.

Amy came to greet them, looking perky and suspicious, as if she was already wondering how Ritt and Deirdre would judge them on the way home; the relative failure of their weight-loss plan, the work that their new designer had done in the living room, which was filled with dark furniture and an almost life-sized leather rhinoceros, creating an effect Amy testily told them was called "ironic masculine."

Ritt surveyed the room, an eclectic group of environmentalists, academics, oil people, a few politicians, journalists. He recognized about a third of them. Higgins brought in argumentative people from different backgrounds and gave them lots of wine from his impressive cellar, and hoped for something memorable. Ritt tried to recall why he had committed to this three months earlier and couldn't come up with a reason. There were people here who had spent a week researching the effect that oil spills had on the burrowing owl, who could tell him at excruciating length the superior Scandinavian ways in which Norway was managing its energy resources, who would tell him how quickly and cheaply the world could convert to solar or wind or chicken manure and how the powerful oil lobby kept those options off the table at a cost that was in the billions annually, a number that they would then translate into aid dollars to Third World countries. Most of this was partly true but the thought of hearing it all once more, with doctrinaire emphasis, brought on a weariness that made his previous weariness seem like an energizing swim in a mountain lake.

The oil industry was emerging slowly from a recession that had left many scars, and the hopeful, obvious lessons that everyone had learned about markets and cartels and human nature were still vivid, and the vows to always abide by these hard-won lessons still hadn't been washed away in the euphoric tide of another boom that would have people suddenly asking themselves why they hadn't thought of getting gold-plated faucets before.

"I'll take that drink," he said to Amy, though she hadn't offered him one.

"The estimate from the Nowruz was between eighty and a hundred million gallons. Now *that* is a wide margin of error." This came from the woman to the right of Ritt, Ellen, an environmental lawyer. She was perhaps forty, slim, wearing a suit that suggested she'd come straight from work.

"It pumped into the Persian Gulf for *eight months*," said Davis, the journalist who was on his left. "It may *still* be pumping. There were no independent appraisals." Davis had thinning hair and a checked shirt and the pent-up hostility that came from earning $28,000 a year. "*One hundred million* gallons, and that's just Nowruz. We've got Castillo de Bellver: eighty million; Kolva River: another eighty million unless the Russians were lying, which they were."

"I'm familiar with the statistics," Ritt said.

"Then how can you drill in the Arctic with a clear conscience?" Davis asked.

Ritt recalled the lessons from the media training seminar he had reluctantly gone to, run by a disturbingly cheerful woman dressed entirely in white. "Seize control of the agenda," she had said. "How do we do that? I just did. How? By asking *myself* the question. Listen, journalists warm you up, they *lull* you. That's their *job*. Then they ask you at what point did you know that fracking acid had leaked into the village water supply, killing six people. Just an example, but anyway." She told them to ask that hard question themselves, framed in a sympathetic way, to *seize control of the process*. To use the interviewer's name, to comment favourably on the question ("Excellent question, Tod, I'm glad you asked it"), to avoid certain charged words—"blame," "lawsuit"—to replace "oil" with "energy," to use political catchphrases such as "the need to preserve our way of life," and to use body language and tone to convey a gravitas that made the interviewer look, to the average viewer, like an annoying pipsqueak pestering an oracle. "Did we make a mistake? We did. Could we have done better? Certainly we could have. And we *will* do better in the future. How? Well, let's take a look . . ." These Socratic monologues were now a staple of every interview.

"We have done environmental impact assessments up there," Ritt said. "And ultimately, the Arctic will be cleaner than the oil sands. And as conventional supplies are exhausted, the Arctic will provide energy security. As long as the Americans are dependent on foreign oil, as long as we are exposed to political volatility, to the whims of spoiled second-generation, half-wit, coked-out sheiks who flunked out of Princeton, to tribal grievances that go back two thousand years, to Arab wars and religious fanatics and socialist dictators, we are going to be vulnerable to price hikes and shortages."

"Which could be *eliminated* with alternative sources of energy," Davis said.

"Which will happen eventually," Ritt calmly responded. "At some point we'll be dealing with solar, or wind, or hydrogen or some new generation of nuclear or something we don't even see coming. But in the meantime, we're stuck with oil and we have to make the best of it."

An hour went by as Ritt contended with Ellen's and Davis's well-rehearsed arguments for oil's overdue death. He wanted to sleep with Ellen and punch Davis. Ritt accepted more wine from Drew, who moved around his guests with two bottles, aggressively filling glasses, fuelling debate.

Deirdre was at the other end of the table. He could see she had tuned out of the arguments that raged around her. He could hear the natural bellow of Herman Keinz from Shell, inhabiting the caricature he cultivated so carefully, delivering a lecture on entrepreneurial spirit.

By eleven p.m. everyone's position had hardened, and the debate grew shrill.

Your grandchildren will die in a treeless wasteland.

You will be speaking Farsi by Christmas, Boo Boo.

Davis launched into a doomsday scenario and the conversation became competitive as to whose End Days looked grimmer. Shuffling through the apocalypse with feral children, living on radiated 7Up and salvaged cans of lima beans found in Mormon basements. Everyone talking at once, Davis yelling that Mother Nature always batted last.

It binds us all, Ritt thought, the snaking lines of oil and its endless by-products: the tubes of lipstick and tubs of margarine, the shampoos that smell like grapefruit, the shag rugs and suitcases and transparent shower curtains, the epic two-step that links humanity in a downward spiral.

Davis suddenly leaned into Ritt, glaring angrily. "Do you know what the most common petroleum by-product is?"

"Anxiety," Ritt said.

They left at midnight. Ritt had had too much wine and Deirdre was driving.

"We don't have anything else this week, do we?" Ritt said hopefully.

"Washington."

"Jesus take me now."

"Wednesday."

Washington was a fundraising event to save the Alaskan polar bear. It was sponsored by five oil companies that wanted access to the American Arctic and Ritt had intended to use the event to get informal intelligence on where government and industry were on the subject of Arctic drilling.

"Who did you talk to at your end?" Ritt asked.

"I was in range of that Shell buffoon. I *was* being shelled. Like being in a mortar attack. And there was a British guy who has some massive grant to study how microbes can be used to clean up oil spills. He's at the university. Kind of interesting in a deadly boring sort of way. I developed a life-threatening headache halfway through the evening, I tried to signal you but you were talking to the woman with all the buttons undone."

"The lawyer? Ellen."

"Pinstriped suit, bra showing, running her hand through her hair every thirty seconds?"

Ritt supposed he should be grateful for this vestige of jealousy.

They drove the rest of the way in silence. When they got home they undressed quickly and fell into bed. Deirdre was asleep instantly. Ritt replayed the evening in his head, shuffling the choleric, unfocused snapshots. His head throbbed, the wine a defence against his tablemates. The entire evening was a defence against something: environmentalists, his host, his own wife, himself. He was agitated and impaired and felt the room shift, his horizontality at risk, moving slowly—a thrust fault sliding on top of some poor clastic formation, rising slowly at its expense, pieces of him crumbling off under the force of that friction, crumbs that would hold the snow, would catch the water, would become soil and eventually produce life. All you needed was time.

Wednesday in Washington, Ritt stood at the back of the ballroom of the Grand Hyatt. On stage, a man was talking about the need for something. The ambient sound drowned out his appeal for money.

He watched his wife move through the crowd, the lightness in her step, that surety. They had been together almost eight years, and the arc of their relationship had gone from ravenous carnality, to the desolation of non-parenthood, to a kind of partnership. It seemed to Ritt, slightly compressed. Certainly the first stage could have lasted a little longer. And what was their partnership based on, at this point? Love? Habit? There were people who couldn't distinguish between the two.

She was talking to a large man, laughing at something he was saying. She motioned Ritt over.

"Ritt, this is Edwin Kirkpatrick. He's advising the White House on the Arctic file."

"Call me Ed."

They shook hands and Deirdre subtly extracted herself.

"Ed, I'm hoping you can give me a sense of where we are right now on Arctic drilling."

"Well the short answer is: nowhere. Congress is looking to hold on the moratorium. I think they've got the votes."

"This is inside the Arctic National Wildlife Refuge."

"A flashpoint issue. Caribou with nineteen million acres to play in. I thought we had enough people on board, but you lose the narrative on these things, next thing you know it's good versus evil and you're the one with the horns."

"How much money is being thrown at this?"

"Maximum firepower. Chevron brought out the heavy artillery, but it may not be enough. You got Nowruz and Kolva River and it spooks the villagers. Thank god it all happened offstage. We get a spill like that in American waters it'll be hell on toast."

Ritt observed the crowd behind Ed, well dressed, swaying slightly, clutching drinks. Some of them, he guessed, would be at fifty of these this year. The man was still on stage, speaking into the microphone, his words merging with Ed's: *the need for research congress has its back up what is life refuge.*

On the way back to the hotel, Ritt and Deirdre sat in the limousine and watched the monumental city go by.

"What did Edwin have to say?" Deirdre asked.

"He says Congress won't re-open the file. It might be good for us. We already have a foothold in the North. One of the American companies may want to get something going up there, get acclimated for when they can get into Alaska, or a hedge against that not happening. Someone will be willing to back our play. I'll send Tate down to do a dog-and-pony."

He wondered if they would make love in the spacious room tonight. Usually he intuited a mood in the course of the evening, a subtle sign. But in the limo, there was only static.

They had sex, a surprise. Deirdre was so intense it held an undercurrent of violence. She might be trying to fuck him to death. Staring at her determined face as she hammered down on him, jaw clenched, lips set like someone who is unsuccessfully trying to twist the top off a jar, he wondered if this was punishment.

In the plane home, Ritt drank a scotch and watched the blanket of cloud below. Deirdre was asleep in the next seat, her mouth open, shoes off. He finished his drink, then asked the attendant for another, and enjoyed the comforting numbness that came with drinking on planes. He felt sentimental and useless. His head seemed to be packed with wet wool. He fell in love once more with his sleeping wife.

Below him the city came into view, sprawled and grey. He carefully moved Deirdre's seat into the upright position without waking her and adjusted the blanket and kissed her troubled head.

FOURTEEN

CALGARY

DECEMBER 1985

Ritt stared at the abused face of the environment minister who was seated beside him. They were both at a public policy forum titled "Citizens Speak Up!"—a joint government/private sector initiative designed to defuse environmental fears raised by a recent benzene leak from a gas plant west of town into a nearby creek that fed into the Bow River, which ran through the centre of the city. Three hundred people perched on folding chairs, arms crossed, looking at them both. Spidery multi-coloured veins snaked across Ron Kemp's ample nose and spread across his cheeks. He was damp and pasty and forcibly upbeat, a short, overweight man with a heroic appetite for alcohol.

"I caught my first trout standing on the banks of the Bow River," Kemp was telling the audience. "A three-pounder. Maybe *four*. I just hope that my grandchildren can have that same experience. That the policies that we are setting in place today will ensure the health of our precious waterways . . ."

Kemp's folksy political veneer was showing signs of strain.

"As I understand it, Minister Kemp," the man at the microphone said, "you don't have children. So I guess, ah, my question is, how exactly are your *grandchildren* going to . . ."

"I'm speaking philosophically, of course."

"Philosophically?"

"I'm speaking for everyone, I think, when I say that water, I mean, it's the source of . . ."

Kemp's sole political gift was a rumpled populism that sent out a single, though evergreen, signal: *Kemp is the kind of guy you could sit down and have a beer with.* His grasp of environmental issues was recent and vague.

The forum had been organized in the hope of cementing the idea that there was a rich and mutually satisfying partnership between the Environment Ministry and the oil industry, and that they shared the same concerns and, more subtly, that only one of them had any money to actually do anything about those concerns. Essentially the ministry had been gutted; they didn't have the resources to do an environmental impact study of Ritt's bathwater. With the takeover of Maple Leaf, Ritt had become one of the public faces of oil. His slight drawl and natural charm were considered by the industry to be more marketable than Manchauser's amphibian head and corporate Darwinism.

Kemp wiped his forehead as he struggled through his defence. ". . . parts per million, which is within acceptable limits."

"And who set those 'acceptable limits,' Minister Kemp?"

"Those are the scientifically devised . . ."

"If you *had* children, Minister Kemp, would those limits be acceptable to them?"

The moderator, a local newsreader who was searching for a look of gravitas, intervened. "Thank you, sir, I think we're going to move to the next question."

There were three microphones in the room. Behind each, a modest line. Ritt thought he saw Deirdre in one of the lines, partly eclipsed by shadow. If it *was* his wife, given the delicate moment in their marriage—a fulcrum that balanced on one side Rich Sexual History and on the other Lengthening Silences—and given the fact that each instance of their infrequent lovemaking seemed like a sublimated death threat, he wondered what kind of question she would ask. Would it demonstrate a calculated, subtle support for Ritt's unswaying interest in drilling in the far north, or would it be a detailed, lawyer-like dissection of the industry's stunning failure to self-regulate and the Environment Ministry's impotence, using data that showed just how far the ministry was bent over and how far up its not-entirely-green ass it was taking it from Big Oil on a prison-like basis.

The person up next asked Kemp why his government had given 75,000 square kilometres of boreal forest to a Japanese corporation that would be dumping dioxins and furans into the Athabasca River.

"They are bringing *hundreds* of jobs to this province and we are proud of our job-creation record. In the last three years *alone* . . ."

"Mr. Devlin, could we have your thoughts on this?"

"Well," Ritt said, as Kemp's wet, sagging face turned to him. "As an oilman, I have to wonder why our government is giving a foreign company $325 million and a piece of land the size of Ireland so they can take profits out of the country. This is money that could be spent on a homegrown industry where *all* the money stays in the province."

"This would be money directed your way, presumably."

"I sure as hell hope so."

There was light laughter and Kemp shot him a look of betrayal. Fuck him, Ritt thought. Kemp was in Manchauser's pocket. The friend of my enemy is my enemy.

The woman who resembled Deirdre had moved up, into the light, and Ritt now realized she didn't look all that much like her. It was her stance that had made him think of his wife, a cross between seductive and pugnacious.

A thin man in what looked like a borrowed suit was at the microphone. "Given that you are on record as a climate-change denier, Mr. Kemp," the man said, "isn't making you minister of the environment a bit like hiring Adolf Hitler to run the Hebrew School? And I'm speaking as a Jew."

Kemp stared at the man for five charged seconds before bellowing, "*Fuck you!*"

Ritt glanced at his ample brisket head, now an entertaining shade of red. Kemp pushed his chair back and stood up. Ritt noticed he was wearing cowboy boots made of something exotic—lizard or python.

"Would you care to repeat that, sir?" the man said.

Kemp said, "I would: *Fuck you!*" He turned and left the auditorium, ushered out on a chorus of boos, some scattered applause, accusations and a few fist-pumping cries of support: *You tell 'em, Ronnie.*

The moderator finally got the audience to settle down, but he was aware, as was everyone, that with Kemp's departure, the air had gone out of the event. Anything else would be an afterthought. He wrapped up the evening in optimistic terms: *Thank you all for a free and frank exchange of ideas.*

Ritt stepped down from the stage and was intercepted by Mary Armitage from Badger Resources.

"Hard to see the upside of that," she said.

"The mouse that roared. Who doesn't want to tell the world to fuck off?"

"His Teflon is going to get a workout in the next few days."

"My guess is his advisors tell him to stand his ground. Apologize for the language, but stand behind the sentiment. Re-emphasize jobs, putting food on the table. Etcetera."

"I hope they advise him to lose those cowboy boots."

At home, Deirdre was in the kitchen, pouring a glass of wine.

"We don't really have anything for dinner," she said.

"We could go out."

"I don't have the energy."

"I'll phone the Thai place."

She shrugged. "How was your thing with the minister?"

"A hillbilly shit show. Kemp told a guy in the audience to fuck off. By tomorrow he'll be a working-class hero."

The light was disappearing quickly as it did this time of year, the sudden gloom of a December afternoon. The Thai guy arrived early, framed in the doorway beneath the harsh porch light. They ate in front of the television, watching the news. A cheerful blonde said there had been a rash of burglaries on the east side.

"Why do they call them a rash?" Deirdre asked. She pushed her pad Thai away. "They put ketchup in it."

Ritt looked at her, aware that this would somehow be his fault.

"I thought you were calling the other Thai place. The one where they don't use ketchup. It kills it for me."

"The ketchup?"

"It's inauthentic."

"It's a take-out place on Seventeenth."

"The thing is, every time I taste ketchup, I think of this place we used to go to in high school. One of those greasy spoons where everyone's crowded into a booth and half the people are smoking and you share a plate of fries and someone douses it with ketchup. And you're so conscious of who is in the booth and your leg is touching the leg of the boy beside you and you're trying to approximate some adult version of the world by smoking a million cigarettes. And all that awful ketchup. I don't know, it's not where I want to go when I'm eating Thai."

On the screen a man stood in front of a smouldering house. Firemen bustled behind him. The camera panned, searching for a suitable metaphor, landing, finally, on a scorched teddy bear.

In the morning, Ritt got one more chance to look at Kemp's angry face, on the front page of the paper. It was still dark outside. Across the table Deirdre's mouth formed an O as her coffee cup approached.

"You slept well?" he asked, knowing that neither of them had.

"Fine. You?"

Ritt decided he had to try to make contact with his wife. "I had this dream. I was standing in one of those dream landscapes, you know, sort of burned out, surreal. I was the only one there. And I was just standing there and I had the feeling that the dream had ended before I got there. That I'd arrived late to my own dream."

Deirdre was studying the business section, the headshots of new appointments at law firms. She didn't look up. "Hmmm. What's it all mean."

"It means I'm invincible," he said, knowing she wasn't listening.

"Hmmm."

Ritt walked to work, a brisk forty minutes. The traffic was clogged and angry along Fifth. He turned west and walked up Sixth. A handful of people moved north, their heads down, bundled and remote. He mentally went through his day: a meeting with Jackson Tate to reiterate where they were with the government and what kind of joint venture they could put together without being sodomized by one of the majors. Lunch with the board, which was getting nervous about the company's onerous debt load. There was an afternoon thing, he couldn't remember. He would spend half an hour staring out the window. Return a dozen calls he wasn't looking forward to. Then walk home in the dark, maybe pick up something for dinner.

When Ritt got there, Tate was waiting for him, sipping coffee.

"The board is going to want to talk about debt," Tate said.

"Maybe today is the day we remind them that they get paid handsomely to do four-fifths of fuck-all and they approved the Maple Leaf deal and every other deal that involved Third

World debt levels and the reason they approved those deals is they missed half the meetings and didn't read past the first two paragraphs of any document put in front of them."

"We tell them we're close," Tate said.

"Close to *what*? Bankruptcy?"

"Close to reaching critical mass. Too big to fail. We just need that last piece of the puzzle."

There was no last piece, Ritt knew. They would keep assembling the company and new holes would appear, new threats, opportunities, debts. It was ongoing. Mackenzie moved like civilization, a messy, determined march over the skulls of its enemies.

He walked home in the dead winter darkness. Deirdre was there, in a black dress, putting her heels in a shoe bag. "Where the hell have you been?" she said. "I called."

"I walked," Ritt said.

"The Giveners. *The Christmas party.* My firm's largest client. I told you three times. You can wear what you're wearing."

Ritt looked down at his suit, dark and appropriate. He had forgotten the party. Who has a party on a Monday night?

"I know you don't want to go. You know you have to. Let's not have this conversation."

FIFTEEN

CALGARY

OCTOBER 1986

R itt left his office at 6:30, the Indian summer sun still strong. On the street, people basked, secretaries sitting at patio tables, drinking mimosas, bicycle couriers taking a break. The sun bounced off mirrored windows and ricocheted through the core. It was Friday and ties were loosened, dreams of barbecues and a cold one. A woman on Eighth was feeding ice cream to a baby in a stroller, the baby's legs kicking between bites, her eyes showing an addict's joy with each miraculous taste.

The price of West Texas Intermediate had dropped to $8 a barrel. If the city reflected this fact, if the downtown could physically manifest what was happening in the oil patch, it would look like Dresden in 1945, a smoking ruin, dazed survivors searching through the debris for food and loved ones. This precipitous drop meant the end of whatever Christmas bonuses had survived the last dip, of expense account dinners that had just crept back into four figures, of buying allegedly important art for lobby walls, of $57,000 kitchen renos, of negotiating naming rights. It meant another round of layoffs, cutbacks, divorce proceedings, unclaimed Western bronzes, unleased Porsches, a time of renegotiated mortgages and dumped season tickets. Eight-dollar oil was shaking this city like a terrier with a rat in its teeth. Yet the streetscape was unaffected. People smoked contentedly, they drank their Cokes and picked their noses and basked in the welcome summerness of it all.

Mackenzie Oil was now worth roughly twenty percent of what it had been worth a year ago. The banks had already called Ritt to pointedly ask how this would affect their loans. Drastically, was the answer, but he told them it was a blip.

He walked to the familiar steakhouse and went into the comforting darkness. His eyes adjusted, and he scanned the red leather booths, a tiny light at each table, looking for Manchauser. An elaborately dressed tray of meat glided by. A waiter in a red vest and white shirt stopped at a table and pointed out the various cuts, their exquisite marbling, their heft and pedigree. Most of the diners were men, their hands wrapped around whisky glasses or clutching a knife and fork like giants out of Grimm's. Laughter echoed, booming locker room eruptions.

Ritt spotted Manchauser and walked over. They shook hands and Ritt sat down and they ordered drinks and aimlessly talked football—whether they'd fill those gaping holes in the secondary. Manchauser had said he had a proposal. He'd had a proposal twenty-odd years ago and that hadn't ended well.

The meat wagon came by and they picked out their steaks and Manchauser started a practised rant.

"Okay, the Saudis took their football and went home. Big surprise. Every year those camel jockeys get together and agree to limit production so they don't flood the fucking market then they go home and every damn one of them breaks the quota. You know why?"

Ritt did know why. But there was no stopping Manchauser when he got going.

"*Because.* They know that every other untrustworthy sonofabitch at that table is going to break the deal. And they do. Costs them two bucks a barrel to get it out of the ground and it's pure enough to pump right into your Mercedes. So those assholes get the price down to eight dollars a barrel, it don't mean shit for them. But it puts us out of business. Forty thousand jobs down the toilet. You think government can't get any stupider but God showed them a new path. Five billion in capital spending . . ." Both of his hands went up in the air, signifying, Ritt guessed, a mushroom cloud. "Best case scenario," Manchauser said, "Iran and Iraq bomb each other back to Jesus and we go in and mop up the oil."

Manchauser was going to propose a merger. Two collapsing companies with roughly complementary assets. It would look good on paper—to shareholders, at least initially. But in reality it would be a marriage between two ailing seniors, each hoping the other would care for them. Not to mention the ongoing hell of working with Manchauser every day.

Before Manchauser got there, Ritt excused himself and went to the men's room. There was a poster tacked up on the wall, the photograph of a boy of about twelve who had a wistful, enigmatic smile. The image had been treated with a colour wash and under it were the words "AB versus Big Oil." Ritt wondered who had put this up here. It must have been recent, in the last few minutes perhaps. It was a protest of some kind, and an employee would take it down as soon as he was alerted to it.

When Ritt got back to the table their steaks were arriving. Ritt looked at Manchauser's pocked lunar face, as he cut and then chewed a largish piece of his thirty-two-ounce porterhouse. As he chewed, he talked, the bloody contents of his mouth coming into unwelcome view.

"Here's the deal, Ritt: Alhambra and Mackenzie, you and me. We join forces. Hit critical mass. I've got the conventional side, gas plays. You've got the North, you've got your friends in the government . . ."

"We're not that friendly these days, Pete."

"They're footing that Arctic bill, though."

"They're protecting their interests up north." Though not for long, Ritt guessed. His wells in the Beaufort Sea hadn't yielded what he'd hoped and the government was getting impatient.

Manchauser considered this. "You want to drill on government money in the middle of fucking nowhere, that's fine. But the industry lives or dies here." He swept his hand around the restaurant. "And right now we're dying. We get together on this, it works out for both of us."

"We're not exactly working the same side of the street, Pete."

"That's why this would be a brilliant merger. And at the moment we're in a war. You need allies when you're in a war. You have to declare a side."

"You know I can't drill north of sixty without government help, Pete. That's just the math."

"Fuck the math. And fuck you, Ritt. I'm not afraid to make enemies."

"You have a gift for it, Pete. You ever wonder why people keep divorcing you and blowing up your cars?"

Manchauser thought about this for a moment. "Where were you that night, Ritt?" he asked softly.

"Fucking my wife in your pool."

Manchauser nodded. "Has it ever occurred to you that your man Tate is just a piss-poor Xerox of me? You could have the real thing. The entire industry is in ruins. We could stand up to the government, we could create solidarity."

"I don't recall you were much for solidarity a few years ago, Pete. Back when you were eating the weak."

"The weak deserve to die, Ritt. Take away your government safety net, you wouldn't last ten minutes."

"I'm not the only one at the tit. You add up the accelerated capital cost allowance, earned depletion and resource subsidies, you're basically a fucking ballet company leaning on government handouts. So maybe it's time to stop pretending we're all Texas wildcatters and it's 1951."

"Maybe you should think about going back to Texas, Ritt," Manchauser replied after an angry silence. "Might be a bit healthier for you down there." He sawed off another piece of steak and lifted it to his mouth.

"How bad you hurting, Pete?"

"I still have enough muscle to sink you."

Manchauser's negotiating style—a bad cop/worse cop approach—was a glimpse of what it would be like working with him; each day a fresh battle.

"If you did, you would have done it by now. And who runs this new company, Pete? And what about Tate, the Xerox copy. We throw him on the scrap heap?"

Manchauser considered this. "I wonder where he was the night my garage was torched. He's a smoker, isn't he. Lights up about every ten seconds."

"He has access to matches, detective."

"This deal is once-in-a-lifetime, Ritt."

"That's what you said to me twenty years ago. It would never work, Pete. The math won't work, the personalities won't work. We'd get an initial bump in stock price then we'd be two drowning men in the middle of the Atlantic, dragging one another to the bottom."

"It's funny, everyone thinks I'm the bad guy. But I keep trying to make you money and you keep turning me down."

"I turn you down because you *are* the bad guy, Pete."

Ritt left the restaurant, walking through the glum downtown. He stopped and noted the subtle swirls on the sandstone of the Knox United Church. Likely quarried from the Porcupine Hills formation. The distant footprints of an overconfident Triceratops staggering through the last of the Cretaceous, leaving an imprint in the silt and sand that was distributed during the Laramide orogeny. Tectonic plates shuddering, the Rocky Mountains coming to life. Ritt looked closely at the stone. There was the illusion of uniformity but the individual grains actually varied in size and colour. Even stone failed to be monolithic—it was a collection of individuals pressed into a society by forces they didn't understand. Stone was equated with stability and it was stable, but only compared to other materials. Measured by geologic time, it was fickle and unreliable. There was rock that was easily fatigued and rock that was incompetent. It rose and fell and crumbled.

He thought, melodramatically, *The city has turned against me.* Though he knew this was simply ego. Who was the city for?

At breakfast the next morning he and Deirdre read their separate sections of the newspaper, a wall of bad news between them. They used to point out stories they thought would interest the other, oddball features about pythons coming out of suburban toilets, or chain-smoking Chinese five-year-olds, or a man who tattooed his face to look like the grille of a BMW. He would comment on the price of West Texas Intermediate, she would mention a movie they should try and get to. But the paper was no longer a medium of exchange. Though this morning he thought he'd try once more to break the endless silence, and told her about a boy who got lost in Wyoming for three days.

"Twelve years old, a boy scout. He survived on dried berries. He made a fire like they taught him, rubbing sticks."

"Sticks?"

"Apparently he never gave up hope."

Despite the calamity in every oil tower, the city hummed along. Tonight he and Deirdre were going to an event to raise money for a dance company. Deirdre was in front of the mirror with a dress in each hand and Ritt had a sudden, disquieting sense of déjà vu, a reprise of their old intimacy.

"Is it worth giving money to something that's going to die?" Deirdre asked.

"They're going to fold?"

"That's what dance companies do best."

"How much did we give them?"

"I wrote a cheque for a thousand."

"By the end of the year the oil industry is going to be asking dance companies for financial support." Ritt found the tie he was looking for and knotted it. "How long is the show?"

"You might enjoy it."

"Every oilman who couldn't get out of this will be asleep in ten minutes. The ones who are awake will be thinking they'd like to fuck the dancers. At the intermission half the wives will mention that they used to dance, that everyone said, *you* should have become a dancer. And then we'll go for a drink with two couples we really don't want to talk to, and the women will talk about exercise and the men will talk about oil and then we'll drive home and dissect them like frogs in biology class."

Deirdre wasn't listening. She waved the midnight blue sheath dress in her left hand. "This one," she said.

They parked three blocks away and walked. Across from the dance theatre a new building was going up. On the hoardings was an optimistic rendering of the finished product, which might remain a hole in the ground for the next two years given current market conditions. Farther along Ritt noticed a poster of the boy again, the one he'd seen at the steak house. There were dozens of them, running in a line down the hoardings for half a block. The photo had the quality that certain paintings had, revealing something intimate.

Stenciled beneath some of them: "Adam Barkley Is Dying for Your Sins."

Ritt stopped. "Have you seen these before?" he asked Deirdre.

"We're going to be late, Ritt."

"There was a poster of that kid in the washroom when I had dinner with Manchauser. The same poster." Ritt examined the image. The colour washes weren't a match. These were collectibles. Get the whole set. If there was a single quality the boy's face represented, it was innocence, the kind of innocence we still liked to believe existed in rural communities, where cable television and the corrupting arm of the devil were unable to reach. Though Ritt knew from experience that was where the devil made his living.

"I'm going," Deirdre said. "You can be late if you want." She marched away toward the theatre.

Ritt ran to catch up. "Adam Barkley. Does that ring any bells?"

Deirdre was stomping like a storm trooper. "You've got the tickets?"

A sudden sickening feeling. He patted his pockets uselessly.

"Wait a minute," Deirdre said looking through her purse as they approached the entrance. "I've got them."

They were only a little late, squeezing along a line of seated people to find their place. The dancers came out and stood on the edge of the stage, leaning toward them, a look of yearning on their faces. They glided and paired off and stomped away angrily and reached to touch one another, their fingertips not quite meeting. They might have been trees, or lovers, or something else that was failing to flourish.

SIXTEEN

SOUTHERN ALBERTA

1986

dam Barkley was an eleven-year-old boy with freckles across his nose and a cowlick in his blond hair who looked like a Norman Rockwell farm kid from the 1940s. His most arresting feature, at least in the photograph that was fast becoming a touchstone for the environmental movement, was his smile, which was described, almost universally, as Mona Lisa–like.

The ranch he lived on was located in the scenic big sky foothills directly south of Calgary, an area that was in the crosshairs of a quiet carpet-bombing of methane drilling activity. The process of fracking coal seams involved an unregulated cocktail of liquids, some of which may or may not have leached into a nearby aquifer.

Adam Barkley found eleven dead frogs in a pond on their property one day. They had seeping wounds, sores that had opened. It looked like a serial killing. He stooped over them and prodded and turned them over and wondered what would have caused it.

A few weeks later, the family's drinking water became whitish and had the effervescence of soda pop and their previously stained toilet bowls suddenly gleamed. When Adam first noticed the rash creeping over his body like something from a horror movie, he was at home by himself. His mother had gone into the city for the day (his father had died when Adam was three). The boy was scientifically inclined, a second-place finisher in the school's science fair, and he was invested with the independence that came naturally to children who grow up on a ranch without a father, and his first strategy was to try to rub it off. He spent an hour in the shower, scrubbing gently but desperately with a rough washcloth. When he finished, the rash was redder and angrier looking. He wondered if there was some kind of impurity in his system, some bacteria that he had eaten, something he'd picked up from the cattle maybe. He drank two gallons of water with grim, weepy determination and sat and waited for his mother to come home.

When she arrived, she took one look and put him in the car and drove him to the hospital twenty miles away. Cursory tests didn't provide an answer and he was sent home. The next day Emma Barkley phoned the Environment Ministry to see about having their water tested. By this time she, too, had a rash.

She drove into town and bought three hundred litres of bottled water and loaded them onto her truck. In the next days she found that Alhambra Oil was drilling wells nearby and phoned and asked to speak to Peter Manchauser. She was handed over to Communications, who noted her complaint and assured her that someone would come out to have a look, though it was unlikely that Alhambra was responsible for any problem, since they took the greatest precautions.

The water from their taps was now as white as chalk and Emma heard popping sounds coming from the pipes. It occurred to her that whatever else was in the water, one of the things was gas. She tried an experiment, filling up a large, empty plastic soda bottle with the water then putting the cap on. If there was gas, it would rise to the top. She waited twenty minutes then lit a match, opened the cap and stuck the match over the opening. Flames leapt out of the bottle, shooting upward and melting the top of the bottle.

The next day she phoned both the ministry and Alhambra with the results of this experiment. The ministry sent out a man named Hanson, who sat in her living room and sipped the coffee that Emma had made (with bottled water) and took notes and inspected the rabid froth that came out of the kitchen faucet. He filled three sample bottles and put them into a small case.

"You're not drinking it now, are you?" he asked.

"No, not for two weeks. The cattle won't drink it. We're trucking it in."

"We'll test this, Mrs. Barkley, and I'll call with the results."

Alhambra sent out a man in pressed jeans who also drank coffee in the living room and took a look at the water and wondered aloud what it could be. While it was true that Alhambra was drilling nearby, he said, because they were working on ranches throughout the area they took extra care—he'd grown up on a ranch himself—and held themselves to the highest standards. He told her he hadn't seen anything like this.

Adam was bedridden now, with a fever. A second trip to the local hospital wasn't helpful, but a trip to the Calgary emergency ward yielded, after seven hours, the news that his liver function was compromised.

"What do you mean, 'compromised,'" his mother asked the doctor.

"It has suffered trauma and is unable to operate at full capacity. Adam can't metabolize properly—both LDH and albumin levels aren't good."

"Well, what can we do?"

"We'll keep him here for a few days, Mrs. Barkley."

The ministry phoned and said the water showed significant amounts of hydrochloric acid, diesel fuel and nitrogen.

"Which means what?" Emma asked.

"We don't know for sure. It could be consistent with fracking activity."

A week went by with her son in a Calgary hospital and Emma still hadn't heard anything from the oil company despite repeated calls from the pay phone in the hospital lobby. Adam had lost the power of speech, which mystified the doctors. He lay there mute and Emma sat on the chair beside his bed and tried not to think of moments they'd had together, of standing in the hot springs in December as snow fell on them, of watching him ride his first horse, looking impossibly small, of him weeping in his Batman costume on Hallowe'en because he'd wanted to be Spiderman.

On the television mounted on the wall in his room, a very chipper host was tasting a muffin made by the woman who stood beside him looking at his hard-working mouth, her eyes widening in anticipation.

Emma watched this and then went down to the lobby again and used the pay phone, this time to call the show, and spent more than an hour explaining what she proposed to do for their viewing audience. She went up to Adam's room and kissed him goodbye and drove back to the ranch. In the morning she assembled everything she needed and returned to Adam's room with a Polaroid camera and took shots of her son in the glaring hospital light. Then she drove to the television studio. Someone at the studio helped her unload and she sat in the green room with a man with sideburns who was going to mix the perfect martini for the host, and a woman singer who wore red cowboy boots.

The host, a bouncy middle-aged man named Jim, introduced her as a hard-working ranching gal who was going to show us all a little experiment. On the long studio counter that had seen muffins and martinis, Emma laid out six large plastic soda-pop bottles filled with water from her kitchen faucet. The studio audience looked at the chalky colour and let out a collective *eeeeww.* She lit a match, one of the long ones she used for the fireplace, and had Jim open the bottles in sequence as she put the match to each one, six gouts of ten-inch flame leaping. The crowd clapped, then listened in appalled silence as Jim asked her about where she lived and what the heck was wrong with her water. Emma held up the Polaroid of Adam taken in the hospital that showed his blotchy face. The camera moved in close and the crowd let out a sympathetic noise, and Emma gave a straight-ahead version of what had happened, keeping her outrage to herself, reciting it all like she was an accountant, and the audience quickly filled that emotional void with their own outrage.

The story was picked up by other media, and she was featured on the six o'clock news and in the newspapers. She had another photograph of Adam, the one with the enigmatic smile, a photograph she had taken in the dying light of a fall day when they had gone riding together and she had looked at the way the light fell on his open face and thought that it was something she wanted to be able to hold forever. And when Adam went into a hepatic coma two weeks later, this photograph began to appear on posters that resembled old boxing posters and initially read, "AB versus Big Oil" then moved to "Adam Barkley Is Dying for Your Sins."

No one was sure who was behind the campaign, including Emma Barkley, who said she didn't know anything about it. It appeared to be gaining steam though.

SEVENTEEN

CALGARY

1987

ackson Tate was in his office, smoking, drinking coffee, looking at the foothills.

"How bad?" Ritt said.

"I have an idea."

"You've had quite a few of those."

"Look, we got too aggressive. Mea fucking culpa. If oil was fifty dollars a barrel we'd be geniuses."

"If oil was fifty dollars a barrel everyone would be a genius."

They had never got out from under the debt load from the Maple Leaf deal. Peterson was right; they were stretched so thin they were transparent. Tate's solution to almost everything had to do with elaborate tax deals. The insistent creativity of these deals caused Ritt some grief in Ottawa, fraying an already tense relationship. Now Tate's creativity was no longer being employed to grow the company; it was busy disguising and shifting their losses, putting more lipstick on the pig.

"There are bargains out there," Tate said.

"*We* are a bargain. We're a fucking Boxing Day sale."

They had sold off a few smaller assets in dizzyingly complicated schemes that sometimes involved selling one subsidiary to
another with no cash involved. They had let staff go, flew economy, were leasing out some of their office space, had sold office
art and renegotiated the lease on their cars, had renegotiated
debt. They had spread misery throughout the province.

Tate said, "But here's the thing; there aren't many ways out
of this. Just listen to this; Babylon Energy has fifty-eight percent of Derringer Resources . . ."

"Jesus, Tate."

"We buy their interest and it gives us cash flow."

"Buy it with *what*?"

"We use a retractable preferred share so the holder can buy
back the shares. The local banks won't back this—they're in
too deep and nervous as hell—but New York is interested.
They've been trying to get a taste and this is what brokers
might call an entry point. We'd need to pledge some wells and
all the Derringer stock as collateral." Tate shrugged and lit
another cigarette, sucking in the smoke like he was in a contest. "There is no happy answer, Ritt. My thinking is this: we
can watch ourselves get eaten by wolves, or we go on the
offensive. We lose, at least we go down fighting."

Every time Tate was faced with adversity, he went on the
offensive, but this was the corporate equivalent of invading
Russia.

"The whole reason for this company was to do something
revolutionary," Ritt said. "To open up the North. To create
something memorable."

"We're about as memorable as you can stand right now,
Ritt. But no one saw eight-dollar oil coming."

"I want to be in the North."

Tate made a noncommittal face and Ritt walked out.

A week later Hedge Chalmers at TD bank called and asked, conversationally, as if he was asking about Ritt's vacation, if the bank could have its $700 million back.

"Hedge, we're in tight. I don't have to tell you that. We need some support. I'm not asking for more money, just time."

"Time," Chalmers said. "Well yeah, who doesn't want more time. I don't know how much of that is left. I just don't, Ritt."

"We're working on something that will bring some relief."

"When do you figure this relief is going to arrive?"

Ten weeks. Never. "Three weeks," Ritt said.

"They will feel like very long weeks, Ritt. My ass is on the line here."

"I'm asking you to hold tight, just for three more weeks, Hedge."

"You might want to do the same."

The succession of events went like this: Mackenzie put $1.5 billion worth of assets on the block and received $300 million for them from various vultures. Their line of credit at seven of the nine banks they dealt with, a spectrum that went from blue chip to a Mafia-grade Liechtenstein trust company, was frozen. The federal government, in a move that seemed personal, closed a tax loophole that Mackenzie had effectively pioneered and had happily exploited. As a result of all this, the company was unable to meet $30 million in interest and preferred dividend payments. To raise money, Tate tried to sell Ritt's Arctic ship to a Mackenzie subsidiary, a move that was blocked by the New York bank, which refused to remove negative pledges to use them as security. The elaborately polite Japanese, who had loaned them $250 million, were no longer polite. The federal government ordered an audit, a Herculean task that led a dozen mid-level auditors through Tate's marvellous labyrinth, following a hundred threads that all led, finally, to what one auditor described as "a dark unhappy place deep inside Mackenzie's own asshole."

The whole economy was crumbling. The banks' share prices got rocked, too, and they weren't accustomed to that kind of volatility. They got nervous and occasionally hysterical, screaming into the phone at Tate who would say, *look, it's* oil, *asshole, you drill a lot of dry holes,* and then hang up like a petulant teenager.

After three weeks Hedge Chalmers called. "I'm out of time, Ritt. And frankly, out of patience. We could bring you down."

"You could, Hedge. Which would entail a seven hundred million dollar write-down, which would take, what, two dollars off your share price, which would fuck your quarterly results, which would submarine your bonus."

"Is that a threat?"

"You're the one making threats, Hedge. I'm saying the only way out is together. You want to go rogue and bring us down you'll be fighting fifty creditors in court for the next decade. At the end you'll have a twenty million dollar legal bill and an ulcer and three cents on the dollar."

Silence. Hedge finally said, "You fucked this, Ritt. You really did. Goddamn it."

"Two years ago, you couldn't wait to give me money, Hedge. You thought you'd won the lottery."

"I'm going to need something. A gesture of good faith. *Something.*"

"I'll see how much faith I can come up with."

As Ritt examined his wife's face, her terse expression unsoftened by the initial sip of her martini, he reflected on the fact that as his company became increasingly frantic and shrill and burdened with debt, his marriage appeared to be marching in lockstep. For a while now he and Deirdre had been almost absurdly polite with one another, a disorienting formality. Part of him felt their relationship could be salvaged, resurrected on the very site where the old one had quietly collapsed. It wouldn't be the gleaming edifice that newlyweds held in their heads when they emerged smiling from the church, but a careful, seasoned structure built for heavy weather. He wasn't sure if Deirdre shared that view.

They were waiting to order dinner in yet another restaurant that was going to revolutionize local dining. Restaurants were easier than the unsettling quiet of their home. There was noise, music, distractions, and their silences didn't have the same fearful weight they did in their own dining room.

"How bad is it?" Deirdre asked, taking a second sip.

Was she asking about his company or their marriage? It was a question that was being asked three thousand times a day by bankers, roughnecks, land men, secretaries, wives, suppliers, investors. The answer, usually, was: it could be worse. But only because it can always get worse.

"We're day-to-day," Ritt said, reluctantly. Deirdre knew this. "Any of the banks could tip us into default but it would mean jeopardizing their investment."

"What's going to be left?"

"The core. Maybe twenty percent if we're lucky."

"Manchauser is teetering, apparently. I heard it from one of the people at work who knows his lawyers."

"Everyone is teetering."

Ritt took a sip of his own martini. The restaurant was less than a third full. It wouldn't revolutionize dining in this town. He examined his wife in the flattering light, her natural elegance, her critical gaze as she assessed the menu. Couples soldiered through death, disease, wayward children, financial catastrophe, flooded basements, car accidents, dead pets and drunken affairs. Each calamity a new thread in the fabric. In the end, staring at one another blankly in the nursing home, husks being wheeled by underpaid immigrants, they still had this vivid tapestry. The unseen triumph of surviving.

But that wasn't them. Their first challenge, the existential hole left by their unborn child, had been too much. They'd poured themselves into their work but hers was deadening and his was failing and they were left with the exquisite silence of four hundred dinners.

A sullen student arrived to take their order. They both watched her click away in her heels.

"I'm sure it isn't any surprise that I've been having an affair," Deirdre said.

Though it was.

"You were gone all the time," she added. And before Ritt could ask, she said, "Don't worry, it isn't anyone you know."

He envied this man, who, he surmised, he actually did know. To be smitten by her, to experience her without the leaden history that joined them, to go down on her and wallow in that perfection—a lucky man.

"I'm sure you've had affairs of your own."

He hadn't. He might have. But adultery was like murder; you needed motive and opportunity. He had motive, he guessed, but he hadn't run into anyone he felt was worth the risk.

"I haven't, actually."

"Your affair is with the earth, Ritt. You wooed it, you fucked it. Your love is six miles underground. Maybe your Pentecostal roots are showing. You're trying to dig down to the devil and confront him, just so you know he's real."

"He's real."

In the extended silence that followed her revelation, their dinner arrived. Ritt's undersized Japanese steak that had been carved from Wagyu cattle in Kobe, a cut renowned for its spectacular marbling, the cattle cared for by men whose families had done this for generations. (All of this had been written in tiny calligraphic print in the menu.) Deirdre's plate looked like a doll's garden, a few flowers intricately arranged around unfamiliar dollops.

"Why bring Japanese beef here?" he wondered, instead of leaning over the table to either kiss her or throttle her.

"This is where the carnivores roam," Deirdre said, taking a

bite of her miniature dinner. "That boy died. Adam Barkley. The poster boy. I heard it on the news on the way over."

"Jesus."

"Never came out of the coma. Six months."

"That poor woman."

They'd moved on from martinis to an expensive bottle of wine. Ritt swirled it around aimlessly in his glass and took a sip. His excessively marbled steak had the consistency of butter that had just come out of the refrigerator, a strangely unsatisfying sensation in his mouth. They ate carefully in the genteel din, Tony Bennett singing softly.

"We need to face up to this, Ritt," Deirdre finally said. "I've spoken to a lawyer."

Her words hung in the air, both surprising and inevitable. He had misread the situation. Or simply hadn't read it.

"You want a divorce."

"It isn't a question of want, Ritt. It's the only thing left. We've just come to the end. That's all. We could kid ourselves that maybe with therapy or a vacation . . ."

"A clean break."

"A clean break."

Ritt lingered over the last of the wine, then stared at the red silt that collected in the bottom of his glass. He thought about mounting a defence. But what was there to say at this point? He could see it was over. This wasn't a passionate tearful argument about how they'd failed one another. They'd skipped that. The lawyers were already on their way.

The staff stood like sentries near the far wall, looking for need. Ritt nodded for the bill.

Some of the bank loans were unsecured, a glaring oversight made by managers who had lent them money in boom times when oil was god and the banks were competing for oil patch business, offering incentives as freely as used car dealers. When the smoke cleared, Ritt sifted through the ash. They'd done worse than he'd predicted to Deirdre: about fifteen percent of the company had survived, and that rump still had significant debt that required them to play the banks against one another. They'd already sold most of the subsidiaries. They lost wells that had been securing loans they couldn't manage. Most of the staff had been let go. They kept the drill ship, mostly because there were no buyers. He and Tate huddled like cattle, waiting for the storm to pass.

In the wake of Adam Barkley's death, while Ritt was moving out of their house and into a condo with spectacular western views, a militant group formed. In October, the Peace River Mainline that ran through the Dene Tha' First Nations territory was bombed. Two days later a gas wellhead outside Medicine Hat was dynamited. The following day a metering shed not far from Cochrane blew up. A fourth attack on a sour gas pipeline left a crater but failed to rupture its target. A group calling itself ABDYS (Adam Barkley Died for Your Sins) sent a note to the newspaper claiming responsibility and warning that war had been declared. The note (and headline) announced in boldface: THERE IS BLOOD ON YOUR HANDS.

By Christmas, there had been twenty-two incidents, sixteen of them successful, causing $28 million in damage and no serious injuries. In the relative calm of January, a rig drilling a hole for Mackenzie was sabotaged. Explosives had been taped to the blowout preventer below the rig floor when the rig was briefly idle during a blizzard. The crew came back before the blizzard blew through and went back to their stations and the blast buckled the tower and it fell with the derrickman in it, crushing him. It was the first fatality of the campaign, and it was assumed to be an accident; the bomber(s) had guessed the crew wouldn't come back in that weather. The derrickman was a forty-two-year-old father of three, a career rig worker.

Ritt attended the funeral, sitting in the back pew. The church was filled with men awkward in suits worn once or twice a year. Ritt twisted his leather gloves and stared at the floor as the eulogy was delivered by the dead man's stoic wife, a plain woman in a black dress. The people reminded him of the congregation in Texas.

A woman sat across the aisle from him at the end of the pew. Ritt noticed her because she hadn't taken her coat off and her collar was turned up, then realized she was Adam Barkley's mother. She bowed her head for a full minute then looked up and caught Ritt's gaze. Her eyes didn't hold anything that Ritt could be sure of. He didn't know if she had unleashed all this, or if she was mourning what had been unleashed in her son's name, or some baffling combination.

When she left, Ritt followed her outside.

"Ms. Barkley."

She stopped and turned around.

"I'm Ritt Devlin. Mackenzie Oil."

"Yes, I know who you are, Mr. Devlin."

"I'm sorry for your loss. Sorry about Adam."

"Thank you, Mr. Devlin."

It was cold outside, and their breath came out in small clouds. Her face was impassive. There were things he wanted to say, things he wanted to ask, but nothing seemed appropriate. They stood a little longer in silence.

"A sad day," Ritt finally said.

Emma Barkley nodded. "Yes, it is. It makes you wonder where we're going with all of this."

EIGHTEEN

BEAUFORT SEA, THE ARCTIC

1988

The pale sky was growing white at the horizon. A desert of ice. To the east, the quiet thrust of Banks Island held ribbons of snow. Other than those on board, there might be fifty people within a thousand miles. The curve of the earth visible. The wind blew from the west. Ritt stood with the deputy minister for energy, mines and resources on the Spartan expanse of *The Adam*, the largest and most heavily mortgaged drill ship on earth. More than four hundred metres long—or more than four football fields, as they always told reporters—and emphatically punctuated by the rig tower. They stood at the railing, observing the impressive nothingness of the Beaufort Sea.

Ritt had brought the deputy minister to the Arctic to take a look at what they were doing. He was losing the government. He could feel it. A polite lull before they sat across from one another at dinner, that sad look: *It's not you, it's me.* He'd heard that federal exploration grants were being phased out; they were what had made this well possible. He hoped that the spectacular visuals might persuade the minister otherwise; that the scale of the North and the heroic nature of the endeavour would win him over. This was the New World, what Elizabeth I had tried to glimpse through Martin Frobisher's eyes four hundred years earlier. It was the gateway to riches. But you needed to experience its grandeur, you needed to see what you were claiming.

The deputy minister, Milt Fothering, was dwarfed by the drill ship, by the North, by his oversized company-issued parka. His small white hands floating weightlessly and unseen at the end of his arms, struggling to be among men.

Did Fothering sense how desperate Ritt was? Probably. Ritt had three partners on this well and one had recently pulled out, abandoning a $20 million stake. Ritt needed the North. It not only defined him, it gave the world the illusion he was still a player. His future hinged on selling the North.

Fothering's lips overlapped in an odd way, a llama-like mouth that twitched slightly when he talked. His canny political face waited for the sales pitch.

Ritt went at it indirectly. "When Martin Frobisher came here in 1576," Ritt said, "he thought he'd found the Northwest Passage. He thought Baffin Island was China." Ritt pointed to the east. "He captured an Eskimo man, assuming he was Chinese. Brought the guy back to Queen Elizabeth as proof. The man bit his own tongue off, then caught a cold and died."

Fothering nodded, pursed his llama lips.

"Frobisher was in it for the money. He was essentially a pirate. He came here three times, looking for gold and looking for China. He didn't find either and went back to pirating. Oil is the new gold. Unlike gold, it has real value. It knows how to do something. Gold is money, but oil is power." Ritt pointed out over the water. "This channel is going to be open one day. We can ship to China and Japan."

Ritt had given the pitch for northern sovereignty so many times—his drill ship in the Beaufort Sea was the *country's ship*—he thought he might have already delivered a version of this to Fothering.

"This well is costing us eighty million," Ritt said. "That's just us. I've got three partners with skin in the game." Now down to two, and that number was by no means firm.

"You're not going to ask for that icebreaker again, are you, Ritt?"

The icebreaker that the government would buy and Mackenzie would use. A scheme Ritt had proposed and the government had understandably balked at.

Ritt smiled. "The world is going to shift over the next twenty years, Milt."

"You know twenty years doesn't exist in political terms."

They walked along the Brobdingnagian deck of *The Adam* and Ritt ushered Fothering into the large mess hall. Inside, the sound of utensils, the echo of voices off steel walls, large men curved over their food, cheerfully complaining. Homemade tattoos and a faint air of incarceration. They sat down and Ritt said, "I know you're planning on shit-canning the northern exploration grants."

"We don't have a choice."

"But this is going to pay off," Ritt said. "It's going to bring in millions in tax revenue and it's going to give you something to wave when every northern country starts claiming the Arctic as their own."

"It's going to bring in millions in tax revenue after we're out of office. It's a gift to the enemy, Ritt. We've got the rest of this term, and that's probably it. You did not hear this from me. But the country's turning on us. No one cares about the long term: not the government, not the voter. Voters want low taxes, low crime, cheap gas and a fistful of pussy." This last was Fothering's uncharacteristic attempt to sound like a rough-neck. "No one gives a shit about Arctic sovereignty."

They sat for a moment in the din then Fothering said he was tired, he was going to turn in. They went back outside into the bracing air. The isolation was breathtaking.

As Ritt walked Fothering to his cabin, he realized there had never been any hope. The marriage was over. *It's not you, it's me.* Fothering and the minister had made the decision months ago. Fothering wasn't up here to listen to a pitch. He simply wanted a holiday. Perhaps he was as stretched and pummelled as Ritt was, fleeing a marital crisis or a pregnant mistress or a drug-addicted son or a palace coup. He was running from something and all he wanted was the unparalleled solitude the North offered.

"You get this country energy self-sufficient," Ritt said, unable to muster any enthusiasm, "and it's a political campaign. It's something people understand in their gut. The country united. What the railroad was to the nineteenth century."

Fothering nodded wearily and said goodnight.

In the steel interior of his stateroom, Ritt tried to sleep. The engines refused to lull him as they sometimes did. There was no movement to the massive ship; it was immobile, an island. He tried to feel the subtle pulse of the drill. He visualized the layers it was going through, each one a new country to briefly explore, before moving on to the next, forsaking its charms.

He got up and stared out the porthole. The curving infinite space of the North was a balm. The scale made him giddy; there was nothing to put it into perspective. The sky receded, the horizon a subtle line. He looked in the tiny bathroom mirror, his unshaven face reflected back in a dull metallic portrait. Every surface in the room was cold to the touch. The endless daylight was malevolent. Ritt lay back on his bed and stared at the rivets winding along the steel like a trail of ants.

The ashes of his marriage: nothing was left there, not even fifteen percent. He thought about his first weeks with Deirdre, that initial gush of confession. He'd trotted out his Texas mythology: a vengeful, belt-swinging Pentecostal father, a long-suffering mother. A boy alone on the Texas plain, God monitoring his every thought. They'd eventually exhausted their stories; everyone did. All the memorable catastrophes that make up our lives. And now she was starting that cycle with someone else.

He'd get a call from Fothering next week, telling Ritt he'd run the idea past the minister (though he wouldn't have bothered) and it just wasn't going to fly. We all need to move on, something like that. A clean break.

Two months later Ritt was in his office, looking at a chart spread across his desk, when Tate walked in.

"What are the charts?" Tate asked.

"Gulf of Guinea."

"Which is . . .?"

"Off Equatorial Guinea. West African country, size of a postage stamp."

"You know anything about Africa?"

"I know there is oil in that gulf."

He'd gotten the logs from a well Total had drilled there, bribing a colleague who had dealt with the French. They'd bailed on the area; they thought it might have something, but not enough to drag their asses to Africa for.

Tate lit a cigarette. He smoked about three packs a day now and looked like a medical cadaver.

"You want to go to Africa."

"Well, I want to get out of here."

Fothering had called, just as he'd predicted. The exploration grants were gone. There was no possibility of drilling another hole up there. The North was gone.

"We need to look somewhere," Ritt said. "We're fucked in the North." He had been right about the Arctic: it did have oil and it was the future. But everyone was looking elsewhere. To the oil sands, sifting through a trillion tonnes of sand. Playing in that tar like greedy children.

Tate digested this. "I have a friend at BP, spent six years in Nigeria. Says it's hell on earth."

"Maybe that's what I need. A sense of perspective. Can you put me in touch with your friend?"

"Miles Wheaton. He's at Imperial now, doing who the fuck knows. Bit of a prick. He probably still has contacts over there. He's one of those drones who's held together by his Rolodex, but he knows Africa. You want me to call him?"

"Yeah, that would be good."

NINETEEN

PORT HARCOURT, NIGERIA

1990

B elow him were large swaths of green interrupted by tan-coloured savanna. Cumulus
clouds gathered in soft bunches. As the plane
approached Port Harcourt, Ritt saw a dozen
pipelines bundled together, snaking along the landscape.
A few oil fires burned, black smoke rising in dense balls that
dissipated. There were patches of stagnant water, lifeless tree
trunks. As they got closer to the city the sun reflected off tin
roofs like flares. One hundred thousand barrels of oil were
stolen each day in Nigeria, Wheaton had told him, siphoned
off and sold on the black market, the money laundered in
London or Switzerland. The greys and blacks of the ruined
landscape gave way to a colonial city laid out with the opti-
mism and scale that came from Europeans who had misread
the future.

Ritt checked into his hotel then wandered the streets for a
while, exhausted from his flight. He ate a light lunch and

forced himself to walk until it was evening and he could sleep and try to recalibrate his circadian cycle.

In the morning, he was feverish, the sweat on his face as viscous as olive oil. He wondered if it was something from yesterday's lunch. Or the water. He ate little of his breakfast then waited in the lobby for his guide to arrive, a sullen man named Godswill whom Wheaton had arranged for. When he turned up, Ritt decided he looked like a middle-aged athlete who had gotten a little heavier in retirement. Though there was ritual scarring on his face.

They drove through Port Harcourt in Godswill's dusty Toyota. Ritt had come to Africa partly to investigate his theory that there was a great deal of oil in or near Equatorial Guinea and partly to put a large exotic gulf between himself and his northern disaster, his failing company and failed marriage.

He hadn't told Wheaton exactly where his interests lay, keeping it vague. Wheaton had said that wherever he was going in Africa, he had to first stop in Nigeria. It was the mother lode of African oil, but also the template for exactly how fucked up any kind of oil venture on that continent would get. Wheaton had set up a few meetings for him with colleagues in Port Harcourt and a tour of the area with Godswill.

The city, home to more than a million, fit around the mouth of the Niger Delta, an occasionally elegant, decayed sprawl. Potholed streets, gridlock, and competing hostilities. The oil companies paid the militia to protect their facilities and paid the warlords not to attack as further insurance. Then they paid mercenaries to do what the militia wasn't able to. They bought guns from Russians and some of them ended up in the hands of stoned fourteen-year-olds caught up in grievances that went back a century.

They drove in silence as the heat built. The city looked like a silent film through the dirty windshield, the colour bleached by the sun. A boy hammered on the window by Ritt, startling him. When Godswill turned his head to stare at the kid, he backed away.

In the afternoon Godswill took Ritt up the Niger River, gliding past small villages and abandoned oil drums. The air was acrid. Men in stained T-shirts advertising American colleges stood on the riverbanks and stared at the passing boat. Oil formed small slicks on the surface, liquified stripes that blurred. The heat was unbearable. A group of children threw stones at the boat, chanting something, smiling, their faces glistening.

Ritt's fever crept back, a subtle spike, barely noticeable in the afternoon heat. His ears felt strained, slightly ringing, and he wasn't sure if the guide was talking to him. Godswill's face was pitted and striated and disapproving. Above them the sky was a distinct and unfamiliar blue. Ritt lay back in the boat and watched the clouds, flat-bottomed and stately. He thought of Deirdre stepping out of the bath in a hotel in Paris, her hair up, as perfect a memory as he had of her. She had converted the West Texas bumpkin, had taken the rougher edges off. He'd been surprised she wanted to keep the house. They had both been indifferent to it; a large awkward place intended for a family.

Deirdre wasn't an innocent. You couldn't be and be a lawyer. She had no venality though. But her divorce lawyer relished the chaos and human misery of divorce. In their one meeting Deirdre had been composed and weary and beautiful.

Her lawyer—Amos Mace, a short angry man with an odd
fish-like face—pushed and prodded, trying to get an emotional reaction from Ritt. But there were no children and
Ritt's relationship with money was pragmatic rather than
acquisitive, which made it difficult for Mace to cause the kind
of pain that he seemed to need. He kept working on Ritt,
accusing him of being irresponsible, insinuating himself into
their marriage. When Mace excused himself to go to the men's
room, Ritt followed and when Mace turned from the urinal
Ritt grabbed a handful of his shirt and tie and twisted it and
slammed him into the wall, putting enough pressure on his
throat that he couldn't talk. Ritt didn't say anything, just
looked into his eyes. Ritt knew that this was how horrible
crimes were committed, this combination of rage and adrenaline mixed into a stew of hatred. Mace's face became mottled
and red, his eyes feral. When Ritt let him go, Mace bent over
and coughed and massaged his throat and looked at Ritt like a
hunted animal. Ritt felt guilty but that look on his face—the
fear and surprise—was worth it.

Ritt went back to the boardroom and sat down across from
Deirdre and complimented her on her dress. They chatted
amiably about a trip they'd once taken to London, a busker
they'd seen in Covent Garden who was in a straitjacket. "How
many fink I can get out of fis?" he'd asked the considerable
crowd. "How many fink I can't? How many don't give a shit?"

Mace came back and sat beside Deirdre.

"Your soon to be ex-husband just tried to kill me," he said.

"Yet somehow you survived," Ritt said. "And without a
scratch."

"Ritt," Deirdre said flatly.

"I am going to sue you for *everything*. And I mean *absolutely everything you own*." Mace's face had rediscovered its cartoon malevolence. "*Do you understand?*"

"Who could blame you," Ritt said. "Attempted murder is a serious crime, Amos. You need to call the police right now. Show them the evidence. The wounds. The weapon. Depose the witnesses. You need to stop this monster before he unsuccessfully kills someone else."

In the end Mace didn't sue and Ritt and Deirdre became strangers. People did it all the time. Years of shared experience quietly erased. You see one another a year later—in an airport or a hardware store—and a memory floats back, an unfocused snapshot of your younger selves.

The Niger River moved by quickly. Small black flecks floated in the caramel-coloured water. Ritt stared at his guide, his dead eyes, the eyes of a former rebel, perhaps. Everyone on this continent was rebelling against something. What kind of wife did Godswill have? A fierce partner who had fought alongside him during an uprising, Ritt decided. And now that he was employed by a British oil company, now that he was domesticated, lent out to tour visiting exploiters, regularly paid, his scars mocking him every morning in the shaving mirror: What was she now? Had they made the transition together, anchoring one another, a nation unmoved by external forces? Or was she bitter? Did he look at her face each morning over breakfast and see his impotence reflected there? Maybe he left the house every day knowing they were drifting apart. *O my brother.* The water by Ritt's ear made a soothing sound. The air tasted of burnt chemicals. He fell asleep.

An explosion woke him. Beyond one of the small islands in the delta the black smoke of an oil fire already towered. There was a second explosion, smaller. Godswill looked at the dirty cloud.

"A drilling platform?" Ritt said.

Godswill nodded.

Ritt looked at the smoke moving inland like an inkblot. The obvious suddenly dawning. "This wasn't an accident."

Godswill turned the boat away from the smoke and sped up slightly, straining the ancient outboard engine. Ritt doubted they could hit twenty-five miles an hour. A whine that had been almost subliminal became audible. Ritt squinted toward the smoke, which had flattened out, and was moving along the horizon. Two boats were approaching, small shapes reflecting the sun, moving quickly.

"Jet boats," Ritt said.

Godswill sped up. The whine was loud now, a threat. The boats were closing. Godswill opened his shirt and took the safety off the pistol that was tucked into his pants.

"You have another one of those?" Ritt asked.

Godswill shook his head.

The jet boats were close enough now that Ritt could see there were several men in each. They had machine guns. The shore was out of reach. One of the men let off a burst into the air. Then he aimed toward their boat and bullets hit the water in front of them. Godswill let up on the throttle and their boat slowed down. He cut the throttle and they drifted. The jet boats loomed up on either side, long ominous shapes. There was a sudden quiet. Ritt looked at the man who had fired. He might be fourteen. He glanced quickly at the other boat. They were all boys. One of them couldn't have been much older than twelve. Their faces and torsos were heavily painted with demonic designs, their eyes bloodshot and lifeless. The boats bobbed in the heavy silence.

Godswill examined the boys in each boat, clearly waiting for one of them to speak. He would be the leader, if they had one.

One of the boys finally said something in a local language. Godswill answered quietly.

They spoke for a minute in short exchanges. The boy had piercings in his chest, a row of what looked like tiny silver spears. Some of his markings were tattoos, some appeared to be the raised flesh of a branding. One eye had red paint around it, the other black. The boy gestured to Ritt with his machine gun and said something. Godswill answered slowly, meeting the question deliberately.

The boy began a tirade, rapid and emphatic. He went on for two minutes and punctuated his speech with machine gun fire into the air. To Ritt's surprise, Godswill answered with force, a stream that sounded like one long sentence, his deep voice pitching higher, his left hand stabbing the air, then sweeping as if to include the whole delta. His right hand was on his hip, his shirt covering it. Ritt assumed his hand was on the gun, though there wasn't any chance of winning a gun battle.

Silence met Godswill's angry speech. The boats were still now, the wake vanished. There was no sound. Not even birds. The water didn't look like it could support life. They were alone.

The leader turned and said something directly to Ritt, then stitched the side of the boat with bullets, moving quickly back and forth, as if painting a fence. One of the jet boats started its engine, then the other. They turned slowly and roared away. Ritt looked down at the water that was seeping in through the holes. He grabbed the bailer, a rusty coffee can attached to the seat with a string, and began bailing. Godswill started the engine and headed toward shore.

"Who were they?" Ritt asked.

Godswill stared ahead. After a minute, he said, "The future."

Godswill turned so they travelled parallel to the shore, thirty metres out. They were losing the battle with water. The hull was filling up. The boat moved sluggishly. Godswill at last turned into shore and the boat scraped against the river-bed. They got out and pulled it onto the mud.

"We walk?" Ritt said.

Godswill nodded.

They climbed the bank of the river, slogging in soft mud that smelled of decay, then moving up to a track that followed the river back to the city.

"Who did you tell them I was?"

Godswill didn't respond at first, then finally said, "A man of God. Come to do His work."

Wheaton had told him there were dozens of gangs. Some of them tribal, some political. Or just formed by the random testosterone that pooled in every teenage boy. There were hired guns and ancient feuds that merged with multinational skirmishes. Nigeria had had seven military coups. There was always a war: a political war, a class war, a private war, a religious war, but mostly an oil war. Nigeria isn't a country, Wheaton had told him after his second bourbon; it is oil. The pure, stateless, distillation of the industry; it's what's left when you strip away civilization. *Take a good long look.*

Ritt and Godswill walked for an hour. Ritt quickly soaked

through his shirt. The breeze on the water had cooled them but now he felt the brunt of the sun. His fever was intermittent and his vision blurred slightly. His hearing was sporadic, interspersed with odd silences. He watched his feet move as if they belonged to someone else. Life was putting one foot in front of the other, his mother used to say. As they passed small encampments near the riverbank, men watched them go by, sitting on tires, smoking. It was getting dark. Godswill delivered a lengthy monologue in another language, though it might have been English. Ritt plodded behind him, the world tilting away from him, the sky a hundred shades of violet, Godswill's voice pulling him along.

It took two hours to get back to the hotel. Ritt spent the next four days in and out of fevered sleep, though he remembered getting out of bed for a hallucinatory meeting with three British oilmen. When he finally got on the small plane to go to Equatorial Guinea, he felt light, insubstantial, like a strong wind could take him away.

TWENTY

EQUATORIAL GUINEA

1990

Through the window of the plane the African coast wavered. The vivid colours and sudden shade of passing clouds. They were flying low. Ritt felt like he was in a child's adventure film.

The plane landed on a rutted airstrip outside Malabo. Ritt's fever crept back. In the taxi to his hotel, the city went by: white colonial structures and obliquely angled shacks made of coloured tin that had faded in the sun, parks with magnificent trees though denuded of grass, dust rising as boys chased a soccer ball. A few tall women walked with a regal gait. Most were built more practically. Men sprawled around the city as if it was a living room, sitting on sacks in front of small businesses, on benches, in cafés. The driver delivered an incantatory lecture on Catholicism as the cab lurched along, the horn punctuating his heavily accented English. A truck carrying goats pulled up closely beside them and those belligerent, bearded faces loomed.

Ritt spent another week in and out of fever. The hotel sent a doctor to his room, a small man who gave him a handful of pills without telling him what they were. Ritt didn't see where they came from; the man simply opened his tiny palm and there were ten pills on it, like something from a fairy tale. "These," he said, as if that explained everything, then tipped them into Ritt's hand and left. How many should he take? What were they? Ritt took one and slept for thirteen hours.

Over the next three days he made a few forays outside, made some calls. He hired a fixer, a Texan named Eldon Baker, to set up a meeting with the country's dictator. Ritt spent hours on his back, watching the slow ceiling fan, hypnotized by it, his eye moving in circles to catch the blades, to keep them in focus. But he couldn't hold it for more than a few seconds; his eyes released the image and they moved around at their indolent pace in a slight blur.

When he woke from another fevered nap, he turned on the twenty-year-old television to see a grainy image of four men hanging from a tree. Ritt briefly wondered if it was a documentary on civil rights but it turned out they were locals, lynched for reasons he couldn't grasp. He was burning up again. He drank water but it didn't have any effect. The ceiling fan spun languidly and failed to cool him. He thought about his father, waking in the back of that pick-up truck fifty years ago, burned by the Texas sun. That agony, his skin tight from the hideous sunburn, dangerously dehydrated, poisoned, every cell rebelling, the sweetish smell of bourbon leaking out of his pores, staring up at the sky. Jesus beckoning him into the fold, and his father, in that agony, said, *Anything but this.*

Through the thin walls of his allegedly three-star hotel, Ritt could clearly hear a conversation but he wasn't sure it was real or conjured by his fever.

"Repeat after me: I, Eldon Samuel Baker." There was a pause. "Say it."

"I, Elton Samuel Baker . . ." It was a woman's voice, accented.

"Am a good man . . . you have to repeat it."

"Everything?"

"Goddamn it yes, everything. Am a good man."

"Am a good man."

"As goodness is defined in the Book of Judges . . ."

"Has good is define in the Book of Judges." She pronounced it *bewk*.

"Which I have not read but like the sound of."

"Which I have not read but like sounds of."

"Yet lo, I will be punished in interesting ways that my imagination has not anticipated."

"Yet lo . . ."

"I will be punished."

"You will be punished."

"In ways that will not make me regret my fifty-dollar investment in the local economy."

"In ways that will make you weep with pleasure."

"Now you're getting the hang of it, darling."

Ritt assumed the woman must be a prostitute from the bar downstairs. Baker was the self-declared expert on this unfocused country, which had flown under the radar of the multinationals. Equatorial Guinea was run by a dictator named Bartho, a man who had generated little international press, his mismanagement and atrocities paling beside those of his dictatorial peers. Ritt had met with Baker, who said he could get Ritt an audience with the man, could pave the way. Baker had implied that he had been highly placed in the American diplomatic service, though Ritt doubted this. Baker was too crude and everything about him spoke to a military background. Perhaps he'd worked as a connection to supply Bartho with arms.

Ritt listened unwillingly to Baker's sexual litany through the wall. He wished he could sleep. Africa was exhausting.

Before Bartho's coup in 1979, Equatorial Guinea had been ruled by a psychopath named Francisco Macías Nguema, who had essentially been deeded the country when the Spanish left. Macías Nguema gave himself the title of "The Sole Miracle of Equatorial Guinea," and murdered a quarter of the population. He crucified his enemies and herded hundreds of people into the soccer stadium and had them shot while a band played "Those Were the Days." After Bartho's coup, Macías Nguema was publicly tried in the city's only movie theatre, where he was suspended from the ceiling in a cage, bellowing like a madman, a string of obscenities and pleas and god-like declarations. He was sentenced to death and executed by Bartho's bodyguards.

Ritt thought there was oil here, maybe not on the mainland but inside territorial waters off the coast near Bioko Island. The French had drilled some exploratory wells near there, but Ritt thought they'd missed it; they were too far south. His reading of the geology was that there could be hundreds of millions of barrels just to the north, following the Cameroon Volcanic Line. If that was true it could transform both the country and Mackenzie Oil.

The morning brought a hopeful light and an exquisite silence that became chaos within the hour. Ritt had slept badly. He showered and changed into his tropical suit and went downstairs for breakfast. Baker was sitting at a table, a plate of what looked to be pork chops in front of him. Baker waved him over with a stubby hand.

He was in a parodic safari outfit with epaulets and a dirty scarf around his neck. The skin of his face looked like red sandpaper spread over a pot roast. "Ritt," he said, "come and sit. Have yourself some coffee."

"What is that?" Ritt asked, pointing to Baker's plate. "Pork chops?"

"Yeah, well maybe. Except for the pork part. They killed something and cooked it. That's about as far as you want to investigate."

When the small, stooped waiter with erratic English came over to take his order, Ritt asked for a Spanish omelette, residue from colonial days. The waiter poured him a coffee that had the viscosity of cough syrup.

"How are we doing with Bartho, Eldon," Ritt said. "I'm running out of time here."

"Time is an alien concept to this bunch. Everything is present tense. You eat, you fuck, and then it's over."

"Well, we're getting close to being over."

After a week of fever and paying Eldon to do little it seemed other than fuck the locals, he hadn't been able to get into the room with Bartho.

"How it works, is, every request is sitting there on his plate. He picks one at random and bingo, it's your lucky day. Unless you're an enemy of the state and today is the day he decides to make a change purse out of your testicles."

"Does Bartho realize what he has to gain here? He's a fifth-rate dictator in the middle of fucking nowhere. This could change his world."

"Bartho ain't exactly a scholar. But he's shrewd as hell. And paranoid as hell. That's pretty much standard issue for your African dictator. I'll rattle the cage a bit, but this is part of the act. He's a busy man, etcetera. You're some foreign pissant who wants a little of the pixie dust he spreads everywhere."

"I can hang on another two days, Eldon. I owe you for eight days and the bonus if you get me in there and that money is getting on a plane in forty-eight hours."

Eldon made a noise that could have meant anything and went back to his breakfast.

Ritt's fever returned with a determined pulse. He walked out the back of the hotel, sweating heavily. The hotel pool didn't have any water in it. At the bottom was a bloated rat and small eddies of leaves. He walked around the side of the hotel, past the overgrown garden. His depth perception was no longer reliable. The morning heat already shimmered off the patchy pavement of the street. It rose in quiet waves and enveloped the city. He thought he saw an army marching toward him. They were chanting. When they grew closer he saw it was uniformed schoolchildren being herded to school by women in colourful dresses, whose faces seemed over-large and suddenly too near.

At the curb, sitting in a battered, cream-coloured Vauxhall, was the driver he'd hired. Bertrand was a spectrally thin man

who could have been thirty or sixty. He was smoking a cigarette and reading a newspaper that appeared to be weeks old.

Ritt got in the front seat and told Bertrand to head out of
town. They rolled past the colonial city centre, the decaying
whitewashed buildings, then on to potholed roads that wound
through shantytowns of rusting corrugated metal and mud,
and finally onto the rutted dusty road where they bounced
past stunted trees and small flocks of black birds. The dust rose
up behind them and drifted quickly on the wind. They drove
past faded metal storefronts selling live chickens, past children
on ancient bicycles, scrofulous dogs, past nuns with parasols.
The infrastructure would cost a fortune. You'd probably need
to build roads. There was a local labour pool but it was limited; he'd need to bring in workers. Maybe the French hadn't
misread the data. Maybe they felt that the infrastructure and
diplomatic costs were simply too high.

A two-hour tour yielded little and Ritt asked Bertrand to
turn back. On the way, they drove past the palace, which
looked like a beaux arts dance hall that had gone to seed.
Plants grew out of cracks in the pavement. It was fenced with
rusty barbed wire. Traffic came to a stop and Ritt stared at the
place. Near the palace wall, a hundred metres away from the
car, a few soldiers stood. A woman kneeled in front of them.
A blade caught the sun as it came down on her. Ritt's sightline
was partly eclipsed by a ragged hedge. His fever raged. Had he
just witnessed a beheading? The car inched forward. The body
came into view, the head to the side. Ritt mopped his forehead
with a no-longer white handkerchief. The car lurched forward
and he wondered if he'd imagined the scene.

He asked Bertrand what they'd just seen. "Bartho is the

magnificent protector," Bertrand said mechanically. "God give thanks."

At the hotel, Eldon Baker was waiting in the lobby, sweating.

"Jesus, where you been, man? We're on." He looked at his watch. "Got fifteen minutes to get to the palace."

Baker ushered him out to his jeep. The afternoon heat was oppressive. Ritt thought longingly of football weather, crisp and clear. Pretty girls wrapped in scarves.

At the palace Ritt followed Eldon across the floor of the vast almost empty room to the large desk where Bartho sat. Three men stood beside him. Ritt guessed they were an advisor, a translator and a bodyguard.

Eldon introduced Ritt to Bartho, who nodded slightly. No one introduced the other men. Bartho was wearing a shiny ill-fitting suit that hunched on his slim frame. He wore mirrored sunglasses.

Ritt told Bartho that oil was the key to modern life, that it was progress and education and that those who controlled it were the ones making the decisions in the backrooms of every nation on earth.

"I am already wealthy," Bartho replied.

"You could bring wealth to your country."

"I liberated my country from tyranny. There is no greater wealth."

"You could build hospitals and schools. Roads, bridges."

Bartho mulled this over. When he finally spoke, he made an incoherent statement about destiny and the need for suffering.

His voice was uninflected, each word given equal weight. His grammar was crude, his message a garbled mix of Catholic imagery and tribal myth.

A ceiling fan moved lazily. Flies circled. The men standing behind Bartho remained silent. Ritt had come to Africa hoping for profit and adventure, the same needs that had driven men to the "Dark Continent" for two centuries. He had also hoped to lay Deirdre to rest, though she had become more vivid and compelling somehow; perhaps the result of the fever.

Bartho was a sociopath. The breadth of suffering that emanated from this office covered the land. And in the throes of his recurring fever Ritt saw the future of this country with druggy clarity; after the multinationals stumbled on oil here, after facilities were built using foreign workers, after their profits were siphoned off and stored offshore, after Bartho had spread misery to every inch of his tiny country, it would become a more desperate, more murderous version of Nigeria.

Bartho had been a torturer for Macías Nguema, that was the rumour. He sat at his desk behind those sunglasses, his insanity and sense of entitlement shielded by the mirrored lenses. Ritt made up his fevered mind about Equatorial Guinea right there.

"Oil rose out of the ground in Titusville, Pennsylvania, in 1859 and it spread across the world," Ritt said, after Bartho wrapped up his lunatic soliloquy. "And it brought light and darkness. And now the earth was corrupt in God's sight, and the earth was filled with violence and all flesh was corrupted. And the Lord said the light of the wicked will one day be put out. Terrors will frighten the ungodly on every side. By disease his skin will be consumed. His belly filled with anger, and the earth will rise up against him and the heavens reveal his iniquity."

Ritt warmed to his sermon, a pastiche of the Texas brimstone delivered to him weekly as a boy. Baker shifted uncomfortably and tried to interject but Ritt was not to be derailed.

"The firstborn of death consumes his limbs, he is torn from the tent in which he is trusted and brought to the King of Terrors. His roots dry up beneath him. His memory perishes from the earth. He is thrust from light into darkness and driven out of the world. His cattle dead, his crops diseased, his wife barren."

Even as he delivered these words, Ritt dimly understood the danger he was putting himself in. What had that woman said to deserve a beheading? Something less offensive than this. But he felt unmoored, his actions divorced from consequences. A formless consciousness that floated in the ether. He couldn't stop.

"Yet wickedness is sweet on his tongue," he said, "and he is loath to let it go, and he swallows riches and vomits them up again. He has crushed the poor, he has seized a *house* he did not *build*. And because his greed knew no rest all the force of misery will be *upon* him. *Darkness* will take him, *fire* will consume him."

Baker scuttled across the floor and took Ritt's arm, hustling him toward the door. Bartho's face retained its practised dictatorial impassiveness.

As Baker pushed him out the door, Ritt delivered one last shot. "Oil will kiss your lips and it will give great hope and bring death to thousands."

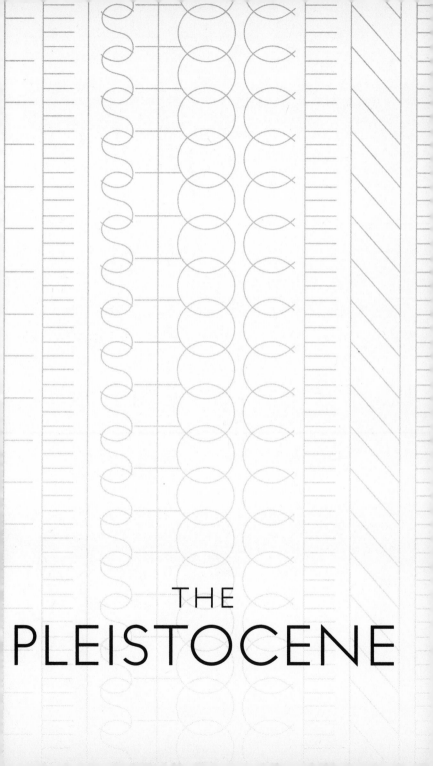

THE
PLEISTOCENE

TWENTY-ONE

CALGARY

1991

They waltzed as a woman on stage swayed slightly and sang about heartache. They stayed on the dance floor for a faster song then decided that was enough and sat down. Ritt ordered them both a whisky and examined his partner. Alexa was in her late forties, a graceful woman with a hearty laugh that was a surprise every time it erupted. She had long legs that were strategically crossed, her black dress hiked slightly. She'd already told Ritt that she had watched her marriage grow stale, that it had died a decade ago. Her husband was a lawyer who travelled a lot and was in fact gone at that very moment. She had come to the Palliser Hotel tonight with friends who thought getting out would be good for her.

They were in the Crystal Ballroom, at a dance to celebrate the petroleum industry's contributions to local charities, and they were three drinks in—at that point when the conversation was becoming confessional and strategic, each party circling the other with a growing sense of purpose. Ritt told Alexa he was putting a difficult divorce behind him. And they both sat with the subtle expectations these admissions had produced.

Ritt hadn't ventured out much either, not since the end of his marriage and the near collapse of Mackenzie Oil. People had lost money, and he had alienated the rest of the town, the people who hadn't already been bitter about his earlier success. Oil didn't breed contentment, and the room radiated resentment and envy and doubt, and he sat at the centre of this storm. He was surprised to find himself drinking whisky with a woman whose company he was enjoying.

Ritt saw Pete Manchauser moving among the tables, one of those ugly men who was aging surprisingly well; all the damage had been done right at the outset. He approached them, then stood over Ritt, swaying slightly, a bit drunk.

"How was your little African adventure, Ritt? Jungle fever? Miles Wheaton told me you had a play over there."

"False alarm," Ritt said. He knew he had been lucky to get on the plane and get out of the country. Baker had blamed Ritt's behaviour with the dictator on his fever. And Bartho probably hadn't entirely comprehended Ritt's biblical speech, though he must have gotten the drift. Apparently his lunacy didn't yet extend to beheading foreigners; it was still strictly local.

Manchauser couldn't resist a parting shot. "I imagine the North's a bit too much of a reach for you now. You burned a lot of bridges, Ritt," he said and moved to the next table.

Ritt decided he wasn't there to think about burning bridges (this from the king of burned bridges) or his company, or what he might do next. He and Alexa danced and had another drink then Ritt drove her home to a spacious split-level not far from his old house. He wondered if Deirdre was still in it. Perhaps she had grown tired of its ghosts. He walked Alexa to the back door and they kissed like high school kids, with a surprising hunger. After five minutes, Ritt broke free and said, "I'd like to call you."

"I'd like that." She kissed him again then went inside.

When he got back to his apartment, he made a drink and looked out the window and toyed with the idea of phoning her. An adolescent impulse that he resisted. He had only dated a few times since Deirdre, dates that had been arranged by well-meaning wives of colleagues. But he hadn't really had the energy. He was distracted by his corporate malaise and felt like Exhibit A—the man who flew too close to the sun. People expected acrid wisdom or anger or remorse, but he wasn't filled with anything. That was the problem. He was a hologram that was projected on social occasions while his real self sat at home sipping whisky and changing the channel.

But after that first night, Ritt saw a lot of Alexa, sneaking around, going to restaurants in strip malls in the suburbs, Vietnamese places with hospital lighting. Ritt's biggest worry was that her husband, Richard, was going to the same out-of-the-way places with whomever he was sleeping with and they'd run into him. After seeing an afternoon movie at a suburban theatre on a gloomy Sunday they rented a motel room and made love on the vibrating bed that needed quarters every four minutes. They had a stack of them on the chipped side table and Alexa laughed every time Ritt awkwardly leaned over to put more quarters in. After two months, Alexa told her husband she wanted a divorce.

"Do you miss the strip malls?" she asked him. They were sitting in an upscale fusion restaurant, a place where they were very likely to run into people they knew, picking at tiny complicated appetizers.

"That restaurant where we saw the mouse?"

"No more vibrating beds."

"Maybe hang on to the beds."

"Richard is being difficult. He suddenly wants to work things out."

"Are you having second thoughts?"

"God no. He's a spoiled child. He hasn't played with this toy in years but when someone else wants it, suddenly he needs it. It's going to be messy for a while, that's all."

They tried the miniature ginger-venison dumplings in the balsamic reduction, Alexa's head at an interrogative tilt as she tasted it.

"And with Christmas coming," Alexa said, "Tatiana's coming back from college. I don't know." Alexa's eighteen-year-old daughter, who was somewhere in Connecticut.

"Does she know?"

"No, not in the let's-sit-down-and-have-a-chat sense."

"Richard thinks Christmas will bring you back together?"

"He made this family Christmas card, one of those ones with a photo of us all and then a list of the great things the family has done during the year. He's never done anything like it. The photo is fifteen years old. We're on a ski hill. Tat is six. Richard is wearing a Santa hat. If he'd described what we *actually* did this year, it would be him fucking his assistant in a suite at the Marriott, me and you on a vibrating bed, and Tatiana smoking dope in her dorm with the window open, listening to Sinéad O'Connor and having sex with an inappropriate boy. Merry Christmas."

"Maybe you should wait until January to tell her then."

"You mean stage a Christmas then tear down the set afterward."

"The spirit of the season."

On Christmas Day, Ritt was in his apartment sipping twelve-year-old whisky and admiring the view. The city was built on views; you needed to be facing west, the direction progress took. The east was an unadorned plain and post-war suburbs that held impossibly small houses that were built when people didn't need much. Ritt could see the mountains in the morning, the light shining off the snow.

One of the benefits of having had money was finally understanding its limitations. His life hadn't changed much despite $7 million in vanished stock options. Debt and wealth were brothers, not enemies. He had no heirs, no bloodline. Whether he left seven million or owed seven million wouldn't matter when he was gone. Everything was temporary; this was the elemental lesson of geology.

He spent much of the afternoon imagining Alexa in her house, tip-toeing around the holiday. Richard working the nostalgia angle, getting their daughter involved. He would have bought them both something extravagant, then hovered over them as they opened their presents. *No really, it's nothing, you're worth it.*

He wanted to call Alexa and wish her a merry Christmas but didn't want the awkwardness of her husband answering. He wanted to hear that the day was incredibly difficult and she was thinking of him and thank god when this is all settled.

Ritt turned on the television, expecting to find a treacly Christmas movie. Instead, there was Mikhail Gorbachev, giving his resignation speech, his earnest, trustworthy face, that stain that no Western democracy would tolerate in a leader. The Soviet Union was breaking up, the drunken bear that had threatened the West for decades. Gorbachev's speech had no fire, few inflections. A eulogy for someone you didn't know very well.

This being my last opportunity to address you as President of the USSR, I find it necessary to inform you of what I think of the road that has been trodden by us since 1985. Squandered resources . . .

Ritt called Tate to tell him to turn on the TV. "Channel eight. Gorbachev's resigning. Let's talk tomorrow. We should maybe think about this. There could be something there."

"Merry Christmas," Tate said.

"Right," Ritt said, and hung up.

We had a lot of everything—land, oil, gas . . . However we were living much worse than people in industrialized countries . . .

He admired Gorbachev's candour. What politician risked taking true stock of his country, his people, even on his way out? In democracies, politicians are forced to sell nobility, to bring hope rather than change. No voter has the stomach for reality.

All the half-hearted reforms—and there have been a lot of them— fell through, one after another. This country was going nowhere and we couldn't possibly live the way we did . . .

Maybe Richard would deliver a version of this speech at Christmas dinner. A survey of the life they had created, one that involved emotional cruelty and romantic neglect, one that had collapsed under the weight of distance and stupidity, but one that possessed the raw materials to rebuild. And in the candlelight, after a few glasses of wine, her daughter beaming, would Alexa succumb? Those awful Christmas movies were popular for a reason: the family reunited, in the spirit of the season, all friction erased. Perhaps she is clearing the dishes at this very minute, thinking there is hope. They once loved. Who knows.

The process of renovating this country . . . has proven to be more complicated than anyone could imagine . . .

A Russian speech: melancholy, human, flawed.

We opened up ourselves to the rest of the world . . .

You loved us and we didn't love you back. A second-world country in a torn prom dress, waiting for the phone to ring.

Ritt hoped Tate would hear what he was hearing: there would be opportunities in the former Soviet Union. They had oil, and now they had (more) chaos. They would be looking for Western technology, expertise and money after thirty years of pretending everything was tickety-boo.

He picked up the phone to call Alexa and then put it back down, then looked at it and almost picked it up again.

He finally went into the kitchen and boiled water and added farfalle. He sautéed some pancetta and added garlic then mixed it all with parsley and Parmesan. He sat on the couch and sipped more whisky and ate his dinner and watched a movie about a reindeer.

TWENTY-TWO

BAKU, AZERBAIJAN

1992

n Neftchiler Prospekti a man stood beside a large black car. He was blocky, his suit was boxy and ill-fitting. He looked like everybody else.

"That guy," Ritt said.

"Gumby?" Jackson Tate asked.

"Was he sitting at the table next to us at dinner last night?"

"Fuck knows. Everyone here is a spy. They spy on each other. They spy on the people who are spying on *them*. Then they both submit reports to the same guy. Who one of them is also spying on. It's the fucking *Twilight Zone*."

"He was sitting at the next table with another guy and a woman," Ritt said. "That face, that suit—he's got to be Russian."

Baku was a mix of 1932 and the sixteenth century. The port was a graceful crescent. Beyond it, oil rigs stood in the water like abandoned toys. Everyone had been here. Since the Paleolithic era people had congregated: Zoroastrian, Sasanian, Arabs, Persians, and then, of course, the Russians, who still hovered over it as the Soviet empire broke into pieces. A walled city with European spaces and the mammoth paranoia that impending wealth brings.

A week after Gorbachev's speech, a Russian geologist named Sergei Krupin had called Ritt. He'd introduced himself and rambled on about politics and the geology of northern Russia then got to the point: "You have *ship*!" Ritt told him that he and Tate had already decided to fly to Azerbaijan, and Krupin said Ritt had to come to Moscow as well. They talked for an hour about the North, how the Arctic was overlooked, how it was the future. Empires would be built.

In the gold rush atmosphere of Baku, it wasn't clear who had the authority to actually sign an exploration deal. The hotel was filled with shady middlemen, corrupt ministers, and local warlords who had all somehow gotten pieces of the action before it was a deal. There were Americans and Brits and the French and each night they picked new partners and waltzed around the idea of exploration rights, fuelled by vodka. It was like the worst high school dance in history.

He and Tate went into the hotel, swallowed by its baroque gloom and walked down the stairs to the tavern in the basement. A woman greeted them with a tired smile and showed them to a table then retreated with a Marilyn sway. It was the only hotel that foreign oilmen were allowed to stay in. One reason for this was that every room was bugged, every phone and most of the tables in the bar too; somewhere an army of Soviet-trained bureaucrats was going through the tapes trying to put things together, every day bringing them hundreds of hours of new conversations, new languages, accents, new bullshit.

"Word is Shell is pulling out," Ritt said, emphasizing his Texas accent, making it a parody. "Taking their football and going home."

"There goes half a billion," Tate said.

It was a game they'd developed to amuse themselves during the long stretches between frustrating meetings. They made up alarmist stories and talked in arcane oil dialect for the sake of the people listening to the tapes in small grey cubicles.

"That batshit Texas Aggie says fuck them and the horse they rode in on, he's going to set up a red dog blitz and whipstock all the way to Moscow. Operation Napoleon," Ritt elaborated.

"Shell does it, you'll have every numbnuts Okie wildcatter out there going sideways faster than blue ticks on bear scent."

"Makes you want to crawl under the stove and lick your balls."

"Brent Crude going to flat out pull a Jim Nabors."

"The full Jim. You don't want to be there when that shit stands up and starts singing Dixie."

"Especially with Exxon itchy to get back to Nigeria. Homesick for leprosy and twelve-year-old soldiers."

"Makes you want to saw your head off with a grapefruit knife."

"Call in the dogs and piss on the fire." *Fahr.*

"Thank you Jesus, catch you on the flip side."

"Operation Napoleon. Sis boom bah."

They sat quietly for a moment, out of inspiration. A waitress came over and they ordered two vodkas.

They were meeting a man named Trotsky. They didn't know if it was his real name, or if he really was from the minister's office. But after three frustrating days, Ritt had bellowed to the microphones hidden in his room that he needed to meet with the minister, that it was important, that a great deal of money was involved. Two hours later the hotel manager asked him if he wanted to meet with one of the minister's representatives.

"You think our revolutionary is going to show?" Tate asked.

"He'll show. I don't know how much use he'll be when he gets here."

On cue, a man wearing a black trench coat came into the tavern and walked directly to their table.

"Gentleman," he said. The accent was Russian with a bit of something else. Educated in England for a few years, maybe. His meaty hand wavered in the air. They shook it and he ordered more vodka for all of them. It seemed like a complicated conversation between Trotsky and the waitress and when the vodka came it didn't taste like the vodka they had been drinking.

The first round tasted like antifreeze. "Is real," Trotsky said.

They drank a toast and then he walked them through the complications of the minister's office. There were shortages. There was corruption. People who must be paid. You understand. He told stories about sickness and death and imperialism. He uttered Russian proverbs and veiled warnings and ordered more vodka, then herring and caviar. He told them a story about a boy who was lost in the forest. "He is frightened, yes of course. Is getting dark. He is small. Forest is big. There are sounds of things, these things he hasn't heard. Maybe bear is out in trees. Maybe wolfs. Who can know? He has only small knife. What can he do with small knife? It is darker. More sounds. Something, not bear or wolfs, something worse. The boy tells himself it is something so terrible no one has ever seen it and lived to tell story. So, worst thing is in this forest. This is why people tells him: Don't go in forest. But of course, he's boy, he doesn't obey. Now he's in forest. Time passes. Boy is terrified. Sounds are closer. He looks at knife. Finally, he stand up. He has found courage! He stabs himself in heart and falls dead."

Ritt stared at Trotsky, wondering if the story was over.

"This is oil business," Trotsky said, then shrugged.

Ritt looked at Tate who was also trying to divine the moral.

Trotsky made a circling motion for the waitress, ordering another round, and then explained that oil was sitting all over the world in mysterious forests and local people didn't know jack shit, and then the Americans arrived and told the natives how to get it out and get it to market. The Africans had let in the foreign wolves and they may as well have stuck a knife in their own hearts. But here, in Baku, Trotsky said, they were more sophisticated. They weren't filled with fear and awe. They knew the power they had, and they planned to use it. They weren't small boys in forests.

Ritt nodded. "Well then, we're working from the same playbook, Mr. Trotsky. Our plans include you."

"This play *book* . . ." Trotsky began.

"It has a happy ending."

They'd left a verbal offer with Trotsky that would tie up a smallish territory. The offer included an envelope with $10,000 in hundred dollar bills in US currency.

"We can't trust him," Tate said. They were standing outside the hotel, out of range of the microphones. "The first thing he's going to do is sell our confidential bid to Exxon or Shell. Then he's going to complain that ten grand is an insult."

"When he gets us in the room with whichever thug is running the zoo we'll give him the full fee, the amount sanctioned by international governing bodies."

"Which is?"

"Who the fuck knows. Assuming that territory isn't already sold and they have at least enough legitimacy to get us spudded in somewhere. Then we'll have something to take to an international court if it comes to that, which is unlikely."

"If we nail something down we can use it to round up some minority partners," Tate said.

"Nailing anything in this country is going to be a crapshoot."

Four days went by. A cold rain hammered the windows. He called Alexa on a static-filled line to see how the divorce was proceeding. He heard every second word and hung up after twenty minutes, not sure what was actually happening. He and Tate stayed in the hotel most of the time because a government minister had been shot a block away and a British oil executive had been kidnapped. They'd heard two bombs go off, distant explosions.

On the fourth night, Exxon held a signing party in the next room. Through the wall, Ritt could hear champagne popping, hearty toasts. The next morning the deal was gone, disappeared into the bureaucracy, the bribes vanished.

Contracts were signed with people who had no power. Contracts were reneged on within hours. Outside the hotel was a poor city in an ill-defined country that was waiting to be illuminated by foreign capital. Inside the hotel was Alice through the looking glass.

By the fifth night, Ritt still hadn't heard back from Trotsky. They could invest a lot and have it all seized by a legitimate government, if one came along as rumoured, or by the next illegitimate government. The world's money pounded like sand down a rat hole. Ritt's strength was geology, not politics. He decided that if he bailed now, nothing would be lost: a few grand in expenses, a cheap education in the *realpolitik* of the post-Soviet era. He could leave this chaos to Tate and explore the chaos in Moscow instead, meet Sergei Krupin.

He stayed in his room and read, getting up every few hours to answer the door and tell the blinking, innocent-looking prostitute that she had the wrong room. On one of these occasions he saw the untrustworthy Trotsky entering a room down the hall.

He had brought Dostoyevsky's *Crime and Punishment* with him, assuming it would be appropriate. It was the last of the Russian books on his reading list. He remembered reading *Anna Karenina* with Oda. She had left him the gift of reading. Deirdre had left a legal bill and little else, though the parting hadn't been acrimonious since neither of them had much of an emotional stake by the end. All those wondrous early moments buried in the wreckage, as they always were. And now Alexa, both of them treading carefully, not sure how to negotiate the next step.

After two more days Ritt cornered Trotsky in the hallway, physically stopping him, one hand on his shoulder. The look on the man's face convinced him that nothing would come of this visit. But he pressed him anyway.

"Where are we at?" Ritt asked.

"The minister's office . . . is many complications," Trotsky said.

"Would one of those complications be that you don't have anyone's ear?"

"Having an ear . . .?"

"You're not in a position to help us get any leases."

"These things . . ."

"Listen, Trotsky, I know this dog isn't going to hunt. I know our ten grand has already been spent on vodka and hookers. But let me give you some advice. We're the people you want here. We're a mid-sized, non-imperialist, happy-to-work-with-the-locals kind of outfit. You're going to open the door to the American majors and the half-dead remains of the Russian oil industry and they're going to come in here and take over and you're going to be waiting tables while they're restaging the Cuban Missile Crisis in downtown Baku."

Trotsky stood there in his oversized trench coat, digesting the few phrases he understood.

Ritt patted him on the shoulder. "Been great working with you, Leon. Good luck with the revolution."

In Tate's room, they poured more of the single malt that Ritt had brought with him. He put on his Texas drawl.

"Ran into Trotsky, that dry-gulching pissant."

"Knew him at Oxford," Tate said, deciding on a broad, uncertain English accent, speaking to the hidden microphones. "Dodgy oink."

"I think that boy's roadkill."

"I suspect you're right. Fed us a load of bollocks. Whole bloody country gone to hell. Sliding on a sea of oil."

"They goan have to get *someone* spudded or this turkey shoot goan flat out Hiroshima."

"It could well be that the winners of this particular cricket match will wish they hadn't. Bit of the pyrrhic, Old Sausage."

"Maybe try Iraq."

"They prefer dictators. Rather comforting, that. Shall we pack up our wellies and murder the sheep?"

"This shitstorm goan blow us all back to Eden."

"Toodles then."

"You got that part right."

Ritt could see Moscow through the window of the unreliable Aeroflot plane, wavering and coughing on its approach to the runway. A city made for winter, the season that defeated Napoleon. The air inside the plane was fetid; it smelled like 1952. Tate had stayed in Baku, convinced he could salvage something. He thrived on chaos and negotiation. Outside the terminal building, the air was sharp. A woman in fur struggled with her neon-coloured luggage. People milled, heavy Russian faces. The sun was a bleached circle hovering above the bulbous Moscow skyline.

Ritt was aware that the Russians were at a delicate moment in their evolution. They were always at a delicate moment; this was their gift to history. Their superpower status had been revoked, and they have been revealed to be a heavily armed drunk, a developing nation with a heroic capacity for self-destruction. Hundreds of tanks were already rusting in the Urals, warehouses filled with weaponry, AK-47s sold to African rebels and Arab freedom fighters, the remnants of their military might. Now the world favoured money over muscle and Russia's economy was a post-communist mess, a black market writ large. They had no money but they had oil, their deliverance. They wanted to be recognized as players on the international stage rather than Slavic hillbillies who had found someone's wallet in the street. If Ritt wanted to operate in Russia, he'd need a Russian partner, someone who knew the terrain, and Krupin might be that person.

He took a cab to the address Krupin had given him, still with his suitcase. The building was nineteenth century. Inside, the lobby was domed and ailing, paint missing from the ceiling. The elevator was ornate. An attendant in an oversized military coat with a frayed collar that smelled of cigarettes opened the chipped golden gate then closed it behind him. The man moved a lever and they lurched up. Ritt hadn't told him where he was going but the man seemed to know. The elevator opened to a large room, which, like the lobby, was imperial but suffering. A woman approached him.

"Mr. Devlin," she said, extending her hand, speaking in a heavy accent, gargling her syllables. "It is so very wonderful to meet with you."

She led him to Krupin's office. Sergei sat behind a massive desk, hearty-looking and bearded. His suit was rumpled, his tie askew. Ritt put down his suitcase and they shook hands. Sergei then held both of Ritt's shoulders as if assessing a cousin he hadn't seen in years. "How shall we make each other rich?" he said, laughing, and released him.

Sergei dismissed the woman and took out a bottle of vodka and poured two small glasses. He raised one. "To our friendship!"

Ritt drained his. A comforting burn. It was eleven a.m.

Ritt already knew that Sergei had been a geologist for a state-owned company and that his path through oil was not dissimilar to Ritt's. During their long rambling phone conversation, Sergei had told him there was madness and opportunity and they had spoken about the North as if it were a mutual sibling who was going through a difficult stretch.

Now Sergei sketched the terrain of the new Russia: the government was selling off its oil assets to three, partially privatized, lupine companies, each of them half-supported by god knows who. Sergei was in the process of forming a small company that would be poised to move when this oligarchy inevitably toppled.

"So Gorbachev says, 'farewell, good luck, it's been fun.'" Sergei sat back in his chair. "And Soviet Union is gone. Like magic. What happens now? Everyone ask this question. Really, only issue is oil. Oil is seventy percent of country's revenue. We sell some vodka, a few Russian dolls, some guns. But we are oil. So really this is only issue. Oil fields are run on Soviet model. Which is, for your information, three crews of workers sent out to exactly where there is no rig. It is rigs that collapse because the welding was perhaps not the best. We have equipment fifty years old, pipelines made of wood. What we do best is inefficiency. World leader in that.

"Let me tell you story. Uzbekistan, 1966, five wells blow in. They burn for three years. How to stop this? No one knows. Gold medal of Olympic gas problems. Finally Karpov, minister of disaster, I think, he has solution. Nuclear bomb. Karpov the genius. They dig a hole beside wells, send a thirty kiloton nuclear bomb down. Set off bomb. Rock turns to glass, shuts down wells. Also kills twelve people. This is Russian oil industry.

"Suddenly there is new system!" Sergei lit a black cigarette and blew the smoke toward the ceiling. "Conoco comes. Shell comes. Shiny and new, but. New system is not filled with joy. Who is boss now? Who gets the money? Who has the power? A hundred questions. Many unfortunate answers. So now we have three companies—Yukos, Lukoil, Surgut—a few smaller ones. Russian government is getting out of oil business, they say. Whole world is at our door—Americans, British, French, Japanese—please take these flowers, please take these chocolates, show me your underpants." Sergei paused and poured more vodka for them. "Who gets in? *I* get in. *You* get in."

Ritt wondered how, exactly, that would happen. The North was their most logical entry point and his experience there would help. The North had been too much of a technological challenge for the old regime, but now that Western money and technology was coming in, it would be accessible and lucrative. And, unlike in Baku, there wouldn't be that much competition. There was a deepwater harbour at Murmansk that could handle supertankers so they could move the oil to market. But they would need money and licences. Judging from Sergei's office, he was in worse shape than Ritt.

Sergei got up awkwardly and lumbered to a wooden armoire that probably weighed two thousand pounds. He opened the doors and pulled out a narrow drawer and grabbed some documents then came back. He unrolled one of the documents on his messy desk. A geological map.

"I speak to you geologist to geologist—the miracle is in the North."

The Siberian tundra was so cold that the sub-standard Soviet steel rigs ruptured in the winter night. But still they endured.

This was the Russian way: to make as many mistakes as possible but persevere as the weak died off.

"Look here," Sergei said, pointing. "From here, between Urals and Yenisey River, then into the Kara Sea. The Turukhan–Igarka foldbelts have major deformation. Not a surprise. Everything is deformed if you wait long enough. But key is right here. Prograding clastic clinoforms during Neocomian. There is our oil. Maybe three hundred billion barrels. Bit more."

Ritt examined the chart. The territory was inhospitable but accessible. They could work six or seven months of the year.

"Most famous oil worker in history is Iosif Dzhugashvili," Sergei said. "You know him as Joseph Stalin. He worked in oil fields. He pushes people around a bit. Then a bit more. He likes it! So he pushes whole country. Uncle Joe. He understood that oil was power."

"What's up there now?" Ritt asked.

"Cold. Wind. But we build city. Not real city with food shortages and ugly prostitutes. But city for workers. Oil city."

Ritt was warming to Sergei. Perhaps it was the vodka.

"Right now," Sergei said. "This moment. Russia is not really a country. It is a casino. Largest in world. We never close! Yes, this expression. Everything is a gamble. But some people will win. Conoco, Exxon, Shell, they have big dreams. That is oil's great gift. It makes men dream. They have expertise, they have money, they have contracts."

Sergei poured more vodka, overfilling both glasses, spilling onto the charts. "The Russian companies will take the money, take the expertise. They will lose the contracts. Oops. Many people will leave with nothing. They get tired of corruption.

Tired of bureaucracy we keep because it is useful. My friend, that is when we move in. Yes.

"So Russia not really a country. Neither is Azerbaijan, Kazakhstan, Chechnya. But here is the news. US not really a country, either. Oil companies are the new countries. They were in Baku with you, negotiating as nations. Conoco is a country. Aramco, Total, Exxon. These are the new countries. They have the money, they control the fuel we need to survive. They have armies, they sign treaties, they go to war. The rest of America is car salesmen and film stars and fat children."

The woman who had greeted Ritt arrived with a plate of smoked salmon, small potatoes, herring and dark bread. Ritt had slept little on the plane, and had been served a disarming breakfast of pancakes and grey fish that still lurched in his stomach under the assault of vodka, but thought he should try and eat to soak up some of the alcohol.

In the end he stayed until five, drinking steadily as Sergei spoke of rampant crime and political corruption. His English was accented and inventive and he took great pride in it. Russia was in worse shape than anyone imagined, he said. There were milk shortages in St. Petersburg. The passwords to government computers had been lost during the changeover and millions of documents were lost or inaccessible. There was violence and extortion. The Soviet Union had bred inventive criminals— one of their few manufacturing successes. People were angry and frightened and drank too much and each morning they woke angrier and more frightened and drank even more. Sergei's broad analysis was probably close to what would happen, though it wasn't clear how this chaos would benefit Mackenzie Oil.

Ritt woke up in his hotel room with his head throbbing, a stale nausea threatening to rise. He looked at his watch and saw it was four a.m. The heavy brocade curtains were open, pale light from the snow outside invading his room. He and Sergei had eventually made a deal, a handshake that sealed their northern adventure. The details were lost. A contract would go back and forth at any rate, chiselled by lawyers. He got up and took three aspirin for his ruined head and drank two glasses of water and looked out the window at the quiet city. Most of Moscow burned before Napoleon arrived; the Russians destroyed it themselves rather than give it to an invader.

TWENTY-THREE

ITALY

1993

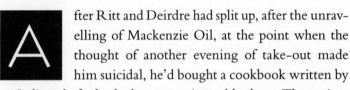fter Ritt and Deirdre had split up, after the unravelling of Mackenzie Oil, at the point when the thought of another evening of take-out made him suicidal, he'd bought a cookbook written by an Italian chef who had an annoying cable show. The recipes were complicated enough that they took time and effort to make. It was the use of his time Ritt was most grateful for—the hour it took to assemble everything, the crucial order of things. Eating seemed like anticlimax, but he discovered that he liked to cook.

In early spring, he and Alexa decided to take a cooking class in Tuscany, a five-day crash course in Italian cuisine given by a diminutive, bustling woman who nudged them toward a more sensual relationship with pasta dough. Ritt found himself entertained as she explained the endless subtleties of olive oil, and the treacherous labelling that made it all but impossible to determine provenance. She punctuated her lecture by dipping her finger into a small bowl of greenish oil then putting her finger into Ritt's mouth.

Alexa quietly disappeared halfway through the second day. The spring weather was glorious and she didn't see the point of spending her time in a dark, stone-floored kitchen listening to the stumbling philosophy of someone's grandmother. And the woman had grabbed a spoon out of Alexa's hand and nudged her away from the pot she was neglecting; this imperious behaviour had re-opened some childhood kitchen trauma. Instead, Alexa took the rented car to Siena and wandered and drank Campari under a striped umbrella in the Piazza del Campo. She was turning fifty and was so mortified by that number that she couldn't bear to say it out loud and the cooking school was partly a disguise; they wouldn't have to dwell on the birthday.

After a moderately successful day in which Ritt made *vitello in tegame col radicchio* and heard from his teacher that cooking was life, it was sex, that it located us on this earth, it *defined* us, he met Alexa back at the large room they had rented in a villa that housed a few other couples. The sun was still strong and they sat on the stone patio by the pool and Ritt had a beer.

"Did she stick anything in your mouth today?" Alexa asked.

"She told us that food is sex."

"Sounds messy."

"She said that what you leave out of a recipe is as important as what you put in."

"That's deep." She gestured to the fields filled with rows of grapevines, the long, ornamental-looking pool, the cloudless sky. "Maybe we should retire here, Ritt. I'm serious. My god. Couldn't you?"

"It's beautiful."

In the morning, while Alexa shopped in a neighbouring village, he made *sugo ligure col pomodoro crudo*. A simple pasta with raw tomatoes, olives, capers and garlic. *Simple is not easy,* his teacher warned, wagging a scolding finger. She got them to crush a ripe tomato in their hand to understand its essence, to feel the sensual quality of its flesh. She took Ritt's messy hand and lifted it to his face. She wasn't much older than Ritt, a compact grandmother. Her face tilted up toward his, dark and lined and heavy, an experienced mouth. Breathe it in, she said. You must understand your ingredients the way you understand your lover. You must know what they can become in your hands.

At noon he helped eat the finished product with two glasses of wine. There were six other people in the class, restless, well-heeled Americans seeking experience in middle age. Ritt talked to a couple from Portland who did something in the tech world. She was in her forties, with a sun-damaged face that suggested she wasn't a native of Portland. He was tall and cautious and the two of them spent some time wondering how heartily they could recommend it to friends.

"It really depends on where they are on their journey," she said. Ritt wished Alexa were there to meet his ironical eye.

In the afternoon, the teacher gave them a lecture on how grass-fed cows in the Veneto were butchered before they began to ovulate. They were known for their specific taste, the taste of a life unfulfilled. Then they made *involtini di vitello farciti* and Ritt rallied, but the eating was a chore. He was still full from lunch and from tasting all the things they needed to taste.

On their last day the teacher pinned a ribbon on Ritt's chest, proof of graduation. She stood on tip-toes and whispered *bella in vista, dentro è trista,* then kissed him on the mouth.

He got a ride back to the villa with the Portland couple, who were now planning to cycle through Umbria. "I think Tuscany is over," the woman declared. "It's gotten so commercialized."

Alexa was still out somewhere with the car and Ritt took a nap. He woke up and splashed water on his face and checked the time. Alexa wasn't back yet, and he called Tate to see what fresh crisis awaited in the oil patch. Tate was still regularly flying to Baku, trying to establish a foothold in the Caspian Derby. He could hear Tate inhale, his head turned slightly from the phone to accommodate the cigarette.

"I was speaking to Unger in Energy," Tate said. "So he tells me the government is in the planning stages of an Arctic council of some kind. Get the concerned countries—Russia, Canada, US, Denmark, Norway—lined up. Multi-pronged scientific effort. I'm thinking—and this could be three years away—but I'm thinking we need to get someone on that council."

"A pipeline for scientific data."

"Well, yeah, that. But look, if there's a major play up there, it isn't going to be scientists on that council, it's going to be bureaucrats. It will get political real fast. Russia has already got deep ports on the Arctic Ocean. They're gearing up. So if we could get our own scientist on there, it would help."

"Maybe Breton Allman."

"That flaky geologist?"

"He knows the North."

"You want me to sound him out."

"I'll call him when I get back. How was Baku?"

"I had a drink with the secretary-of-fucking-state. The Americans have got everyone there: senators, spooks, CIA. It's like Vietnam only with oil instead of communism. Remember that guy, what's-his-name? Trotsky?"

"Who screwed us the first time around."

"He's still there. I saw him talking to a table of Japanese oilmen. Still working his magic."

Ritt could hear Tate light another cigarette, the intake and slow exhale.

"You're over there making pizza," Tate said.

"Something like that."

"Okay then."

The next morning Ritt and Alexa drove to Florence and checked into a formerly grand hotel that looked down onto the Arno River. Their room was large and marbled and a bit *fin de siècle*, cracks in the wall painted over with pastels. After lunch Ritt took Alexa to the Basilica of San Lorenzo.

"There's someone buried there. I want to see his tomb."

"Who."

"The patron saint of geology. A man named Nicolas Steno."

"So what, exactly, did Saint Nick do?"

They were in the courtyard of the vast basilica, resting place for the Medicis, the gorgeous stone.

"He invented time."

"That's quite a trick."

They entered the ancient stone coolness of the basilica. There were a handful of tourists wandering through, pointing up to the detailed ceiling, murmuring respectfully. He and Alexa strolled arm in arm among them, looking for Steno, finally finding his sarcophagus among the glorious Medicis. Ritt stood for a moment. A few years earlier Steno was made an actual saint, beatified by John Paul II. He had essentially starved himself, perhaps as an act of penance for insulting God with his discovery. There was a plaque above the sarcophagus that read "*vir inter geologos et anatomicos praestantissimus.*"

Alexa looked at him quizzically, then gave his arm a tug.

Outside, the spring sun was warm. They walked through the Piazza della Signoria and ate gelato. Around them, tourists soaked up the Renaissance and shopped for shoes and T-shirts and stood figuring out the exchange rate on pocket calculators.

He and Alexa stopped in front of heroic sculptures in the piazza and examined the opulent antique muscles. Ritt stared at the stone, which was slightly pitted, a century of pollution slowly eating the marble. It was likely quarried in Carrara, seventy-five miles away. Marble that had begun as limestone 200 million years ago, just as North America and Africa were splitting up—*let's stay in touch.* Then 27 million years ago, an insistent tectonic block crashed into the Italian peninsula, leaving basalts and sediments on top of the limestone. The tectonics just didn't let up. Millennia went by. Still pushing until there were six miles of rock on top of that limestone, which heated to four hundred degrees and turned to marble and migrated slowly toward the surface, waiting for Michelangelo's precocious hammer.

"I feel more Catholic around all this, you know," Alexa said. "All this architecture, the nuns shopping in packs, those monk-like guys wandering among the tourists. You can't help it. It creeps back."

"When was your last confession?"

"Oh god, I'd have to book a month to catch up. You'd need three priests working in shifts. I wasn't the world's greatest Catholic and neither of my parents was really religious. I think the Catholic school just made their lives easier—discipline, fear and virginity. They could sit back and let God do their work for them. After I graduated we all drifted away. But you can't beat the Catholics for drama."

"The Pentecostals worked a smaller room, but you didn't have snake handlers."

"What do you think priests are? Oh god that's awful, I know." Alexa laughed. "Am I with a dirt-eating hillbilly? Are you going to flop down on the cobblestones and start speaking in tongues? Didn't those snake handlers get bitten?"

Ritt stared upward at the statue of Perseus holding Medusa's severed head, clutching those snakes.

"Bad hair day," Alexa said.

"Bad everything day."

Alexa was turning fifty in two days, a looming moment that had produced something close to a twitch in her before they'd left on their trip. Though she seemed comfortable here in Italy. In less than a week she had turned an appetizing brown. In the morning they took the train to Venice, the productive countryside going by slowly. Venice was long walks and long lunches. At night they watched a Fellini film that was projected against a white wall in a small piazza. Sitting on folding chairs they drank wine and watched the decadence of Rome in black and white, slightly lost without subtitles. Walking back to the hotel they held hands and Alexa leaned into him as her heels negotiated the stones. They made love and in the morning Ritt got up and dressed and stood looking at her lying naked on her stomach, the sheets in a sensual crumple. He went downstairs and had an espresso and read the *Herald Tribune,* checking the price of oil. He ordered another espresso and a cappuccino and took them upstairs with the paper and alternated reading about a transit strike and looking at Alexa, still asleep on the bed. Things were simple with Alex, a function of age perhaps. She inhabited the world with an ease that was valuable to him now. Sitting there with his morning coffee, the bad news open on the small marble table, Alex splayed on the sheets, her taste still on him, he was a contented man. This was how you fell in love.

Still, he wondered if he'd been happiest with Oda. Or was this simply romantic nostalgia. The rest of his world was so unknown back then, all the big questions still suspended. The early days with Deirdre had been intoxicating. They'd ventured into the world like an army. Every marriage like Rome: Who thought it would fall?

After Alex woke up and showered they walked to the Rialto market and browsed the fish stalls, looking at small sharks on their backs, those U-shaped strangely melancholic mouths. Clams, scallops, tubs filled with eels. Ritt found all of it exotic and mesmerizing.

"It's not like we have a kitchen," Alexa said, a restraining hand on his arm. "I mean, we're not actually going to cook any of these things. Thank god. Some of them look like aliens."

Then she protested about the smell, which to Ritt was only slightly more maritime than the general Venetian air, and they left the market. They walked without a map, going down whatever street looked interesting. For her birthday dinner, Ritt took her to Terrazza Danieli, near the Bridge of Sighs. They sat outside and ate shellfish, bright pink with dead black cartoon eyes, and drank Pinot Grigio.

"I don't want to hear anything about my birthday," Alexa said.

"Nothing about how you look thirty-nine? In your prime?"

"Let's just put it behind us."

The waiter came by, overly solicitous, a professional romantic. He lit Alexa's cigarette and took the wine out of the ice bucket and poured a little into her glass.

"Venice is the kind of place you come to for romance or to kill yourself," Alexa pronounced, looking around.

"We could get married," Ritt said, surprising himself. The magical evening light on her face, the wine, the view. It all conspired.

"Ritt, is that a laconic Texas proposal?"

"I suppose it is."

"Well then. We could."

"You're accepting?"

"You don't have a ring, do you?"

"This was a bit spur of the moment."

"My, my."

In the morning Ritt got up early to fly back to Calgary. Alexa was leaving in the afternoon, catching a flight to London to visit her sister, who had married a British banker and was living in a fairy tale nightmare according to Alex, whatever that meant. He showered and kissed her, waking her up. "You're abandoning me," she said.

"Never."

At the airport Ritt lingered in the bookstore, looking for something to read. The English book selection was limited. He examined a few paperbacks, reading praise on the back covers; everyone was writing at the peak of their powers, god bless them. A shelf filled with genius. He picked up an Italian tabloid newspaper with an actress on the cover. She was wearing a black dress, her hair slightly dishevelled, her mouth curled in a ferocious snarl. In block letters was the word *Tradimento!* He didn't know what it meant, but bought the paper anyway on a whim. There was a story there.

TWENTY-FOUR

CALGARY

1994

Alexa woke him up, rocking him with both hands.

"It's Tatiana," she said. "She hasn't come home."

Ritt looked at the clock. 2:22. He'd been asleep for an hour. Tatiana was staying with them for the summer, ostensibly looking for a job, but mostly hanging out with friends, smoking dope in the afternoon and giggling her way through daytime soaps.

"She's twenty-one."

"I know how old she is, Ritt. I have a bad feeling. We need to find her." Alexa was slurring slightly, syllables gently collapsing.

"Find her where?"

"At one of those clubs. On Seventeenth. They all go there."

"And tell her what? That it's past her bedtime? Maybe she's staying at a friend's. What's-her-name with the lizard tattoo and the expensive shoes. The nihilist."

"Suzanne. She would have said something."

"She might have met some guy."

"I want you to find her, Ritt. I want you to do that for me, honey."

Ritt yawned, and stretched, and got up heavily, pulling on jeans and a shirt. He wondered if he was over the legal limit. Most likely. They had been at a dinner party that had gone on a bit, laughing late-night arguments about whatever. He went out to the car and drove slowly, tempted to park on the next street and sleep. Alex had had too much to drink and she needed to address this immediately and irrationally. *Find my little girl.* Once Alex got something in her head, it didn't go away. He could argue all night or go look for Tatiana.

He drove past calm houses, the street empty. Cool air came in through the open window and revived him slightly. He turned onto Seventeenth and drove slowly. A group of boys walked in a kinetic pack that expanded and contracted as they shoved one another. *Oh yeah!* one of them shouted, his fist pumping.

The chances of finding Tatiana were remote. And if he did, what would he do? Tell her that her mother was worried? Tell her that her mother was drunk and filled with inchoate regret? His own relationship with Tatiana was somewhat strained. He had come so late to her life. She was an adult living as an adolescent, which didn't help them find common ground. If she lived on her own, if she had meaningful employment, if Ritt was able to meet her as a fellow adult. But she lay around the house, useless, stoned, resentful, filled with undergraduate opinions. *You're not my father,* she'd told him when he said she could maybe empty the dishwasher.

He saw a cluster of people on the sidewalk, smoking and chatting. A bouncer stood in front of a door, arms crossed, emphasizing his tattooed biceps. Ritt pulled over and got out of the car. He walked up to the door, past the trio sharing a joint, past the hectic partial anecdotes, the promise of sex swirling among these twenty-year-olds.

"I'm looking for my daughter," Ritt said to the bouncer.

"Still have to pay, sir."

Ritt nodded and went inside and gave twenty dollars to the slender goth behind the desk. She picked up a stamp and looked at him expectantly. A small chain dangled from her pierced lower lip. There was a cartoonish tattoo of a piranha on her shoulder, the oversized mouth gaping at him. She reached for his hand and held it and stamped it.

"Go crazy," she said.

It was dark and loud, the music an insistent pulse, a collective heartbeat that told people they were alive. The dance floor was crammed. Almost everyone seemed to be in their early twenties except a few thirty-something men who looked predatory. Ritt wondered what he looked like. A concerned parent most likely, though he was neither of those things.

Ritt could see over the heads of most of the people and scanned the room for Tatiana. A lot of young women looked like her—medium height, slim, short hair, lost.

He stayed for half an hour, watching, then left and drove farther down Seventeenth and tried another club without any success. He got into his car again and searched the quiet streets, moving slowly past a park that contained kids smoking dope in a huddle. He stopped to see if he could spot Tatiana.

"Take a picture, it lasts longer," one of the kids yelled. A beer can bounced off the sidewalk and hit the car.

Ritt was surprised by the 3:30 a.m. scene. People staggering home from somewhere, or marching purposefully to some kind of shift work. Delivery trucks backing into tight spots, the relentless beeping. Furtive cats. He saw a coyote near the river. As he drove, he began to feel more like a parent. He had missed all the steps—drunkenly assembling toys late on Christmas Eve using poorly translated instructions. Trips to the beach, splashing in the shallow water with a shrieking toddler. Fixing bicycles, applying bandages, driving lessons, perfunctory lectures on drugs and sex. But now a terrible highlight reel of all the bad things that can happen to a young woman played in his head. Drugged by some creep. Passed out at a party. Getting into the wrong car. The possibilities were endless and each one branched into a new permutation that was worse.

He slowed to examine a line of prostitutes. Their faces weren't garish with make-up but pale and unadorned. They'd already had two or three or five awful dates; moist overweight men who apologized afterward. They were tired and the drugs had lost their zip. The only face that was made up belonged to a man, defiant on his heels, his red dress shimmering slightly in the streetlights. Ritt realized that he must look like a middle-aged man cruising for sex. Why else drive slowly through the edges of downtown repeatedly?

The car in front of him stopped beside a woman who was about Tatiana's age. She walked up to the passenger window, hesitant, keeping her distance. Like the police, she didn't know what she'd see when that tinted window was rolled down.

On Tenth Avenue, a man was bent over a low stone fence, vomiting violently. Farther along three girls walked, their arms linked. The girl in the middle looked like Tatiana. He slowed further, then looked through the open passenger window as he pulled even, trying to get a look at her face. The one closest yelled, "We have mace, fucker!" None of them was her.

He drove past machine-cut sandstone facades, the rock formed during the late Cretaceous. The front ranges of the Rocky Mountains heaving their final eastward sigh, pushing sediments onto the younger beds, folding and thrusting, compressed into rock. Near the time of the great extinction. Though local dinosaurs were already heading for the exits, the climate cooling up here. Moving south to a better life, retiring in what would become Phoenix 100 million years later. Then the asteroid hits, the sun is obscured, and every dinosaur that can't fly bites the dust. But life crept back as it always does. Though a different crowd, most of the old gang gone.

By 5:30 Ritt was exhausted but he knew there was no point in trying to sleep now. He stopped at a twenty-four-hour restaurant and ordered a Western omelette. The light was glaring. A few customers appeared to be in that DMZ between drunk and hung over. The sun was coming up, the light bouncing off the mirrored gas tank of a motorcycle in the parking lot, a solar flare.

A young woman was sitting alone in the booth next to his, her red dress clashing with the orange Naugahyde. She looked about nineteen. The dress had a Western yoke with blue fringes. Her mascara was smeared and she was writing something in a notebook. Ritt guessed it was poetry. Hoping that something good would come of whatever heartbreak was filling every inch of her right now. Probably some guy who had read her poetry, had said it was *great*, had told her how much he loved her ironic Western look, how he had never met anyone like her.

Somewhere Tatiana was sleeping or not sleeping, regretting her actions perhaps, already burying them with all the minor stupidities we accumulate. Waking beside a man she will re-assess in the sickly light of day, realizing he isn't as interesting or handsome as she had thought. That maybe his only attribute was he was a good listener (and maybe he wasn't even really listening) and that she had paid for that relatively scarce skill with drunken sex. Then either a hasty exit, or bad coffee in a crummy apartment with a mannish empty fridge. Or a late breakfast at a greasy spoon, her indiscretion softened by the clamour around them.

It was a world that Ritt had never experienced. He wondered how much he had missed. He'd never had the chance to sleep with all the wrong women.

When he got home, Alexa had given up her drunken vigil and was asleep. He showered, put on his suit and walked to work. He spent most of the morning in a meeting, barely able to stay awake. Numbers and proven reserves and government tinkering with the royalty regime. Everyone weighing in, trying to say something memorable, though Ritt would remember only grey fatigue. At 11:30, his assistant told him Tate was on the line from Baku.

Tate had just gathered with a group of international oil executives in the Gulustan Palace to sign the "contract of the century," creating a consortium titled the Azerbaijan International Operating Company. The consortium had Russians, Americans, Brits and Japanese and, marginally, the Canadians of Mackenzie Oil, who had paired with an American firm. Tate had said it was like the fucking Malta Conference.

"How is life on the Russian front," Ritt asked.

"The Chinese are knocking on the door. You can barely hear them but they're here. The Russians and the Americans have a brand new hate-on. The Russians have already started skimming and the oil is not even out of the ground. A zoo."

Tate loved the international intrigue, though. He told Ritt it was like living in a novel you bought at the airport.

"Are we going to make any money out of all this?" Ritt asked.

"A trickle, but it'll still be trickling twenty years from now."

"We need to get something out of this. It can't just be an interesting hobby."

A million barrels of oil a day were coming out of the ground and the potential was far higher than that. A century ago Baku produced half the world's oil, and now it was back in the game.

"How are they going to move that oil?" Ritt asked. "That pipeline through Russia isn't worth shit, is it?"

"Americans don't want it to go through Russia. Russians say it has to. There's too much oil to ship through the Bosphorus. Turks would raise a shitstorm. Some kind of pipeline deal is going to happen. Right now it's like a poker game with forty-two players."

"How are our American friends?"

"Greedy. Worried."

"When are you getting back here?"

"Wrap up in a week or so. Might stop in London for a few days. R and R."

"All right. Stay out of trouble."

"I changed hotels. Maryanne has the details. Security was a bit lax in the last one. Some guy got knifed in his room. A Russian. I'm told he overreached. The whole Caspian is a cross between a war zone and a sitcom. Nazarbayev wants more money, apparently. Word is he's into eight figures at this point."

The President of Kazakhstan. Another thug who'd ended up in a chair when the music stopped.

"Are we on the hook for bribes?" Ritt asked. "Let's keep arm's length on this."

"Yeah. That's a lovely thought."

At 12:30 Ritt told his assistant he had a lunch meeting he'd forgotten to mention and he'd be gone for the afternoon. He walked down Eighth and went into the welcome coolness of the cinema.

One of his few guilty pleasures was sneaking out to see an afternoon movie on a weekday. Sitting in the plush seat in a theatre that held four hundred, and there would be eight of them, or twelve, or twenty-six, seated as far from one another as possible. Some of them guiltily missing work. A few just killing time. The life onscreen so much more vivid than their own.

Ritt liked movies where he didn't see the ending coming. Dark cop films with terse dialogue where you weren't sure who the killer was. And he didn't like going to these matinees with anyone else. It wasn't the same experience.

He sat back in his seat with the tub of popcorn and waited for the house lights to dim. It was the anticipation. The lights go down and we're back in the womb.

He was woken up four hours later by a teenager. "Sir. Sir, you were asleep."

"What time is it?"

"Five twenty, sir."

On the screen were the last of the credits, the barely acknowledged names zipping past. He'd fallen asleep before the movie ended, then slept through an entire second showing. The floor was covered in popcorn.

"Was the cop dirty?" Ritt asked. "Was he the killer?"

The teenager looked at him, acned, puzzled.

"In the movie. Did the cop do it?"

"He tried to save her in the end. The bartender's the bad guy. The one he always talks to."

Ritt nodded and got up stiffly. Outside he stood in the harsh light for a moment then started to walk home. The sun was still high and he slung his suit jacket over his shoulder. He was sweating by the time he got back. When he entered the front door he could hear Alexa and Tatiana arguing. He stood in the hallway, silently rooted, feeling like an intruder.

"Ritt was out *all night* looking for you. Do you understand? Do you?"

"Well, I didn't ask Ritt to go looking for me so he could drag me home like a fucking twelve-year-old."

"You *are a fucking twelve-year-old*. You *live* like a twelve-year-old. You don't work, you're out all night. You have no responsibilities."

"What would you know about work?"

"*I worked*. When I was your age, I worked. I worked hard."

"I've applied for jobs. I told you. It's not, like, the world really needs another minor in psychology."

"You have to do *something*, Tat."

"I'd *love* to do something. You don't think I want a job."

"I honestly don't know what you want. I really don't."

"I know what *you* want. Another drink. So help yourself, hon. The world's a better place after three glasses of wine."

"*Don't* . . . Don't you ever talk to me that way. At least I don't smoke dope all day long."

Ritt could hear Tatiana going up the stairs. He closed the front door loudly behind him and walked into the kitchen. Alexa was standing there with a glass of wine in her hand, her face rigid with anger.

"You know, I think you made the right choice," she said. "The whole no kids thing. That's definitely the way to go."

"I could try to talk to her."

Alexa didn't hear him. Her anger had taken over her head, a white noise that obliterated outside sounds. He figured she was replaying the argument, only this time she was sage and calm, offering wise maternal advice. Through the sliding door Ritt could see a book on the small patio table beside the lounge chair. The ashtray was full. This wasn't her first glass of wine.

"I could talk to her," he repeated.

"No. Don't do that. Things are bad enough as it is."

TWENTY-FIVE

BAKU, AZERBAIJAN

1995

nd now Tate was dead. Ritt listened to a bad connection from Azerbaijan, the voice small and indistinct, a slight accent. Ritt asking him to repeat what he'd said.

"Your man Tate, we regret to inform you, is now killed. He was found in the sea. A victim of the foul play."

"How do you know it was foul play?" Ritt asked.

"He was shot this once in the back of the head."

Ritt hung up, and sat for a moment, then called Tate's girlfriend and had a short tearful conversation. *How could this happen, Ritt, but how?* He didn't even know how long they'd been together. A year maybe. He thought about calling Alexa, but didn't know what he'd say. He'd have to go to Baku, at least to bring his body home. He had his assistant book the flight, not telling her yet about Tate. Then he phoned Sergei who told him there were a lot of murders in Baku, many of them unreported. There were too many sides to the oil war.

———

Ritt rented a car at the Baku airport, an ailing Russian sedan that smelled of cigarettes and old clothes. Tate had loved the action here, the danger; he'd once said the country was one large concealed weapon. With Mackenzie's fall from grace, there wasn't the same juice in the oil patch at home. That sense of risk and import, the jolt that money and power confer. Life at home was sterile and cautious. Baku had become a global focus, ground zero for the Caspian Derby and Tate had managed to get a seat at that table, albeit far from the centre of power.

Ritt drove straight to the police station and waited for an hour to speak to a distracted detective who was eating his lunch. The man had dark circles under his eyes and thin blond hair and a handful of prominent, worrisome-looking moles on his face. He wore a checkered sports jacket and a thick turtleneck sweater that was too warm for the season. He told Ritt that Tate's body had been found at Neft Daslari—Oil Rocks—fifty kilometres offshore. The Caspian Sea was shallow there and the Russians had built a town and three hundred kilometres of roads on land-fill in the 1950s, anchored to ships that had been sunk to provide a foundation. There were two thousand people living in that odd, stranded community. It had been the world's first offshore oil platform, then had grown into a curious village. Rigs still dotted the sea around it. There was a nine-storey hotel, a bakery, a hostel for oil workers, houses perched precariously.

"What would he be doing out there?"

The detective shrugged.

"Do you have any suspects?"

The detective made a sweeping motion with his arm. He was eating a sandwich and small pieces of something fell out of the bread onto his lap. "This city is filled with suspects."

The detective, whose name was Arkady, agreed to accompany Ritt to the morgue and then to Neft Daslari and show him where the body was found. Ritt suspected he was simply looking for something to occupy himself. Anything to take him out of his grim office for the afternoon. Arkady stared at the remnants of his sandwich and dropped them in a metal wastebasket.

The morgue was three blocks from the police station. They walked into the cold room and Arkady talked with an attendant who checked a clipboard and opened a wooden file cabinet in the wall to reveal an old woman. Her face had collapsed around a toothless mouth and her collarbones protruded. Wispy white hair clung to her fragile head like dead vines. It took four tries to find Tate—three more drained expressionless faces pulled out of the wall then pushed back in. When they finally found the right drawer Ritt wasn't sure it was him. His face was damaged by the exiting bullet. He was thin, very white, and so vulnerable looking. There was no trace of the man who had made those fearless, calamitous deals, but it was him.

Ritt nodded and what was left of Tate was filed in the wall. They walked to his car and he drove through the city following Arkady's abrupt instructions, past mirrored towers and ancient walls, finally turning onto the street that went to Oil Rocks. Ritt's car was the only one on the narrow road that snaked over the water. The sea and sky were slightly different shades of grey. Arkady smoked in silence.

Ritt remembered when he'd met Tate, how he'd convinced him to give up law and jump into the oil business. He wondered how many hundreds of hours they'd spent discussing strategy, takeovers, entrenchment, layoffs, dissecting personalities and deals. In the boom times, they had been referred to as the Gold

Dust Twins, a perfect complement to one another: Ritt's geological intuition and Tate's creative accounting. (During the bust they'd been referred to as Laurel and Hardy.) But that half of the company was gone now. Ritt was on his own.

He could see the derricks in the distance. When they got closer there were pumps nodding in the water. The place looked like a village a child would build out of popsicle sticks, giving up out of boredom before it was finished. Some of the houses were dilapidated and appeared to be uninhabited. A slum built on artificial islands connected by trestle bridges.

Tate had been seduced by the politics here. The Great Game of the nineteenth century being played out in this backwater. Chess pieces moved carefully, a finger lingering on the piece for a moment before finally committing. High-level Russian and American officials came out here and gave diplomatic speeches while their hatchet men roamed the hallways making death threats. Tate had had a drink with the secretary of state, he'd said. He'd had a lot of drinks with a lot of people.

Arkady told him to pull over. They got out and walked.

"Why would he come here?" Ritt asked.

Arkady shrugged. "Maybe a woman. A poker game."

Neither of these was plausible. "Could he have been killed on shore and driven out here?"

"Everything is possible at this point in our investigation."

It wouldn't cost much to buy a local policeman, Ritt thought. Perhaps all of them. Compared to the billions that were at stake. You buy people *before* you need them, Sergei had told him, not *when* you need them. They're cheaper, for one thing. He knew that Arkady wasn't here to help Ritt, he was here to quietly steer him home with the least amount of complication. Maybe Arkady

had killed Tate himself. Why not hire the police to kill people?
They have guns. They need the money. They won't get caught.

He followed the cop along the deserted road and Arkady
finally pointed down to the rusty deck of a half-submerged
ship. "He was here."

"Who found him?"

"Girl from bakery. Comes to work early in morning, maybe
four. Sees him lying there. Oh god, she says. Calls police."

Arkady looked for his cigarettes, patting pockets. He had
smoked three since leaving Baku and had returned the package to the same breast pocket each time. Yet every new cigarette prompted a fresh person-wide search. A testament to his
detective skills. Arkady found the package and lit a cigarette
and looked at the sky and almost looked at his watch.

Ritt stared at the submerged ship. He wasn't sure how to
mourn Tate. They had been partners, had argued and suffered
together, though they'd rarely seen one another socially. Ritt
had once thought it was his fault, that he had failed to seize the
friendship somehow. And there was some truth to this. But
Tate was one of those relentlessly public men who have no
close friends and a complicated private life. There were a lot of
women. What else was there? Tate would have been taking
chances financially. That was his nature. Maybe he'd owed
money? Or he had slept with the wrong woman.

Ritt awkwardly climbed down to the spot where Tate had
been found.

"So he's lying here. Right about here?"

Arkady remained up on the road, peering over the railing.
"Yes."

"Face down."

"Yes."

"You bring someone out here, execute him, someone sees you, you only have one avenue of escape. There's one road to shore. It doesn't seem like an ideal plan. A witness makes a call, you intercept him."

"This isn't a city of witnesses."

"Right. It's a city of suspects. You want someone dead, you kill him, throw him in the ocean. You could stop anywhere on that road and throw him over the railing. But you leave him here, on an oil platform? You want to send a message."

"Our job is find out what that message is."

"I thought your job was to catch the killer."

Arkady flicked his cigarette into the sea and patted his jacket to find the package again, then took out another one.

There were several houses nearby, close enough that someone could have seen the body being dumped. Gulls swooped in intersecting circles. There was oil on the rock. Some of it probably leaked naturally out of the formation. But some of these pumps were fifty years old, in need of replacement, and oil was being lost. The wind arrived in broad gusts. Ritt walked carefully over the slick surface and climbed back up. He walked to the car and started it. Arkady got in and they turned around and headed to Baku.

"I don't envy you your job, Arkady," Ritt said. "Dangerous town. You never know what you're going to run into."

"It's a job."

"How often do you fire that gun?"

"To shoot?"

"You've probably had to shoot a few men. Bad men. Men who had it coming."

"Sometimes this is necessary."

"When was the last time it was necessary?"

Arkady tossed another cigarette out the window into the sea. "Some months ago," he said with a shrug. Shrugging was the Eastern European disease. Often it was the only response. It was their chief form of exercise and it communicated the notion that empiricism was dead, that whatever you think you see is not how the world works.

"I'm told that the difference in a gun battle isn't who is the better shot," Ritt said. "It's who can shoot another man. Apparently it isn't as easy as you'd think. It must be a comfort knowing you can take a man's life. A sense of security, knowing you'll pull the trigger when the time comes."

Arkady stared out the window. "We take comfort where we find it."

The clouds were low. A strong wind buffeted the car. Ritt motioned to the east. "You go fifty kilometres that way, there's the Azeri-Chirag-Gunashli field. In the Aspheron trend. Six billion barrels of oil. That's your future. The reason for every crime in your city, it pays for every drink, every hooker. That's your paycheque, Arkady."

Ritt recalled giving Tate a geology tutorial on the area. No one was really clear on the origins of the proto-Caspian Basin. Probably some ongoing geologic nightmare that started in the Jurassic. An early alpine collision results in an underlay of oceanic crust. Something rises, something gets buried. Geology is like politics. A revolution then things are quiet for a while. The late Miocene, not a peep. Along comes the Messinian salinity crisis and the Caspian Sea gets cut off from the other oceans, orphaned. You get pressure, violence, forces pushing against one another, grinding, until one finally throws in the towel. It's not worth it, the struggle. All that effort, for what? To be the top layer? For how long. Another event comes along, something that just keeps pushing and it finally buries you. That's geology. It never stops. It takes a break for ten millennia and people think: well, it's finally over. But it isn't. It's never over.

The bar was sedate, Old World, chandeliers and heavy furniture and velvet. A sense of whispered violence and intrigue.

"The short answer is, I don't know who killed your friend." This was Bentley, a freelance fixer who had recently been cut loose by Shell, one of their point men in Baku. Ritt had gotten his name through Sergei, who'd made some calls on his behalf. Bentley might know something, he said. The landscape at least.

"How compromised is the police force?"

"I doubt they're killing people, if that's what you're thinking. But they aren't going to catch the killer unless they're told to. Once in a while they get handed someone to hold up as a trophy. Someone expendable. But they're paid for. Most of them anyway."

Ritt wondered why someone would kill Tate. Mackenzie was such a marginal player. "He was found out in Oil Rocks. On the deck of one of those sunken ships. It looked like someone was sending a message."

Bentley sipped his drink and glanced around the room. He was a hard-looking man, a rugby player in an expensive suit. His hair was close cropped and one ear was slightly damaged. His powers of persuasion clearly went past the financial.

"This used to be a simple business," he said. "Ten years ago, you wanted exploration rights in Kazakhstan or Azerbaijan or any of these whack job fiefdoms, you gave two million bucks to the energy minister's bag man, he'd spread it around. Most of it filtered up, a little filtered down. A lot ended up in Switzerland. Everyone's happy. Two million, five million, ten. It seemed like a lot of money. They thought they'd made the deal of the century. It slowly dawned on them that people were taking billions out of their country. That maybe they should up their price. Then you get the Russians asking for a hundred million up front. That kind of shifted the landscape. Now you've got all kinds of middlemen demanding a piece of the action. Ten cents a barrel, fifty cents. Whatever. So you've got these streams, tiny streams of international cash that flow into foreign banks. Something between extortion, business and diplomacy." Bentley shrugged. "The lines between governments and oil don't exist anymore. When Bush got elected, they could stop pretending. The world's one big drunken cartel."

"So the message . . ."

"Who the fuck knows? You need an interpreter these days. Don't assume it was rational, though. Tate was meant to be found. He's at Oil Rocks. It might be because of something he brought with him. Something that happened six years ago in Texas or Alberta or Nigeria. Someone with a grudge."

"Why kill him here?"

"Because in Baku there are no consequences."

Ritt remembered staying at the Intourist Hotel here with Tate, the circus before Aliyev brought a vague sense of order. Corruption can't be killed. To get rid of it, it needs somewhere to go. Like getting a bird out of your house: you leave an open window and it flies out because it's better out there. It was only a few years ago the two of them had first tried to get a piece of this action. It had been like an Orson Welles movie that went on for eight days. God knows why Tate was really coming back.

"You think maybe Tate was dirty?" Ritt asked.

"Everyone's dirty."

"How much grey money comes out of Baku."

"Practically the gold standard. Maybe Nigeria's king. But twenty, twenty-five percent."

"Difficult for a soft player to push his case, I would think," Ritt said. "Tate said a guy was knifed in his hotel."

"Yeah, that was Kredenko, Russian, working for the Azeris in some capacity. Probably trying to muscle in on someone's action. Bit of a loose cannon. Liked to beat up prostitutes. Just generally a messy guy to have around."

"What's the next step with this play?"

"Probably build a new pipeline. Maybe let the Georgians develop liquified natural gas options for them to hedge against Turkish pipeline deals. But there are about five different directions on this thing, and each direction has fifteen players. Fucking horror show."

"You know a guy named Trotsky? Big, bit soft, worked the angles before Aliyev took power."

"Trotsky." Bentley looked up. "I don't know. Maybe to see him."

"Russian accent. Hint of British something."

"This is, what, three years ago?"

"Yeah."

"Could be a casualty by now. Who knows? This isn't a world with a fully funded pension plan."

"Can you look around? See what you can find?"

Bentley tilted his head, an indication that it was a question of money.

"What would twenty thousand get me."

"A good start."

Ritt walked along the crescent, staring out to the water. He passed two legless beggars on wheeled boards. They had their eyes closed, hands out, reciting something in unison. Their faces were deeply lined and their teeth the colour of tea. The skeletal shapes of derricks receded out to sea.

Tate had taken almost as big a hit as Ritt when Mackenzie swooned. He may have leveraged his personal life as far as he'd leveraged the company and he was under water. He had a house in Phoenix, another one in Hawaii. How far had he pushed things? What had he gotten into? Tate had once told him that corruption was protection. It was what kept the business competitive, it weeded out the weak.

The sun was high and it was warm. Ritt walked along the shore. A city with jutting towers and four-foot stone walls to repel Cossacks. Now it welcomed every invader. It sold its ass but kept its secrets.

In the morning he spoke to Len Wyman at Hees, the American company Mackenzie had paired with for the Contract of the Century. They had breakfast in the dining room of Ritt's hotel. Wyman was a lanky Oklahoman, a man who was itching to get back home to the simplicities of a hobby ranch and a restored Camero.

"He was a good man," Wyman said.

Ritt didn't want to debate this point. "You know of any enemies he might have had? Personal or business?"

"Don't know much about his personal life. He liked the nightlife though. Never cared for it myself. Too old anyway. But Jackson got around. Liked to see how everything worked."

"How about business?"

"Everyone's your enemy over here. Until you end up working with them. Even then. But it's a mystery to me, Ritt. Maybe he got into something on the side. We've only got a very small piece of this thing."

"Maybe you're the most vulnerable. Someone wanted to cut the weakest out of the herd."

"Why? What would be the point?"

"Yankee go home."

"Yeah, well, that's the deal just about everywhere." Wyman took his napkin off his lap and folded it carefully and laid it on the table and patted it. "They hate us but they need us."

"One day they're not going to need us."

"It'll just be the hate. The only fuel more reliable than oil."

Ritt called Alexa from the room. She was filled with her own concerns. Tatiana had moved out, she said, moved in with her father and his idiot girlfriend, Little Miss Fitness.

"What is she? Thirty-two? His girlfriend is going to want

a family about five minutes from now and then Richard is going to, what? Be a father at fifty-six? He wasn't up to it at thirty-six."

"Well, maybe it'll be good for you and Tat to have a break. Maybe it'll make things easier."

"The issue isn't easier, Ritt. It's what's best for Tat. Richard's going to give her the full-on princess treatment. Which is the *opposite* of what she needs. He's going to let her do whatever she wants—'it's fine if you smoke dope in the living room, honey, I'm cool with that'—he'll try and get Tat to bond with that cunt. 'Why don't you two go to the show—I've got two tickets but I have to work tonight.' When Tat tells him what a nightmare it was living with me, he'll say, 'you know, honey, you have to try to understand your mother, she's having kind of a tough time.' He's going to go into full lawyer mode, steer her toward the idea that I am pitiable. He was a shitty husband, an absent father, but he's a pretty good lawyer."

Ritt could hear the faint chime of ice. She would be drinking vodka. He mentally did the time difference—it was eleven a.m. over there.

"I saw Tate yesterday. In the morgue. Pretty grim."

"What is it you think you can do over there, Ritt. Solve the case?"

"I'm here to arrange for the body, all that. Do something. I've got a flight out tomorrow."

There was a silence at the other end. He wasn't sure if he'd lost the connection.

"Alexa?"

"I heard you. Tomorrow. Okay then."

He dropped by to see Arkady in the morning. He was sitting at the same desk, wearing the same clothes, eating a sandwich, a cigarette going in the ashtray. An instant replay of his last visit.

"Busy day," Ritt said.

Arkady held up the sandwich as evidence he was on his lunch break and something fell out of it onto the floor.

"Any news on Jackson Tate? You manage to beat a confession out of anyone yet?"

"Not so much beatings anymore."

"The good old days."

Arkady shrugged, and put his sandwich down and started the search for his cigarettes.

"You looking for those cigarettes, I can save you some time." Ritt patted his own breast pocket.

He called Alexa, again, from the airport.

"Who is this? Tat?" She was drunk. Her voice was thick and angry.

"It's me."

"Ritt?"

"I'm in the airport at Baku. There's some problem with the plane. Needs a part. Or a pilot. Something. I'll be late getting in."

"Getting in."

"Yeah. Everything okay?"

"Oh. Well, it's just . . . peachy. Yeah."

His phone rang and he assumed it was Alex calling back and he answered wearily. But it was Bentley.

"You have any dealings with Alhambra Oil?" he asked.

"Nothing that panned out. Why?"

"They showed up on the radar. I'll keep you posted."

A month after Ritt got back, Bentley called his office.

"So listen, there's a trail. Even by local standards, it's a fucking rat's nest. It looks like Alhambra had a deal with a Japanese company, Kiken Oil, and they rolled Tate's disappearance into the deal . . ."

"His death was part of an exploration deal?"

"Yeah, it seems so, but then Kiken has a deal with *Rosneft,* and they roll Tate into *that* deal, so now Alhambra is two companies removed."

"So the Russians . . ."

"This stuff is all back channels. I don't know where it originated in Alhambra . . ."

"I've got a pretty good idea."

"Ritt, there is no hard evidence. This isn't something you can prosecute. This is strictly peace of mind, you understand."

Ritt wondered how much peace of mind there could be in a phone call from a career fixer who had no way or no intention of providing any proof.

"So this was just business. For the Russians, the Japanese."

"Looks like."

"What is this 'peace of mind' going to cost?"

"My fee is sixty K and my expenses, mostly greasing palms, are sixty."

"One twenty for this peace of mind."

Bentley's story sounded plausible. Though he could have interviewed two guys from the Calgary oil patch and found out about the bad blood between Manchauser and himself, then fabricated a story around it.

"Was Arkady involved?"

"That sad sack fucking mope detective? No, not that I can see. Looks like former KGB. They're everywhere, offering their services. No job too big or too small."

"You want cash, I'm guessing."

"That's the protocol."

"I'll get it, but I'll need something more from you, some kind of documentation."

"That's not how this world works."

"This world doesn't work. It's not an unreasonable request. Let me know when you've got something."

Ritt hung up and pondered this narrative. Manchauser signing the paper. Shaking hands. A nudge, a wink, a bullet.

TWENTY-SIX

CALGARY

2003

T he blast knocked windows out of the building across the street. Dust billowed out of the underground parking lot and moved east on the wind, a dark, gritty cloud that swelled then drifted. It was 9:23 a.m. A sunny day, warm for October. The detonation in the underground parking lot converted the explosives to hot gases, creating a blast wave of super-compressed air that was propelled at supersonic speed, shearing limbs off two executives who were walking from their cars to the elevators. The wave had the impact of a solid object. It lasted less than a tenth of a second, but destroyed everything on P1, every Porsche, every briefcase filled with documents that needed signing. It simultaneously melted and shattered the booth where the twenty-one year-old attendant sat reading *Atlas Shrugged*.

The blast ruptured the lungs of a man talking on his cellphone. A woman was blinded. The almost instantaneous propulsion left a vacuum that sucked debris into it, maiming several people.

Two blocks away Ritt felt the blast wave, deadened to a violent gust. It was as if it had taken all sound with it, creating a moment suspended. Ritt ran toward the cloud, past a man who was examining the coffee that covered his suit, still holding the cup. A bicycle courier balanced on his $1,500 bike, upright, subtle movements to keep from falling over, both feet still locked onto the pedals. He had an orange dayglo helmet that had blue dinosaur spikes. Then he pedalled toward the sound.

Ritt saw black smoke billowing out of the underground parking lot. Sirens filled the air. A woman stood in bare feet, blood trickling down her leg. She was coughing. It was Mary Armitage, from Badger Resources. Ritt rushed up to her. Her face had a fine grit over it and he couldn't tell if it was masking a wound or not. He sat her down on a concrete planter. Phones, shoes, purses, tattered rags, pieces that might have been flesh littered the street. Trash fluttered awkwardly. Above that, blue sky.

"Jesus, Mary."

Her eyes were vacant. Ritt knelt down and examined her leg. A four-inch piece of glass protruded from her calf. Ritt took it out. It was hot enough that it burned his fingers. He dropped the glass and shook his fingers and instinctively put them in his mouth. Mary shivered and a harsh sob came out. She sucked in some air. The leg wound was bleeding freely and he couldn't think what to wrap it with.

"Mary, are you hit anywhere else?" He didn't know if she could hear him.

She stared at him, eyes wide.

Ritt took off his tie and wrapped it around her leg. Should he carry her to the hospital?

Two fire trucks pulled up, followed by ambulances. Six police cruisers shuddered to a stop at the intersection, and two constables rolled out yellow tape, motioning for people to get back, yelling, "*Step away!*" People had started to scream, raw hysterical cries. Red lights blinked. Cars stopped, and drivers got out and horns blared in the distance. A man sat against a building, one shoe off, his face a deep red, a Chinese red. Not blood, maybe just the heat from the blast. Paper swirled and people rushed and barked commands. Ritt felt suddenly tired, as if the blast had punched the energy out of him. He sat down beside Mary on the planter, put his arm around her and pulled her closer. "We're all right," he said.

He couldn't get her to the hospital. His car was at home and there wasn't any chance of getting a taxi. They'd just have to wait for a paramedic. He took his jacket off and draped it around her shoulders. He looked to see if there was anywhere to get water. A café down the street was open, people standing in front. "Wait here, Mary, I'm going to get some water."

He went in and grabbed three bottles from the refrigerator and left a twenty-dollar bill on the counter and ran back to Mary. He loosened his tie. And trickled some water on her cut, rewrapped it, then wet the cuff of his suit jacket and used it to gently wipe her face. He opened another bottle and put it to her lips. She drank a bit and heaved, a few racking sobs that subsided.

You planned for things, Ritt thought, but then you're on the way to the bank and a bomb shatters everything. Like a meteor landing. Out of the blue.

Ritt got his cellphone out of his jacket pocket, called Alexa and got the machine. "It's me. There's been an explosion downtown. In case you see it on the news. I'm okay. Jesus. What a mess."

A block away, a woman stepped erratically then collapsed and another woman rushed to help her. "My god, Ritt," Mary said. "All those people."

The bomb had been in the trunk of Pete Manchauser's Mercedes. He had driven in to work, and before he had parked in his spot, the first reserved spot in the lot, the one closest to the entrance, the bomb had been detonated. There was very little left of Manchauser. One of his John Lobb shoes was found forty metres away.

The dinner hour news played footage from the blast that looked like a war documentary, like something from the other side of the world. An official police statement announced that they were pursuing leads; a message from the mayor condemned this cowardly act. Various experts appeared on the screen. A military bomb expert noted that there were several components to the blast, that it killed first with its sheer sonic power. Then there was the shrapnel and the debris from destroyed objects. There was the heat and noxious chemicals—the gasoline and oil and plastics that had evaporated. In all there were seven dead and twenty-three wounded. Mary had needed fourteen stitches to close her wound.

Two days after the blast, a poster was sent to the newspaper, the one with the photo of Adam Barkley and the words, "Adam Barkley Died for Your Sins" on it. The poster hadn't been seen for almost a decade.

Ritt sat at home watching the news, drinking a whisky. Alexa was on the couch, with a glass of wine. The police said that they were seeking Emma Barkley for questioning, though the spokesman wouldn't confirm if she was a suspect in the case. A professor named Eggerton who was an expert on terrorism groups opined that since ABDYS had been dormant for so long, this may not have been their work. She noted that the original ABDYS targets had been property, never people.

"But then, we have to remember, we had what we assumed was the accidental death of that man on the oil rig," Eggerton said. "This is likely what caused the group to become dormant. It may have caused a schism. Not unusual in any nascent terrorist cell. You have a fatality and some of the people in the organization are going to say, 'I didn't sign on to kill a father of three.' You have the idealists who are okay with destroying oil property but not with taking a human life. But you also have a core that has become radicalized. We see this in the Muslim world, we've seen it in Afghanistan, in Pakistan, in Lebanon. So you lose some idealists and gain some fanatics. And this is a dangerous moment for an organization."

"Where does it go from here, Professor Eggerton?" the newscaster asked.

"Either the organization is torn apart by something like this—the ringleaders captured, the core weakened, the cell dies. Or it draws people to it. It gains strength, or at least numbers."

"Brilliant time to be in oil," Alexa said. She got up, wandered into the kitchen and took the white wine out of the fridge. She poured herself a generous glass.

I like a drink. That's what Alexa used to say about herself.

Two weeks ago Ritt had found bottles hidden in the shed, nine empty wine bottles and two bottles of Snow Queen vodka, one of them full. She was hiding her consumption now.

"Let's watch something else," she said, coming back to the couch. "They're deconstructing this thing to death. Not much point until they catch someone. Then it'll be news. Now it's just a tragedy and we're watching and that makes us part of it. That's what they want."

Ritt wondered how it could have been anything to do with Adam Barkley at this point. If Bentley's analysis of Tate's death had been right, then who knew what Byzantine trail led to Manchauser's murder? Like Tate, it was meant to make a point, and like Tate's death, the point wasn't entirely clear.

After Ritt had gotten Bentley's report, which tied Alhambra to Tate's death, he'd thought about what to do. There wasn't enough evidence to go to court—there wasn't *any* evidence. Not enough to charge Manchauser. And he had lingering doubts over Bentley's information. But it had sat inside him for months, festering. He'd finally confronted Manchauser, following him outside the Petroleum Club, asking him about the deal with Kiken, about the unwritten rider: *Murder Jackson Tate*. When Manchauser stared back blankly, Ritt had backhanded him across the face. Manchauser was stunned, a suddenly vulnerable seventy-two-year-old man. Ritt threw him down hard onto the asphalt and told him this would come back to him; he wasn't going to get away with murder.

Though he did, for a while at least. Then he'd been blown to smithereens. By whom? Some snaking trail that led to an oil company he'd wronged (a longish list), the burden of murder passed along to other companies through hostile takeovers, buyouts, unpaid debts. Or was it simply the twisted grief of a mother, ultimately expressed? The narratives that oil unleashed on the world. A history of blood and heroic exploration and energy and exploitation and corruption and death. Hidden behind years of violence, hidden beneath unseen geologic struggles. He was glad Manchauser was dead. Something he could never say out loud.

Alexa flipped through the channels, finally stopping on a British historian who was talking about the mysteries of Stonehenge.

The police came to Ritt's office, detectives Barnus and Dunkley, insisting it was strictly a routine visit. Ritt motioned for them to sit.

Barnus was tall and folded into the chair like a water bird, his notebook out. Dunkley looked like a bouncer, with a rounded, small-featured face and pugnacious shoulders that rolled when he walked.

"We understand you were at the scene," Barnus said.

"Three blocks away. I ran toward it. Saw a colleague, Mary Armitage. She'd been hit by some glass."

"It was your company that was working that hole when the derrickman was killed."

"Yes."

"And you knew Peter Manchauser?" It was clear that Barnus was going to ask all the questions. Maybe Dunkley was used for intimidation.

"I did. You figure out how that bomb came to be in his trunk yet?"

"How would you characterize your relationship with Mr. Manchauser?"

"Unpleasant."

"You were at that New Year's Eve party when his garage blew up. When was that? Twenty-odd years ago?" When Jackson Tate drunkenly set fire to it. "It didn't blow up," Ritt corrected him. "It caught fire and there were subsequent explosions from his cars. But yes, I was there. Along with five hundred other unhappy people."

"Did Manchauser have any enemies in the oil patch?"

"Pete only had enemies. But if this was personal, why not blow him up at his home? You think ABDYS—if it was ABDYS—targeted him personally? Or are they going after the whole industry."

"At this point, we don't have anything that can be made public." Barnus shifted in his seat. "So you would describe yourself as one of his enemies."

"If one hundred people show up at that funeral, ninety-eight of them will want to dance on his grave. You might want to stake out that cemetery. It'll be a hoedown."

Barnus flipped some pages of his notebook up and examined his notes.

Ritt thought about seeing Emma Barkley at the funeral for his derrickman. Composed and sorrowful. She was a wilful woman. You'd have to be to pursue the government and Manchauser's company the way she did. He couldn't remember what had become of all that. Had Alhambra settled? If they had, there would be a non-disclosure agreement.

"Have you talked to Emma Barkley?" Ritt asked. "Is she a 'person of interest'?"

"There are a lot of people we'd like to talk to."

"I can't imagine she'd condone something like this."

"Your son dies, it changes you."

"But to target civilians? That's a leap. And why now, so long after her son's death?"

"Manchauser tried to initiate a merger with you, didn't he?"

Ritt wondered where they'd got this information.

"Back during the collapse. Didn't he approach you?"

"He did. I turned him down."

"Why is that?"

"We were both drowning at the time; a merger wouldn't have solved any of our problems and it would have introduced a truckload of new ones."

Barnus made a show of folding up his notebook. Like anything Ritt said now would be in confidence.

"You kidnapped his nephew," he said, bringing his grey eyes to bear on Ritt's.

"A lifetime ago I invited him to watch soap operas in a motel for four days and he took me up on it."

"Did you ever assault Mr. Manchauser?"

"Not the way I would have liked to. I slapped him once."

"Slapped."

"Back of my hand." Ritt offered it up for perusal.

"And why did you assault him?"

"Because he insulted me." No need to complicate things. Or implicate himself.

"When was this?"

"Years back. Seven, eight."

"Do you remember what the insult was?"

"Something about sucking at the government tit. Alcohol was involved. A stupid moment between two old men."

"There are people who say you were Manchauser's biggest enemy, Mr. Devlin."

"It may have been true at some point. But I didn't work the same side of the street. I wanted to open up the North. Pete never bought into it." Though he'd tried to. "He was old school. Had the imagination of a cocker spaniel. Stay at home and suck the plains until they're dry."

"How are things in the North?"

"Expensive." Finished.

"Do you have any trips coming up, Mr. Devlin?"

"Am I a suspect?"

"We haven't ruled anyone out. Even his mother didn't have anything good to say about him." Barnus put his notebook in his pocket and stood up.

"Maybe she did it. She might crack under interrogation."

"I spent an hour with her and I would seriously doubt that."

TWENTY-SEVEN

CALGARY

2004

It was late morning on an April day that held the promise of spring. The sun was strong though there were still pockets of snow in the shade. Emma Barkley's body was discovered in the small graveyard on her property that contained her parents and grandparents. A neighbour saw her truck and found her. She was sprawled on her son's grave, a twelve-gauge Benelli shotgun beside her. There was a calamitous wound to her head. The coroner estimated that she'd been there for a few days. It was ruled a suicide. There was a note in the pocket of her barn jacket and one of the newspapers got hold of it and published it on the front page with a picture of her and her son Adam.

There were days when I thought I could bear it. I couldn't. You can only lose so much.

I wish I could hope. I can't. I wish I could have forgiven. I couldn't.

In her house was a journal that contained details of Adam's sickness, and that, too, found its way into print. But the journal ended with her son's death.

The police hadn't found the person who put the bomb in Manchauser's car. Now that Emma was dead, that note was scrutinized for evidence of guilt, especially those last lines: *I wish I could have forgiven. I couldn't.*

Had she killed Manchauser? Was she behind ABDYS? There was no hard evidence. And in that lacuna a mythology grew. It wasn't clear where she'd been in the months after the bombing. Neighbours hadn't seen her, though the nearest one was six acres away. The police feared that the martyrdom quotient had been ratcheted up and there would be more violence. They lobbied City Hall for more funds and increased overtime and set up surveillance of anyone remotely of interest. They flew in terrorism experts from Israel and London who advised them on security measures and psychology and preparedness.

Most of the larger oil companies hired their own security, bringing in people from abroad. They prepared for war. But a month went by and all that happened was an outpouring of conflicted grief for Emma Barkley, in the papers and online. There were more poster efforts—the original poster of Adam Barkley copied and pasted up on hoardings and walls and light standards. But when three people were caught pasting them up, interrogation revealed they were just university students with an activist bent. They'd downloaded the poster and copied it and had no connection to anything.

A long investigative piece in the paper revealed little about Emma Barkley that wasn't already known. There was great speculation—that with her rural background she was familiar with fertilizer and ammonium nitrate and she could have fashioned a bomb. That it wasn't a suicide: she'd been killed by the real bomber who made it look like suicide. A second month went by and there was no word from ABDYS and city cops were divided over whether this was because Emma was in fact the organization or if this was strategic or whatever.

Ritt called Mary to see how she was bearing up and she assured him she had recovered fully. By August, city councillors quietly voted to end the emergency funds to the police and everyone settled into the nice weather.

They owed more than a dozen people a dinner party, a fact that Alexa brought up regularly. Ritt was the one who chose the menu, bought the ingredients, did the cooking. All of which he enjoyed, but it seemed lately that it was too much of a production. When he finally relented, it was only to appease her. They decided to invite ten people over, a bit ambitious, larger than he liked, but it would kill a few birds. It was late August and there was still the looseness of summer. Ritt had bought seafood and made a ceviche to start, which he would follow with steak Florentine. On his way home from work he picked up the steak and then lingered in the wine store, choosing two cases of pricey wine with the help of a chatty, allegedly knowledgeable employee.

When he hauled in the groceries, Alexa was in the kitchen, on the phone, gesturing with the glass of white wine in her free hand as she talked. "I appreciate that she asked me to lunch, I really do, Richard, but you know, here's an idea— why doesn't she fuck right off."

Alexa turned in tight circles, as if she was avoiding a mouse on the floor. "Why do I not believe that, Richard? Tell me." She was close to tears.

It was almost seven. People were coming at eight. The house needed straightening.

"Well, you'll want to check the DNA on that one, honey," she said. "Listen, must run. Having guests. Always a . . ."

Alexa stared at the phone. She hissed "fucker" and pressed the end button and looked up at Ritt.

"How is Richard?"

"Richard is an evil bastard and he deserves to have the baby from hell."

"She's pregnant? Little Miss Fitness?"

"Three months. Tat neglected to tell me."

Tatiana was also pregnant. She was thirty-one now, and had more or less settled down with a thin, monosyllabic guy who had an elaborately careless haircut, worked at a framing shop and played bass in a rockabilly band.

A *bass player,* Alexa had said. *Jesus.*

After an extended run at adolescence, Tatiana was suddenly, and perhaps accidentally, embracing life at its most elemental level. Like almost everyone, she was unprepared.

"She's going to bond with that cunt," Alexa said tersely. An ongoing fear. "They're going to go to pre-natal classes together." Alexa stared out at the backyard, her face drawn, then burst into violent heaving sobs. She composed herself quickly. "They'll be on the phone every day. They'll compare weight gain, shop for clothes, those little hats—*oh my god the bunny ears!*—send each other links to parenting advice, playing Mozart to the fetus, all that horseshit.

Richard fucking planned this, I swear." Alexa searched for a tissue and found one and blew her nose and wiped her eyes on her sleeve.

"Serve Richard right to be a father at his age. And a grandfather."

"It won't serve him *anything*," Alexa wailed. "*She'll* be the one getting up at night to deal with the baby. She'll be changing the diapers and sitting in the clinic with a screaming infant hoping the fever isn't serious. He'll pay for college if he hasn't died of natural causes, maybe get out to a gymnastics tournament if it's not too early in the morning."

"Maybe you should have lunch with her. Miss Fitness. What's her name, again?" Ritt wasn't sure he'd ever actually known her name.

"Velvett. Two Ts."

How could he have forgotten that? "She named herself, or something."

"Her therapist told her she had to take ownership of her life. Though picking a stripper name maybe defeats the purpose a little."

Ritt held his wife and rubbed small, ineffectual circles on her back. Alexa sniffled more, leaning her head on his shoulder. Her daughter was slipping further out of her orbit, her role as grandmother, a development already greeted with joy and horror, somehow usurped by this development.

"I know this hurts, Alex. But you don't know how it's going to play out."

She pulled away and turned from him, opening the fridge. She grabbed the white wine and poured more into her glass and took a gulp.

"We've got ten people coming over in less than an hour," Ritt said, looking at her smeared, vulnerable face. "Maybe we should straighten things up a bit. I'll get dinner organized."

Alexa put the glass down on the counter. "Okay," she said, taking a deep yoga breath, her hands pushing down through the air. "Dinner. Calm." She looked around at the dishevelled kitchen. "I have to change," she said and went upstairs.

Ritt laid out the thick steaks on a large rectangular plate. A prehistoric pile. He poured the olive oil he'd gotten at the specialty shop where they had tastings on Wednesdays, an in-house expert telling the assembled that there is cold-pressed and then there is *cold-pressed*. He massaged the oil into the meat and ground coarse pepper and salt and covered it and let it sit on the counter. He chopped vegetables and made a vinaigrette and dipped his finger in to taste it and washed the spinach and looked at the clock on the stove. He opened four bottles of Saint-Emilion Chateau Angelus and set them on the table. He put on Sinatra's *Songs for Swingin' Lovers!* and did a dance step on his way back to the kitchen, attempting to shift his mood through action, then poured a large whisky. The clock read 8:02. The patio door was open and the air was cool. He could hear his wife's footsteps in the upstairs hallway, and then they stopped and turned around and stomped back to their bedroom; to change again no doubt. Five minutes later she came down in a low-cut, fitted black blouse and tight skirt. She took the open Sancerre out of the fridge and poured herself another glass and lit a cigarette and opened the screen door and stood out on the deck. Her face was expertly made-up, though it still held a puffy vulnerability.

"The best time of the year," she said, maybe to him, maybe to herself, breathing in deeply, inhaling the last of the season. "That mood just before fall, decay and renewal at the same time."

The doorbell rang and Ritt opened the door and greeted Dickie Steiner and his wife, whose name suddenly evaporated. They stood there expectantly, those two beaming faces. Dickie thrust a bottle at Ritt. He was wearing a checked shirt and dress pants. His wife had very skinny expensive jeans that advertised what Ritt dimly recalled was an eating disorder.

By nine everyone was there, the last two couples arriving apologetically—*traffic, god this town*. Ritt got everyone a drink and steered them toward the ceviche and managed to escape, moving to the backyard, standing over his massive, absurdly expensive outdoor grill, the Flintstonian plate of meat covered with a tea towel. Behind him, bellowing laughter came through the screen door. He knew someone would saunter out and spoil this perfect solitude. He did a mental calculation of best case/worst case scenarios.

After five minutes it was the worst case who showed up: Al Bancroft. He'd been Total's man in the Sudan then come back to work in some grey VP capacity; he tailored his relentless accounts of overseas experience to fit his mood. Sometimes it was glorious and worldly and the French really knew how to live, and sometimes it was a violent African shit show punctuated by deadly dinner parties in Paris where he didn't have a fucking clue what anyone was saying despite the private tutor's best efforts and he suspected they dismissed him as a Western clod.

In his sixties, Al was spreading over the waistband of his khakis, a softness that matched the wounded collapse of his face. His hair was colourless and thin. Ritt took a sip of his whisky and glanced at the uncharacteristic water in Al's glass. Unless he had nine ounces of vodka.

Al tilted the glass and looked at it himself. "You're over there, fuck all to do sometimes, or too much to do. Language nightmare. So you drink. Kind of got away on me a bit. So I'm dialling it back. And the wife is dragging me to Pilates classes."

Without being asked, Al offered that he didn't miss the booze, not really. Well, parts of it. But not the part where you wake up feeling like roadkill and you swear you won't touch another drop then at noon that double gin seems like just the ticket.

Ritt looked over Al's shoulder to see if anyone else was going to join him. He had craved solitude, but now that Al was here—washed out, jittery, filled with thoughts of drink denied—he needed a buffer.

After ten minutes of Al's descriptions of monumental hang-overs, of his liver as it appeared on the ultrasound ("like a discarded football you find in the park in the spring"), Nancy Polk stuck her head out the patio door and asked if the hard-working chef could use a refill.

"That would be great, Nancy," Ritt said, holding up his glass. "The Lagavulin. On the counter."

She disappeared and reappeared a minute later, holding the bottle and a glass of wine for herself. She was compact, with short black hair, naturally exuberant. She was on her fourth husband and had once told Alexa that it didn't really matter who you married. They're all a version of the same thing. She'd joked that they should set up an idiot exchange where you brought in your old idiot and walked away with a new one. No papers to sign, no money changing hands. She figured most women would eventually end up with their first husband again.

"Ritt, you're stuck out here doing all the work. Listening to Al tell you how glorious it is to be sober." Nancy gave Ritt a large pour.

"Glorious might be overstating it," Al said.

"You got that right," Nancy said. "Herb and I did a one-month cleanse last January—no alcohol, no sugar, no something else. By Week Four we were one gluten-free muffin away from divorce."

Ritt took a sip of the scotch and let the peaty flavour roll around his mouth. It was after nine and still light, though cool enough that you needed a sweater. They chatted a bit about Manchauser's violent end and whether Emma Barkley had done it, poor woman. Al decided to randomly tee off on the electric car industry, taking angry gulps of his water, wondering when the world was going to wake up to face certain facts. Wondering how it was that so many people lived in a cozy bubble that had *nothing* to do with the reality on the ground, which he was having trouble outlining.

A few others drifted out, including Alexa. Dickie's wife guiltily bummed one of her cigarettes and lit it and smoked with the unease of the social smoker. Ritt put the steaks on, that satisfying sizzle. Al mercifully drifted away. Nancy joined a few women and an eruption of laughter came from them. Lem Billings wandered up and appraised the steaks appreciatively. He had been CEO of Ocelot before Manchauser had gutted it. "I've found that everything tastes better since Manchauser got his ass blown to hell," he said.

Whenever there were enough oil people and enough booze together in one room, they would play an ad hoc parlour game: Who Killed Pete Manchauser. They'd go around the table and argue over who among them was the best suspect: who had the clearest motive, who had a rural background, which was now linked inexorably and irrationally to fertilizer bombs. Who had hunted; who had killed something. Who had lost the most. Ritt hoped they weren't in for another round tonight.

He could see Alexa over Lem's shoulder. She was already weaving, the hand holding the glass at her hip, like a gun-slinger. Her anger with her ex-husband, the sense of injustice and loss that snaked through her from the coincident fertility of her daughter and Richard's new wife. All this would manifest itself in unfortunate ways as the evening wore on. One of the reasons Alexa liked throwing dinner parties was it gave her licence to drink more. She had home field advantage.

Ritt flipped the steaks and hovered over them, moving them occasionally to hotter parts of the grill. When they were done, he piled them back onto a clean platter and took them inside. He asked Alexa to give him a hand with plating and she nodded and kept talking to Billings, who was telling her something in a German accent. Nancy Polk finally came to lend a hand. He took his sharpest Japanese knife and made thick angled slices of the steak and mixed it with the spinach and halved cherry tomatoes and added the vinaigrette and put it in the centre of the table. It took five minutes of herding to get everyone to sit down. It was almost ten and some of the guests were as notice-ably drunk as his wife.

They were too large a group for a single conversation. Different cliques talked about Manchauser, about Phoenix and real estate. Ritt was at one end of the table with Alexa at the other end. She was holding court about something. Ritt couldn't hear the details. She wasn't eating. Ritt suddenly realized how drunk he was, too. The whole dinner seemed like background noise. There were familiar sermons about government policy, everyone on the same side, but yelling above one another so that it seemed like an argument. Dickie's thin wife picked at her steak, checking for signs of life. She ate a few spinach leaves. Ritt still couldn't remember her name, had listened attentively for someone to say it but no one had. Perhaps everyone had forgotten. Betty? Too prosaic. *Marzipan?* Bit random. Maybe even Dickie no longer knew. It was gone, like one of those indigenous languages that passes from the earth.

Dickie was loudly telling a joke about bear hunting and blowjobs, roaring with laughter before the punch line arrived then repeating it twice. *"You're not here for the hunting, are you?"*

An hour went by. Ritt brought the dessert out and twenty minutes later most of the giant flan remained uneaten. He was sodden, the alcohol sitting in him like a dead weight. He had stayed too long on the scotch, perversely viewing it as a defence against Alexa's obvious drunkenness. He heard snatches of different conversations. *Backcombed halfway to heaven, throw a fuck into the Bakken.* The faces flickered in the light, the sudden shadows giving them a sinister cast.

Ritt felt a tickle at his feet and looked down and saw that sand was filling the room like liquid, covering the floor, his toes disappearing. He stared for a long moment. The Quaternary Period finally passing. It had to go sometime. Geologic time, suddenly in a hurry, a speeded-up time-lapse version, the sand still loose, not yet compressed into stone by the weight of another era. It was hardening, though, he could feel it. Who could argue with the progress they'd made in the Quaternary: agriculture, tools, civilizations. A few disagreements along the way. And now a layer would form containing ninety million discarded computers, four feet of half-eaten take-out in Styrofoam containers, jeans that didn't really fit, outmoded cellphones. It piled so high but compressed to almost nothing, releasing dozens of chemicals that rose and settled comfortably. The formation was the colour of weak coffee. Another strata inched upward—his legs disappeared. It threatened the table—threatened Al's half-filled, deeply resented water glass, Nancy's fourth husband, Dickie's nameless wife and her uneaten dinner. It would soon take Dickie's jokes, louder and more inappropriate as the evening staggered on. It would bury all of Alexa's resentments. Her face was florid, her anger leaking out at first in sharp bitter comments, and then the dam burst, and she was telling Ritt there should have been a vegetarian option, pointing to the untouched meat, then telling the two vegetarians to get with the program, Bambi.

The encroaching strata would cover Alice Staedlater's recent facelift (which made her look like a dead cheerleader), it would cover Morris Swain's unsubtle implants (which stuck out of his head like a failed Third World agriculture project). This was how time passed, slowly at first, you hardly noticed the years go by, then suddenly everything changed, everyone got old in a hurry.

There was relief whenever a period ended. Nostalgia certainly. The Cretaceous mourned its own passing—*We were living large. The world is smaller now.* The incoming Paleogene insisted that those dinosaurs were out of touch. They deserved to die. Clumsy, slow. God and evolution working together couldn't come up with a worse idea. They took up too much space, ate everything in sight. They thought they invented sex. And those stories. It's a miracle they didn't die of boredom. We're younger, we're faster, we're *smarter,* the Paleogene is going to last forever.

Who could see the Neogene coming? Birds, mammals, grass everywhere. Massive forests shot up and sucked up all that carbon dioxide, lowering the level from 650 parts per million to 100. Thank god for that. *Homo habilis* arrived. Not much of a reception. Barely human. Hairy sex and lunch for the faster animals. Stone tools, and that's on a good day. Grab a fucking brain.

You had to look at the big picture. In the very beginning, the Ectasian, quiet as church. Just that uneventful land mass and seas with colonies of green algae floating serenely. It only took four billion years for those single, clueless cells to evolve into Larry, Curly and Moe poking each other in the eye.

A candle fell over, spilling wax onto the table. A glass crashed. The strata quickly covered it, covered the empty plates stacked awkwardly on the kitchen counter, the uneaten meat and crusted mustard, the pools of blood. On the table, all those wine bottles, the half-eaten flan, the handful of blueberries in the ceramic bowl they'd bought in Italy. The twelve of them (except two were missing, who were they, *where* were they?) now encased almost to their chests. Here is where height is an evolutionary advantage. Compact Nancy already a casualty, just the top of her head showing, the smallest hint of grey roots at the part. Dickie's wife breathing through her nose, worrying about her weight—*how much spinach is too much.* Dickie had one more joke for us, *So this consultant takes his new wife fishing hahaha . . .*

Alexa's open angry mouth filled with sediment. Her eyes showing surprise, though you couldn't say we didn't see it coming. Suddenly stifled. Ritt felt relief at this, and felt guilty for that relief. Their eyes met along the runway length of the table and Ritt saw neither love nor fear in his wife's expression, just the mutual recognition of a dying species. The strata was at Ritt's own chin, settling fast. Below his waist, it was already stone. The winds howled, the sky opened. The house was blown away, the timbers flying east, the dark clouds close enough to touch, it seemed, if his arms were free. The end of an era and you want a bit of a show, something to remember. It was past his mouth now, too, only his eyes surveying what was left. He wanted a divorce, this much was clear. He wanted out. It crept up behind him, moving against the back of his head then pooling around, enclosing him, covering the last of him.

TWENTY-EIGHT

CALGARY

DECEMBER 2004

Ritt thought he heard the ambulance, a distant siren. He drifted in and out of consciousness. Alexa was talking to him again. There was a moment when he waited for her to press the gun barrel to the back of his head and execute him like a Latin American insurgent. Bang. But she was out of ammunition. He could hear her going through her purse and thought she might be looking for more bullets, but he heard the hiss of a lighter and the deep satisfying inhalation of smoke. Hoping the cigarette would bring clarity to the situation. He stared at his blood. Lying in that pool, immobile. It occurred to him that he might be paralyzed. She had dialled 911 and offered a partially coherent version of events over the phone without the frantic need of most emergency calls. Instead she rambled conversationally, as if catching up with an old friend, *Anyway, I shot him. I didn't plan it or anything, and now he's lying here. But maybe you could send an ambulance. I wonder if they could stop on the way and pick up a bottle of Snow Queen vodka.* Had she actually said that?

And so they waited together. The pain echoed through his body, making it hard to locate the source. How many bullets were in him?

"Do you remember that first Christmas together?" she asked.

"The one when you were still with Richard." His voice filled with effort. The weight of his body pressing down.

"No, the first Christmas we actually spent together. When we went to Arizona. You didn't want to go."

They'd gone to Phoenix. Alexa was a golfer and Ritt had always successfully avoided it. She said it was something they could do together. You'll catch on, she insisted. Everyone does. Standing in the dry air, on a lush course in the desert.

He did catch on, though not that first day. It took four tries to hit the ball on his first drive, the club malevolently and uselessly slicing the air. When he finally connected, he topped the ball and it rolled thirty feet. Alexa bent over, laughing and apologizing for laughing. "Oh god, I'm sorry, Ritt. It's just . . . Here, hon, let me show you . . ."

"The beginning of my love affair with golf." The words slurred, his face pressed down, his mouth twisted.

"God you were terrible. And so angry."

They had rented a convertible but it was too hot to drive with the top down. Alexa had asked him to go slowly through a quiet, residential area. She just wanted to look at the lives, she said. She found a radio station that played music from the sixties and listened to the Tremeloes sing "Silence Is Golden" and wondered what went on in those bungalows. They didn't see a single person on the street.

There was a knock on the door, four quick hard raps. Alexa opened it and a group quickly filled the room, policemen and paramedics. Suddenly there were several conversations happening at once, the police talking to Alexa, one paramedic asking Ritt if he was conscious, the other saying, *Stop the bleeding, locate the source.* The police emphasizing *the gun.* Ritt lost track of what they were saying. He could dimly hear Alexa offering them a drink.

When they turned him over onto the stretcher, he saw her, perched on the arm of the sofa. She looked drained of everything. She tried to say something as he was quickly wheeled by, but couldn't get the words to come out. In the cocoon of the ambulance, he was hooked up to an IV. He heard the whispered reassurances of the paramedics and saw the doubtful look they exchanged before he lost consciousness.

Ritt woke up in the hospital, as if pieces of him were waking up separately, a slow chain reaction that gradually spread through his whole body. He felt calm. He examined the tubes. He was tired but he didn't feel much pain. An ache muffled by the morphine drip.

A nurse came in, a brisk woman in her forties. "You're awake." Stating the obvious. "Five bullets. Crime of passion."

Ritt wanted to ask her how he was, an odd question, but he was slow to formulate it.

"So your girl wasn't a great shot. Still, five out of seven. We took four of the bullets out, Mr. Devlin. Number Five is still in there. A souvenir."

"Where are the bullets?"

The nurse laughed. "I knew you'd want them. The police have them. Evidence."

"I don't think I'm going to press charges."

"It must be love." She adjusted his bed and straightened the sheets.

"Where is Alexa?" he asked.

"Your wife? Probably in jail."

He lifted his gown awkwardly, bunching it up, trying to scan for wounds.

"They're all in the back," the nurse said, pulling his gown back down.

"Any permanent damage?"

"Well, the doctor will be in to give you the rundown."

"But you have an idea. Ballpark."

"There's no major organ damage, a miracle. There's a broken rib. But no nerve damage, no spine. Annie Oakley had a bad day."

"We both did."

"I could get you something. A sandwich."

"I'm not hungry, thanks."

She walked to the door. "Ring if you need anything. I imagine the police are going to come by at some point."

Ritt drifted toward sleep, a heaviness that consumed him. His eyes closed. He saw an image of Alexa driving the rental car in France, a bit tipsy from their long lunch, angry with the endless traffic circles, going around one of the big ones four times, trapped in the inner lane, unable to exit. Finally forcing her way to the periphery amid horns and French curses, taking the wrong exit. *Are you looking at the map? Toulouse? Is that us? Well it is now.*

He thought of a dinner party—two years ago?—that point in February when everyone is fed up with winter. Alexa had got into a roaring argument about *Mary Poppins,* something about Julie Andrews. It was very late. She sang a verse from "Feed the Birds" to quietly surprised dinner guests and then fell asleep at the table.

Tatiana had given birth to a girl she named Ramona. Velvett gave birth a week later, prematurely, to a girl she wanted to name Precious but that was vetoed by Richard. The footage Ritt took of Alexa with Tatiana's baby looked like a hostage video, with her holding the crying baby tightly then Tatiana swooping in and grabbing it.

Ritt fell into sleep. Did he dream of Alexa? Maybe the early version.

When he woke up again, there were two detectives in the room, wearing cheap suits and hard expressions. They were sitting on chairs observing him like he was an experiment. They introduced themselves as Dunham and Brisby, and asked what had happened exactly.

Ritt told them he had asked for a divorce and that Alexa had wanted to work things out.

"Interesting way of working things out," Dunham said.

"I'm not pressing charges," Ritt said.

"She shot you. It's attempted murder."

"We had a few drinks. We talked. She shot me. We talked some more."

"How many drinks?"

"I had two. Alex, hard to say. I'm guessing eight."

"You're oil, is that right."

"We're all oil."

"Let's start at the beginning," Brisby said, taking out a note-book. He had a moustache and smelled of cigarettes.

"You don't want to start there," Ritt said.

TWENTY-NINE

PARIS

2007

I t was the year of the Great Melt. In 2007, twenty-four percent of the Arctic ice disappeared, a fact that went largely unnoticed outside of environmental circles. A barge carrying coal from Vancouver to Norway successfully navigated the Northwest Passage, which was ice-free, the dream of Franklin finally realized. This was the year the *Akademik Fedorov* sailed for the North Pole behind the nuclear icebreaker *Rossiya*. The *Fedorov* carried two Mir Deep Submergence Vehicles, and Mir-1 descended 4,261 metres below the polar ice to claim the North Pole for Russia; it planted a titanium Russian flag in the sea-bed, along with a time capsule containing a photograph of a shirtless Vladimir Putin staring nobly into the future.

It was also the year that Sergei Krupin cobbled a deal with Rosneft to drill in the Barents Sea. It was a co-production with Rosneft as the majority partner, Sergei's company, which was called Gubkin Oil, and Mackenzie Oil. What Ritt brought to the table was his somewhat rundown supertanker drill ship, which needed at least $200 million in retrofits, his expertise on Arctic deepwater drilling, and the political mitigation of a Western company. Sergei brought political instincts, rusty and unnecessary geological skills, and his position as broker. Rosneft brought a ruinous record (621 reported oil spills on Russian soil and possibly double that number of unreported spills), a lack of transparency, a murky relationship with government, an impressive bureaucracy, and a bullheaded sense of Arctic destiny that was accompanied by bouts of deathly pessimism. More importantly, it brought money and leases.

The initial video conference with Ritt's Russian partners had been stilted and unsatisfying. In his boardroom, Ritt looked at the screen that showed eight Russians seated at a large table. The lens had a fish-eye quality that distorted them; they each appeared to be four feet wide.

"Do you . . ." Ritt began.

"Welcome!" the man next to Sergei said brightly.

"I think we . . ."

The man who welcomed him now spoke in Russian to the woman beside him, who then turned to address the camera.

"So our friend Mr. Medvedev speaks warmly of the Arctic project."

"Please tell Mr. Medvedev . . ."

"Rittinger, how is the terrible weather there?" This was Sergei. It went like this for almost an hour, partial sentences, unheard comments, overlapping dialogue that was laboriously translated. The video of the men began to look like a still photograph, a snapshot of some politburo meeting from decades ago that was slightly out of focus and brown with age. They finally said their hesitant overlapping goodbyes and the Russians tried to sign off, a huge head looming into the screen like a manatee, pushing buttons unsuccessfully and swearing before the screen went dark.

A month later he met with Sergei in Paris. A vacation of sorts, which was good, because Ritt had become wary of vacations. He didn't like to travel alone and wasn't interested in organized tours. So he was happy for the chance to go to Paris under the auspices of business. Sergei was there trying to squeeze money out of Total, though he was more interested in eating and drinking. He came with a list of restaurants they had to try. He was on a Rosneft expense account and felt they had a responsibility to eat well.

They chose a restaurant Sergei had found on a recommended list in a Russian travel magazine. It was small and dark with wooden floors. A row of large, colourful, violent paintings filled one wall. Everyone in the restaurant was younger than they were, which wasn't hard. They sat by the window and a slim middle-aged woman in heels marched past with a small bag of groceries, off to cook dinner for a lover, Ritt decided. When she looked at them there was a hint of a smile. She had a lovely, lived-in face, creases under her eyes.

Sergei watched her pass. "They eat butter all day and remain butterflies," he said. "Russian women want to double their weight before they die. This is their goal. They have had great success."

Sergei was happiest in restaurants, eating and drinking. Where was Ritt happiest? At home with a drink and a nice dinner and a football game he could attach a narrative to, finding a team to like, someone to hate. Not an uplifting revelation.

Sergei started in on the geology of France, the Paris Basin and its annoying sedimentary rock. That suspect permeability, that indifferent porosity—so French! Oddly, they had found oil in oolitic limestone. Not much, but. Instead of Cretaceous sandstone, Sergei said, France had a thick seam of decayed beauty, millions of women crushed by bad luck, bad men, by life. It smelled faintly of Chanel No. 5.

"A tragic formation," Sergei said. "You drill into this, out comes a long sigh." He mimicked the noise.

The waitress came over and Sergei ordered in halting French. They watched the woman walk away, a tidy, short-stepped walk.

"Rittinger, do you believe there is just one true love for each of us?" Sergei asked, still examining the waitress. When they socialized, they essentially had three conversations, he and Sergei—geology, love, and the tragic state of Russia.

"No." Though in retrospect, he did have One True Love: Oda. He'd been madly in love with Deirdre and Alexa at the beginning, but love was a marathon, as they say, not a sprint. He seemed to be a middle-distance runner.

"My belief, totally scientific, is that there are a thousand women who you may fall in love with," Sergei said. "Women are thrown in your path by a god who is bored and has a terrible sense of humour. So you try this one, that one. Sometimes, you find one in those thousand. If you are very lucky. Even then." He shrugged. "You are sitting with the woman and after four drinks her voice is suddenly the voice of God. You watch her lips move, you look into her eyes. She is so perfect! But in a week, a month, a year, she stares at you and you see she wishes she was far away. She makes mistake. Also you make mistake." Sergei shrugged again and took a sip of the outrageously priced wine he'd ordered. "Then we make same mistake again."

They drank three bottles of wine with their dinner (*rognons de veau* for Sergei, *gigot d'agneau pleureur* for Ritt) then left the restaurant and walked in the autumn air. They strolled for half an hour then stopped at a bar for a cognac (since when did cognac cost $64 a glass? Though he may have miscalculated the conversion) and Sergei described (again) the chaos of his first marriage (four children), the tragedy of his second, and started on the epic collapse of his third. Love, they agreed, was Darwinian; it evolved or died.

Sergei was impressed that Ritt had been shot by his third wife.

"No one has ever loved me enough to shoot me, Rittinger," he said mournfully.

"I don't know that it was love. Maybe it was just the vodka."

"It's a fine line," Sergei said.

There were two more stops on the way back to their hotel, more cognac, another scientifically backed theory from Sergei, this one involving the mating habits of sea lions. The street they were on was unfamiliar, or, more accurately, it looked like fifty other streets. Neither of them had a map of the city. Ritt's phone was dead. Sergei had left his at the hotel.

They walked in what felt like the right direction. But each street curved subtly away from where Ritt thought they wanted to be.

"We are officially lost," Ritt said.

"Let's not involve officials."

"The hotel isn't far from the river." Half of Paris wasn't far from the river.

"We find the river."

They didn't find the river. They asked four people and received vague directions, arms pointed in conflicting semaphoric instructions. They could have taken a cab, though there weren't any on the small streets they were on.

Ritt was getting increasingly confused, each new certainty about where they were quickly undermined. This absence of solid ground. It occurred to him that his lostedness (a recent problem, this manufacturing of words) was only partly due to Haussmann's confusing semi-concentric city plan. There was a deeper confusion here that nagged—his memory, which ideally would have allowed him to trace their path back to the hotel, had failed him. And his spatial relationship with the city was somehow skewed. Sergei was literally having trouble walking. He moved his bulk through the street like a farmer pitching hay, a rolling repetitive movement that threatened his balance with each step. His alcohol consumption had been roughly thirty percent higher than Ritt's own considerable intake, and he was now effectively useless.

They finally arrived on the rue de Rivoli, which they were both sure they'd been on, and they declared this was progress. They no longer needed a cab. The hotel couldn't be far. Past the Louvre. They asked a man in red pants where the Louvre was and he laughed and pointed them in the direction they were going. "*C'est fermé*," he said.

As they walked, the signs on the buildings almost certainly familiar, Sergei asked him, "Why did you leave Texas?"

"I thought I'd killed a man." He told Sergei the story of Jimmy Dean and the tire iron, the first time he'd told anyone. They walked past the Place du Carrousel and into the semi-familiar Jardin des Tuileries. Dozens of people strolled here, wrapped in scarves, deep in conversation.

"Fifteen and already a murderer! Such progress!" Sergei said.

"Except he didn't die. I went back thirteen years later and found him."

"So for thirteen years you are a murderer, then after you are a saint. You said to this man, I apologize for killing you."

"No. I wasn't that sorry."

As they lurched past the Petit Palais (had they gone too far?), Sergei talked of love as essentially sedimentary in nature and not, as so many poets supposed, igneous. Ritt was fairly sure the hulking Palais beside the Petit wasn't something they'd passed on the way to the restaurant. He would have remembered it. Or perhaps he did remember it. Or he was remembering it from a trip with Deirdre decades ago?

Ritt was now sure they'd missed the hotel. Almost sure. Maybe they should take a cab. Ritt stopped, and Sergei kept walking, again describing his idiosyncratic French geological formation, filled with longing and regret and affordable table wine. Ritt wasn't sure if they should go forward or turn back, and decided it didn't matter.

THIRTY

CALGARY

2008

That one bullet remained, lodged in his back below his shoulder in a delicate spot near his lung. He had seen the X-ray, the bullet slightly misshapen from the impact, a stain on his ghostly outline. A souvenir, the doctor said. Ritt hadn't seen Alexa in almost four years. She had miraculously avoided jail, the result of a brilliant lawyer and a sympathetic jury. The divorce was finalized. His one post-shooting meeting with her had been for breakfast, statistically the safest meal. Ritt ate pancakes and Alexa picked at her blueberries and yogurt and talked about her expensive rehab in Atlanta, which she framed in comic vignettes about her fellow inmates. How an airline hostess from North Carolina managed to smuggle in a gym bag filled with vodka miniatures so they could have a party to celebrate their sobriety. It was one story after another, she said. That's what you did in rehab, you told stories: a man driving his Volvo into a public pool. A woman from New Haven waking up in a Mississippi truck stop. A woman took a shotgun to her husband's Bouvier, both barrels, *and the damn thing wouldn't die.*

As this came out, she was suddenly aware of the parallel, then rushed to describe the broken marriages, fistfights, neglected children, car accidents where it was a miracle, etcetera. The inmates compared liver damage and previous treatment centres and played board games that had coffee stains on them. Alexa had been there a month, long enough, she said, to get bored with both the idea of any more genteel incarceration, but also with the idea of drinking again. I don't want to be one of those people who talk about their mental health like it's a new religion, she said. How I'm doing yoga again. All that. Ritt asked her if she'd given in to a higher power. I need a little more proof, she said.

It was a pleasant breakfast, and when they left the restaurant the sun was high, the streets filled with people walking to work, juggling coffee and cellphones. They stood in the spring morning and Ritt wondered for a daft moment why they couldn't get back together. Oddly, the impediment wasn't the fact that she had shot him five times. Something else had left them. Alexa was one of those people who come out of rehab both happily cured and vaguely diminished. He remembered the preacher in the movie in Texas, the one called the "sin killer," and how his mother had said that when you killed sin you killed something else, too. Alexa had the look of someone who had just returned from a spa vacation—rested but empty of experience.

Still, they were comfortable together, standing there on Fourth Avenue. They had a shared history with an alarming range, and now they both knew it wasn't enough. Alexa kissed him on the cheek and said, I'm sorry I shot you, Ritt.

———

Since the end of his third marriage, Ritt hadn't dated much. He'd suffered through a lot of jokes about having dodged a bullet, about *femmes fatales*. He'd come into the coffee room once to find his executive assistant singing "Frankie and Johnny"—*She shot once, twice, three times, and Johnny fell on the hardwood floor.* She had a brassy nightclub voice.

Ritt had fallen into an old man's routine. He was seventy-two. He got up, made porridge most days, drank black coffee, read the paper while the television news chirped in the background, then walked to work. He spent the better part of eight hours holding the company together. Tate and his sleight of hand were long gone. Mackenzie Oil was ordinary now, at the trough with everyone else.

Usually he had lunch at his desk. Occasionally he went to a restaurant with a colleague. He walked home, even in dire weather, poured a large whisky, and made dinner from one of the cookbooks in his unruly collection. He liked cooking for people, but the social math of a single man in his seventies was taxing. After giving a dinner party he was then invited to reciprocal dinner parties and he could almost hear the conversation between the host and hostess about which woman to invite to fill the table and what age was appropriate—well, why *wouldn't* he want to date someone his own age, the hostess insisting indignantly. And then he would find himself at a dinner party, picking at the (slightly overdone) *boeuf bourguignon*, glancing at the woman to his left, a woman his age who had spent twenty minutes choosing her dress, and he could see on her pleasant face the faint glimmer of hope. These women with their slightly sagging histories, the well-chosen dress, perhaps well-chosen lingerie, and past that the flesh that has been unobserved for several years, wary and creased. And what did they see when they looked at Ritt? A man with three wives behind him, a company renowned for its failures, silver hair that was still plentiful, a tanned creased face giving way to a soft white old man's body. There were occasions when the hostess had misjudged, when the brilliantly maintained face of a sixty-year-old woman who had twenty years of Pilates under her belt and a dietary regimen that was fastidious though not extreme, made it suddenly clear that she hadn't left her faithless husband to date a seventy-two-year-old harbouring a bullet.

At whatever stage we face the world—the nervous school days, riotous adolescence (though his own hadn't been), the stupid confidence of youth, the surprising fragility of late middle age—there was always something lacking: experience, confidence, wisdom, agility. This was life's conundrum: *if I'd only known then what I know now.* He wasn't sure what he knew now. Middle age is when we're best equipped. We have experience, our health (with luck), fewer doubts. Now Ritt was besieged by doubt. He wondered where the certainty of his youth had come from. Had it only been ignorance?

There was a subtle cruelty to these dinner scenarios. On one occasion he was paired with a woman roughly his age who was *well preserved*, that odd curatorial compliment. They chatted amiably at dinner and Ritt offered her a ride home. When she invited him in for a nightcap, he thought for a moment that he had misheard. He wondered what a nightcap meant these days. Possibly it only meant a nightcap. He parked and followed her into a house that was part of her divorce settlement, a modest, well-tended split-level that a family had been raised in. They had a cognac and talked and when she asked him if he'd like to stay, he honestly didn't know the answer. Which was better: to stay and experience (possibly) pleasant sex, the touch of a woman, that intimacy that was gone from his life. Or to avoid the complications, the (possibly) awkward morning and return to the comfort of his own place. He didn't see a future for them, though it was more he didn't *feel* a future. You felt it or you didn't. Though maybe it was the future itself he couldn't feel. He gazed into the faded eyes in the pleasant face. Why not?

It turned out that it was enjoyable, though he remained curiously uninvolved. What was that phrase everyone used— *in the moment.* He wasn't in the moment, he was watching the two of them conservatively explore one another, watching himself ease inside her (not as hard as he—or she—might have liked), hovering over the two of them. He almost spoke to her during sex—*what do you like?* But it seemed too intimate. He couldn't find the words. He worked on his facial expression— involved, though not too intense. Politely engaged. Perhaps she was struggling, too, trying to look passionate rather than dutiful. Their uncertain faces only inches apart.

Afterwards they lay on their backs and chatted and Ritt may have fallen asleep while she was talking. In the morning, she set out a breakfast of mixed berries and fresh pastries that Ritt suspected had been bought in anticipation of company. Why would a single woman buy four pastries? He kissed her at the door and left feeling relieved and regretful, and wished he felt more—the welcome nausea of love.

Ritt came to understand that there were people who put themselves through this on a regular basis until they found someone or until the thought of facing another audition was finally worse than the prospect of being alone.

But there was alone and there was alone. Ritt had no family. He wasn't in touch with Deirdre or Alexa. Sergei was probably the closest thing he had to a real friend. He had well-meaning colleagues and a surprising residue of enemies.

Meanwhile oil was doing everything, all at once. Russia loudly gearing up. The Americans putting their faith in shale gas. Pipelines turned into political footballs. Railcars filled with Bakken oil lurching across the country, waiting for that spark. Tapping the Groningen gas field off the Dutch coast caused twenty-one earthquakes, those decades of depletion destabilizing the formation. The Saudis were gearing up for (yet) another showdown. A well in Kazakhstan blew for ninety-seven days. Aging dictators, African uprisings, Middle-Eastern drama. All the usual suspects. The price crept up and fell back. The oil sands were the poster boy for global warming. Energy was so unfocused now. Like Ritt. China sent clumsy delegations around the world, trying to supply energy to a billion people who were facing pollution levels that approximated nuclear winter. The Arctic becoming interesting again.

He suddenly had so much time. It lingered. The light still glowed behind the mountains after the sun had set, visible through the oversized west-facing windows. Then the dark filled his apartment like an inky fluid. He reminded himself not to drink after dinner. He watched videos, read a lot, found himself occasionally forgetting the name of some common item. Staring at a spatula in the kitchen, random words forming in his head—*Italianate, spider*. It was, his doctor said, normal for his age. If you forget where you put your keys, it's not a problem, he said. If you forget what a key *is,* maybe we have a little problem.

He still liked to get up to the mountains and go hiking. He would labour up the aggressive thrust of Mount Rundle and recount its geological travails as if they had shared them together. *Remember the Cretaceous, my god I thought it would never end.*

He'd become increasingly particular. Particular about his coffee, which had to be a dark, oily bean only found in two stores in town. He went through three espresso makers before he found one that produced exactly the right kind of caramel-coloured *crema.* This from a man who had been happy with instant coffee for twenty years, happy to pour hot water from the tap over granules that yielded a watery drink the colour of sewage. You gravitated toward things, the way two boats on a still sea will move closer to one another. The laws of attraction. You gravitated to a certain brand of whisky, a specific solitude.

He found it harder to be charming—or at least to be found charming. The salesgirl at the liquor store, who had one side of her head shaved, and who looked like she'd spent some time in both a weight room and a mental institution, ignored his cheery perceptions.

He got home with his single malt and poured a glass and ran a bath. He lowered himself into it and surveyed his body, the trail of silver hair, the alarming pallor. How vulnerable we are. As soft as pincushions. So easily pierced.

THIRTY-ONE

THE BARENTS SEA

2014

R itt lay in his berth on *The Aleksandra,* formerly *The Adam,* formerly a decommissioned Japanese supertanker made from steel smelted by broad-backed Ukrainians in Dantean furnaces, using banded iron formation silicates found in Precambrian rock that was weakly metamorphosed (too conservative to change, or maybe just too lazy). Everything of the earth.

The Aleksandra was rooted in the Barents Sea by suction anchors, looking like an outdated piece of Cold War equipment. Its sheer scale appealed to the Russians, more than four hundred metres of floating steel. The retrofits had been done in Murmansk. Twenty-two months of welding, technological upgrading, reinforcing, and bribing contractors, which had cost between $261 and $461 million, depending on whose accounting was used.

Ritt's assistant had compiled twenty-three articles on the subject of militarization in the North, and they lay in piles on the bed beside him. Nineteen of them made reference to the Cold War. Six of them were largely technical, listing the equipment and soldiers that had quietly been moved north in the last six years. All twenty-three had the word "tension" in them. The new Cold War was getting colder, various diplomats said. Some of them recalled how disastrous and beneficial the original one had been.

High-tech semi-submersible drilling platforms sat like chess pieces in the northern seas, essentially flags. A growing fleet of ships roamed. Canada had ordered eight Arctic patrol ships. Neutral Norway ordered five Fridtjof Nansen–class frigates equipped with Aegis Combat Systems. Denmark developed their Knud Rasmussen–class of ice-capable patrol vessels. And these were the peaceful nations, the perennial doves. The United States equipped its Virginia-class submarines with Arctic navigation systems and sent them under the ice. The Russians developed a ballistic missile submarine and reinstated their military bases on the New Siberian Islands. Vladimir Putin declared the North a priority, as did the Canadian prime minister. The toy that no one had played with for four hundred years was suddenly all the rage.

Ritt got up and grabbed his orange parka off the hook and walked down the bright clanging corridors to the mess room, a grimly lit cavern that echoed with the clatter of cheap, heavy silverware. He joined a line of men and looked at the steam trays: beef, eggs, potatoes, herring, sour cream, pancakes, a bean soup that had the consistency of mud. This was breakfast. He took a little of the beef, some cabbage. The men in front of him piled food into mounds on their plates. Two men in the line began shoving one another, grunting and heaving like elephant seals.

Men fought about anything. He'd once seen two men in a rig camp come to blows over who made a better truck, Ford or Chevrolet. *Fix Or Repair Daily—that's your goddamn Ford,* Mr. Chevy had yelled, his nose bloodied. *I had one and you couldn't pay me to drive that piece of shit now.* The man was near tears, whether from the blow or the injustice of Ford's truck hegemony, it was hard to say.

Ritt ate quickly and without appetite then went up onto the deck and felt the cold September air on his face. It was still dark. Imperial was drilling a hole in the Beaufort that was six miles deep. This Rosneft hole was intended to be almost eight miles, the deepest anyone had ever gone in the Arctic. It would take three years to complete. This was Rosneft's optimistic, misleading estimate. It would be four or five, maybe more, Ritt knew. There were always complications. A heartbroken welder is sloppy and the welds don't hold. An engineer is drunk when he presses "send" with his wobbly calculations. A safety inspector is paid off, a bureaucrat threatened, an idiot nephew promoted. The whole world was human error.

He saw a large seabird flying in a wide circle. Odd to see one this far north; they preferred the northern Pacific. Following the ship perhaps, living off its waste. He knew the bird and in his head he watched four words go by—*Abilene, focus, peregrine, stirrup*—before landing on albatross.

Ritt walked stiffly in the cold. His body should be becoming more familiar, but it was becoming less so. The seventy-eight-year-old version with its miraculously sprouting liver spots. A bruise on his leg, the result of god knows what, took nine weeks to heal. The shiny white calves that seemed to belong to someone else. Aches, creaks, spools of black thread floating across his eyes. All the tiny betrayals. Names leaked out of his head. Words abandoned him, familiar things suddenly alien. Sometimes he encountered words on a page and couldn't put an image to them, *wallet, faucet, turmoil.*

The sound of the rig engines was a constant drone. A helicopter hovered nervously. Ritt strolled along the edge of the ship, observing the sea. Ice floated, unconnected, like puzzle pieces laid out. He could see the trail of another ship that had cut through. Within a few weeks it might knit itself, the trail vanishing.

Sergei was approaching. He appeared to be smoking. The Russians had a tolerance for idiosyncrasy.

The Russians had made few compromises with nature; they weren't going to start now. So they didn't drill a relief well that would help if the well blew in. They wouldn't get any help from nature up here. When the Deepwater Horizon blew in the Gulf of Mexico, leaking 42,000 gallons a day into the local shrimp fishery, nature was an ally. The countless bacteria that existed in the waters naturally broke down the hydrocarbons. Communities of microorganisms worked in concert to eat the oil. But the Arctic didn't have trillions of bacteria. People weren't the only organisms to be drawn to the South.

Sergei handed Ritt his flask. He took a drink and felt the cold vodka in his throat. They were here as investors and, nominally, as geologists emeriti, observing the operation with a mixture of wisdom and discovery.

"You saw the Rosneft Bolsheviks?" Sergei said.

Ritt nodded. Four executives who had arrived on the ship with dazzling escorts. There were four luxury suites on board, one of them appointed in royal purple in the vain hope Putin would use it. And now they were occupied by four extravagantly useless men who had brought prostitutes who were likely costing $10,000 a day, all of it going onto the drilling budget.

"This is the charming thing about Russian corruption," Sergei said. "In America you would hide this. In Russia you flaunt it."

After his second vodka (usually before lunch) Sergei would tell Ritt about money disappearing into offshore accounts, laundered through numbered companies set up in Liechtenstein.

"Russia is a giant whale, what is this one. White . . ."

"Moby Dick."

"We are Moby Dick washed onto shore. The huge body rotting, picked at by scavengers. And now you and I are among the scavengers." Sergei took a sip from the flask. "You saw the protest?" he asked. "Romania?"

Ritt had seen it on the news the previous week. Angry citizens protesting against fracking. Grainy phone footage of pushing and shoving and twisted faces. Police herding angry students with truncheons out.

"I saw it."

"So behind this, apparently, is our wonderful competitor Gazprom. They organize protest, give money. Also in Bulgaria, Lithuania. They don't want this shale gas hitting market, billions of barrels. So propaganda. Next is America. It has wonderful students who drive to college in big Ford then protest against Big Oil."

Oil had collapsed, yet again. Down to under $60 from a glorious peak of $147. Russia was hurting more than the world knew, Sergei had told him. First, sanctions against them for invading Ukraine, now $60 oil. The financial district in Moscow, 150 acres of gleaming high-rises, was sixty-two percent empty. On the forty-third floor of a bank tower, a youth hostel operated. *Filled with Bulgarian students with dirty socks and guitars singing folk songs,* Sergei had said. The skyscrapers of the financial district were a Potemkin village. The whole country was a Potemkin village. There was pressure to succeed in the North. Putin saw it as a nation-building exercise. The North was the future, the tense every politician was happiest in. And who is more northern than the Russians?

To the east, on the black sea, there was a puddle of bright yellow shaped like an hourglass. They both stared.

"What the hell is that," Ritt said.

Sergei took another swig from the flask. "The Novaya Zemlya effect," he said. "This is only second time I've seen it."

It looked like liquid gold had been poured over the dark water. It was near the horizon, and appeared to be expanding.

"What is it?"

"It is . . . what are they called. A mirage. A polar mirage. Bit like geology. High refraction of sunlight occurs between atmospheric thermoclines. Looks like sun is rising out of the sea. But reality is, not even rising. Nature's little trick. Sunlight bends to earth's curvature."

"The glorious sunrise that wasn't there."

Sergei shrugged. "One day, perhaps it won't rise. But today, I have good feeling."

They walked toward the rig and the noise of the engines grew louder, the symphonic range. Ritt detected an odd note, an oboe coming in late, a violin slightly out of tune. A change in pitch could indicate what they were drilling through, or the state of the bit, a hiccup on the way to the formation.

"Hear that," he said. "That whine."

"These machines, they talk only to you, Rittinger."

On the steel stairs Ritt felt a subtle shudder.

Below them was a quilt of basins and platforms formed by continents slowly colliding, the Caledonian orogeny rising in protest. The Mesozoic comes along with its itchy tectonics and the Caledonian goes down. The whole Barents Sea drifted (from 20 degrees N in the Carboniferous to 55 degrees N in the Triassic); it was lost for ages. Wandering the globe, too proud to ask for directions. It finally settled over billions of barrels of gas in Middle Jurassic sandstone. Fault-bounded positive blocks waiting to be introduced to so-called Russian expertise.

He went inside and looked at various gauges, many of them unfamiliar additions from the retrofit, the markings all in Cyrillic script. The driller was there, a short intense man who had no English.

"Ask him how it's drilling," Ritt said. He wished he'd gotten the latest samples from the geologist. He had meant to go there after dinner and the idea had evaporated. He had repeated it to himself five times as he ate dinner then had walked right past the geologist's cabin. Thoughts wouldn't stay put.

Sergei said a few words to the driller who responded harshly, moving quickly around the generous space. Three other men came in and there was a flurry of conversation.

The oil was supposed to be in Jurassic sandstone and they were months away from hitting that. Ritt wondered if hydrocarbons were leaking out of traps. This could be an early gas hiccup.

"What are they saying?" Ritt asked Sergei.

"Maybe gas. Maybe . . ."

Two more men came in and examined wall gauges and talked loudly to the driller. A noticeable tremor shook the room. Like a mild earthquake that rattles the china. A high-pressure blow-in could send oil seven hundred feet into the air and blow for months or until it ignited and burned everything down. Intense overlapping conversations filled the room. There were seven men now, and Ritt asked Sergei for a translation. Below them the blowout preventer sat on the ocean floor, a hundred feet of failsafe steel that had several functions. In the worst-case scenario the shear rams would be activated, a signal sent down through the fibre optic cable that activated the pistons, cutting off the pipe and sealing the hole. It was an expensive last resort.

There was another master control for the blowout preventer, at the other end of the ship, in case the doghouse was compromised. Ritt wondered what was going on in there. A few more men had come in and the debate was heated. It looked like a hostage situation. Orders yelled and refuted and men moving their threatening bulk closer to one another. A siren went off and a red light flashed through the window.

Through the smeared, oversized pane that gave onto the drilling floor, Ritt could see two roughnecks standing uneasily. Young men, maybe twenty years old. They knew something was going to happen. That was what they'd say afterward anyway. Anything happens and people say, *they had a feeling*. There was another jump, a shift. Ritt opened the door and screamed and motioned for them to come in, and they scuttled to obey like golden retrievers.

Ritt searched for a word—*annual, granular*. "Annular," Ritt said to Sergei. "Tell them to shut the annular. It's a gas kick." He looked at a pressure gauge. Which one was for the drilling mud? Needles twitched and strained. The numbers didn't make sense. It was warm in the room. A man slammed something on the floor, the sound of metal clanging and echoing.

Three bulky men argued in front of a gauge, one of them tapping it insistently with his thick finger. Ritt assumed it was the hydrostatic pressure meter. A man bumped him out of the way and Ritt yelled forcefully into his face. The man responded with a fierce threatening spiel. The rate of return on the mud was lower. Ritt was sure. Almost sure. A digital readout showed flickering, declining numbers. If the rate of return was going down it meant that drilling mud was being lost to a thief zone somewhere below the casing shoe. With the mud leaking out, formation fluids—some salt water mixed with gas probably—would fill that space and migrate upward along the annulus. They needed to activate the annular blowout preventer, shut the hole without compromising the pipe, send some kill fluid down to suppress the gas.

"*Shut the annular*," Ritt yelled. He grabbed Sergei. "Tell them to shut the fucking annular, get the mud engineer up here. We need to mix up some kill fluid. Do it!"

Sergei yelled. Two men yelled back. They shoved one another. All of them talking. One man was yelling into the ship's phone. The flashing red light created a violent strobe in the room. Faces lit up like Mephistopheles.

Ritt thought maybe no one was prepared to make a decision here, fearful of making the wrong one and stuck with that responsibility. He moved to the blowout controls. Two men stood in front of him, wavering.

Ritt wasn't sure about the mud flow. What was the formation pore pressure gradient? A tumble of geological scenarios went by. Part of this was instinct. But for instinct to work, you had to feel the earth through all that steel. It was a relationship that grew over the course of the hole. He was an interloper now.

There was a sudden drop in the gauges. A shudder. Then an unsettling calm. Ritt looked around the room. Had someone activated the shear rams? Cut the pipe off? It might have been done from the other set of controls. The collective at work. Jesus. Sergei was still yelling at a man, his hands grasping his coat, shaking him. The man's face was rubbery, his oversized head poised to receive a blow.

This might set them back. At any rate, they had panicked. Perhaps it was the sudden realization that if something went wrong up here, there wouldn't be a rescue operation. This wasn't the Deepwater Horizon, sitting comfortably in the Gulf of Mexico, in range of help, the weather perfect for vacationing. They would burn in the frozen North. A handful would escape on the helicopter, one of them leaning out the door for that award-winning photograph.

THIRTY-TWO

NOVAYA ZEMLYA, RUSSIAN ARCTIC

Ritt wasn't sure how long he'd been unconscious. Likely only a few minutes. He was cold, though not frozen. Still belted in to his seat. The helicopter had settled at an angle. He struggled to release the seat belt. His fingers were cold and fumbled with the buckle. When it released, he lurched to the side. The pilot was in his seat, moaning. There was a gash on his face. His head lolled, a Khrushchev head, potato-shaped and lumpen. Ritt worked on the man's seat belt and when it released, he slumped toward Ritt. He pulled the man out with great difficulty, collapsing with him onto the hard snow where he had to sit for a moment to catch his breath. Khrushchev was sprawled as if he'd been dropped from the sky.

Ritt finally stood up and went into the helicopter and looked for the survival kit. The metal case was slightly twisted from the landing. He dragged it out and opened it with difficulty. The pilot was sitting up now, looking stunned. Ritt took out the shiny Mylar thermal blankets and draped one around the man and another around his own shoulders. He didn't know the pilot's name. A Russian with no English. Khrushchev's head was bleeding from the gash and Ritt found a bandage and clumsily applied it to the wound. Khrushchev focused on Ritt, his oversized face a question.

"We crashed," Ritt said, simply.

The man looked down at the snow. The small red spots of blood.

Ritt tried the radio in the chopper but it was dead. He looked for his cellphone, knowing there wouldn't be any reception. He found the phone in the inside pocket of his parka and turned it on, but it wasn't picking up a signal.

It was still dark. The first week of October, an hour or so of twilight, and twenty-three hours of darkness. Ritt checked his watch. 8:23. The glow to the north was magnificent. The sea was on fire.

Ritt rubbed his hands and did a small dance to stay warm. He replayed the images. Sitting in the helicopter with the pilot on *The Aleksandra*, waiting for Sergei and a Rosneft executive. They were all heading back to Alakurtti. From there they'd get a plane to St. Petersburg, then finally to Moscow. Sergei had been sixty metres away when the well started to blow. Oil shot eight hundred feet into the air, maybe higher. A massive dark vomiting. The oil splashed and covered the deck, an initial assault that left thick streams. The pipe shimmied then began to emerge. It looked like a snake slithering out of its hole, a slow-motion regurgitation that saw the drill pipe rise up then buckle and twist and fall onto the deck. Did the blowout preventer fail? And its failsafe. Though nothing was failsafe. Sergei lumbered toward the helicopter, moving unevenly, all that accumulated excess. He hit the oil and slid, coated and helpless. The pilot lifted off. His face was white and terrified, the instinct to survive superseding anything else. Ritt yelled at the pilot to wait. Screamed the word.

Then the explosion came. It was like being punched, a sonic wave that left him temporarily deaf. His organs suddenly jelly. The chopper lurched away from the ship, nudged by the sonic wave. It must have sustained damage in the blast and it limped through the air. Ritt assumed they would spiral into the sea. They flew low, maybe twenty metres above the ice. He stared at the jagged pieces of ice, the dark seams that separated them. He couldn't hear a thing. But he felt another explosion. The oil had ignited, and the whole ship was on fire.

They flew along the water for an hour, neither of them saying anything. Ritt recalled the safety lecture, the survival time in freezing water. Was it three minutes? They were working on survival suits that would give you nineteen minutes, though those extra minutes wouldn't be a blessing.

They finally hit the shore, the undifferentiated whiteness. Ritt's hearing returned though it was muffled and he both felt and heard the engine sputter. Ten minutes later it began to spasm. They were no more than five metres above the ground. The pilot let out a stream of words, instructions to himself. Shifting and pulling and pressing. When the helicopter came down, they were at an angle and still moving forward and they landed hard and bounced before settling on the hard snow.

Ritt inventoried the contents of the survival kit. There were rations and gloves and flares. Wool hats and energy bars and pills—probably painkillers. A syringe with something in it. The label was Cyrillic. It occurred to Ritt that the helicopter would have a beacon. There was a small box and Ritt opened it to find a single red button. It must be the emergency beacon. He pushed it. Somewhere in Murmansk a soldier on the night shift would see this. It would give him their co-ordinates and he would send paramedics in a Sikorsky chopper.

"Can you walk?" Ritt asked.

Khrushchev mumbled something in Russian.

There were six flares. Ritt took one and placed it in the gun and shot it. The light it gave off was surprisingly warm, with a slight greenish tinge. Khrushchev's face followed the light up in the air, then drooped downward. With the bandage and the lines of blood and his mismatched, homemade face he looked like Frankenstein. The light bounced off the harsh reflective surface of the Mylar, and the blankets briefly shone.

Ritt helped him to his feet. The two stood unsteadily for a moment. Ritt put one of the wool hats on and pulled one onto Khrushchev's head. In his pockets he put the beacon, four energy bars, and five flares. He started to walk and immediately felt light-headed. The terrain was hard snow with small ridges, tiny obdurate drifts. They weren't far from the coast. The glow of the fire opened the sky. The metal would be fused. There couldn't be any survivors. Not now. The ship would fail, it would sink at some point, all that steel vanished. Could enough oil migrate to the surface to keep the fire going?

Khrushchev staggered beside him.

"You left Sergei to die," Ritt said.

Sergei moving toward the helicopter, oil sluicing along the deck. Slipping and falling hard as the helicopter moved away. Sergei's happy messy life over.

They walked for half an hour in silence. Khrushchev's breathing was a series of soft mechanical grunts. It was still dark.

Ritt dimly noted that he was turning eighty-one in a few days. Or eighty-three. An intermediate year, forgettable. They had been at this well for years. Five? The endless complications. The northern passage was open now. Cargo ships lumbered through, going from Germany to Disneyland. That couldn't be right. Vancouver. Shorter than the Panama Canal route. And no Somali pirates yet. Waiting until the warming really took hold.

What would come out of that hole? Eighty thousand gallons a day, more. Worse than Deepwater Horizon. None of this was hard accounting. The world was filled with estimates: lost productivity, carbon emissions, Mumbai rape statistics, suicide attempts, proven reserves, sports concussions. Ballpark, all of it. It was always worse than you thought. This could burn for weeks, months. The oil would pump for years. The Russians might go nuclear; they had done it before and they would do it again. Leave the northern sea irradiated for ten thousand years. The half-life of Man.

Khrushchev started talking in a low monotone, reciting something. A prayer perhaps. A speech to his wife, a list of regrets. He might be fifty. A heavy man, who embraced himself as he walked. Ritt was fatigued and one of the hard small ridges caught his boot, and he sprawled awkwardly, still clutching the blanket as he fell onto his face. After a minute, he got onto his hands and knees, then tentatively unrolled to a standing position, like a fighter who has taken the count and regains his feet out of limbic instinct.

"You have a wife," Ritt said to Khrushchev. "There is someone for everyone. Will she miss you, do you think? Or will some part of her be happy to see you gone. She'll go to the funeral and break down, sobbing. She is sorry for something. Maybe she's sorry you died out here. Maybe she's sorry for the life she spent with you, a life that just happened to her. She went on a date. It wasn't so bad. Then twenty-five years of snoring and drunken stupors."

Khrushchev looked at Ritt and said something in Russian.

"Were you the love of her life? Or did you beat her and she's been waiting for this day. Maybe you loved another woman but she turned you down, so you married the first girl who would have you. Is that it, Khrushchev?"

"Khrushchev." A word the man recognized. He repeated it and said something in Russian, inflected, conversational.

"What was his first name?" *Banana, assassin, Potemkin.* "Nikita. That's it. *Nikita Khrushchev.*"

Ritt heard engines, the sound of a plane. He fumbled for a flare and tried to put it in the gun and wondered why he hadn't done this already. He held it up but pulled the trigger too soon and the flare went in a soft arc across the tundra. He and Khrushchev lit up briefly in bright white, their hands going up instinctively to shield their eyes. The light bounced aggressively off Khrushchev's Mylar blanket and he had a sudden celestial glaze. The flare sputtered to a stop, its light immediately swallowed. They stood and looked at one another, their eyes adjusting.

The noise of the engines disappeared. Ritt walked a few steps and turned to see Khrushchev sitting down.

"You have to keep moving. You have to get back to the woman who doesn't love you. You need to carry the guilt for the men you left to die."

Khrushchev looked up and softly spoke a few words. His head dropped heavily.

"*Khrushchev!* For fuck's sake, get up, man."

Khrushchev looked up and spoke more forcefully. A soliloquy. Blood bubbled at his mouth, pink dots on his blubbery lips. Ritt scooped up some snow and ate it. He put some more in his hand and smeared it against Khrushchev's mouth. His tongue came out and licked the moisture. Ritt helped him up and they walked.

There was the ghostly pale of sunrise, but the sun never broke the horizon. Ritt looked at his watch. 11:34. His legs were heavy. They walked for another hour in the pale twilight, an unmitigated blankness.

The light wasn't the opposite of darkness up here. It was its enlightened twin. The day never arrived. Just the idea of light.

"The Holocene," Ritt said. "Rise of human civilization. Stone Age, Iron Age, Age of Aquarius. Let the sun shine in." Then what. *Plastics. Plasticine?* "Pleistocene—the mammals are extinct. The epochs. We're going backwards, Khrushchev. The Pleistocene gave us the first real humans. Short, hairy, touchy as hell. But we kept at it." Then what . . . something. "Anyway, an ice age. Not the first, not the last. You miss one, wait an epoch and another one comes along." What came next? *Myocardial. In fractions. Obscene. Mama Mia.* "Miocene! You get mastodons, horses. The Carpathian orogeny. You know those hills, Khrushchev? Then there was . . ." What was it? *Oligarch. Margarine.* "Oligocene. The rise of the oligarchs. Eocene. Dawn of the Modern." On a roll now. "It was the end of the Laramide orogeny. I hated to see it go. You know the Rockies, Khrushchev? I used to love going up into those mountains. Am I missing one? Did I say Paleocene? The dinosaurs disappear. Really just that one note. But a beauty. Too big to fail."

Krushchev was staggering now.

"There are a bunch all mixed together—the forgotten epochs. The time that time forgot. Cantaloupe? Wedlock? *Wenlock,* Ludlow? The Cambrian explosion. The phyla are a problem. Trilobites, worms . . . We came so late to the party. They never should have let us in. The species that always needed another drink. It was never enough." Ritt didn't know if he'd been talking out loud or not.

Khrushchev fell hard and lay still. Ritt wavered over him then knelt. "Khrushchev," he whispered. He rolled him over. His face was the colour of the snow. Tiny frozen rivulets of blood marked sections on his face. They reminded Ritt of the dotted lines on butcher's charts identifying different cuts of meat. Rib-eyed Khrushchev. The man was still breathing. He opened his eyes and looked at Ritt and then closed them. Ritt sat down beside him, fatigue filling every part of him. The tiredness went beyond his body.

"Khrushchev. Get up, man. You want to die here? You careless bastard."

Ritt could see that Khrushchev wasn't going to get up. And he didn't have the strength to rouse him.

You wake up to life's possibilities and are too old to embrace them. Ritt had only known three women and they had arrived in the wrong order. Alexa should have been first, an ongoing party that had to end. Oda should have been last. He ate one of the energy bars from the survival kit and put more snow in his mouth. Ten minutes went by. Khrushchev hadn't moved. Ritt knew he had to get going. He rose with great difficulty and started walking.

He remembered Oda in the barn, naked on the blanket,

telling him the story of *Crime and Punishment*. It was warm in the barn and the sun came in through the joints where the boards had shrunk and made a pattern on her long body. Dust from the straw suspended in the sunlight.

He walked with his head down. When he stopped to look up, it looked like Texas, the monochrome plain. The emptiness. All those souls trying to divine God's will. *The earth also is thine; the world and all that is in it, thou hast founded them. The north and the south.*

He may have heard engines. Was there a plane? He fumbled with the gun and stumbled and fell backward as he pulled the trigger. He landed hard on his back and lay there winded, staring up. The flare arced above him, an umbrella of light, the northern sky suddenly blazing. The perfect landscape illuminated for one glorious moment before darkness returned. Ritt lay on the snow and the thought that came to him was, *It's time to go.*

AUTHOR'S NOTE

Long Change is a work of fiction. While I have dealt with actual events in places, the characters are all fictions. Geology plays an important part in the book and I have, on occasion, bent its immutable properties to my own purposes. I am indebted to Peter Maass's excellent book, *Crude World: The Violent Twilight of Oil*, and Ben Gadd's *Handbook of the Canadian Rockies*.

I am grateful to the early readers of this book, Ellen Vanstone and Ken Alexander. As always, my thanks to Jackie Kaiser at Westwood Creative Artists and to Anne Collins, my astute and steadfast editor. And finally, thanks to my wife, Grazyna, for her ongoing support.

DON GILLMOR is the author of the bestselling, award-winning two-volume *Canada: A People's History*, and two other books of non-fiction. His debut novel, *Kanata*, was published to critical acclaim, and his second novel, *Mount Pleasant*, published in 2013, was a national bestseller. Another groundbreaker for Gillmor, it was described by the *Toronto Star* as "a near perfect satire of the faltering lives of Toronto's no-longer-young yuppies. Funny to the point it hurts, because it's all so true." Gillmor has also written nine books for children, two of which were nominated for a Governor General's Literary Award, and he is one of Canada's most accomplished journalists. He lives in Toronto with his wife and two children.